SHADES

AND

SHADOWS

A PARANORMAL ANTHOLOGY

SHADES

AND

SHADOWS

A PARANORMAL ANTHOLOGY

EDITED BY TERRI WAGNER AND JESSICA SHEN

NEVE TALBOT · SCOTT E. TARBET
J. AUREL GUAY · ERIC WHITE
GINGER MANN · E. BRANDEN HART
SCOTT WILLIAM TAYLOR
MARIAN ROSARUM · R. M. RIDLEY

Xchyler Publishing, an imprint of Hamilton Springs Press, LLC
Penny Freeman, Editor-in-chief
www.xchylerpublishing.com

1st Edition: October, 2013

Cover and Interior Design by D. Robert Pease, walkingstickbooks.com
Edited by Terri Wagner and Jessica Shen
Published in the United States of America
Xchyler Publishing

TABLE OF CONTENTS

FOREWORD
Ben Hansen

Why has mankind always been so sated with the here and now? By here and now, I mean our world: our problems, our living flesh and blood, our present time, our tangible experience. Why are we so fascinated with what lies beyond this existence or the rumors of life on other worlds?

I don't mean to suggest that these age-old questions are not some of the most intriguing ever to plague mankind. This is not the matter that puzzles me. However, it seems that religions, faith, and even science have provided enough answers to quench the thirst of our exploration into these subjects.

Yes, the details of life after death may be fuzzy. We don't all agree on what *that* world or worlds may look like, what *we* may look like or consist of once we reach that place. Yet, why is the interjection of legend and folklore into the arena so prevalent? Why do we entertain ourselves so frequently with ghosts, spirits, and other versions of the undead?

Television shows and movies, fictional books and stories, ghost tours and paranormal investigators—fascination for the "supernatural" and death appears consistent, if not ever increasing. Even the most religious of people join ghost hunting groups, and some are found among the most ardent fans of vampire and zombie literature.

Are we trying to confirm our beliefs or just speculating on the details in an entertaining fashion? On one hand, it makes sense. Maybe it's an escape, a distraction from the mundane, an alternative to the unbearable circumstance that life can become.

One the other hand, could such intense curiosity originate from a mystical force which frequently demands our attention, regardless of what we think we may already know? As the host of a television show that investigates paranormal events and evidence, I find myself living this dichotomy nearly every day.

My own interest in the paranormal started really by accident. Like many children, I was taught that ghosts didn't exist. I believed in spirits, yes. But, those were departed relatives who might return in a dream or vision to impart an important message of comfort or warning. Ghosts who haunted a location by appearing at random or who inspired fear with their trickery and antics were simply nonsense in my reality.

It wasn't until I was in college and took a group of friends to a war memorial park for some fun around Halloween that my reality was challenged. We brought a tape recorder. A voice was captured on the tape that wasn't ours.

Fast forward a decade, and I can tell you that during investigations I've seen several instances of objects moving by themselves or flying across the room, audible voices responding to my questions, spheres of bluish light zipping through walls, shadows marching past doorways, and the occasional light touch of fingers on my back and top of my head.

If you would have told me when I was younger that I would have more belief in the supernatural as an adult than as a child, I never would have believed it.

May you enjoy the following collection of ghostly stories which will inspire your imagination. Maybe you will regard them as entertainment, a diversion from the world as you know it. Or maybe one day you will have your own experience that too closely resembles what you once considered fiction. Whichever the case, if you always stay curious, you'll never be bored.

—Ben Hansen

Lead Investigator and host of SyFy's *Fact or Faked: Paranormal Files*

MUSIC MAN

Eric White

Ishould have died that night, not Michael. For the last twenty years, I have thought of nothing else. This undercurrent drifts below every waking moment, followed by a simple question: why? Such a small word to consume a life.

In the end, it doesn't matter anyway. I must shut my eyes tight and resist the urge to turn towards the tinkling music box song coming from outside the bedroom window.

Most people call midnight the witching hour. My night terrors steal my dreams away at 3:30 in the morning. I learned the reality of nightmares at that hour. Darkness filled my dreams when I glimpsed his shadow through a sliver-crack in covers curled around my head.

It happened at my cousin's house. I was nine. I still see the red digital alarm clock from the night stand flashing that dreadful hour over and over, like the silent lights of an emergency vehicle washing their dead glow over some fatal accident. 3:30 a.m. marks the last moment I saw my cousin Michael alive.

We always had sleepovers at Michael's house. Just a few years separated a half a dozen boy cousins in our family. Jeff and I came first. Greg, Ross, and my brother, Terry, made stair-steps behind us. A handful of years later, the youngest joined the family—Michael.

He was only five. Five. The years of his life splayed out on one gentle hand. What did evil want with someone so young?

Why did our Uncle Jim tell us such a horrible tale? Did he know it was true? Why didn't he warn us, instead of treating it like a ghost story to scare us into going to sleep? And, why didn't the Music Man take me? Questions I'll ask God—if there is one—someday.

All of these memories flood my mind like the overflow at the spillway where we had spent most of the day before that horrible night. The contrast between that glorious sunlight and the wretched hours of darkness to follow slice my mind like a razor on soft skin.

❡ ❡ ❡

Terry and I woke up with the sun that Saturday morning. We wolfed down our Captain Crunch in front of the TV. Terry snorted sugar-soaked milk through his nose as Wiley Coyote first went kersplat off the cliff and then got squished by a boulder. The big goof was never going to catch the Road Runner.

After breakfast, we hollered hasty goodbyes to our sleeping mother through her open bedroom door and jumped on our bikes to head off to our cousin's house. I can still hear my little brother's cry as I followed him out of the house: "Step on it, Petey!" And with that, we took off.

Dad bought us both Huffys, but getting the hang of riding mine eluded me for some reason. Then, one night he brought home a silver bike with Harley bars and a banana seat, and I shot off on it like a rocket. I flew like the wind. The nickname "White Lightning" stuck with me through high school. I made that silver bike scream.

❡ ❡ ❡

Three light taps on the window behind me break my thoughts apart like shattered glass. "Tap . . . tap . . . tap . . ." The raps of long, bony fingers on the windowpane come soft and slow.

MUSIC MAN ⟩ ERIC WHITE

My mind brings up the image of the Billy Goats Gruff and their "trip-trapping" across the bridge to eat the sweet, green grass of the field on the other side. A troll lurked under that bridge. And I know a spectral figure leers in at me through the fogged-up window over my shoulder now.

Just knowing his shadow drapes over my body as I sit with my back to the window makes my blood stop and my stomach curl. I fight back the bile creeping up my throat. And still the tinkling song chimes on, a slow lullaby that leads not to sleep but death.

I shut my eyes tighter and try to remember that wonderful day again. The importance of remembering weighs heavy on my heart. Somehow, I know it is necessary, just as I know the necessity of returning here to this place and hour, on the anniversary of it all. I don't know how I know this, but I do.

The maddening truth lies behind my eyes like a bloody weight. It hangs on a thin, fraying cord, waiting for the certainty of gravity to make its full measure known. That measure will find me tonight. But first, I must remember the sunlight.

∙ ∙ ∙

We sped off, racing up Locust Street towards Main. A few blocks later, we curled past the Sunoco Station, jumped the curb at the Sesser Post Office, and veered left at the public library. From there, we raced past the park, only planning to stop if we saw Roy or Ryan in the ball field shagging flies. That day they played elsewhere.

We rode on. The green leaves of the huge oak trees cast flickering shadows over the street. We crossed over the culvert we sometimes played in at the base of the hill where our great-grandma once lived. Once we crested the rise, we slalomed down the slope on the other side. The wind whipped around us.

Only the sight of our Grandma Hutson tending the roses in her garden slowed our course on the way to our cousin's. She waved and we stopped, dumping our bikes in the yard. She made us come in and take a break. She filled our bellies with buttered raisin bread and ice cold Coke, and our hearts with love. She smiled and laughed at all the adventures we shared with her. I can still hear the "Wheee!" she let out when something we said tickled her.

♦ ♦ ♦

A low chortle mocks the memory of my grandmother's play-ful laughter. It sounds like a throat full of broken glass. I picture the rows of sharp teeth in his sick, inhuman smile. A thin screech peals on the outside window. The nails of one hand run down the pane to test its merit.

What does he hold in his other hand? my mind asks madly. I know the answer. My stomach sickens once again. I try to block the image already forming in my mind's eye. It takes shape regardless: a rusty wire bird cage. Faded flecks of gold leaf fall from its frame.

And what does he cage there? my mind questions again. But no, I can't let that picture surface. Not yet. I have to remember the day first. I have to remember it all.

I struggle back inside my head, even as the tinkling music box song tries to burrow its dirge deeper into my mind.

♦ ♦ ♦

Grandma Hutson made us a couple of lunchmeat sandwiches before allowing us to go—pepper loaf and Swiss for me, hard sa-lami and Colby-Jack for Terry, along with two ice cold Cokes from her fridge. We kissed her goodbye. After a short sprint, we turned to the left at the VFW. A few more blocks and we arrived at our destination.

Jeff and Greg lived next door to Ross on Walnut Street.

They shared a driveway that held a basketball goal. I spent hours there practicing my three-point bank shots and free throws. We skirted into the gravel drive, and ran out into the empty lot to the left of Ross's house. Our cousins were already outside playing kickball. We joined right in.

Ross shot a screaming missile into the neighbor's siding. Loud curses bellowed from inside. We all got on our bikes and high-tailed it out to Sesser Lake where Aunt Judy, Uncle Jim, and Michael Man lived.

❧ ❧

We all called him Michael Man from the very beginning. It made us smile, calling the youngest and smallest of us cousins "man." It made him happy when we did.

The humor is long lost to me now. We got to grow up. He never had the chance. We didn't know that then. On that day, we were all innocent, and Michael the most. I can still see his face. Every time I close my eyes, I see my little tow-headed, blue-eyed cousin. God, I miss him so!

❧ ❧

Another chortle, thick and gravelly, like a spade to wet earth. The scratch of metal on the glass wrestles the image from me. And did I hear a faint squeak? He softly taps the birdcage against the window.

I almost turn, wanting to scream twenty-plus years of agony and self-loathing at him all at once. But I resist—somehow. I pull the sheet tighter around my head and shoulders like a small child frightened by the shadows of the night. I blame myself. Michael needed his oldest cousin to protect him. I did nothing.

Until now. Tonight, I will stare my misery in the eye. I will stand and face the Music Man. He tore Michael from us while the world slept and dreamed and woke to sunlight that has dimmed for me ever since.

I'm sorry to say that sometimes the boogey man we see in the closet is all too real. And sometimes he plays his music box in the dark.

Remember.

¡ ¡ ¡

We climbed the huge hill that led to Michael Man's house. Aunt Judy had a beautiful place on the east side of Sesser Lake. We went there any chance we got.

We started the day by fishing with home-made cane poles off the spill way. Ross and Jeff took their fishing seriously. Each time we fished, they competed to see who could catch the most bluegill before sundown.

The scream of "Cannonball!" broke the silence. Greg jumped in the water in his skivvies. His splash soaked the studious fishermen. They hollered their heads off at him for scaring away the fish.

Terry and I were content to float leaves and empty Styrofoam worm containers down the slanted slope of the spillway to the stream below.

We came across a dinosaur of an alligator gar dead in the brush at the bottom of the spillway. The beast's length spanned four feet! We gaped at its pale flesh. One dark glassy eye gazed up into the trees above.

We yelled for our cousins to come check it out. They all took turns poking at it with sticks. Ross carefully pried open its mouth. We stared at the long dead teeth in its maw with wonder. We dared each other to touch them. No one did. I imagined it somehow coming to life and snapping off our fingers.

After the newness of this discovery wore off, we explored the woods behind Michael Man's house. We pretended to be cowboys and Indians, wilderness explorers, swordsmen, and super heroes. Our imagination had no end.

The sun dipped down across the lake. Aunt Judy hollered for us to come in for supper. It was hard to pull us away from our imaginings.

We ate the best spaghetti dinner I think I had in my entire life that night. I soaked up every drop of sauce with homemade garlic bread. And though we normally avoided vegetables like the plague, we even ate the salad. We had chocolate brownies that melted in our mouths for desert. Everything tasted delicious.

Afterward, we went out into the front yard and caught lightning bugs in canning jars. We made glow rings out of the unfortunate ones' butts until called to come inside for the night. The day played out in the magnificent, slow speed of summer. Our childhood danced around us like heaven on earth.

If I had only known how dark the night could be.

· · ·

Tap-tap-tap again on the window, a little more persistent now. He grows impatient with me—or the hour. I look at the digital alarm clock that I brought with me, complete with new batteries, to the old vacant house. No one has lived in it since Michael Man disappeared. The digits burn a steady 2:00 am.

I still have a little time. Enough, maybe, to remember the rest before I come to it. To what I came here for. The cage in his hand scratches a slow arch against the glass. The screech brings welcome pain to my ears.

I relish the dull ache over that sing-song tinkle that has echoed in my mind ever since that horrid night. It has jolted me awake, screaming, almost every night for the last month now. When I look at my bedroom clock, it always reads 3:30 a.m. My witching hour.

More squeaking from inside the cage. Another graveyard snicker.

I force myself back into my memories.

‡ ‡ ‡

We spent the night hours playing board games: Monopoly, Life, and Clue. We drank the generic cola Aunt Judy bought for our sleep-overs like it was champagne, and ate bag after bag of potato chips and popcorn as if there was no tomorrow.

Around ten, we got out an old deck of cards and played rummy and the version of poker that only grade school boys understood. We laughed at the things young boys find hilarious: farts and belches, jokes about each other's moms, the "you should have seen your face when" memories of adventures past.

At midnight, we got out an Ouija board and played around with it. Every one of us accused each other of faking it. "You're making it move! Am not, I swear!" Inside, I think we secretly desired some supernatural cause for its movements. Our youth allowed us to still believe in things adults explained away.

I want to disbelieve, but I know things walk around unseen at the edges of reality. They hide in the corner shadows just out of sight.

I never shared this with anyone—not my brother nor any of my cousins. After we grew bored of the Ouija board, we went into the living room to both watch and reenact wrestling on the television. I was pinned in my first match, so I came back into the kitchen. The game sat there on the table. Half-empty cola cans and ravaged potato chip bags surrounded it on all sides.

I looked at the board. The eye of the stylus stared back at me. My mouth felt dry. I took a sip of flat soda and washed the taste of fear down with a slow, solitary gulp. The stylus acknowledged my fear. The last question we asked left it pointed at the word "yes" next to the grinning sun in the top left corner.

For some reason I put out my hand to touch the pointer. I felt a tingling sensation go up my arm. The thing jittered forward on its own, no joke. I jerked my hand back and returned to the living room where my cousins wrestled on the floor.

I joined the fray with a Macho Man elbow smash from the top ropes. Nine-year-olds have the unique ability to forget things that scare them. Some things, anyway.

⋅ ⋅ ⋅

A *long, drawn-out hiss pierces its way through the window and into my spine. I chance a quick glance at the clock. 2:45 a.m. Not much time left for me or for him. He knows it, too. The Music Man's song will soon conclude for this night.*

He yearns to take me before his appointed time. He longs to pull back the covers from around my head and pry open my eyelids. I feel the burn of his hell-fire eyes against them, lustful for a brief flutter to seal my doom.

The hour prevents him from acting, somehow. He is bound to the appointment as well. I have kept the arrangement I made last week. I did not call to cancel to avoid paying a fee. Oh, I will pay an awful price tonight. I just hope my soul can afford it.

I curl my fingers into my hair and pull hard. Tears well up in my eyes. I welcome the pain. Anything to get that cursed music out of my head. I can feel the weight behind my eyes dropping lower now, the strands of gore-covered twine snapping off one more thread.

Soon. We both know it will be soon.

⋅ ⋅ ⋅

We carried on laughing and shouting into the night. Uncle Jim came in to quiet us down. The man towered over us in the archway that divided the living room and kitchen. A coal miner by trade, he spent more time underground. He kept to himself. We rarely saw him, to be honest, even though we lived at Michael Man's house nearly every weekend.

A memory of my uncle floats into my thoughts. I got a splinter in my finger while playing outside Michael Man's house. I came in looking for Aunt Judy to take care of me. Uncle Jim sat at the kitchen table. He sipped his coffee and eyed me over the brim of the cup.

"What's wrong with your finger?" Uncle Jim said in the deep voice I rarely heard.

"Just a splinter," I whispered.

"Come here," he said.

No one disobeyed that voice. I froze. He motioned me over with one large, calloused finger. I walked up to him.

Uncle Jim pulled a huge hunting knife from a case on his brown, leather belt. The blade looked a foot long to my young eyes. I felt the color drain from my face. My eyes grew wide. A tiny curl of a grin formed at the edge of my uncle's lips.

I closed my eyes as he worked the splinter out from underneath my skin. Later, I learned that he used a needle—the knife his jest. I did not learn this until I grew up. Until then, I thought he carved the splinter from my throbbing finger with the point of the hunting knife he used to skin deer.

Memories upon memories and the ones I must remember now are black.

i i i

Uncle Jim. Yes. He came to calm us down for the night. Just his presence stopped our rough-housing in its tracks. We looked up forever at our larger-than-life uncle, Michael Man's dad.

"You better go to sleep before the Music Man gets you," Uncle

Jim said in a low voice, that same hint of a grin on his lips.

"Who's the Music Man?" Ross asked. Ross beamed up at Uncle Jim. His curious smile stretched across his freckled face. Our uncle's stature had the least effect on him.

"Get in your sleeping bags, and I'll tell you. If you won't be too scared," he said. The grin broadened a little.

Calling nine-year-olds scaredy cats was tantamount to questioning one's manhood. We all scurried like moles into our sleeping bags spread out on Michael Man's bedroom floor. Michael Man himself had conked out a few hours before. He lay curled up on his bed like a caterpillar in a cocoon. The many clocks in Aunt Judy's house rang out the hour: 2:00 am.

❦ ❦ ❦

Uncle Jim told us this tale—this awful, terrible tale no one ever needed to hear. But he told it anyway to a bunch of his wide-eyed nephews in his own home. He told it with his little boy asleep on his own bed.

He must have thought it was just a story. Why else would he tell it? Just a ghost story to frighten the wildness out of the boys and get them to sleep. He had to think that, right?

No one answers the questions asked in the dead of night.

❦ ❦ ❦

"An old man lived across the lake many years ago, long before your great-grandparents lived. He led a simple life. He fixed things for a living: clocks, watches, music boxes, things like that.

"He had a small shop in town. If you wanted something worked on, you brought it to him there. At the end of each day, he loaded his wagon up with what needed repaired. Then, he returned to his shack to work his magic. People say he could fix just about anything.

"He lived in that small shack all alone. He had no wife or

children. He did have pets, though. He had pet mice, a half dozen or so, which he kept in a gold birdcage. He brought them wherever he went. He talked to them, caring for them as his children. He fed them tiny bits of crackers or cheese through the bars of the cage.

"He came across a bit peculiar to the townspeople, but people minded their own business back then." Uncle Jim said this with a smirk, showing on his face what he thought of people these days.

"Hey, wouldn't mice just slip through the bars of a birdcage?" Ross questioned.

"The old man loved them. He took good care of them. They had no desire to run away," Uncle Jim countered. No one argued with him, not even Ross. He continued.

"One morning in the middle of winter, the old man left for town and forgot his pet mice. Maybe he feared getting them out in the winter air. Maybe he just forgot. Nobody knows for sure. But when he returned home late that night, he discovered his front door kicked in. Someone had broken into his shack. Vandals had ransacked the place." We barely breathed as he spun his tale.

"But his shock turned to horror when he closed the door and discovered his pet mice. He found their lifeless bodies nailed in a circle on the back of the door in a bloody wreath. The birdcage they called home lay on the floor next to the rickety table and stool where he ate his supper and fed them." Uncle Jim looked at us. He had us all hooked.

"The old man went crazy. He took their skewered bodies off the door and held them in his hands. He pressed them to his cheek, begging them to come back to life. Hours passed as he prayed for them, on his hands and knees. His tears wet the dirty floor. His prayers went unanswered. They were gone."

"The old man kissed each one on top of its furry head. Then, he noticed something on the floor, something that told him who had broken into his home and murdered his mice that winter night."

"What was it?" Jeff asked quietly. He scooted close to me.

"A music box," Uncle Jim answered. "He had fixed it just a week before for a young boy who lived across the lake. The boy carried it around like you guys lug your G.I. Joes."

"The mother of the boy and his three older brothers came by his shack to pick it up, instead of going all the way back to town to get it. Some people in town called those boys mischievous. Some might have even said cruel. The old man thought these boys had broken into the shack and killed his darlings."

"What did the old man do?" Greg asked as he pulled his cover up closer to his chin.

"He lit a lantern. Then, he put on his trench coat and tall, black, top hat. Wiping the tears from his eyes, he opened his front door once again. With birdcage in one hand and music box in the other, the old man started walking across the frozen lake. They say you could hear him crying for his mice over the howling January wind. He headed for the home of those wretched boys to confront them."

Uncle Jim stole a glance at the digital clock on the nightstand. "He left for town at 3:30 in the morning."

"What happened to the old man?" I asked. I remember dreading the question even as it fell from my lips.

"The old man never made it to their house that night. No one ever saw him alive again," Uncle Jim said slowly, watching the color fall from our faces.

"But, one by one those boys disappeared. People say the ghost of the old man, the Music Man, came and got them." Each one of us barely breathed.

"They say the Music Man—whether a ghost or a demon—walks these very woods late at night. He holds a rusty birdcage in one crooked hand. A music box plays softly in the other. As the eerie song plays, the Music Man cries out for his pet mice." My little brother buried his head in his blanket.

"They say he looks in the windows of the houses around the lake for them still." Uncle Jim's voice lowered to a whisper. "And if he finds boys like you still awake at 3:30 in the morning—the time people say he died frozen in the woods—and he looks into your eyes, he turns you into mice to be his pets forever."

Uncle Jim paused then and looked around. Four of his nephews sat frozen to the floor in their sleeping bags. One—my brother Terry—had vanished completely beneath his covers. He glanced again at the clock.

"Better go to sleep. It's almost 3:00 a.m. now," he said. "And if you hear his music, keep your eyes shut." He closed the door and went into the living room to watch something raunchy on Showtime before going to bed.

We tried to laugh the story away, not wanting to look childish. But we all went straight to sleep as if someone had hit us on the head with a hammer. Everyone that is, except me.

I couldn't get the story out of my head. I lay there with my eyes closed, picturing the Music Man walking through the woods, up towards the house. And then I heard it: that hellish tinkling sound of a music box just outside the window where we lay sleeping on Michael Man's floor.

At first, I thought I must be dreaming, or that maybe Uncle Jim was playing a trick on us, like he did me with the hunting knife. Surely that was it. But I didn't dare turn my eyes toward the window. The music grew louder.

I heard three light taps on the window. Tap-tap-tap. (Again the image of the Billy Goats Gruff floats past my mind's eye. *Who's that trip-trapping on my bridge?*) And then, a bump on the windowpane, and the shrill squeaking of mice. I cinched my eyes shut tight. My nine-year-old heart pounded in my chest.

Then, I heard a small voice join in harmony with the music of the night.

"Gotta go pee," Michael Man said sleepily. Through my peek hole in the covers, I saw his little body stir and stumble out of his bed, rubbing his eyes.

I watched him stagger from the bedroom. Then, he was out of sight, shuffling the short hallway to the bathroom. I lay there, frozen. The music grew louder, and something thumped against the side of the house by the window. I wanted to scream but nothing came out.

The toilet flushed from across the house. Moments later, I heard the swish-swish sound of Michael Man's footed pajamas scooting across the living room carpet.

† † †

I didn't know what to do! I was nine years old. Nine. A real boogeyman had appeared. Fear glued me to the floor. My screams to warn Michael and the rest of my cousins had died in my throat. And now he had Michael in his cage.

No one expects a child to face a monster. No one blames a child for fearing what lurks in the dark. My troubled heart whispers these words to comfort my aching soul. I listen to these pale excuses, trying to reason the guilt from underneath my bloodstained hands.

It never works. The oldest protects those younger than him. The night guard awake at his post does not fail to sound the alarm. I relive that night over and over, wishing for the courage to do something. Anything. But I did nothing. I lay there in terror and did nothing. Nothing at all.

Michael Man walked slowly past me on his way back to bed. He stepped right past me, mere inches from my grasp. My fear paralyzed me. I watched him crawl back into bed, and in horror I heard him speak.

"Music," he spoke to the night. Then his voice caught in his throat, a choking sound. And still I couldn't move.

From the slit hole in my covers, I saw Michael Man frozen like a statue on his bed. His eyes bulged out of his head. A line of drool slid down his pale, white chin. His body jerked as if under some electric current.

On the wall above his head a gruesome shadow formed: a tall slender figure in a top hat holding a spider web-shaped shadow at the end of a nightmare arm. The rest of my cousins slept on, oblivious to the horror around them.

And then Michael Man just disappeared, his bed clothes crumpling down like a sheet from a clothesline onto the bed.

I stared in complete disbelief. My arms and legs ignored my brain's commands to run. My screams echoed only in my mind as the tinkling music played on around me.

Michael Man's bed clothes stirred. Above the music, I heard the squeaking—small frantic cries from within his pajamas. The whiskered face of a mouse peeked its head from the armhole of Michael's pajama top. I bit my lip to keep from screaming out loud then, drawing blood that I barely felt.

Then, I witnessed through my somehow open eyes a horror to top all the others. The gangly arm of the Music Man, bony and white-fleshed, reached *through the closed window as if it was not there.* It opened one skeletal palm, and long, yellowing nails crusted with dirt tipped the fingers.

The mouse that had once been my little cousin crept from the pajamas. It sniffed the air and looked in my direction. It squeaked out one last cry for help before inching into that dead hand.

The arm retreated through the window pane as if through water. I watched his shadow turn away from the window while he put his new pet into the birdcage. That's when I noticed the music box.

A small, rectangular box of rich, red wood rested on the windowsill. Ornate feet set at each corner. An oval key of silver spun slowly towards the window on one side. The key was open in the center—an eye of silver looking out into the dark.

Edging framed the box about an inch from both the top and bottom. Between them lay a glass front. Miniature mechanical figures played out a scene behind the pane. Some meager light in the box shone behind them. I watched their tiny shadows move along the inside lip of the window.

A tall, gangly figure in front danced and twirled with one leg raised perpetually in the air. He wore a top hat and held a small stick up to his face.

The other figures were children who moved back and forth to mimic running. They followed behind the man in front. Tiny things ran in a circle around them all along some grooved line.

At first I struggled to make them out, they were so small. Then it came to me, and I gasped in horror. The tiny objects were mice or rats. An eternal scene from "The Pied Piper" played out behind the music box window.

The shadow turned back towards the window, and I snapped my eyes shut. If this nightmare man knew I was awake, he never let on. He paused for what seemed like an eternity. I felt his stare like crooked fingers wishing to pry my eyes open.

The music box played its funeral song for Michael. Then, the music faded into the night. When I could hear it no more, huge silent tears leaked from behind my closed eyes and down my face. I lay there in anguish, replaying every detail over and ever in my head.

Sometime much later, with the miracles that God reserves for children, I somehow fell asleep.

We woke up to the frantic scene of our aunt and uncle searching desperately for their little boy. Each time they called out his name, the word "guilty" resonated in my head.

I cried openly and loudly. Uncle Jim begged me to tell him if I knew anything that might help find Michael. Between deep sobs, I stammered out how Michael had gotten up to pee sometime in the night, and that I thought I heard something at the window. The unbelievable truth remained my burden, damning me behind my silent lips.

■ ■ ■

The mad search and rescue in the woods lasted for weeks afterward. Sesser volunteer police and firemen combed the woods day and night. My aunt and uncle were interrogated as prime suspects in their son's disappearance, heaping pain on their grief and weight to my guilt. Divers from the Search and Rescue Team searched the lake to no avail. No body rested at the bottom of that lake. Michael was gone.

Only I knew his demise. I alone carried that burden my entire life. My guilt takes shape as a music box hanging on a thin string. Its weight falls behind my eyes and sinks into my heart. Eventually, they pronounced Michael dead. His death was a tragedy shared by the entire town of Sesser.

■ ■ ■

I look at the alarm clock again. 3:10 am. Almost time. And as it should be, only a few memories remain. I think I have the resolve. I think I can go through with what I have planned. I made the contract. I signed my name to the bargain. My witching hour nears.

I can hear the nails on that skeletal hand scraping the window sill for purchase. He claws in to get me. The Music Man wants his pet. He will have me, but only at the appointed time.

. . .

I spent the last month catching live mice after work. Dead ones wouldn't work. I catch them at night in the storage room in the back of my store. I have remained wifeless and childless, and have lived alone my entire life. No one is there to question my behavior.

"Pete's Antiques and Pawn" sits on the edge of town past the fire station. We specialize in the location and restoration of items from the last century. I have restored just about everything: 1960s Shriner cars, 1940s bubble gum dispensers, 1930s and 40s radios, and once a 1954 Wurlitzer jukebox. I had it playing in the front of the store until the customer came from Evansville, Indiana, to pick it up.

My reputation for restoring antique clocks, old French mechanisms, English bell strike mechanisms, and mechanical clock towers brings me customers from across the country. I enjoy working on those clocks with animations—moving figurines.

I once labored on an antique Schneider eight-day chalet-style cuckoo clock. It had a spinning water wheel, dancing figurines, and lumbermen chopping and sawing wood on the full hour. I spent an entire night hand laying the wooden shingles on that one. It played an enchanting version of "Edelweiss" in crisp music-box tones.

The mice seemed particularly active in the walls while it played.

I tell anyone who asks that my love of these types of clocks stems from spending so much time at my Aunt Judy's. She had a dozen or so lining her living room walls. But, the real reason is much darker. The movements of that music box have consumed my entire life.

I set up shop in an old building—previously an old IGA grocery—and the rodents love it. A field surrounds it on two sides.

This allows the field mice easy access through the cracks and crevices of my 1950s grocery-turned-pawn shop.

Maybe they associate the building with a food source? Who knows? They come around, especially at night. I hear them scurrying about when I work late, even with all the lights on.

I thought about just buying them from a pet store, but when I went to do it, I got anxious. I shook so bad, I had to leave the store and walk around the block until I figured it out. It didn't fit the conditions, you see?

So, I put out little tidbits of meat and cheese, and caught them with a large mason jar. I have become quite good at it. I would boast about the skill, if it wasn't for such a grave purpose.

I tied the mice by their tails to a loop of wire and hung them in the window of Michael Man's old bedroom by the latch. I did this in the middle of the day. The room sat silent—stifling hot and dusty from years of being closed up. I didn't dare do it anywhere near night. I needed to build up my resolve to face this nightmare.

I hope my courage lasts.

ɩ ɩ ɩ

The deafening music pounds in my ears. The tinkling of broken glass plays like wind chimes on my tombstone. The notes trace my spine like the skeletal thrumming of broken guitar strings.

The Music Man's glowing eyes burn into the back of my skull. His ragged breath lands on my neck, although the window remains closed. The rotting odor of death permeates the room. I choke back my own vomit. The urge to end it prematurely deepens, but I hold on. For you, Michael Man. Only for you.

♦ ♦ ♦

I cut my hand with a hunting knife much like the one Uncle Jim pretended to use on my finger years ago. I made one clean cut, a straight line up the palm and to the tip of my index finger on the left. It hurt like hell.

Relief and pain mingled together with that cut, like opening a festering wound to let the infection out. I let the blood trickle down my finger and watched it drip to the hardwood floor. Drip-drip-drip.

Who's that drip-dripping on my floor?

I bent down on my hands and knees and wrote my contract on the floor in my own blood. I wrote this:

Play your music, Music Man, and walk among the trees.
Sing to your pets, Music Man, as I now leave you these.
An offering, Oh Music Man, my life within your hand.
Return the child of innocence is but my sole demand.
Play your music, Music Man, and walk among the trees.
Sing to your pet, Music Man, my blood promise I leave.

I looked it over several times. Satisfied, I left the house, making sure to leave well before sunset. Then, I waited for the day. This day. The anniversary of Michael Man's kidnapping.

♦ ♦ ♦

I steal a glance at the clock. 3:29 AM. My witching hour arrives at last. I rise up and let the sheet wrapped around me fall to the floor like a ghost. I stand with my back to the window.

His hunger rages like the heat from a furnace on a January night. The whole house shakes with the music from that damned box. I turn to face the window.

The air moves around my throat as the hands of the Music Man reach through the pane of glass. Deep ragged breaths of corpse rot fill my nostrils. His dead laughter slices like a guillotine through my mind. I open my eyes to my fate, my release, my deliverance from this earth-bound hell of remorse.

I chance a quick glance at the music box on the window sill before I steel my eyes to his ravenous gaze. I watch the silver key spin away from the window. Satisfied, I surrender. The last thin string snaps at the weight of my guilt, and the music box falls, splattering the blood of innocence on the floor boards of my mind.

As my body shrivels and twists into its new form, I see the small towhead of Michael Man standing on his bed. He rubs his eyes with his tiny fists. He has slept for a long time. I think he recognizes his room, even though emptied of all his things, save his bed. Dawn will come. The sun will smile over the horizon.

Michael looks around, confused at his whereabouts. I pray he remembers nothing. "Mommy?" he cries out. I want to comfort him. I squeak my love for him as the Music Man places me in my new home.

I think I hear the faint warble of a police siren before we leave. I sent an anonymous letter to the Sesser police station earlier that week. It warned of the abandonment of a little boy at the old Laur house on the lake. I hope they did not dismiss the letter.

◆ ◆ ◆

My face peers between the rusty bars of my cage, my whiskers twitching in the dark. A small, white candle sheds its meager light across the ancient shack, its light flickering shadows around the top hat resting on the table. A withered pale hand holds out a piece of cheese. I take a bite.

The other mice-children and I timidly nibble the treats he gives, and then scurry to the other side of the cage. We huddle together in terror. Soulless eyes stare at us through the tiny door. He closes it.

Then, his wraith-like form silently melts into the shadows at the other side of the shack. We can't see him, but we feel his presence all around us like a suffocating cold fog.

Time has no meaning. No daylight shines here, only the light of the candle on the table and the death glow of the fireplace. It tricks the eyes, this dead light. Often the objects in the room around the cage—the hat on the table, the mantle over the hearth and the old rocking chair in front of it, the straw broom leaning like a hanged man against its side—take on a queer double exposure, as if they are both real and insubstantial at the same time. It made me sick to look out at the room at first.

Only the music box stays in sharp focus. It sits centered on the mantle like a worshiped idol, next to an old bottle that flickers in and out of reality. We reside in a ghostly flux, some sort of purgatory between our world and whatever realm where souls reside. But the music box remains constant. It holds the key to our freedom, if I can figure out a way to get to it.

Ross had wondered about the mice squeezing between the bars. Our mice forms can easily slip through the space between the bars, with the smallest never touching them. That isn't the problem.

I tried the first night. As soon as the Music Man disappeared into the darkness, I squeezed my whiskered face between the bars. I barely got my pink nose outside the cage.

An ear-splitting wail emanated from every corner of the shack. The walls shook as if a tornado raged outside. The floor boards bounced up and down. Eerie blue flames flickered like fire glass in the cracks between them. The hearth roared to life with icy flames, casting pale light over the entire room.

The Music Man appeared in front of the cage, howling with rage. His eyes burned like red coals as he shrieked at us. He towered in front of us, growing to a terrible stature from floor to ceiling. His bony claws gripped the cage on both sides as he screamed out his fury, turning the metal white hot at his touch.

I fled to the back of the cage with the others and waited out his anger. It went on forever. After some time, the shack quit trembling and the screaming alarm ended. The Music Man retreated to the dark, but unlike before, his eyes burned like embers in our direction as a warning.

I learned a few things that first night. First, we had to escape through the birdcage door. Second, it only opened by one skeletal hand. The final revelation came as a complete surprise: I could communicate with my mice brethren.

As we cringed at the back of our cell, squeaking in terror, a strange thing occurred. An auditory version of our doubling vision began. I heard the squeaking mice sounds in my ears, but at the same time, I heard the cries and voices of the children echoing in my head. Their voices floated in and out of my mind: sometimes sharp and strong, sometimes muffled, as if spoken underwater. But I heard them, and they me. We could communicate. Through this strange telepathy, we planned our escape.

Every day—if you can call this endless shadow a day—a scene plays out in the shack. The day that started it all repeats like a black and white silent movie on a constant loop.

The door doubles in front of my eyes, remaining shut while a ghostly copy of it bursts inward. Three apparitions of young boys enter the room and begin tearing up the place. They smash an incorporeal copy of the rocking chair against the fireplace while the actual one remains where it always sits.

The tallest boy overturns the table, and we brace ourselves for the fall that never happens. We sit safe in our place while the doppelganger of the bird cage crashes to the floor without a sound. We watch as helpless viewers of this spiritual reenactment of violence and hatred.

Our squeak screams fill the shack. The ghost copies of the mice are crushed in the boy's hateful hands and nailed to the backside of the door in silent torture. When the carnage ends, the boys rush out of the open/shut door. The youngest one drops something: a pale version of the music box.

As I pray for this nightmare movie to end, the ghost door swings open again. The old man stands in the doorway. His eyes change from the joy of being home to the horror of being violated in an instant. I watch the tears well up in his eyes, and in that brief moment, I empathize with his terrible loss. Then, he transforms into the monster he has become.

The house erupts as it did when I tried to escape. Mind-shattering screams of fury bombard the previous silence. Flesh turns to bones. Elderly eyes filled with sorrow melt into glowing orbs of hell-fire. Wisps of shadow waft out from his skeleton in all directions. He hovers in front of the door and lets out a banshee wail at the ghost images of his dead pets.

Suddenly, his anger subsides and he turns towards the table. He floats before the bird cage, opening the door with his withered hand. One by one, he counts us with a bony finger, making sure we live. Then he fades into the shadows once again.

Does he hear our squeaking in that darkness? More importantly, does he hear our thoughts? Prayer affords me no answer.

I move towards a pile of straw I have claimed for my bedding. I scatter the other mice-children as I burrow in. At first I cannot find it, and my heart drops. Then I uncover it a few inches to the right of where I had left it. It lay hidden beneath the hay. The others must have moved it.

I take the shiny silver music box key—the one I hid in my mouth the night I exchanged my life for Michael Man's—between my mouse teeth, and practice turning it with my paws.

I never forgot that horrible night, not one second of it; Michael Man twitching and changing before the specter's ghastly shadow, his skeletal hand piercing the window like water—all of it. But mostly, I remember the music box and its hellish music. I held on to the image of that devilish box all of my life.

As owner of Pete's Antique and Pawn, I did just enough business to keep food on the table. I spent most of my time scouring the Internet for clues. I traveled to antique dealers and estate sales. I talked on the phone to historians and museum directors and anyone else I thought might have the answer. After years of searching, I finally found it.

It took me three days to open the package after it arrived at my shop. The UPS man practically had to shove it into my arms. It sat there on the grey table where I do my life's work: restoration. Restoring antiques was the façade. My true calling lay in restoring Michael's life.

When I finally opened it at arm's length with a razor knife, I screamed until I thought my lungs would burst. All the terror I held in my entire life surfaced in one terrible cry. But once I stopped, I knew I had one more night of terror to face. There in front of me sat an exact replica of the Music Man's music box.

Even after all my planning, the doubts linger. In that brief glimpse, did I truly see what I thought I saw? What if I am wrong? What if it doesn't work the same way? But I have to try. One last turn of the key in the dark.

I look up at the mantle above the fireplace. There it sits. The music box takes center stage over the hearth, without the key. I figured he would keep it on him somewhere. I had planned for that. I felt my own key in my mouth with my small pink tongue. Would I have enough time?

As the gruesome scene plays itself out silently before us for the hundredth time, I put the plan into action. I gather the mice children together in the center of the cage. We stand in a circle of loss and pain. We take turns biting one another with our sharp, pointed teeth. As the blood flows and mats in our fur, we play dead and wait.

I fear one of us will lose our nerve before the door opens. I speak into the mice children's minds. I beg them to stay strong and hide their fear as the screaming begins again. The Music Man has come home.

Déjà vu overtakes me as I squint to see his awful shadow mourning over the pale reflections of his dead pets. I return to that night, cringing on the bedroom floor and peeking through my sheets. I think of Michael and close my mouse eyes. It is now or never.

His wails intensify as he sees our bloody, lifeless bodies at the bottom of the cage. I hear the creak of the cage door opening. I scream "Now!" in my head with a loud squeak. We all leap to life and rush out to either freedom or death.

We scatter in every direction as we hit the table and bound to the floor. The Music Man's shrieks pierce my mind as he swipes after us. The table throws itself into the vibrating walls with such invisible force that it shatters into splinters. The birdcage floats up from the wreckage and into one of his dead hands.

I hear the children crying in terror in my head. The floor boards begin to pop to the ceiling one by one, revealing blue fire beneath. The world has gone mad. I rush towards the fireplace. Six feet.

The rocking chair in front of the fireplace bucks madly and then is flung into the fire. The flames explode outward, blinding me for an instant. My mind reels with screams for help as he captures one of the mice children. I reach the broom and scurry up its length. Four feet.

The Music Man spins around like a demonic whirlwind, capturing another mouse child in his clawed hand. A piece of the wall flies across and smashes into the other side. I can't help but look. Beyond the hole in the wall, I see darkness so deep that it defies description, a primordial place where light has never shone. I perch myself on the tip of the broom. I jump and the broom flies across the room and embeds itself in the door.

My claws almost lose their purchase on the lip of the mantle. I spin my hind legs frantically, scratching my way on. Two feet. I move the key to the front of my mouth and run.

The Music Man's rage shakes the shack to pieces. His screams tear through every cell in my body. He has captured most of the other mice children. Their pitiful cries burrow into my skull.

An old bottle stands between me and the music box. I squeeze my body behind it and against the wall. I can see the key hole now. I shove myself through. The bottle teeters. One foot.

I reach the music box and spit out the key into my mouse fingers. It slips from my grasp with my spittle. I pick it back up with my teeth. The bottle topples over the mantle edge, shattering on the floor.

The Music Man spins in my direction. His eyes burn with pure hatred. His mouth gapes open, barring black razor teeth. He lunges across the shack. The flames from the fire place reach up to lick at my fur. I am not going to make it.

I struggle, slipping the key into its slot. My mouse paws feel useless. I hold the key with my teeth and shove. The key slides in its groove. I turn the key backwards towards the wall, the way I saw it turning when he gave Michael back, the opposite direction of when he was taken.

The Music Man screams as he flies towards me with outstretched claws. I release the key as his hands crush me into the wall. I feel my small bones snap. I hear the tinkling notes of the music box begin to play. The world goes black.

Black. The room is black. I wonder if I am dead. Then I feel pain. My right arm and leg scream in agony. A sharp pain throbs in my side. Broken ribs, I think. I lay prone on the ground. My eyes begin to adjust to the gloom. I hold my hand, my human hand, in front of my face. I start to laugh. Then something touches my arm and I scream.

"Mister, where are we?" a child's voice asks. I turn to see five children huddled together across the room from me. The oldest one approaches me.

I realize we have returned to Michael's old house. Together. Resurrected. Restored.

"Free," I answer and try to smile. I prop myself on my good arm and sit up.

A little red-haired girl in a Victorian dress walks up beside the older boy. She takes his hand and looks up at his face. He looks back at her.

"Is it really over?" she asks. The boy nods. Tears well up in her green eyes.

Suddenly she runs into my arms and gives me a bear hug. I wince in pain but laugh anyway. I hug her back as best I can with my good arm.

"Thank you," she says, and I begin to cry.

One by one the children come over and thank me. For a second, I fear they will disappear like the dust particles filtering through the rose-colored light in the window, returning to their proper times and places.

Minutes pass in silence as the children surround me in a circle—another wreath. They all have the same look in their eyes; the watery gaze of relief and the wide-eyed stare of "what happens now?" The tears come in buckets. I cry for a long time.

With the children's help, I somehow limp my way back to where I had parked my car along one of rutted roads that ring

Sesser Lake. I had parked it there and walked the rest of the way to Michael's house to give my life up for his. It was a much shorter walk that night. I pile the children in the car and drive slowly back to my store. Thank God I don't own a stick shift.

After I make the children as safe and comfortable as possible, I tell them to wait for me there. Then, I take my cell, hobble outside, and dial 911. The ambulance driver shakes his head in disbelief.

"Running a man down on his morning walk and then driving away? There's a special place for people like that down below."

◆ ◆ ◆

I hold my breath as a sharply dressed young social worker walks my little blonde-haired cousin into the conference room. I want to hobble over to him and hug him like there is no tomorrow. I lean on my crutch and wait. She closes the door softly and then kneels down in front of him.

"Michael, here is the man we've been talking about. The one who wants to take care of you. Would you like to meet him now?"

Michael says nothing but nods his head.

"I'll be right outside this door if you need me, okay?"

Again Michael nods. The social worker stands up and gives me a smile before leaving.

I notice Michael staring at the cast on my arm and leg.

"I had a little accident, but I'm all right now," I tell him, knocking on the plaster leg sleeve with the tip of my crutch.

"Does it hurt?" Michael asks.

"A little, but it was worth it."

He finds that funny and smiles. "My name's Michael. What's yours?"

"My name is Peter, Michael Man," I answer and hold out my hand.

Michael gives it a hard shake. "My cousins used to call me that!" he exclaims, his smile now showing in his eyes.

"Is that so?" I reply, feigning surprise. "I would do anything for my cousins."

"Anything?" Michael asks, looking up at me.

"Yes. Anything at all."

And with that, we began to know each other, again.

A year later, I find myself sitting on my back deck watching Michael Man and his "cousins" play in the backyard in much the same way I did with mine growing up. Another circle in this merry-go-round we call life.

Allison brings me a tall glass of lemonade and sets it on the table. She leans over and gives me a kiss. She stands beside me, placing one hand on my shoulder. I reach over and brush my fingers across her bare leg. She may not be thankful for all those long days of social work in high heels, but I am.

I look up at her face and smile.

"I love you, Sugar Bear."

"I love you more," she answers. Her smile brightens my life like the summer sun.

I still don't understand why we had to endure such darkness. I did it for Michael, but maybe there was a bigger reason. It looks that way from where I sit. Life—like childhood—is both precious and brief. I hope our days in the sunlight last a long, long time.

* * *

CHINA DOLL

GINGER MANN

I. SHOW AND TELL

The rain fell lightly on Kris as she trudged up the hill to the small building. The other children were already wandering into the doorway for morning classes. She stared at her yellow rain boots, carefully matched with the jacket that was tucked over her tiny form. Under her feet, she watched the puddles on the grass as she made her way to the only schoolhouse in Heidenburg.

Today was the day. Kris had been waiting for a week, ever since the last show and tell. Her ragged pack slung over her left shoulder stood in almost direct contrast to her perfectly matched clothing and the blue satin ribbons around her long, black pigtails. She was dressed up for a reason, wearing her best Sunday clothes, the ones that her mother had made her just to match the prize that she had nestled in her pack.

Reaching her desk, she set down her bundle ever so carefully and opened the flap. From a rosewood box, she half-lifted, half-caressed a China doll.

She held it close, content to wait her turn. The doll's brilliant dress painted a rainbow against the blue sky of the child's dress.

Kris politely clapped her hands as the other children showed off pictures of their cats and dogs, rocks that they had found, crafts that they had made, and last year's birthday presents. She smiled primly as they each took their turn and sat down. She kept her seat until she was certain that no one else had anything to bring forward—then she made her move. Sitting up straight as an arrow, she raised her hand high and waited for the sound of her name.

"Kris has something to show us today!" announced the melodic, lilting voice of Mrs. Banks, Heidenburg's one and only elementary-level teacher.

Kris paraded forward, her crisp, ice-blue dress echoing the ruffles around her socks in her black Sunday shoes. She dared not look to the left or right at the other children, but instead stared straight ahead as she walked, cradling the doll in such a way as to hide it from view. Then, she turned around and barely lifted the bundle in her arms, with caution, as her mother had shown her, so it would never fall to the ground.

The littlest children squealed in delight at the rainbow wash of colors Kris displayed. Kris stroked the doll, almost talking to it. "This is a China doll," she said. "My mother got it in the Orient when she was a little girl and her daddy was in the Army.

"It's very valuable, and there are none like it anymore, but my mother gave it to me to take care of because she says I'm a big girl now and I am . . ."—she looked at the teacher quizzically—"trustworthy?" Mrs. Banks nodded her approval that Kris had used the right big word.

The little girl beamed. "And she helped me practice holding her, and I did, and I got it right today."

"Why don't you lift her up so that the other children can get a closer look, Kris?" Mrs. Banks suggested. Kris grinned from ear to ear as she raised up her prized possession. The other children gathered around eagerly.

The doll was a treasure. Its brightly colored satin gown was bound at the waist by a sash as blue as the sky. Its raven hair perfectly reflected the lights from the windows, and its eyes were as dark and liquid as the summer rains. Even more remarkable, though, was the fragile white skin of the doll, whiter than snow on a mountain, and smooth to the touch.

The children were dumbfounded. They had never seen its equal. They reached out to touch, clumsily at first, and then guided by Teacher, who herded the little ones and said, "Gently now. We mustn't break Kris's pretty doll. Touch lightly, just as if your fingers are butterflies."

The children all took turns touching the doll's smooth face and hands. It was a sweet, long time for Kris before, still smiling, she laid it into the perfectly molded, velvet-lined rosewood box that her father had carved for it, and put the box back in her pack. Today, she would be the most popular girl at recess.

The end of the day just couldn't come soon enough. Kris could barely pay attention to her math problems before the bell rang that set her free from the schoolhouse. She had plotted at least a dozen ways of telling Mama how much the other kids had loved her doll, and how good she had been all day long. She took her backpack and opened it eagerly, every nerve in her fingers itching to grasp her treasure again.

A glance upward stayed her hand for the moment. Mrs. Banks peered down over her glasses. "Don't you think you should wait, Kris? You've been so careful today, after all."

Kris sighed. Teacher was right, of course. She closed her pack, mindful of its precious contents, and headed for the door of the schoolhouse.

The afternoon sun peeked through rain-soaked clouds as she trudged home to the family cottage. It wasn't very far away, and Kris always walked home. But today, she half-ran, half-skipped all the way down the hill, her long braids flying behind her, yellow boots splashing in and out of the mud puddles that had grown deeper throughout the day.

When she reached the bottom of the hill, she just couldn't stand it. Longing to hold her doll again, she carefully extracted it from the box, laying her pack beside her on the ground.

Lifting the doll high, she admired it in the glinting sun. The black hair shone, crowned with sky-blue satin ribbons. Behind her, the prairie grasses and flowers bowed, sparkling with drops of the new spring rain. Kris shouldered her pack and headed toward the house, just dying to tell Mama about the day.

She never saw the deep puddle by the gate.

In the split second her yellow boot hit the ground, she knew it was too late. All she could do was try not break her arm or an ankle as her foot slipped through the mud. Her thoughts turned to the doll, but only in time to see it fly from her grasp and strike the wooden gate post. Horrified, she watched as the smooth white face shattered into piece after piece of ruined, muddy porcelain.

Kris couldn't even let out a whimper as she stared, open-mouthed, at the remains of her treasure. Little bits of china lay strewn before her—a hand here, an eye there; the doll's body lay in the mud, dirt, and grime marring the bright satin cloth.

Silent tears running down her face, Kris began to gather the broken pieces and place them lovingly, apologetically, back into the rosewood box. She latched it with ceremonious attention and sat on the ground next to the fence post, her blue dress now soaked in mud underneath her raincoat. She was wet and cold and she had water and rocks in her boots, but she no longer cared about any of that. She laid her cheek down on the rosewood and wept.

II. THE MAKER

The old man awoke from his afternoon nap with a start. Muttering to himself, he straightened up, wiped his eyes, and tried to remember what he had been dreaming about. As usual, it had evaporated from his mind.

Instead, he shuffled around the confines of his small den on a mission to find his sweater. It wasn't often these days that he could walk around in his shirt sleeves, and this town of Heidenburg was just a tad nippy almost every month of the year . . . well, every month except for about three weeks at the end of August.

He cursed himself for the hundredth time for having picked such an unseasonable place to set up shop, and cursed even louder when he stumbled across the couch on his trek across the den. He forgot why he was cursing when he discovered that he was staring down at his sweater. His sweater and Abigail, that is. The black and white tuxedo cat had tucked herself amidst the folds of the worn, ragged garment. Her sides rose and fell blissfully as she rested her head atop her white paws and napped.

The old man paused for a minute, considering whether or not the chill in the air was more important to him than dealing with the wrath of a dethroned cat. Finally, he waved a hand absently in Abigail's general direction, and shuffled out of the den and into his workroom.

His projects lay strewn about in every possible direction. It had been a busy week, and he had a lot of orders due out before the first harvest. A man of his gifts had to be careful: his projects were exacting pieces of work. All were personal and very precious, so he never tolerated a haphazard state of order in his shop. He had to know where everything was at all times.

Not haphazard is not the same as uncluttered, he thought, looking around distastefully. He vowed to himself, again for the hundredth time, to build more space into the shop. But he knew he wouldn't be building any shop space today. Donning his eyepiece and taking the smallest screwdrivers from his tool chest, he set his teeth for another long night. A long, chilly night. Darn cat.

On cue, Abigail mewled and wound herself around his ankles. "Are you here to help, or are you here to make a mess?" the old man quizzed the kitten. As if in answer, Abigail scuttled up onto his work table and started to chase a washer. The old man sighed. "You could have at least brought me my sweater."

Abigail froze in mid-chase to look at him innocently. Then, she leapt the short distance to his shoulder, and proceeded to bury herself in what was left of his hair. "Good for nothin' little furball," he muttered, stroking her affectionately in spite of himself. "If I really knew what was good for me, I'd be making saddle oxfords out of you." The cat purred and kneaded her paws on the side his neck.

The bell to his outside gate jingled timidly just as he sat down to work. He had no appointments that afternoon, but that didn't mean anything. He peered out his window at the gate to catch a glimpse of his young visitor. He recognized the little girl, but only barely—she looked as if she had been dragged through a swamp.

The old man left his worktable for the moment and walked out of the front door to meet the child. She was drenched from head to toe in mud, and her dark hair was coming loose from her long braids. She clutched to her chest an intricately carved box, clasped tightly shut on the side, and her eyes were red and swollen from the tears she was still crying.

She must have been crying all the way to my shop, the old man observed with a sigh.

He glanced briefly at the end of the path to his gate, where child's mother waited and watched vigilantly. Their eyes locked for a long moment before he turned once again to the little girl, who had frozen in her tracks. "It's raining, child," he said gently. "Why don't you come inside?"

Kris glanced back at her mother, who nodded her approval. She made it all the way to the door before she began to sob uncontrollably. She caught her breath just long enough to spit out, "They . . . told . . . me . . . " She tried bravely to stop sobbing so that she could explain herself. "They . . . told . . . me . . . you could help."

The old man cocked his head to the side, "Who told you?"

"My Mama and Daddy told me. They . . ." she stopped to catch her breath one more time, "they said . . . that . . . you . . . know how to fix it." She finally left off trying to use words and held forward the rosewood box.

The old man took it from her hands with care. The carving on the box was exquisite, almost equal to his craftsmanship. Little vines wound their way around the borders intricately in the rosewood, and then down in meandering ringlets across the hinged lid of the box. Tiny flowers adorned the vines at the corners of the lid, and a butterfly sat perfectly in the center. So vivid was the butterfly in its carved detail that the old man could plainly see that it was a new butterfly, drying its wings after hatching from its chrysalis. Turning the box gently on its side, the old man even found the butterfly's chrysalis hanging from one of the meandering vines that wound around the side of the box.

A keen light played in his eyes as he studied the sobbing girl. Her father had put an extra amount of attention into this for her. He stared at her for a long, uncomfortable moment, his face inscrutable. Then, breaking suddenly from his reverie, he smiled with warm approval, opening his door wide for Kris to walk through.

He laid the box on his workbench, still smiling. His smile disappeared, though, as the gruesome contents revealed themselves to him. He leaned against his chair and wept silently at the horror inside.

Kris hung her head in shame. Then, sobbing again, she cried out, "I don't know how anyone can fix her back the way she was, but," she paused to try to regain control of her voice, "she's my favorite, and I'll do anything if you can fix her. Do you know how to fix her?"

The old man suddenly turned his gaze upon Kris. "How much do you love her?" he asked.

Kris emptied her pockets and produced the money that her mother had given her at the gate. It was a lot of money—enough for anyone to fix anything in town. She held it up in her fist. "I can pay you," she said.

"Oh, my, that's a lot," the old man chuckled, "but I never accept money. Your mother knows that. Money is nothing to me, and I always have all that I need without it. Besides, no one could afford to pay me what it really costs to do my work."

Kris looked quizzically at the old man. "But I don't have anything else to pay you with," she said.

The old man repeated, "How much do you love your doll?

"More than anything," Kris answered. "Do you know how to fix her?"

"I know how to fix her," answered the man. "I know how to fix her and make her better. But you must first answer my question. How much do you love your doll?"

"I'll give you anything," said Kris desperately.

"You have nothing that I need, so you have nothing to give me. That doesn't interest me. Do you love her? Do you want her to be better?"

"I love her more than anything in the world. I want her to be whole again and not in little pieces," said Kris solemnly. Her dark eyes gazed at him from beneath her mud-streaked brow, "I want you to fix her."

"Then, she will be fixed," said the old man. "Come back tomorrow afternoon."

III. WORK SESSION

The day didn't pass so quickly in Heidenburg's old wooden schoolhouse. Kris shunned her friends, kept to herself at recess, and spoke to no one all day. Her world was centered on her precious doll, streaked with dirt and broken into so many pieces. How could she have been so careless, so foolish? She buried her head in her hands, trying to forget.

Finally, the school bell set her free. Kris didn't even remember the trip to the Maker's house. She ran there so fast, like she was one of the great tornadoes, sweeping down the hill, tearing through the grass, jumping over the fence, and then tumbling, almost face-first onto the doorstep of the little wooden shack.

"Oh, there you are." The old man opened the door just before Kris would have fallen straight through it. The girl burst in so quickly that she almost landed on a black-and-white cat, who leapt from her perch on the couch with a shriek.

"My sweater!" said the old man, grabbing it from where the cat had been and wrapping it around his shoulders. "Thanks, child, I've been after that since yesterday." From the bookshelf above the sofa, Abigail licked her paws and eyed him with a contemptuous glance.

Kris stood up, breathless. Her hair was a mass of black wisps wrapped around her head in every direction. Her face was flushed, grinning with anticipation. "I'm back, I'm back, I'm back," she squealed in delight. "You said come back and I'm back!"

The maker laughed so hard he began to cough. "So I did. And I've been waiting here just for you. Are you ready?"

"Yes!" Kris almost screamed. "Where is she?"

The old man held out one hand, and Kris took it. He led her through a small corridor to the workroom. The tangled mass of machinery and hardware seemed to have arranged itself into a perfect sphere right above his accustomed perch at the workbench. "Here is where we start," he said.

"Start?" Kris followed, but slowly. "What are we starting?"

"Work, of course," The Maker said, matter-of-factly. With some apparent difficulty, he climbed onto his stool and began the task of cleaning and laying out some small, shiny instruments. He patted the seat of a stool next to him, and then turned his head back around to focus on his own work. The girl would come, or she wouldn't; this was out of his control. Meanwhile, he had work to do.

Kris approached her seat tentatively. Finally, she climbed up to the table and took in the scene before her. She wasn't sure what she was looking at, but she knew it wasn't what she had come to see.

Where was the doll, in her pretty dress, with her clean face and shiny black hair? What she looked on, instead, was a plain, wooden storage box that held a catastrophe. A piece of scalp with dirty black hair, a piece of hand with fingers attached, a mud-caked dress that once shone like rainbows in the sun.

Kris bit back a sob. "But she is still . . ."

"Broken," said the Maker. "Yes, child, what did you expect?"

Kris knew what she had expected, but she politely kept her mouth shut. The old man, not at all ignorant of the little girl's heartbreak, sat back patiently. He said nothing as the pain of realization came over her like a flood. He knew she had been through a lot already, but he also knew the box before her contained a disaster that could never be repaired with ordinary tools or hardware.

With an accident this bad, he usually sent the visitor straight home; but he hadn't turned her down. The fix she needed was not an ordinary one, but she was not an ordinary girl. For her, there was hope. But it wasn't worth a hill of beans if she didn't take to the task at hand.

The tears welled up Kris's eyes, but she was brave. "I don't think I understood you."

The Maker hesitated a moment, carefully lifting his gaunt frame from his perch. He placed a hand on the child's shoulder and squeezed tenderly. "I know you didn't. You came here for something else, but the important thing is that you came back. Now, I have one more question—will you fix her?"

"Fix her?" asked Kris.

"You said you love her. How much?"

"You said you were going to fix her!" Kris wailed.

"You said I was going to fix her. I said she would be fixed. Are you ready to start?"

Kris sank onto the stool next to the Maker. She folded small hands with resignation on the yellow apron of her dress. "I don't know how."

Instead of answering, the old man handed her a tiny brush and said, "You don't have to know. Just follow me."

Kris sniffed, and grasped onto the brush. It was so small that it threatened to slip through her hands.

"Take it, and dip it into this bowl," the old man said.

Kris did as she was told. "Now, pick up this piece of porcelain and scrub it. Gently . . . that's right, get all of the dirt off . . . like that. Now, put it down . . . here." He gestured to an empty box right next to the one that contained the sad remnants of the China doll.

Dutifully, Kris cleaned every tiny piece of porcelain, and set them inside the empty box. She scrubbed, polished, combed, and brushed with such precise focus that she was blind to everything else. So busy was the work of her hands that she never noticed the work taking place beside her: the grasping of long, slender tweezers, the deft application of glue, the setting of piece against piece, cradled inside of a bowl of old dry beans. It was only when she looked up after cleaning her very last piece that she saw what had happened.

She caught her breath. "Her face!" the child exclaimed. "She's back! You've done it!" Her hands shot out from under the table compulsively, grabbing at the resurrected image of her prized beauty.

The Maker was faster. With surprising swiftness, he blocked her fumbling hands. "You're worse than Abigail," he chuckled.

Hearing her name, the cat looked over her shoulder caustically, then went back to sleep. "This bonding agent cures overnight, so right now, she only looks like she's fixed. We have done enough for one day. Come back tomorrow."

Kris sank down in her seat one more time, stubborn again. "Tomorrow again?" she whined.

"Of course tomorrow. You love her. You will give her anything, so you will be back."

Kris jerked upright. "Wait," she said. "Not tomorrow."

The Maker's face darkened. "Not tomorrow?"

"Tomorrow is Emily Wilkerson's birthday party. She's my best friend. And it will be so much fun! Her daddy's going to give us all ride in his old-fashioned horse buggy, and we will dress up in pretty hats and eat birthday cake, and then play with her new puppies," Kris bragged, her face beaming.

The old man sighed, and sat back on his stool. "Then you have things to think over, don't you?"

Kris stopped short. "What do you mean?"

"There is a price for everything I take on, child. I have nothing to ask of you, but I need to know what you will give. Then, she will be fixed, but only then."

"I love her! What if I come back the next day?" Kris pleaded. "Please, I have to go to Emily's birthday."

"The next day, you may look for me, but you may not find me. I'm very sorry, but the price is the price."

The old man turned away and sat down at his workbench again. He had no more to say, so he began to sand a neatly carved set of wooden spoons. Kris stood staring at him for what seemed an eternity before she slipped out the front door of the little shack, and trudged all the way home.

The Maker crept silently to his door, and watched her walk away.

SHADES AND SHADOWS

IV. TOMORROW

Emily Wilkerson wasn't very nice. She didn't understand, either. She never understood. That was why Kris was fighting with her, and that's why she wasn't going over to her house that day. No one could make her, not after what Emily Stinky-Pants said.

What did she know, anyway? Kris knew the truth. She was a big girl. She was not a crybaby who wanted to play with her dolls and her tea set all the time. She did know what was important, and she was, too, a good friend. She played with Emily every day at recess, didn't she? Even when Emily wanted to go play with boys instead—and they were the worst—Kris played with Emily, anyway.

Well, not that day. Emily could have her stupid old birthday party, and she could have it without Kris. Who cared if she got all grumpy? Who cared if she said the Maker was some creepy old man in a run-down shack in an old cow pasture?

Kris fumed as she walked away from the school. Why did that old man have to be so fussy, anyhow? He could very well wait a day. He wasn't going anywhere, he stayed put in that little building, and everybody knew it. She had even offered to go see him after the party, but he had said no just to say no. He wanted her to be sad and to lose all of her friends. He didn't care.

Suddenly, Kris was standing in front of the door of the ramshackle old building. She didn't even realize she had arrived. She took a deep breath, thought for a minute, and finally knocked on the door. It opened instantly.

The old man didn't look at all surprised, but he did look pleased. "Good evening, child," he said. Why did he always call her 'child'? That was worse than those stupid boys at recess. He knew her name. She didn't like him today. She didn't like anybody. She said nothing and made her way into the shop, found a stool, and sat on it.

The old man followed her and took his seat. He studied her carefully. "Is it really that bad?"

Kris wanted to hit him, but then she decided not to. She took a deep breath and counted, like Daddy taught her. "I'm missing my best friend's birthday for you," she hissed reproachfully.

"Me?" The Maker cocked his head, peering at her sideways. Her dark hair was braided with ribbons, and she was wearing a lovely pink dress. She had left the house for a special occasion that morning.

"I can't believe anyone would come here for me. Maybe you came here to see my cat?" Abigail raised her head and peered sideways at Kris, in the way that a sparrow regards a poisonous snake.

The little girl's face turned scarlet. "You're the one keeping my doll, and you won't let her go!" she screamed, leaping from her seat.

"Kris," he said, "sit down."

She sat, seething, not listening. "Kris." The old man tried to catch the girl's eye. "Kris, listen to me very carefully."

"No, you can't make me."

"No. But listen anyway. Kris—"

She put her hands over her ears.

"Kris." He took her hands in his own, opening them into his old, weathered palms. "I asked how much you love this doll. I asked because if you love her, you can heal her."

She still refused to listen. "So, I guess you're going to make me work again."

"Make you? It's the only way, dear one. How else can any broken thing ever be repaired, except if someone cares to work on it?"

Kris looked around at the broken wheels, new cooking pots, plows, and tables, all seeming to wait their turn for attention by Heidenburg's beloved Master Craftsman. As her eyes traveled among the chaos, they rested on a neat little island in the middle of it. There, next to the rosewood box, glistening white and black in her bright ribbons and silk, sat the China doll. Kris caught her breath, transfixed by the restored beauty of her favorite toy. "But there she is!" Kris said. "She's all ready to go, and you fixed her like you said."

"Kris," the Maker warned, "she is not finished. You are here so that you can—" A crash interrupted him rudely. Abigail sat frozen with a raised paw and twitching tail, carefully ignoring the box of bolts she had just upset. Her gold eyes dilated wide with astonishment for a split second before she hit the floor, and tangled herself hopelessly around the old man's legs. For an agonizing moment, she struggled with his shoelaces, and then finally made good her escape.

Kris knew a thing or two, and she could see that opportunity was knocking. Silent as a thief, she placed her doll inside of the rosewood box and raced out of the house. The Maker paused with his back turned, fully aware of what had just taken place behind him. He shuffled back around to face the doorway. His face fell as he stood, deep in thought for a moment.

"I'll see you tomorrow, dear one," he said wistfully.

She didn't stop on her journey that time, didn't do any tricks on her way down the hill. She ran right into her house and through the door to her bedroom, shutting it behind her. She didn't want to talk to anybody, she was too busy being . . . feeling . . . what . . . ?

"If you love her, you can heal her." What on earth was that supposed to mean? Didn't she love her? Didn't she give up a whole afternoon with her best friend? Was she supposed to be a slave to some old man and his cat for the rest of her life, just because he fixed her doll?

She remembered the rosewood box still clutched in her arms, and began to caress her treasure once again. Tenderly, she placed it down on her bed, and opened the latch. Kris lifted the doll from its velvet cushion with the utmost caution. Cradling her, she began to smile again. She reached out one hand and began to caress the doll's smooth cheek.

The instant Kris touched the doll's cheek, its face shifted. Fracture lines from the accident emerged once more. One cheek began to sink with the light pressure of her fingers. Then, the surface tension broken, little shards of the rest of her cheek began to cave in with it. Kris stared in horror at her broken doll, her fool's errand staring right back to mock her. Didn't that glue set? What kind of glue was it if things were just going to fall apart? She had been careful! She knew she'd been careful.

Hot tears streamed down Kris's face as she remembered the Maker's last words to her before Abigail cut him off. "She is not finished . . ."

Not finished? Why? What had she done? What did she still need to do? The world fell apart, completely and totally. Carefully putting her once-pretty doll back into its royal velvet bed, Kris laid her face down on her pillow and cried until she slept.

V. The Mending

Saturdays were supposed to be fun, but Kris didn't feel like any fun today. She had lost her best friend and her favorite toy in a single day. Not even Mama's honey biscuits at breakfast could make her smile.

She ached to do something, but she knew she was defeated. She had done everything right, hadn't she? It just didn't work, and it was her fault. The old man said, "If you love her. . . ." Kris knew one thing today: she knew that she loved. She loved her doll, she loved Emily, and she loved Mama and Daddy. She even loved that silly black and white cat at the Maker's shack. Yes, she loved. But she had found out that love was scary.

Love meant that things hurt sometimes. It meant that her heart had broken into as many pieces as her beautiful doll's face, and that there was nothing she could do to mend it. No glue or bonding agent would "cure" her. She had felt the silken touch of snow white porcelain beneath her fingers, and she could not bear to think of how she had corrupted it.

She cried all the way through breakfast, and she cried all the way to her room to put on her play dress. She cried all the way out to the barn to feed the chickens. She cried all the way back into the house. And then, she was sick to death of crying and stopped because she couldn't cry anymore.

"If you love her . . ."

Kris dropped the mending she was doing for Mama and buried her face in her hands. She couldn't cry anymore, but she couldn't stand to sit anymore, either. She had to leave the house, and she knew where she was going. With resolution, she marched straight to her room. Carefully, she lifted the box from her dressing table and walked into the kitchen.

"Mama, I have to go and see him again."

With her back still turned to her daughter, Kris's mother paused. Her head hung for a brief second before she placed the dish into the cupboard.

"Go, darling," she said. "Go and do good work."

Kris shut the back door behind her resolutely as she began her long journey down the hill.

◦ ◦ ◦

The Maker considered himself to be great at fixing and only average at cleaning. But Abigail hadn't given him much choice yesterday, so he was cleaning. He could see nuts, bolts, screws, washers, dowels, and a pile of acorns under his workbench, when he bothered to look. Then, there were the cat's hunting trophies. He shuddered, and made a mental note to ban the cat from his workshop. Again.

As if on cue, Abigail jumped lightly onto his stooped shoulders, and rubbed her face against his ear with a heavy purr. The old man forgot his resolution and made his way to the front door, because company was coming. No doubt about it, he just had to get that door open . . . now.

Kris paused for a second, and then walked slowly through the door. Now that she was here, she realized that she hadn't thought this through. She didn't know what on earth she should say to this man. She only knew that . . .

She embraced the rosewood box. The details of the evening before, and what she had done, crashed onto her like stones. Hot tears flowed as she tried to think what she was supposed to do now.

"Let me start," said the Maker, "by saying you are right on time." The old man's eyes twinkled.

"I'm sorry!" Kris blurted out, "I wanted her back and so I took her, and now she's broken and . . . I'm so sorry." She began to sob.

The old man's hand rested on her shoulder. He led her to her stool and gestured for her to sit. He pulled up his work stool so that he could sit right across from her and look her in the eyes. She calmed down a little, but her face was puffy and red. "You came back," the Maker said, with a generous smile. "You don't know how happy I am to see that you came back."

"I love her," Kris said with resignation, as she sank into her chair. "I can't help it, I love her, but . . . I don't understand. I did what you said, and she is still broken."

"You did everything except listen. You were too busy being angry, and anger doesn't listen. I'm so very sorry that you had to learn this way, because I see how it hurts you. But, at least you are back."

Kris walked over and placed her bundle carefully onto the workbench. She opened it. The doll's beautiful face was marred by her affections of the previous night. "Why?" said Kris. "You said the bonding agent keered . . . creered . . . what was it?"

"Cured."

". . . overnight, and so she was fixed. Right? Why did she break again?"

Instead of answering, the old man said, "Help me."

Kris perched attentively on the high stool. She did as she was told this time, every little thing. She took each errant piece, scrubbed it exactly as she was shown, and handed it to the old man. In turn, he glued and placed each piece directly back into its original spot. He used tweezers, taking time to move the pieces until they sat perfectly in harmony with each other. The doll's face shone again, new as the day she was made.

"Kris, do you remember that very important thing I told you?"

"If I love her," repeated the child.

"You can heal her. I don't say this to everyone. I say this only to the most . . . shall we say, gifted, of my students."

"Gifted?" Kris's eyes went wide. She liked gifts.

"She isn't fixed, Kris."

"But she really looks like it. Isn't she ready to go home again?"

"After last night, what do you think?"

"Then," said the child, "I don't understand. She will never be fixed. At least not so I can play with her. She will only ever be fixed for people to look at. That's not the same thing."

"There is no fixing her all the way, not with any tools that you know about. China is never the same again once it has been glued."

Kris didn't like the sound of this, but she could tell he had something more to say.

"You have come to an unusual place, and I believe that you are an unusual person." The Maker gazed at the wooden box, his eyes resting on the butterfly's chrysalis. "She will be whole again, because you will make her so."

The child's eyebrows shot up in a silent question.

He shook his head. "I must show you, because you will not understand. Give me your hands."

Kris jerked away at first, because she didn't like anyone taking over her hands. But she trusted the Maker, and finally let him guide her little fingers. He raised them into a gently arched sphere across the doll's head.

"Think of her, and close your eyes."

Kris thought of pretty black hair, creamy white porcelain, a brilliant dress with ribbons, and the shine of dark eyes, glinting in the sunlight. Her face began to brighten, then, as the Maker guided her, her hands began to glow. Heat came from her fingers, and she began to sweat. It surprised her, but the Maker knew what she could do. He held her hands steady, even as she tried to flinch away, and before she knew it, it was all over.

The Maker caught her just before she fell off of the stool, dumbfounded. "What happened to me?" she said.

"You loved her, child," said the Maker. A tear slid down his face as Kris turned her eyes back onto the table. Her doll was radiant. She had never seen such beauty, even on show and tell day. Her face, her hair, her dress . . . if she had been made today, she would not have been more beautiful. "I did this?" gasped the girl.

"Not all the way," said the Maker. "I helped you, and something way beyond my comprehension helped me. But you opened the door for it, and it happened through you."

"You mean, I did magic? Just like a fairy princess?" Her eyes glittered at the thought.

The Maker sat back and placed his hand on his chin, eyeing her with caution. "Magic is a messy word. There is no craft of magic that is ever practiced here. We are servants, not masters. But if you must use that word, let's say that you have *felt* magic. The oldest and best 'magic' there is. Love is what does the mending here. I can tell that you love this doll very, very deeply."

"Magic?" Kris's eyes were still locked on her newly mended doll, her ears deaf to the world around her. "Magic that fixes things?"

The old man smiled and shook his head. Clearly, the lessons were over for the day. "I believe she can go home with you now," he said affectionately. "You have done well, Kris."

VI. The Journey Home

Kris hugged the rosewood box as if it contained her very own child. The day was so beautiful, with mid-afternoon fading into a soft evening glow, and the prairie flowers twirling as she passed, and she decided to take the long way home. It was almost as if she truly was a fairy princess, and her royal subjects were bowing and dancing as she walked by. She felt like one just now.

And she felt . . . strange. What had just happened in the Maker's house? Her hands had never done that kind of thing before, not when she was mending socks, or gathering eggs, or milking cows. When she had placed her hands over the doll's face, her fingers got pinpricks all over them, just the same way they did when they fell asleep and started waking up again.

But then, something . . . bloomed? It was like holding something inside of her hands. She felt it start to live there, like when she picked up a baby chick, or a roly-poly. But the sensation was uncomfortably warm, like being outside too long when the sun was high in the sky.

She wasn't at all sure that she ever wanted it to happen again, but it did make her feel special. She looked up at the clear, blue sky, and she stopped a minute. She was at the crossing of 7th and Main Street. She could turn right, if she wanted to, and get back to her house that way, but if she turned left . . . Well, what if Emily Wilkerson wasn't so mad anymore? Maybe she would like to play, and look at her pretty doll. And she just couldn't wait to tell Emily everything about the mending!

Her feet made the decision for her, and she began to wander to the left. She strolled straight down the middle of the ancient cobblestone street, down the middle of the dusty, sleepy little part of town, where no one ever did business except on market days. She walked along the paved road past the old fruit stand, past the used-to-be post office. She walked toward Emily's house, and never let her doll go—not even once.

Mr. Wilkerson was training a new horse. Emily told her all about it last week. It was black and shiny, just like those beautiful horses that handsome knights rode in the fairy tales. It matched his black old-fashioned surrey. It would mean lots more rich visitors would hire him for buggy rides in the country on the market days. Emily was excited, because the old sorrel horse was getting kind of tired, and didn't move so fast anymore. It was time for her to go graze in the pasture and be nice to Emily's friends. If Kris could get there, she just might be able to catch a glimpse of the shiny new stallion. The more she thought about it, the more she buzzed with excitement. Horses and dolls and her best friend and Saturday afternoon! She started to skip, not realizing she was in the middle of the road.

She was thinking too much, lost in a magical land of fairies and flowers and butterflies, where she lived with her beautiful doll. She wore the prettiest dresses, and rode horses in the woods. She could hear the footfalls of her beautiful black stallion then. It sure was running fast!

The black colt was not having a good workout, and the evening sun was directly in the eyes of Dale Wilkerson. He was fighting every pull of the reins. Wilkerson pulled right, the colt veered left. Wilkerson pulled back, the colt surged ahead. Wilkerson cracked the whip, the colt stopped short. Last time he did that, Dale had almost sailed over the back of that good-for-nothing piece of dog meat, and he had told him so, too.

In fact, he was yelling out some of those things right now, while he pulled up short on the reins and begged the horse to stop, stop, stop! The colt wanted none of it. Wilkerson was out of control and along for the ride. The runaway buggy took a turn and headed straight down the middle of Main Street.

Blinded by the sun, his attention jumping from trap to horse, Wilkerson never saw her. She fell beneath the wheel, right where she had been walking in the middle of the road.

In her right arm, protected and unbroken, was the china doll.

VII. The Return

James answered the knock and saw Dale's face at the window. James opened the door, and smiled at his friend. Then he stopped short.

A cry came out from behind him. Kris's mother stood frozen, her gaze locked onto the lifeless body in Dale's arms. Dale stood frozen, with tears streaming down his face.

"James, she was in the road," he managed to say, "I didn't see her, she was right in the middle, and my horse . . . my horse ran away and my buggy. . ." Wilkerson stopped, his body shaking with sobs.

For a long moment, James looked at the mangled body of his only child. The buggy wheel had ripped her little play dress in the middle. Her left side was damp with blood, and her hair was matted with grime and dirt. His wife's sobs increased as she collapsed onto the floor, rocking herself. Squaring his shoulders, James stepped forward and gathered his daughter into his arms. Then, he looked his friend directly in the eye. "Give me a ride, Dale," he said.

▮ ▮ ▮

The Maker watched a young black stallion, looking very chagrined, pull an old-style surrey to his front door. Two men alighted. He didn't need to ask who they were. He always knew, and this visit would not be one of the more pleasant ones.

He had at least managed to stop his tears before the party arrived, but he wasn't feeling very strong at the moment. He opened the door as James approached. He had not wanted to see his student twice in the same day—especially not like this.

Kris's father stopped at the door, looking directly into the Maker's eyes.

"It's okay, James. You know it's okay. Bring her in."

James and Dale began to walk toward the door. The Maker placed out a hand just before Dale crossed the threshold. "Thank you for your help. You have to go now."

Dale drove away slowly, signaling his good-bye as he went. James faced the Maker. "He brought us. You couldn't make an exception?"

"Not for him, not for anyone. Not even for my own flesh and blood," the old man replied.

"Her mother is beside herself at the house."

"The Chrysalis has rules, James, you know that. No one enters who does not have business here. I can't change that."

"Dad," James said, looking at the broken body of his daughter, "I love her."

The Maker sank into a chair, his head in his hands. "Jim, you don't understand. You don't know what this means. To love a thing you are fixing, that is small. But a human being? Do you know what you're taking on?"

"Dad," James said, "I love her. I cannot make it any more plain than that."

"You are uninitiated!" The Maker stood up from his chair. His shoulders rose, and his back straightened—painfully—for the first time in decades. James had forgotten how tall his father was; the strength and power of his taut muscles and giant frame. "You think that you can just waltz into this place and demand its use? Are you looking to ruin it?"

"Dad, I love her, and I love you, too. I am well aware of the price." James began to place his hands around his daughter's face.

"Stop it!" The Maker jerked his son away with an uncanny show of strength. "The rules are the rules. Have you already forgotten that you have been claimed? Think, boy!"

"Grandma," said James slowly. "Dad, I'm sorry. It is all a blur to me."

"Son," said the Maker, his shoulders starting to slope downward again. "Your life was bought by another, and now you cannot give it away."

James doubled over in agony. "Dad, my life means nothing to me, now. Without her, I will never love again. Where does that leave us? Where would this town, and all of its broken things, be if *you* couldn't love anyone?"

"You cannot save her, Jim, so the choice is not yours." He paused to look his son in the eye. "It is mine."

"Dad . . ."

"You have no right to take what's here, Jim. You have no right to ask for what must be done. But you have done the right thing by coming here. The rest is up to me."

Kris's grandfather regarded the child whose body lay on his floor. "James," he said slowly, "You may not ask for my sacrifice, and neither can I ask for yours. But the shop will not survive the absence of a Maker. You know what happens if I leave this spot, and what must be done to keep the portal open. You know that the town depends on it. There is only one way. Would you take on the mantle so young, when your wife needs you at home?"

"I told you, Father, I love my little girl."

The Maker sighed, his head bowing low. "Yes, son, I know it. Step aside, now."

Kris's father did as he was told. The old man spread his fingers across the face of the child, and closed his eyes. Light began to fill the room, and heat radiated from his hands, fingers, arms, and then to the top of his head. Sweat poured from his skin, saturated his clothing, and began to mat his hair. The Maker looked as if he was melting away.

The old man began to scream in agony, despite himself, as the force of life filled him, and then shot through him and into his granddaughter, illuminating her face, hair, and skin, healing her wounds, renewing her body. Somewhere, in the back of the room, thunder clapped, and the walls began to shake.

After what seemed to be an eternity, the man sat still.

Kris's eyes fluttered open. A sharp light shone from the workbench of a house that she shouldn't be in. The face of her father floated into her view.

"You're all right now, Kris," said James. He laid the China doll in her arms.

She lay silently, blinking.

The Maker laid a hand on her shoulder. He looked so pale now. Abigail crawled into his lap and nuzzled his hand. "You're in my shop again, child."

She turned her head to the left, eyeing a door that hadn't been there earlier. It had a carving of a butterfly on it, just like the one on her doll's rosewood box. "What is that?"

Her grandfather looked over his shoulder at the back door. A light shone from somewhere behind it. "That's a door, and that's all you need to know."

She studied it for a minute, stroking the face of her doll. "Chrysalis," said the Maker, and she jerked, surprised he knew her real name, "Kris," he corrected himself, smiling, "You are well named. Do good work."

She smiled back at him as her eyelids drooped into a deep, restful sleep.

"I think you will find Dale at the crossroads," the old man told his son. "He's waiting for you to come back. I can hold on just long enough for you to retrieve him. Send him to fetch your wife, and come back. She will want to see her daughter right away. That's all the time I can give you. You cannot leave this house again, James, you know that. You are entering the Chrysalis, and it will transform you. Your life, as you have known it, is now over."

James settled onto the workbench with a sad smile. "Dad, how bad is it, really, staying here all day long, every day, fixing whatever people bring you?"

"Not nearly so bad when you have company," said the old man, smiling down on his granddaughter. "Now, go summon that cart so this little girl can get home to her bed."

"Where will you go, Dad?" asked James.

The Maker pointed to the door in the back of the cabin. His life, as he had known it, was also over. The butterfly shone through the rosewood, newly hatched from a chrysalis carved at the top right corner of the door. "I'm going wherever that leads," he said, "I have only seen it once before today. It was on the day that your grandmother, the Maker in her day, saved your life by giving her own. She walked through there. All I know is that, if that door has come back, I'd better use it while I still can. I will see if I can find your grandmother, and ask her where she's headed. Now, go get that cart. I can't wait. Please."

"Dad, I love you," said James.

"I know it, son. I am very proud of you. Do good work."

VIII. The Maker

The knock on the door was crisp, and in a pattern today. She was getting creative. What song was she tapping out this time, he wondered. With a lopsided grin, the Maker pushed open the door of the little cabin that housed his shop.

The child was radiant. She stood, beaming, in the doorframe, hair braided neatly, tied with pale blue ribbons to match her Sunday dress. It was her very favorite time in the whole day: time to fix things.

Kris launched herself into her father's arms. James dropped his tools in a pile, clattering right onto the floor, scattering Abigail to the four winds as he did so. He gathered up Kris and lifted her high.

"I love you, Daddy," said the girl.

"And I know it," said James. "Are you ready to get to work?"

"Oh yes, please! What will I fix today?"

"As always, it is your choice."

"I love Emily," said Kris. "I will fix her doll house today."

"How is Emily?" her father asked.

"She's as silly as ever," Kris said. "She loves boys but she still loves her dolls. She broke the house last week, and still won't admit that it's been making her grumpy."

"If we can love them, we can heal them," said James.

"I didn't used to know what that means," said Kris.

"Neither did I," said James. "How about today? Do you know what it means now?"

"I do," his daughter smiled back. "Emily's going to love her doll house. It will be better than new."

"Just the same as it is with everything you fix," James replied, squeezing his daughter's shoulders. He burst with pride as he handed over her little toolbox.

* * *

SPLIT ENDS
Scott William Taylor

he subtle aroma of dusk wafted through the open window as
Frank sat and watched the sun lower and finally disappear
behind Pikes Peak. The life-long bachelor contemplated going for a stroll in the crisp air of spring, but a glance at his Howard
Miller told him he didn't have enough time to shuffle along the
uneven sidewalks of Manitou Springs. The shop downstairs would
soon close, and Bets would be walking through the door.

The last time Frank Jowalski picked up a pair of scissors and
cut hair for profit, his hands were steadier, his eyes were clearer,
and his knees better supported his weight. He missed much of his
old lifestyle, but as time ravaged his aging body, his decision to
take down the shingle and pack it away soothed his lonely soul.
Since retiring, he no longer needed to descend the flight of stairs
from his studio apartment to the beauty salon he established thirty
years earlier.

However, for Elizabeth 'Bets' Westmore, he'd do just about
anything. And on the fifteenth of each month, without fail, he rose
from his favorite chair, dressed in his best shirt—a shirt always
cleaned and pressed—and headed downstairs to provide a simple
trim to his one and only remaining client.

Another glance at the desk clock and he knew only a few minutes separated him from the beauty of the brilliantly orange sunset
and his monthly date.

Frank heard the bell ring, a bell that gingerly hung over the shop's front door. Frank knew Bets waited patiently for him in the shop. As he took the stairs, he imagined the woman only a few years his junior arranging the slightly outdated glamour magazines and setting the handbag that perfectly matched her shoes at a right angle on the table as she waited for him.

He took the stairway which led from his apartment to the salon's back door. The door remained unlocked, something the new shop's owners were kind enough to do at the close of business on the fifteenth of each month, or as they called it, Frank's Date Night. The aging door squeaked as Frank entered the room.

"Why, Bets Westmore. What brings you to my humble shop today?" She failed to look up. 'Uh oh,' Frank thought. He reached into his breast pocket and placed his stainless steel scissors and comb on the counter. Better turn on the charm.

Bets understood charm like few women could. The casual observer would not use *charm* as a defining attribute for the native Texan, but the few who knew her well knew she possessed the consummate skill of putting her stunning looks and soft southern lilt to her greatest advantage.

Married to a military man provided Bets the opportunity to live the world over. Wherever she went, the diminutive Texan with brilliantly blond hair represented the country well. The term *Ugly American* could never be said of Bets, but it was once said of Mrs. Elizabeth Westmore, "If she was in the mood for stripes, she could charm them off a zebra."

"You look so pretty tonight. Are we headed on a cruise?" Frank withdrew a small brush from his back pocket and brushed off the already immaculate chair. "Maybe you've been invited to this year's governor's ball . . ."

He remembered back when he attended many social functions. Since an injury during a training exercise at Fort Carson cut short his military career, he missed dancing, especially at the annual officer's cotillion. The boy from Pittsburgh who enlisted one week after graduating from high school and who served at bases all over the world cutting the hair of tens of thousands of soldiers, loved to dress to the nines in tux and tails. He missed having the opportunity to dress up. He missed many things.

"Zip it Frank. I'm not in the mood." Bets stood and crossed the space separating them in four quick steps; quite an accomplishment for a woman of her height.

"I see. Just a trim. No chit chat tonight?"

Bets adjusted her red skirt that hit her still attractive legs just above the knee, and with an offered hand, climbed up on the chair and dared him to improve her attitude. He smiled as he took out the cape and snapped it before gently placing it around her neck.

"I guess you're not having a good day."

"You guess right."

Frank picked up his scissors and checked the tension on the blades. When he worked every day, he had to sharpen his tools twice a year. He couldn't recall the last time he had them sharpened. The fact that they now cut hair as efficiently as when he first bought them amazed him. He combed and made two cuts to hair that really didn't need to be trimmed.

"Beautiful night, huh?" he said, testing the atmosphere.

"I suppose."

"You really do look amazing—like you haven't aged a day."

"That's not helping, Frank." He stopped combing and waited. After several moments of silence, he resumed.

Outside the shop, darkness engulfed the quant street. Sparse streetlights illuminated selective areas of the neighborhood, giving the road a feel of uniformity, of order. The occasional car passed. The eyes of those inside would unconsciously follow the car's headlights in the shop's mirrors as the vehicle either drove from east to west or west to east.

Sometimes, especially in the non-winter months, people would stop and look inside the large windows of the store, curiously watching the scene playing out before them. People began showing up on his and Bets' date night shortly after his retirement. Some would look quickly, then hurry about their business. Some would linger, taking in the entire store's contents, as if the two were not even there.

Frank wondered if rumors began among the townsfolk because of their monthly ritual. The thought made him smile as he turned his attention to his friend.

"Did you go anywhere nice in the past month?" He received no response. He continued with a few more cuts, which he could have done in his sleep. The man knew her hair better than anyone else on the planet.

He remembered the first time she came into his shop. The moment the door opened, the woman's personality enveloped the entire space—oxygen fought with her for importance in the room. She arrived as Frank swept the clippings from the day's customers into a small pile. He had just flipped the Open sign to Closed when he heard the bell ring. He looked up and saw the woman standing confident in the doorway as if she owned, not only the block, but the entire town. He wondered if she had even noticed the sign now read CLOSED. She spoke and he knew even if she had, it didn't matter.

"Ma'am, can I help you?"

"Are you Frank Jowalski?"

"Yes, ma'am." He watched as her eyes took in his salon.

"My girlfriend, Mary Smith, recommended you. I moved to Colorado Springs four months ago and in that time I haven't found a stylist I feel is . . ."—she stopped and locked her eyes on his—". . . sufficient. I didn't want to have to drive six miles up that small canyon road every month, but I'm at my wit's end. Can you help me?" she said, more a command than a question.

"Of course, please take a seat and I'll be right with you." He quickly finished cleaning as his newest customer approached the chair and adjusted her expensive skirt. "I always stay open longer than normal on the fifteenth of each month. Just in case."

Twenty-eight years passed since that woman first opened his shop door. Like Frank, Colorado Springs turned out to be Bets' husband's final military assignment. Frank could count on one hand the times the two failed to meet after closing hours on the fifteenth of each month. Many times, as he cut her hair, he remembered that cool autumn evening when she first arrived and her incredible beauty that took his breath away.

Looking at her now, he noticed not much had changed. Sure, wrinkles and other imperfections could be seen, but her core, her essence remained the same. She was still tough as nails.

He stood back and checked his progress. He looked in the mirror and noticed tears gently falling down her face. In all the years he'd known her, he only saw her cry once.

"Bets, what's wrong? You know you don't come here each month because I'm such a great stylist." His words brought a sad smile to her lovely face.

After a moment of silence, she said, "It's Tom . . ."

"Is he okay?" Tom and Elizabeth separated a year earlier. Neither remarried, though Frank felt Bets probably had several opportunities to do so. He met Tom on several occasions, but never connected as some men do. People described Tom as "a man's man," something never said about Frank.

The look on Bets' face brought a sense of worry to the room.

"He's okay," she said as she withdrew a linen handkerchief and dabbed her eyes. "In fact, he's more than okay. He's getting married."

Twenty-four hours before Bets stepped inside Frank's shop, Tad Richmond heard about the little hair salon in Manitou Springs from Chuck Lindly, a fellow hockey player on his team. The story sparked intrigue in the burley Colorado College sophomore.

"It's always on the fifteenth—that's when you gotta go," Chuck told him. "And always after hours. The place has got to be closed."

"Why the fifteenth?"

"Don't know—that's just when you have to go."

"And there's weird stuff going on?"

"Sometimes," his teammate said. Having grown up in the city of Monument, a few miles north of Colorado Springs, Chuck knew many of the local legends. Tad came from Minnesota and angered many of the locals when he accepted a scholarship to play hockey for the Tigers.

"You ever see anything weird?"

"No. I never did. Sometimes the lights would go on and off, but the building's old and people said it's the wiring. I had friends who swear they saw some freaky stuff; they even tried to get it on video, but it never turned out." Chuck's narration increased his friend's interest.

"We mostly used to take dates up there when we were in high school. You know, to get the girls all scared and stuff, but then the cops passed a law saying you can't loiter around the area for longer than fifteen minutes after the businesses have closed. The strange things began to taper off, so we lost interest. I don't think anyone goes up there anymore."

"Today's the fourteenth—you doing anything tomorrow night?" A sly smile crept across Tad's face.

"You really want to see this place, don't you?"

"Let's do it! I'll ask Shelly. You and Vicki could come with us and show us where it's at."

"I'll check and let you know."

The conversation between the two friends that took place the night before played again in Tad's mind as he maneuvered his small Japanese import up the canyon that separated the towns with the last name of Springs.

He'd been to the city before. When he first arrived in the area, he took the cog railway to the top of Pikes Peak. Every tourist and most residents did the same thing. This time, a charge of electricity hung in the air as the four college students drove toward the unknown.

"You really think we'll see something?" Vicki asked from the backseat.

"Oh, you'll see stuff," he said as he pulled his girlfriend close to him. She giggled with excitement.

They turned off Route 24 and entered the city. Midweek proved a good time for few cars ventured onto the streets. They passed quaint homes and businesses built in the city known for its beautiful setting and mystical hot springs from which it took its name.

"Just around this corner. It's on Main Street." Tad kept driving.

"I can't believe we're actually doing this." Shelly said.

"There!" Chuck pointed to the small, unassuming beauty salon; the name *Frank's Place* glowed in red neon above the shop's only door. Goose bumps rose on the driver's muscled arms.

ɩ ɩ ɩ

"Oh, Bets," Frank said as he dropped his shoulders and looked at his friend in the mirror. "I'm so sorry."

"No, no . . . it's fine. I mean, what's a single man to do? He's still got a few good years, and, well, he's the nicest man I've ever known." She looked at Frank. "Next to you, of course."

He placed his comb and scissors on the counter and his hands on her slender shoulders. "You are wonderful. It truly is his loss. Any man would be lucky to have you."

"Any man?" She raised her eyebrow.

"Well, almost." He gave her shoulders a squeeze and returned to the haircut.

Frank looked down upon his friend as he continued his monthly ritual. 'This must be killing her,' he thought. This confident woman, afraid of nothing and no one, sat in a humble salon afraid, naked, vulnerable, her broken spirit forced to face this new reality alone, the cruel earth mocking her pain with the joy of others. His heart ached for his friend.

Over the years, Frank had many female friends, more than male ones. He honed his skills as a stylist while in the Army. When he received his last assignment, in Colorado, one look at Cheyenne Mountain and Pikes Peak to the west and he knew he would never leave.

After his discharge, he found a small, run-down salon in Manitou Springs, only six miles from the larger city of Colorado Springs. It took four months of hard work to transform the space. His skill with a pair of scissors and his chair-side manner brought in a steady clientele, which included regulars, many from outside of town. Soon everyone knew if you wanted a good haircut, Frank was your man.

Of course, in a small town, everyone knows everything about everyone. The local stylist became the subject of rumor and conjecture between men and women alike. Soon, however, those looking to line up the handsome ex-Army sergeant with many of the eligible bachelorettes in town failed to produce a love connection. Marriage just wasn't in the cards for the new man about town.

The days and nights proved lonely, but Frank knew no other life. This latest stop at Manitou Springs continued a long line of solitary stops. But no matter how alone he felt at night, he always had his customers during the day. The women became his saving grace.

"You'd better get back to cutting or we'll be here all night," Bets said as she neatly folded the handkerchief and with a trembling hand placed it back into her pocket.

"You're right." He began again to cut. "Hey, you'll never guess who I saw walking past the shop last week. Mary Smith. I was upstairs just looking out the window and I saw her. I guess that new hip of hers really did the trick. I'm so glad—"

"He met her at church, of all places," she said, cutting him off. He kept combing, but the scissors stopped. "Tom and I almost never went to church. He's alone for the first time in thirty-four years and he decides he needs religion, needs to be sitting in a pew listening to a preacher talk about God and the devil and heaven and hell. That's when he met her."

Frank waited for the words to circle the space between them before asking, "How'd you find out?"

"I saw them." It pained him to hear her words. "I had my suspicions—don't ask me how. Maybe it's just something an ex-wife knows about the man she loves. Maybe I knew it was going to happen. I don't know."

Frank began again to cut, but he made sure she knew he was still attentive to the story.

"On Sunday I found myself in front of Mountain View Presbyterian Church on Arlington, and I *never* go to that part of town. I saw him go in and I followed. I watched as he sat down in one of the pews up front. I stayed in the back and made sure he never saw me."

"Like a spy—all stealthy? Bets Westmore, you should have been a spook." He kept cutting.

"Listen, darling. How do you know I'm not a spy?" With that, he saw the old Bets—the one with attitude—slowly come back to him.

"So, I'm watching my husband and thinking about so many

things. For the life of me, I couldn't remember why we broke up. I'm trying, but my mind is blank.

"The next thing I know, all the women in the room start noticing Tom—there's like a twenty-to-one ratio in that place—and a few of the brave ones start to make their way over to him."

"I can almost see it."

"Can't you though? There are a couple of women close to death, and by that, I mean *old*. There are some others twenty years younger than him. He attracts them all. He's got a smile that could melt steel, that man. After the service, they all want to talk to him, make him feel welcome and all that garbage. I naturally hate all of them."

"Naturally."

"But there's this one woman sitting all by herself. She's different. She doesn't fawn all over Tom. In fact, she doesn't even see him. She's just sitting alone reading the Bible."

"Alone, huh?"

"Yeah, alone, and I think she's crying. Tom sees her. I see that he sees her, so after the herd of hyenas is through *proselyting,* he looks over and she's still there, just reading the Bible. He goes over, sits down, introduces himself, and I knew—I knew right then and there . . ."

Bets stopped and Frank sensed the inner struggle raging inside her tiny frame. In the decades of friendship between them, he had learned when not to interrupt. She needed to win that small battle; otherwise, she would lose the war.

"I knew it," she finally said. "That was three weeks ago. *Three weeks!* They've been together almost every waking hour since, and today—" Bets' voice broke again, but she continued speaking. No fear, he thought.

"Today I saw them on Kiowa Street at Barney's and they picked out a ring." She struggled to find her handkerchief as a new wave of tears reached her eyes. "We dated for a whole year before he asked me to marry him. Hell, I would have married him the day I met him. Three weeks . . ." She trailed off and looked at her fidgeting hands.

Frank walked over to the cabinet at the other end of the room. He returned with a glass of cold water.

"Thank you, dear. I've been crying all day. I need to refill the reservoirs." She emptied the glass and handed it back.

"You want another?"

"Maybe later."

"Sure. Just let me know." He picked up the comb and returned to his job.

"What's she like?" he asked, sensing she wanted to continue, but not wanting to make it appear as if she did.

"You mean, *the other woman?*"

"Yes. Is she nice?" This time he did not stop trimming. Frank knew this line of questioning could get him in trouble, but he thought she needed to open up, to get these feelings to the surface where she could face them, confront them. If so, those emotions wouldn't stand a chance.

Bets waited to answer. "There were probably ten or twenty women who came up to Tom that day at church and not one of them was right, or good enough for him, but Brenda—that's her name, by the way, Brenda. She's different. She's really nice, and that makes me even madder. If she were a witch, I could justifiably hate her, but she's not, and I can't. I'm pretty sure she and I could be friends."

"You can make friends with anyone," he said as he checked her bangs.

"Now you're just being cruel. You know I don't play well with others, and by others, I mean, other women."

"You know they're just jealous."

"I know, but what can you do?"

After a moment's silence, he asked, "Maybe this Brenda woman will come into my shop and I'll get to do her hair."

"You? You're retired, remember? I'm your only customer now."

"Sadly, that's true. Even if by the off chance she does drop by, I'll never get a chance to meet her."

"You ever think about coming out of retirement?" Bets' question descended from a different place, a place void of contention, a plea for normalcy and for peace.

"You know how it is, Bets. Life's a jealous mistress. It tempts us with the promise of joy, gives us the tools to succeed, then sits back and watches the show."

A lull in the conversation followed and Frank wondered what the two would talk about next—the weather, politics, or fashion—things they never discussed. He'd let her decide.

Often, as he cut her hair, neither party spoke, but there existed no awkwardness. He wondered if this occurred to married couples—where minutes, possibly hours, could be shared between two people without a word spoken between them.

Since he never married or spent significant time with someone, he never knew what married life was like. He spent so much time with women, and when they placed the sacred trust of their beauty in the skill of his hands, he became their confidante, their counselor, their minister, therapist, lover—only without the bond of a physical knowledge.

But marriage, to be a spouse, to enter into the ultimate commitment? He could never fulfill that role. He contemplated these thoughts as he continued cutting, the slicing of scissors the only sound between friends.

"Frank, did I ever tell you about my father?"

"The salesman? I think so, a little." He remembered hearing stories of her mother—many stories. She occasionally spoke of her father, but he sensed a pain behind her words.

"My father. I think my father's the reason I hated men for so long, at least, until I met Tom. Growing up in Texas was tough enough, but having a man gone seventy-five percent of the time, and not really being there when he was home . . . well, it's not an ideal child-rearing situation."

"No, I don't believe it is."

"I can honestly say I really didn't know the man, but there are some things I remember. He used to tell me that life was an illusion. That nothing was real. He told me not to trust anyone or anything, that everyone lied, and the day after he told me that, he left my mother and me and I never saw him again."

"Bets, that's awful. You never told me that before."

"There are a lot of things I never told you."

"You told me your parents divorced and your dad ended up moving to California."

"He did. That much I knew. For the first couple of years, he would send me postcards—nothing to my mom, just me—and he always sent postcards, never real letters. He said he moved there, but if I were to believe the very words he told me, then he lied to me, because everyone lies."

Frank looked and saw the previously assembled group was gone. After a moment, he asked, "Bets, do you trust me? Do you think I lie to you?"

"You're the one person I've always been able to trust."

"Even more than Tom?" He said it as a joke, but he immediately knew because of the way she shifted in her chair, it was not taken that way.

"Frank, you know me. You know me better than almost anyone except maybe my mother, and when I tell you that you're the one person I've trusted more than anyone, you'd better believe it."

"I do."

"Good, because I don't come here every month because I need

a haircut *every month*. You think I'm going to keep this same hairstyle for eternity?"

He laughed and lovingly measured the end of several strands of hair between his fingers. He made a cut. "I know why you come in each month." He paused. "What will you do now?"

"For now I'm going to wait until you finish this haircut, then go home."

"I meant, about Tom."

"I know what you meant." He began working on the last section of her hair and waited.

"Can I ask you a question?"

"Of course," he said. Bets hardly ever asked for information. She usually demanded it, and she never asked as kindly as she did now. "What would you do, if you were me? Would you run out there and marry the first person you saw? I mean, would *you* marry me?"

The scissors stopped. The ends of her hair floated down and rested on the clear plastic cape covering her shoulder. He saw her shoulder begin to shake ever so slightly which caused some of the hair to slide off. Frank looked at his hands suddenly dormant and he willed them to respond, to continue. They failed to obey; they then began to tremble.

He gathered his instruments in one hand and looked straight ahead, into the reflection of themselves in the mirror. While waiting for him to respond, they again saw activity of the street through the darkened windows of the shop.

In the awkward silence, both he and Elizabeth noticed a car pull up and stop directly across the street. They watched as two couples of college kids jumped out of the car and looked in their direction.

They were definitely college kids, but probably not from the Academy. Their hair was too long and they moved without the respect of discipline. They watched them walk up the street and disappear.

"We're here. Now what do we do?" Tad asked as the group congregated behind the car.

"Let's walk this way. I don't know if the cops will bust anyone anymore, but I don't want to take any chances." They heeded his words and began walking west, but each person stole backward glances, hoping not to miss anything strange that might happen. "We'll double back and hide in front of the flower shop by the car. That should give us a good vantage point to see something."

"What's the deal with the guy?" Tad asked as they continued west.

"I never met him. Some guy—I think he was a Pole from back east someplace—stationed at Fort Carson, then got hurt and came up here and opened this shop.

"He ever get married?" Shelly asked.

"Um . . . I don't think he could get married, if you know what I mean," Chuck said.

"Why not?" A look from Tad answered Shelly's question.

"Anyway," Chuck continued, "the new owners kept the name, *Frank's Place,* I think out of respect for him. My friend from high school knows the guy who bought it, and he says he keeps the lights on after they close and they even leave the doors unlocked on the fifteenth, just so they can get in."

"You're kidding!" Tad said.

"No way," added Shelly.

"So that place is open right now? We could just walk in and look around?" This time Vicki spoke, upping the ante on curiosity.

"Yeah. That place is open right now."

"You ever go in?" Tad asked the obvious question.

"Me?" Chuck said. "No, but I had friends who did and it scared the crap out of them."

Shelly laughed. "What happened? Someone get permed to death?"

"No, nothing like that."

"Then let's go in," Vicki challenged.

Chuck called her bluff. "You're on!"

ı ı ı

They watched the teenagers disappear from view, and Frank thought again of Bets. Would he marry her? She sat waiting for the answer he needed to give. He searched beyond the storefront, past the streetlights and shops, hoping for the words. None came.

Looking down, he noticed again the collection of short gray hair accumulated on her shoulder. He withdrew the small brush and whisked the hairs away. She gripped the armrest of the chair as the tiny fibers of the brush whispered over the skin of her ear and neck. The hairs hovered, then gently fell to the floor to join the rest of the newly cut ends. He stood and, with shaking fingers, began to comb the last strands of unattended hair.

"Oh, you know me," he said clearing his throat. "If I were you, I'd do what you always do. I'd find a way to win, to beat the odds, to charm the stripes off a zebra." Bets slightly lowered her head.

"Over all the years I've known you, I've never seen anything you can't overcome. There's no man on this earth that can best you."

"Sounds like you're refusing my proposal." He heard a smile in her words.

"You don't want me with all my faults. I'm pretty sure I snore, though this can't be confirmed. I've never lived with anyone, except my Army bunkmates, and I think they're all dead.

"Tom snored."

"I'm an awful cook."

"I doubt that. Besides, I'm a fantastic cook."

"I drink too much."

"So do I."

"I'm terrible company." This time she didn't respond and silence again filled the room.

"Yes," she finally said. "You are terrible company—can't carry on a decent conversation to save your life. Maybe that's why you never married."

"I'm sure of it." He winked at her in the mirror.

"Besides, for forty-four years I lived with, stayed with, slept with only one man. I don't think I'd know what to do with someone else."

Frank came around to face the lady sitting in the chair, her haircut finished. "Oh, you'd know *exactly* what to do." He winked again and detected the slightest hint of a blush rise to her cheeks.

"If anyone wouldn't know what to do, it'd be me."

❦

Since Chuck accepted Vicki's bold challenge, the attitude of the group's innocent adventure changed. They walked closer together, suddenly mindful of each sound emanating from the sleepy mountain town.

"Are we really going to break into this place? Don't you think the cops might be a little harder on us than they would be for loitering?" Shelly asked.

"We'll just say we dropped by, saw the lights on and checked to see if someone was working late." The nervousness in Tad's voice belied the words he spoke. "Besides, Coach said I ought to get a haircut. If the cops catch us, we'll just tell them that."

No one thought this sounded believable, but what else could they say? Each student thought of alternative rational excuses as they made their way closer to the salon.

❦

Frank inspected his work one last time. He knew how important appearance was to the regal woman. He checked all sides. Another perfect job, he thought. Nothing less would do.

"I think we're done." He unclasped the clip holding the cape close to her neck. With the skill of a bullfighter, he removed the cape and with outstretched arms, snapped it, allowing any errant clippings to fall silently to the floor. He then folded it once, twice, then again and placed it on the counter. He set his comb, brush, and scissors atop the plastic cloth.

After receiving a satisfactory nod from his friend, he turned the chair to face the front of the shop. Elizabeth waited until he came and stood before her. He extended his hand to help her down, repeating a gesture he performed hundreds of times.

Assuming the part, she gently placed her hand in his and rose. She is still incredibly beautiful, he thought as she smiled at him. She adjusted her red skirt and went to retrieve her handbag.

"Can I ask you a question?" he asked as she walked away. It was a question he wanted to ask for some time.

"Sounds like you just did." He saw the smirk on her face in the darkened window of the store.

"Yes, I did." He turned and walked toward his tools.

She spun around. "What is it? You know you can ask me anything."

"Did you mean what you said, about me being the only one you trust?"

The look he received from those confident cobalt eyes dissolved all the air in his lungs. She walked to him, placed both arms around his neck and brought his head to hers. He knew she was going to kiss him, something she had never done before. In all his years he wondered what it would be like to kiss another human being on the lips, to kiss a woman—especially to kiss this woman.

Their lips met. She lingered. They separated. He looked down upon her, six inches shorter than him—even in heels—and he saw something never before seen—a vulnerability. He saw her humanity.

"Tom was the best man I ever knew," she whispered. "But he can't hold a candle to you." She kissed him again, this time on his cheek. She removed her hands from his neck and stepped back, searching his face for understanding.

"Thank you, Elizabeth."

"For what, the kiss?" The Bets he knew now stood before him.

"For everything."

"Now don't you go thinking just because I kissed you, that you can have your way with me. I'm not that kind of girl."

"Wouldn't dream of it."

"Good. I've got to get going," she said as she finally reached the table and picked up her bag. "Don't want anyone spreading rumors about you and me."

"Couldn't have that, now could we?"

"Under no circumstances."

"Same time next month?"

"Same time."

† † †

"We really doing this?" Tad said as the group huddled close to the business next to the salon.

"What? You scared?" Shelly ribbed.

"No," he said even though everyone knew he was.

"Okay, on three," Chuck finally said. "We'll walk like we're going to go right past it, then we'll quickly duck inside before anyone sees us. Sound good?" Everyone nodded.

"Let's do it. One . . . two . . . three."

The group tried to act as if they were just two couples on a stroll through a quaint mountain town. The girls' grip on their boyfriends' arms tightened as they neared the entrance to the shop. Each one peered inside the lighted space of the empty salon and saw no one. Tad heard an almost imperceptible squeak come from his girlfriend and she squeezed his arm even tighter than before. They were mere inches from the door when they heard it.

Suddenly, the small bell hanging over the salon door rang.

Vicki screamed. Chuck grabbed her hand and ran toward the car. Shelly and Tad froze in place, unable to leave. They both looked at the door. It remained closed. They looked up and saw the bell swinging, the echo of the sound reverberating inside the shop.

"Let's get the hell out of here," Tad finally said. Shelly couldn't speak, but nodded her trembling head. The two turned and ran. They reached the car moments after their friends. Tad fumbled with the key fob as he tried desperately to unlock the door.

"Hurry, man!" Chuck whispered with intensity. The girls lightly jumped up and down on the tips of their toes not wanting to look across the street, but their scared minds forced them look in order to avoid any specter or ghoul screaming at them through the un-locked door.

"I'm trying! I'm trying!" Tad's fingers juggled the keys until he hit the right button.

The moment the doors unlocked everyone threw open their car door and dove inside. It took several seconds for Tad to jam the key into the ignition and fire up the engine. He gunned the accelerator, slammed it in gear, and squealed the tires as the car vaulted into the quiet streets of Manitou Springs.

ı ı ı

As Bets approached the front, Frank noticed the same four college kids walking slowly before of the shop. Bets gently placed her hand on the knob and opened the door. The small bell hanging above rang.

The moment the clear sound of the bell pinged, the kids began screaming. Frank and Bets froze as they watched them race to their car. Moments later they heard tires squealing as the small import raced through the streets of their quiet town.

Bets turned as the noise dissipated. "What the hell was that? You'd think they never heard a doorbell ring before."

"Oh, just some college kids, most likely. They hang out here every once in a while. I thought about calling the cops on them a few times. As long as they leave me alone, I let them have their fun."

"If you call whooping it up and driving like maniacs fun." She turned to him one last time. "Maybe I don't know you at all, Frank Jowalski."

"Maybe you don't." Bets winked at him and left the shop.

He watched her go. She turned east and headed down the street. He noticed that she never looked back. He turned to the empty salon.

"Another month, and we'll do it all again," he said to the empty room.

* * *

CHILD OF THE UNDERWORLD
MARIAN ROSARUM

The court of the Underworld had assembled to watch the evening's entertainment, a beautiful ballerina who spun endlessly in the center of Queen Mania's stony throne room. Princess Lara watched the dancer from the shadows by the door, clutching her toy rabbit in one hand.

The mere presence of the ballerina illuminated the normally derelict chamber, making it easy for Lara to ignore the crumbling stone dragons guarding the entrance and the mildew-eaten tapestries. The ballerina seemed to be illuminated from within, glowing with her need to believe that she would be allowed to return to her golden, sunlit home as soon as the dance was over, and Lara longed to fill herself up with the taste of that hope until she was full to bursting.

But the two guards restraining her prevented Lara from joining her mother's milk-skinned courtiers as they gorged themselves on the hope that continued to radiate from the dancer. Lara, alone, was left out of the feast.

The pleasure Mania's retinue took from the ballerina's artistry showed through their complexions. Flushed with the good cheer and health they drew from the human girl, they remained otherwise silent and seemingly impassive to her display.

The ballerina began to waver on her bloodied feet, struggling to stay upright, even as her legs gave way beneath her. She finally cried out, her knees buckling.

"Get her up," Queen Mania commanded. Two courtiers in the front row of the audience responded immediately, gliding out into the center of the room to haul the ballerina to her feet.

Mania folded one trim leg over the other as she settled back in her throne, and Lara felt a twinge of envy at the sight. Her own gangly limbs looked emaciated when paired with her pudgy torso and large hands. Lara was keenly aware of how little she resembled her beautiful mother, whose skin shimmered like moonstruck waves, while Lara's snow-pale flesh only made her look perpetually ill.

"Continue," Mania ordered the dancer, licking her lips.

"I can't," the ballerina moaned shakily. "I—"

"I want to watch, too!" Lara cried from the alcove, interrupting the ballerina's plea. "Put me down! Put me down!" Mr. Rabbit slapped repeatedly against the breastplate of the soldier on the right as she flailed.

"Your Grace, my utmost apologies for interrupting the festivities," the guard said, bowing. He and his fellow soldier came forward, dragging Lara between them. "We found the princess by the elevator in the southeast corridor again."

"We don't mean to handle her so roughly," the other volunteered, "it's just that we didn't want her to go above ground and—"

"Enough!" Mania bellowed, and the soldier fell silent. "Leave the princess with me." Lara's mother pounded her fist on the obsidian arm of her throne. "Take the human back to her cell. You are all dismissed!"

"Please let me go!" the ballerina begged. "I danced for you, didn't I? I danced for as long as I could! Please, just let me go home!"

"You should be honored to be here at all," Mania spat. "You'll dance for us again, tomorrow. Perhaps after that, we'll let you go."

The ballerina whimpered, but her protests went unheard. The guards deposited Lara gently on the ground and shepherded the weary dancer from the room. She was too weak to struggle against them, and her head fell limply between the narrow wings of her shoulders.

The court, too, vacated the chamber, bowing fluidly as they departed. The ladies twitched their skirts back from Lara as they passed, lips curling in disgust as their eyes ghosted over her, but no one dared to grumble about the interruption of their feast.

"How many times must I tell you to stay away from that elevator?" the queen asked sharply once she and Lara were alone. "How many times must the guards drop you at my feet? It's hardly the way a princess should receive her subjects."

"I just wanted to see how it looked above ground." Lara gave her toy rabbit a vigorous shake to emphasize the statement.

"If something happens to you, I have no heir, and this kingdom will be overtaken if it does not have a queen," Mania said. "Do you want to invoke my sister's wrath by crossing the border? If we anger her, our people will have nowhere left to run this time."

Lara stomped her bare foot on the ground. A grimace flickered across her countenance, but she otherwise ignored the pain that shot up her leg. "Why should I care what happens to your stupid kingdom? Everyone here hates me, anyway, and there isn't anyone my age to play with. I want to go upstairs and make friends of my own!"

"Don't you have enough entertainment?" Mania snapped. "Your room is filled with toys and books. Just look at that rabbit you're always dragging around."

Lara was undeterred. The look she shot Mania was mimicry in miniature of the glares her mother so often directed her way. "Mr. Rabbit isn't alive, Mommy! Everyone says there are loads and loads of children above ground. But I'm the only one in the Underworld. Don't you want me to have friends?"

"You're too old for this nonsense, Lara," Mania sighed, sagging in her throne. The flush in her cheeks had died away, and Lara suspected the frenzied energy she had drawn from the ballerina was evaporating. The bliss that came from eating art did not last long. "If Tvath catches you above ground, she'll lock you up and make sure you waste away out of spite. Do you want to be deprived of loveliness and passion? Do you want to die?"

"But the world above ground is so big, and she doesn't even know what I look like," Lara returned, lip jutting out in an impressive pout. "I could go and take a look. I wouldn't be gone long."

"There are no guarantees in that world," Mania replied. "Here, I can ensure that you are safe, and that you will never go hungry. I have starved, Lara. I carry the scars it left me with and I still live in fear of it. Hunger is the absence of color. It drains the beauty from everything."

The queen breathed outward in a gust, and the air that fled from her lips blossomed towards Lara in a frosty halo, in spite of the moderate temperature of the room.

Lara drew back, her obstinate irritation replaced by a cresting wave of fear. "Mommy, what . . . what are you doing?"

"I remember what it is like to be truly hungry. And now you will, too." Mania exhaled, and the memory sprang like a cat into the princess's open mouth.

Lara doubled over without warning, her hands seizing up into fists as she clawed at her belly. Her stomach shrank inside her until she felt as hollow as the bones of an owl. Pain ignited in her veins, furious and without mercy. Nothing she had ever read about in her many books had ever prepared her for the gnawing misery inside her own body, worse than any hunger she had ever felt. Her teeth scraped along her dust-coated tongue.

"Mommy, make it . . . make it stop! Mommy!"

But Mania was unmoved. "Do you see what is at stake? Do you understand what will happen if you have no one to bring you food, no one to feed you the melancholy and ecstasy of mortals? This is how I first felt when Tvath deprived me of human prey and banished us into the dark."

A steady stream of tears worked their way down Lara's cheeks, leaving furious red trails. "Mommy!" Lara lamented. "Mommy, I . . ."

"I should leave you like that," said Mania, "but I'm feeling generous. If you apologize, I'll take back the memory."

"I didn't know," Lara croaked. Her ribs pressed more painfully against her stretched flesh than they had mere seconds ago, and every breath she drew was agonized. "I didn't know! Please!"

"Stop your wailing. You're making my ears ring. I hope this lesson has been painful enough to make you stop trying to go above ground without my permission."

Mania snapped her waxen fingers, and the feeling withdrew from Lara at once. She collapsed, sobbing with relief. "I didn't know," she whispered. "I didn't. I'm sorry!" Lara tasted her own terror at the back of her throat, astringent and acidic.

"Go back to your chambers," Mania said wearily, waving a hand to dismiss her. "I will send someone to play with you later, if you are good for the rest of the day and stay in your rooms."

Lara did not argue. She gathered Mr. Rabbit in her arms and shuffled out of the room, her nerves still singing with the shrill echo of pain.

⁝

The stern-faced soldier who escorted Lara to her room barely spared her a second glance as she led her away. Once she had ushered Lara inside, she took her place in the hallway, her great ax raised, should anyone try to approach Lara's bedchamber without permission. Lara knew she should have been grateful for the protection, but today, it felt like the soldier stood guard to keep her caged rather than to prevent harm from coming to her.

Lara kicked the door before flinging herself onto her bed. The assortment of plush toys lining the headboard shuddered with her landing, as if they had drawn in a collective breath. She grabbed several of them, all in far better condition than Mr. Rabbit, and snarled.

She wanted to hurl the stuffed animals across the room and howl till her voice gave out, but the thought of Mania's anger stayed her hand. If word reached the queen that Lara had thrown another tantrum, she might punish Lara more violently than she had in the throne room.

Lara swallowed her tears and clutched Mr. Rabbit to her chest, rolling onto her back. She needed to be a good girl and stay quiet, she thought, worrying at one of the toy's button eyes. And it wasn't so bad here, was it? Her bedroom might have felt like a prison at the moment, but it was snug and clean, making it far more hospitable than most of the Underworld.

Some enterprising soul, no doubt one of the artists from the world above that Mania coveted so, had even painted a bright landscape of stars on the ceiling. Lara had never seen real stars before, but the sight of the mural comforted her when she was unable to sleep. She always hoped the painting was just like the real night sky. It would be disappointing if the true stars were less brilliant than the artist's impression.

The stabbing pain in the pit of Lara's stomach, the last remnants of her mother's shared experience, abated little by little as she continued to stare at the ceiling. Though a relief, a duller, if no less deadly, ache soon replaced it. Lara was truly alone in her room, and the absence of companionship gnawed at her almost as deeply as the memory of Mania's hunger.

Her mother had given her explicit instructions not to leave, but after what felt like hours of waiting, Lara could not stand to be confined any longer. She slipped off her bed and padded over to the door, pressing her ear against the wood. Lara waited for any sound that might indicate the presence of the guard, but she was greeted with silence.

That the soldier had been assigned elsewhere and abandoned her post at Lara's door came as no surprise to her. The Underworld did not have enough men- and women-at-arms for Lara's every movement to be watched, regardless of Mania's wishes; they were needed in other parts of the kingdom.

Lara waited another minute to be sure that no one would be waiting to snatch her, then tugged the door open into the mercifully empty hallway. "Mommy must have forgotten she was going to send us a playmate," she whispered to Mr. Rabbit. "We'll be very quiet and find friends of our own. We don't need her help." Heartened by the prospect of company, Lara set off down the corridor.

Her wanderings became aimless. She marched down empty cobblestone alleys pitted with fetid puddles of water and down narrow passages swallowed by the shadows that clung to every corner of the Underworld. Belatedly, Lara realized she had come to the dark prison that held the ballerina.

Lara ducked around the corner to avoid being seen by the two soldiers standing watch over the dancer. The guards had unsheathed their swords in preparation of some ill-advised escape attempt on the part of the ballerina, though Lara could see that her ankles were bound with heavy manacles. But, the grim sight of the ballerina's slippers, stained with blood as vivid as the petals of a rose, caught Lara's eye.

Mania insisted loudly that the artists who fed the court had chosen their fates, but that did not appear to be the case with the dancer. Why would someone choose to dance until their feet bled through their shoes?

A grin suddenly blossomed on Lara's lips. If she guided the dancer out of the Underworld, the young woman might, in turn, help Lara find her way when they reached the sun-soaked land above them. Lara did not think the ballerina was likely to refuse her offer; both would benefit from the bargain, and it felt cruel to leave the dancer as she was.

All Lara needed to do to talk to the ballerina alone.

Inspired, she stepped into the open and waved to the guards.

"Princess, you shouldn't be here," said the soldier on the right, barely managing to suppress a groan. Lara was rarely a welcome visitor, and she had already troubled those particular guards that day. "Go back to your room, or we'll have to fetch your mother again."

"I know I'm not supposed to be here," Lara said swiftly, "but I saw someone odd when I went for a walk. They were all red from the sun and smelled strange. I thought I should get soldiers in case they had come from the bad queen."

"What?" the first guard blurted, her voice rising. "Someone from above ground found their way down here? But how?"

"Are you sure it wasn't someone you recognized?" her companion asked skeptically, but the color had drained from his cheeks. The prospect of one of Tvath's spies in their midst understandably frightened the man-at-arms.

"No," Lara said with a brisk shake of her head. "It was someone new. I'm sure it was." She held her breath, waiting for another rebuttal from the soldiers, but none came. They seemed to believe Lara would not be so foolish as to risk her mother's ire for a second time in one day; she had no other reason to lie to them.

"I thought we had a treaty with Tvath. But who else could have sent such a person? No one else knows we're down here," the first guard said, and uttered a curse under her breath.

"We may have a treaty with her, but that doesn't mean she'll honor it," her companion replied, and raised his blade. "Tvath was furious with Mania the last time we saw her. Maybe she's planning an invasion to finish us off. Come on! We need to raise the alarm."

"But what about the dancer? We can't just leave her here," the first soldier protested.

"We can, and we will," the other guard replied curtly. "Look at those chains. She's not going anywhere."

The first soldier cast a glance over her shoulder at the ballerina, then nodded. "Right. But if the ballerina gets away, Mania will have both our heads." With the threat of their queen's displeasure still hanging in the air, the two soldiers sped off, leaving Lara and the ballerina alone.

The dancer sat frozen for a moment, her mouth agape, but the paralysis did not last long. Her hands sprung to life, and they closed over the shackles that bound her ankles as she attempted to free herself, tugging at them fiercely.

"Hello," Lara chirped.

The greeting, however friendly, made the ballerina cry out in alarm. She scrambled backward, pressing herself flush with the dirt wall. "Please don't make me dance anymore," she begged, raising her hands to protect her face, damp with sweat. "Please! I can't; I'm too tired."

"I didn't come here to make you dance," Lara replied. "I won't hurt you; I promise! I just wanted to talk to you. What's your name?"

The young woman hesitated. "I . . . I'm Helen. Helen Gray," she said at last, the answer faint and breathless. The ballerina whimpered as she rose slowly to her bloody feet, but she managed to stay upright.

"I'm Lara. I like your name, Helen. It's very pretty. You came from the world with the sun and the stars, didn't you?"

Helen, seemingly at a loss for words, nodded dumbly. "I . . . I did." To Lara, she looked like a faun in a picture book, wide-eyed and nimble. "I used to be a real dancer with a real ballet company. They—the soldiers—took me when I was walking home from rehearsal." She laughed humorlessly. "It's almost funny. I thought they were going to mug me. Muggings, that's what happens to normal people. Normal people don't get trapped underground with . . . whatever you are."

"I'm a princess, not a thing," Lara replied coolly, but she was willing to forgive Helen for her rudeness. "Do you want to go back upstairs, then, if you didn't want to come down here to begin with?"

"Can you do that?" Helen whispered frantically. She edged towards Lara as far as her chains would allow. "Please, can you take me above ground?"

"I can," said Lara. "I've always wanted to see your world myself, but I don't know my way around. You could lead me, though. I bet you know all the best places to visit."

"You want to come with me to the surface?" Helen asked, blinking in puzzlement. That was clearly the last thing she expected to hear from Lara.

"Yes," Lara said brightly. "I have books that talk about it, but pictures aren't the same as the real thing. Mommy would get mad if she knew I even had pictures of the world upstairs. She hates to be reminded that she can't go there anymore."

"If you swear to take me up to the city, and that we won't get caught, I'll take you somewhere nice. Somewhere with lots of people and lights," said Helen, turning solemn.

Lara considered the proposal. Promises made by mortals could be easily discarded, but she was bound to the same rules as her mother. The price she would pay if she violated her oath would be her own blood. But her indecision did not take long. "I swear."

Helen reached down and tugged at the shackles that bound her. "I can't help you if we don't get these off. Do you know where you can find the key?"

"Oh, I don't need a key." Lara toddled over to Helen and, setting her rabbit aside, bent on one knee. She held one hand over the chain and closed her eyes, reaching out with probing, mental fingertips, coaxing the metal into doing her will. When she lowered her hand to the manacles, they clicked open effortlessly, and Lara beamed. "Tada!" she announced, and picked her toy back up.

"You're very clever," Helen stepped gingerly away from the shackles, as though they might come alive and ensnare her again. "How do we get out from here?"

Lara reached out a hand to her. "We'll use one of the elevators. They're all supposed to be guarded, but there are never enough soldiers for that. You'll have to shut your eyes tight and hold onto me as we go. Otherwise, the magic won't work, and everyone will be able to see you. Then we'll both be in trouble."

Helen looked at Lara uncertainly. Their two hands could not have looked more different, Lara's gray and stitch-worn, Helen's smooth and pale, save where they were stained with blood. A moment later, she twined her fingers with Lara's. "Okay," she sighed. Taking a deep breath, the ballerina's lashes fluttered closed.

"Don't worry—I won't let you trip and fall," Lara assured her, and pulled Helen forward. The ballerina followed her, and as promised, Lara did not allow her to slip on the uneven ground, despite her limp.

The dancer remained silent as she and Lara moved through the streets of the Underworld, and Lara had to admire Helen's stoicism. She had seen the state of the young woman's feet, and could taste the rich, red sparks of pain that flared through the dancer with each step she took.

The elevator Lara led Helen to was one of several ways of traveling in and out of the Underworld, but it had been years since anyone had used it. The iron grating across the threshold had rusted, and dirt caked its velvet carpet. Lara felt her excitement dwindling now that she and Helen had arrived. What if someone caught them? Lara did not wish to think how her mother would punish her for a second infringement. She had seen courtiers torn apart for less.

"Why have we stopped?" Helen asked, her eyes still closed. "Are we there yet?"

"Yes, but keep your eyes closed," Lara said hastily. She glanced down at Mr. Rabbit. If she had the courage to go to the surface, she would finally have the chance to drink in the sequined stars and see if they looked like those painted on the ceiling of her bedroom. Even better, she might be able to play with the children rumored to live in the sunlight.

"I know Mommy said Tvath would make us go hungry if we went upstairs, but if I'm only gone for a little while, there's no way Mommy's bad sister will catch us," Lara whispered to her toy.

"Who . . . are you talking to? Is someone else here?" Helen asked, her brows knitting together, but Lara ignored her.

"We won't go looking for trouble. And you want to see what's upstairs too, don't you?" She winked at Mr. Rabbit's button eyes, her smile growing.

Accepting the toy's silence for consent, Lara drew the elevator's iron grating back and dragged Helen inside. The machine rumbled to life as she punched the button on the side paneling labeled *G*, and Lara squeaked in both surprise and delight. It worked!

"You can look now," Lara said to Helen, releasing the dancer's hand as the machine began its ascent. It felt infuriatingly slow to Lara, as if it was climbing the shaft inch by inch.

Helen opened her eyes just in time to watch the Underworld slip away beneath them, and laughed with relief. "You really did it," she breathed. "You got us out and we didn't get caught!"

"I told you I could," said Lara. She hopped from foot to foot, animated by nervous energy. The world above might be dangerous above ground, but she needed to know for herself what it was like. Perhaps once she reached her destination, she would be satisfied with a glimpse of Tvath's kingdom and be content to remain in the Underworld thereafter.

"You're very smart," said Helen. "Thank you." She slumped against the rear wall of the elevator, and a second burst of laughter worked its way up her parched throat. "I'm going home. I'm really going home."

"Where's home?" Struck by an idea, Lara added, "Do you live with Tvath and her court?"

"I don't know any Tvath. And if she's like you . . . I'd never even seen anything like the people who live in the Underworld before I was abducted. Not outside of bedtime stories, anyway."

Lara folded her arms across her chest and considered this. "I guess it makes sense that you've never heard of the bad queen, if you thought Mommy and me were just stories. Is the big war also in human stories?"

"The last big war happened a long time ago, before I was born," Helen said, sounding more bewildered than ever. "And it was fought on the other side of the ocean. I don't know about any war involving people like you."

"Mommy and the bad queen fought for the throne, and the sky burned and the ocean danced." It seemed impossible to Lara that her mother had lost a great battle, but the evidence of Mania's defeat surrounded her in the Underworld. Mania's small army and her tarnished relics were not grand enough to be spoils of war. "Anyway, the bad queen won in the end and sent everybody who loved Mommy best down into the Underworld."

"I see," said Helen, her gaze distant and unfocused. Her mind was not on Lara's story.

The elevator creaked to a stop several minutes later and the doors opened, revealing the interior of a small, wooden structure. The top of Helen's head brushed the low ceiling as she hurried out of the elevator. It was as if just being back in her world had caused her bloodied feet to heal.

Helen pushed past the shovels and rakes that stood between the elevator and the door opposite it. "This looks like a garden shed. We might be in the city park."

"Park?" Lara asked.

"It's a green place," Helen explained. "There are lots of trees and flowers there. I'm sure you'll like it."

"I hope so," said Lara, wrinkling her nose as the all-too-familiar smell of dirt hit her nostrils. She saw no evidence of the fabled sun; it was as dark and gloomy as the Underworld. What if this land was just like her mother's kingdom, ugly and shadowy, and she had come all this way for nothing?

"No! That's not how it is," Lara told herself firmly, and shook Mr. Rabbit. "It's got to be beautiful out there, it's just got to be!"

She joined Helen at the threshold and grabbed the ballerina's hand, her resolve greater than ever.

The crowd that greeted Lara and Helen outside was in sharp contrast to the empty, damp streets of the Underworld they had so recently walked through. Paper lanterns in the shape of dragons and firebirds drifted in the star-strewn sky above them. The huge, round moon, as bright as Lara had imagined the sun to be, illuminated the throng of men and women around them.

Peddlers danced around the tables and tents erected between the palms and soaring mango trees, and they called out to their friends and festival-goers. To Lara, their promises of wonder sparked on her tongue like firecrackers as they handed out flyers and compliments, all of which rang true in the giddy atmosphere of the carnival. The smell of sizzling grease and sugar permeated the air as much as the siren song of the band playing beyond the trees.

Lara let out a little cry of elation as the taste of the music filled her mouth, coating it with sweetness. The queer pitch of her voice turned a few heads, but she ignored the onlookers. "Look!" Lara raised Mr. Rabbit's head up so that he too could survey the park. "Look at all the people!"

Years in a monochromatic universe made the stunning, colorful displays throb like open wounds before Lara's eyes, but she did not dare close them. "I wonder if it's like this every day," she murmured. A party every day! How marvelous that would be. She swung her arm back and forth, fully in the spirit of the adventure. "I've never seen so many colors. I wish we had festivals like this in the Underworld."

"Maybe you can, someday," said Helen. She tugged her hand free with an anxious smile that failed to reach her eyes. "I kept my promise, Lara. You helped me get out of the Underworld, and look: I've taken you to a place with lots of nice things."

Lara wrenched her attention from the festivities long enough to look up at Helen with wide eyes. "You could stay for a little while," she prompted, sensing the dancer's imminent departure. "We could have fun together."

"I . . . I'd like to, but I need to go home," Helen said. "My family will be wondering where I've been. But there's a nice spot for you over there. You can watch the festival." She swept her arm out, gesturing towards a nearby bench. "I'm sure you'll have a good time here tonight."

"I bet I will," Lara agreed. She thought about throwing her arms around the dancer in gratitude, but decided against it. "It was nice meeting you, Helen. I hope you get home safe."

"It was nice to meet you too," said Helen, her smile strained. "I . . . Goodbye, Lara. Don't tell the soldiers where I've gone when you go back to the Underworld." Her hasty farewell made, the ballerina whipped around and hurried off in the opposite direction of the shed. All too soon, the masses of partygoers swallowed her.

Lara waited to see if Helen would reemerge, but too much was happening for her to focus on the departed ballerina. She weaved through the crowd to settle on the bench Helen had pointed out to her, sweeping her tulle skirt beneath her with what she hoped was the grace of a proper lady.

The humid night air pressed in, and Lara basked in the welcome heat. She swung her legs cheerily as she propped Mr. Rabbit on her lap. "It's so nice, isn't it?" She told the toy with an air of confidence. "I can see everything from here,"

"Oh, but you haven't seen everything. Not yet."

Lara glanced up, and found herself staring into the face of a beautiful woman with skin like polished sandalwood. Her hair cascaded down her back in dark waves that stood in sharp contrast to the vivid orange of her dress. The fabric of her gown clung to her supple curves before blossoming outwards at the waist like the petals of a flower stirred to life.

Lara wanted to reach out and finger the shimmering silk of the woman's gown to see if it felt as warm as it looked. But, she was dismayed to see that the longer she gazed at it and sucked in its colors, the more the dress lost its luster.

"What else is there to see?" Lara asked. "Are you in charge of the festival? Is that why you came over?"

"In my own way," the woman said carelessly. "Where did you come from, little thing? You're less human than most here."

Lara plucked at Mr. Rabbit's plush ear. Was it natural for a stranger to recognize her as something other than human so swiftly? She didn't think so, but the woman was being kind. It was only right that Lara should be polite to her. "I live somewhere that's not as nice. There aren't as many colors there," she said. "Mommy's not human, and I don't know who my daddy is. I guess that makes me different."

"You must be from the Underworld," the woman said. "I didn't know they stole children to decorate their dark halls. It's so cruel. Just look at you—you're so pale! When was the last time you saw the sky, little creature? When was the last time you were fed a square of chocolate, a sliver of beef?"

"Nobody stole me," said Lara with a frown, doing her best to ignore the odd endearments. "I've been down underground since always, and I've never had the food from up here. Is it good? It smells good." She tried to reach out and taste the woman's true feelings, but was met with a wall. Whoever the stranger was, she clearly knew a fair bit of magic.

"Oh, it's very good, indeed," the woman said, resurrecting her smile in its full glory. She offered Lara a soft, brown hand. "Would you like to try some of it?"

"I don't have any money." Lara had failed to factor funds into her brilliant escape plan, but the hunger already gnawing at her belly was sharp and belligerent.

"Maybe I could give you these?" The princess raised a hand to indicate the diamond studs in her ears. "Everything here is mine. You can have whatever you like. There's no need to pay for it. You're a child—you must like sweets. See, we have wonderful sugar flowers here. They taste like spring. Have you ever tasted spring before? It's wonderful."

Lara's little, pink tongue snaked out of her mouth to moisten her lips. She slid off the bench. "Yes, I want some," she said as her hunger swelled. All she could think about was food. "I'm a princess, you know. I can pay you back later."

"Oh, a princess!" the woman said with a gasp. "Princesses should be able to have the best of everything. Princess of the Underworld, is that it?"

"Yes." Lara reached up to lace her fingers with the woman's, so warm, unlike her own mother's ice-cold hands. "Mommy says so."

"Of course, of course," the woman said, nodding. She took Lara over to one of the food stalls. "Just one for the child," she told the vendor manning the cart.

The cook laid one of the flowers on a sheet of newspaper and extended it towards her. Lara remembered her manners as she accepted the sweet. "Thank you." She traced a finger across one of the frosted petals, then popped it into her mouth, sucking greedily at the sugar. Her appetite whetted, she sank her teeth into the remainder of the flower, demolishing half of it in a single bite. Just as the woman had promised, it tasted of the joy carried by the death of winter.

As the moon rose higher, the partygoers increased in number. Many had donned Venetian masks for the occasion, their true faces secreted away behind gold plating and spiraling ropes of glitter. Their hands were painted with a variety of brilliant, tropical colors, rich claret, sharp cerulean, inviting fuchsia. The world glimmered like a pane of cathedral glass, shapes and shades bleeding together, and Lara lapped at it as a kitten would at a saucer of milk.

"There's more," the woman said, drawing Lara over to another stall. This one sold fat dumplings glistening with grease. "Eat, eat," she insisted. Although her voice remained gentle, the invitation seemed more like an order than it had before.

Lara did as she was told, and picked up the dumpling, stuffing it into her mouth. The savory flavor burst on her tongue. It was as hearty as the terror of her mother's human prisoners she had devoured in the past. Somehow, though, it was richer, filling her body as human emotions had failed to in the past. Yet the deeper hunger Lara felt remained, and she tugged more lines of light and bliss towards her.

The line of candy-colored thoughts evaporated without warning. "Don't eat my guests!" the woman snapped, and tightened her hold on Lara's hand. Her nails speared into the child's palm, and Lara whimpered in surprise. "There is plenty of food here."

"I'm sorry," Lara whined, "but I'm hungry." Cut off from the sea of history and excitement that floated in the wake of the guests, she felt more ravenous than ever. Lara tried to fend off the rush of panic that threatened to engulf her, hoping that the next dish the stranger offered her would put an end to her ceaseless hunger.

"Then come, and we'll get you more," the woman said. The next stall offered a carton of fat buckwheat noodles, and Lara accepted them with desperation. Too impatient to fumble with the chopsticks provided, she pinched the noodles between her fingers and crammed them between her lips. Lara's small belly began to fill.

While the food was certainly nourishing her physical body, it did nothing for the mental itch she battled with every mouthful. She still felt as hollow as an empty bowl. Why was she still not satisfied after eating so much? That had never happened to her before.

The woman watched as Lara licked her sticky fingers clean, her gaze as avid as a hawk's. "You still want more, little piglet?" she said, with a mocking lilt. She placed her free hand on the small of Lara's back, pushing her on towards the next vendor.

"No child should ever go hungry—not here. What shall we have next? Black beans and pork? Coconut and melon? What about this?" She took a paper dish of sorbet from the counter and guided it towards Lara, her smile dim and cheerless. "What will fill that hole where there should be a girl?"

"It's not my fault I'm hungry!" Lara spat savagely, but in spite of the vile look she directed at the woman, she did not give the cup back. Lara jammed plastic spoon roughly into the cool cream and began to shovel it into her mouth. The sorbet was so tart it stung her lips, but she had no intention of stopping. "Mommy didn't make me right," she said between bites, sniffling. Her eyes burned with unshed tears.

"No," the woman agreed. "She didn't. You're collapsing in on yourself even now without the hearts of others to fill the void in that belly of yours. The only things your mother ever gave birth to were dead things. You are no more alive than cemetery dust."

Lara's face reddened and her eyes shimmered behind their caul of tears, but she did not cry. Princesses did not cry in public. She pinned her lower lip between her teeth to steady herself. "How would you know? I just met you."

"Do you think I cannot see through you?" the woman asked her darkly. She filled up Lara's vision like a mountain range, blotting out the host of stars she had come so far to see. "There are no children below the ground for a reason. There is no sunshine to nurture them, no food, other than sadness and a longing for the light, to help them grow."

The woman ground her nails into the back of Lara's hand again, leaving sickle-shaped indentations in the girl's flesh.

"Your teeth were stolen from the wailing mouths of lost boys and girls, and your bones belong in tombs that should have remained sealed. You were cobbled together from the dead; you are a nothing but a mouth, and the soul your mother chained to that skin, outstripped by your appetite."

Lara ran her tongue along her teeth. They had never merited her attention before, but the woman's description made her fear that they were now sharp and distorted. "I don't believe you," she tried again, her chin jutting out defiantly.

"If I let you have your fill of the people here, your hair would turn scarlet with stolen desire, your lips charcoal gray with despair filched from some poor passer-by." Her denouncement made the air around them tremble. "You are filled with stolen potential. Lives that never were, dreams that never came to pass."

"I'm not a monster!" Lara shouted. She shook her head rapidly from side to side, her composure finally failing her. Her swollen belly heaved and Lara thought for a terrible moment that she might vomit. The food she consumed in the Underworld might weigh heavy on her conscience from now on, but it did not make her feel bloated and sick as human fare did. "I want to go home!" she wailed.

"To what end?" In spite of Lara's pleas, the woman did not look in the mood to release her. "So you can eat the poor singers and dancers and poets who happen to stumble into your mother's realm? Why should I allow that? I know your mother, and I drove her and her appetite from the land."

"You're Tvath! You're Mommy's bad sister!" Lara cried, jerking her arm back in a futile attempt to free herself. "You can't make me stay here! Let me go! Let me go or Mommy will eat you up!"

Tvath laughed. "Eat me?" The sound of her voice could have made empires crumble, and Lara paled beneath it as it reverberated through her bones. "Your mother is crippled by her stupid, vapid hunger, just as you are. I defeated her before. I do not fear her."

"I want to go home," Lara whimpered. Her wild defiance fell away like tattered, autumn leaves. "Please, let me go home. I won't come up here again if you let me go. I promise!" Never returning to the surface would be a terrible concession to make, but it was better than starving to death.

"You don't want to go back," Tvath said. She seemed to shrink back to the size of an ordinary woman as she regained some of her original warmth. But its return gave Lara no comfort. It was impossible to forget the cold rage that had animated her aunt moments before, and the possibility that she might unleash it again made Lara flinch back.

"You would not have come here if your mother had given you what you truly wanted. You would suck the love denied to you from my fingers like honey if I opened myself to a beast like you."

"I would not," protested Lara, her cheeks flushing. But despite her half-hearted outcry, she recognized her aunt's words as the truth, uncomfortable as they were. Lara had come to the surface out of loneliness; returning below ground would only force her back into her former gray and endless state of melancholy.

Tvath dropped to one knee, her dress shifting around her as though it too were alive. "I know what you want," she crooned, her voice every bit as sultry as any singer whose music Lara had gobbled up. "You might be a monstrous little dragon now, but you are still my niece. I could change you into a true princess. When you do not hunger for those around you, no one will run from you. Instead, they will love you as a princess should be loved.

"You could grow up, Lara, and become a queen. Don't you want to change, as a woman should? Wouldn't you rather grow up, than remain your mother's little doll for all eternity?"

"I want . . ." Lara started, her lip quivering as she tried in vain to stave back her tears. She had spent decades in the Underworld and gone unaltered by the malevolent passage of time. Lara should have been a young woman like Helen by now, but she had not grown. "Everyone in the Underworld is afraid of me. Everyone!" she wept, burying her face between her rabbit's ears.

Her mother had been quick to assert that Tvath was their enemy, but Mania's sister had extended Lara a tantalizing offer: the promise of a future Mania herself could not deliver. "I don't want to be a monster. I want to be a princess! Princesses do good things and I can't, not the way I am," Lara said. "Please, I want . . ."

She groped madly for the right phrase that would convince her aunt of her sincerity, but her desires caught in her throat like stones. They were too vast to be contained in mere words. How could she express the intensity of the longing that had dogged her for her entire life? She wanted the love her mother and the citizens of the Underworld denied her more than anything.

"I can make you a real girl," said Tvath, stroking Lara's loose curls. Her voice was full of pity and kindness. "Would you like that, little princess? Your blood will boil and your belly will scream with hunger for a time. But I promise you that in the end, you will be a real child and dream your own dreams, not those of the children that were broken to forge you."

Lara's silent weeping thinned until finally, only the echo of it hung, distilled, in the heady festival air. "I want to be real," she gasped. Lara reached out and dug one hand, her fingers still spotted from grease from her binge, into Tvath's rippling dress. "Please, make me grow up! I want to be like you! I want to live up here and have friends!"

"All things are possible," Tvath soothed. "I will feed you apples, I will fill you with bread and all the wonders of the world. You will be the most beautiful and just princess when you have shed the appetite that governs you. You will be my heir instead of your mother's, for I have no children myself. And you—you haven't even had a proper mother."

Lara nearly sprang to Mania's defense, but the spark of devotion she felt towards Underworld's queen had grown dim. Tvath was right. When had Mania ever behaved like a mother? When had she comforted Lara or played with her? When had the queen thought of anyone but herself?

If her aunt had told Lara the truth, Mania carried the responsibility for her court's exile. Mania was a black hole of a creature capable of nothing but gorging herself on human lives and artistry.

Lara began to understand why her aunt had cast her mother down into the depths of the earth. Mania and her court would have descended like a swarm of insects to devour the watercolor dashes of life that wafted from every man, woman, and child at Tvath's festival if they'd had the chance.

"Let me stay with you," Lara pleaded. "You'll take care of me, won't you? You could make me a real lady." She might always be haunted by the memory of starvation no matter how many alterations her aunt made to her, but what point was there to living if Lara existed only to consume and never be fulfilled?

"I'll do anything to stay here! I don't want to hurt anyone anymore. I want to make beautiful things like you, not destroy them."

"If you promise not to eat my friends," Tvath said, "I will take you into my house and allow you to live with my court. You will be a princess of life, not of death. I will be strict with you, but I will also love you, little one." Her smile had a touch of sadness to it. "You are not the only one who has been lonely. Queens have little time to cultivate loved ones."

Euphoria broke on Lara's face like the summer still to come, chasing the agonized darkness from its hollow, white inclines. "Yes," Lara said in hushed and reverent whisper. "Yes, I promise."

When Lara's aunt leaned in to embrace her, she smelled of pomegranates, and all the temptations that came with the prospect of a new life.

It was a gift Lara was all too happy to accept.

* * *

COST OF CUSTODY

R. M. RIDLEY

Jonathan approached his car, holding his phone to his ear while trying to extract his keys from his pants pocket.

"Nothing dark, I know, Ralph. I've known since we stole beer from your uncle, how many decades ago now?"

Jonathan managed to free the key ring and looked at the multitude of metal pieces barely illuminated by the street lights. He tried to figure how he owned so many when he only used three: one for his apartment, two for the car. He never locked his office. That way, he'd never have a busted door. Jonathan felt he didn't make enough as a P.I. to pay for another's inept lock-picking skills.

"Okay, I'll pick up two six-packs. I need smokes anyway."

As he inserted the key into the car door, Jonathan heard his name called out hesitantly. He was certain he could get in the Lincoln quick enough; unfortunately, it wasn't the sort of vehicle that allowed for a quick getaway. Sometimes getting Ralph to tow it was the getaway.

Jonathan turned and saw a blond, but mostly bald on top, thirty-something guy crossing the street. He walked as though his legs were rentals; his eyes were red as the sinking sun, and his cheeks slick as a boat in a storm. By the glow of the streetlights, his flesh held all the color of old snow.

Jonathan lowered the phone and hesitated over his answer. All he wanted was to sit in Ralph's salvage yard, drink a few beers, and watch the dogs and gremlins chase each other. What he didn't want was a weeping nerd, but Mick Jagger had a catchy tune about wanting and getting.

"You are Mr. Alvey, right?"

"Most days," Jonathan replied. He brought the phone back up and said, "Looks like I've angered karma once again, Ralph. I'll call you later," and hung up.

"I'm glad I caught you, Mr. Alvey. I—I don't know where else to go, and Gail said I should see you. She said you'd help. I don't want trouble, but she can't just do this."

"All right, come with me." Jonathan steered the man back across the street. "You say Gail sent you?"

"Yes, she said you'd helped her once. That you were an honest man."

"Gail's prone to exaggeration," he mumbled, opening the door to the Lucky Monkey restaurant. "Let's go inside, and see if we can't sort out what's wrong."

As they stepped into the quiet room, the man exclaimed, "What's wrong is that she's taken my little girl!"

Jonathan choked back a sound. Unbidden from his memory came the image of the boy tied to the bed, Jonathan's father standing over him, reading from the Bible, and anointing him with holy water.

Bao, the owner of The Lucky Monkey, brought Jonathan back to the here and now by placing a hand on his arm and motioning towards a seat by the kitchen.

"Just tea, please, my friend."

Bao gave a small bow and disappeared into the steamy kitchen.

"All right, let's start at the beginning. What's your name?"

"Ben."

"You have a last name?"

"Tate."

"Okay, Mr. Tate, what do you do for a living?" Jonathan didn't much care, but he needed some time to calm Ben and, if he was being truthful, himself after that memory of his father.

"I teach at the U—chemistry."

"Now, Mr. Tate, you said someone took your daughter."

"Yes, my wife—ex-wife."

"Why haven't you gone to the police?"

"I just . . . I don't want problems. I don't want her to get in trouble, but she can't do this. I've got a right to see my daughter."

Bao arrived, discreetly filled their cups with tea, and then disappeared again.

"How long's it been since you saw her?"

"My daughter?"

Jonathan nodded, sipped some of his tea, and told himself that the guy wasn't being obtuse on purpose.

"Since last weekend. I get Rose on weekends. I was supposed to get her today, but my wife called and said it was off, that I couldn't come. She said if I tried . . ." He gulped in a breath. "She said if I tried, she'd call the police."

"I see." Jonathan didn't like the direction he saw this tale heading but forged on. "Is this sort of behavior usual for your ex? Is she volatile, moody?"

Ben shook his head and stared morosely into his tea. Jonathan wanted to light a cigarette, but Bao didn't allow smoking in his place. He briefly wondered why he hadn't led the guy up to his office, but he really hated being alone with weeping people, especially grown men.

Everything in Jonathan said this guy wasn't the abusive type. Ben wasn't at his ex's place pounding down doors, but here, sipping tea and weeping softly. Still . . .

"And you can't think of any reason that she'd bar you from seeing your daughter?"

Ben looked blankly at Jonathan. The man truly had no idea what Jonathan was implying.

"Look, I got to ask. Any reason your ex would think you had abused your girl?" Before Ben could get indignant, Jonathan clarified. "Did she trip, fall out of bed, bump her head running around, anything like that?"

Ben's shoulders slumped, his anger at Jonathan's accusations never reaching potential.

"No. I can't think of anything, and I swear—I swear on my life—I would never lay a hand on my daughter. Rose is everything to me—to us. My wife and I have differing opinions on things, but not Rose."

Jonathan had noticed how often Ben referred to his "wife" and not his "ex," which meant two things: a recent divorce, and Ben still loved her. Jonathan wondered if it was important.

"That's why this is such a shock. It's not like Darla to say I can't see my own daughter."

Jonathan understood right then he was being presented with Pandora's box. He got an ugly feeling in his stomach that had nothing to do with the bourbon from earlier mixing with the tea. This felt like an octopus had wrapped its tentacles around his innards and started pulling. Jonathan knew the feeling too well, and it meant he had better travel with his doctor's bag of tricks.

"All right, Ben, this is what's going to happen: we're going to go to your wife's place."

Ben started to object, spilling tea over the edge of the cup and onto his hand, but of the two of them, only Jonathan noticed.

"I know what she said, which is why you are going to park on the street, while I go up to the house. And you are going to wait until I come and get you. Got it?"

Ben nodded. "Yeah. Sure. Thank you, Mr. Alvey."

"Don't thank me; I haven't done anything yet. Now, you promise you'll stay in your car?"

"I will."

Jonathan tried to gauge the sincerity of Ben's answer. He believed the man meant it now; it was the two minutes after getting there that Jonathan worried about.

Too often people's best intentions went south when emotions came into play. Most people couldn't do what had to be done when dealing with loved ones. Jonathan knew, all too well, the fortitude of will it took to act against your instinct.

†††

In the solitude of his own car, following Ben's sedan towards the ex's place, Jonathan glanced at his bag of esoteric paraphernalia on the seat beside him. The nagging feeling of this case being more than it seemed still hounded him. Somehow, he just knew the problem's roots lurked in the dark loam of the paranormal; once you'd touched it, you could always feel its influence.

Jonathan hated using magic: it was a drug that made morphine look like children's chewable vitamins. Once you'd used magic, then came the draw, a pulling at your skin and an itch in your soul. The more magic you used, the more of yourself you used up. Every atom that magic burned out became something different—something both powerful and crippling. But sometimes, the only way to defeat magic was to use magic. Jonathan hoped this wasn't one of those times.

The suburb Ben led him through had been new twenty years before, a mouse maze for the middle class, and they'd flocked to it like blue cheese. The streets wound like a hung man's bowels and each house looked identical to its neighbor. Not even the cars in the driveways set them apart. Just as Jonathan began doubting anyone's ability to find a house in there from memory, Ben pulled to the curb.

Jonathan parked the Lincoln in the driveway and got out. He walked back to Ben and found him gripping the steering wheel while looking resolutely ahead. Jonathan reached through the window and turned off the car, leaving the keys in the ignition.

"Sit tight while I go have a quick chat with your ex."

The darkness of the front porch accentuated the dim light coming from inside the house. A quick glance through the garage door window showed the shape of a minivan. Darla was home.

Jonathan stepped onto the low porch, and the hairs rose on his arms. It felt like the skin around the base of his neck rippled as the wards and sigils of protection he had tattooed there reacted to whatever had tipped him off at the restaurant. There was, or had been, something there: it wasn't simply a spell or a warding—his tattoos had reacted to something else. What, became the question.

Self-preservation made Jonathan hesitate before knocking. He had no proof of anything, just the words of the man in the car. Jonathan did a quick check over his shoulder to make sure Ben actually remained where he'd left him. He had, but if this were an elaborate set up, then Ben would be required to stick around to confirm Jonathan had sprung the trap.

"The problem with paranoia is you never have time to gloat when you're right," Jonathan sighed to himself.

He checked the screen door and the featureless wooden one behind it for spell work or hexes. Not finding any, he knocked. He waited, his eyes on the window to the left of him. Nearly a full minute passed while nothing happened, but then Jonathan saw it: a flicker in the light quality—someone moving inside the house.

When he knocked again, Jonathan suspected one of two things would happen: either Darla would shut off the inside light, or she would come and peek out the window. If the former occurred, that meant fear ruled her. If the latter, then curiosity was the dominate emotion. Each choice held significance.

He knocked, and a moment later, the darkness at the window took shape. For an instant, the shadows became deeper and contoured. Then, they resumed the flat, unrevealing darkness. Fear hadn't strangled her yet.

"Darla. My name's Jonathan Alvey." With no reason to broadcast his voice, as he knew she stood just on the other side of the door, he spoke normally. "Darla, Ben came to see me. I'm a private investigator, and he wanted me to talk to you about your daughter. I think you should open the door. Ben is very upset, and I hate to see grown men cry."

While he waited, Jonathan gauged his reaction to the house. Whatever had first disturbed him lingered but hadn't grown. If Darla only opened the door a crack and gave him a cheap excuse, he might have to re-evaluate the situation. That sort of answer implied she feared a danger that was close and immediate.

"Darla, Ben says he has a legal right to see Rose. If that's true, my next step is to alert the authorities."

Jonathan heard the chain being unlatched, then the door opened on a woman whose appearance made Ben look well put-together.

Just from the way she clutched the dissolving tissue in her hand, he knew Darla was strung out. With wide, red-rimmed eyes, she looked everywhere outside but not at him. Her make-up made Jonathan think of white wash on rotting clapboard, and she continuously raked her hand through her hair, causing it to stand on end.

From inside came a familiar smell, but Jonathan told himself he was mistaken.

"Who are you?" she uttered, suddenly pinning him with her gaze.

"Just who I said I was. I'm here about Rose."

"He can't see her. You—you have to make him understand that. It's just—just for this weekend. I'll make it up to him. I promise I will. He can have her . . . he can have extra days, just not now. Please, you have to go."

"So he didn't—"

"No. It's not him. Look, you really—just please, please go."

Jonathan couldn't do that, nor could he ignore that smell any longer: blood.

Darla showed no signs of being injured, and the blood didn't smell fresh. Jonathan caught her eyes with his and spoke in a soft, deep tone, his speech pattern regulated, even.

"Darla, whose blood is it?"

"Kiri's," she answered without inflection. Shocked, her hand flew to her mouth.

He continued. "Is Rose here?"

"No," she sobbed.

Jonathan nodded. "We're going to pretend to leave. Unlock the back door. You need help, and I think I might be the best you're going to get."

"They said no police!"

"Trust me, I'm no cop."

She gave a pathetic nod, and Jonathan walked back to his car. He managed to start it on the third try, and, pulling up beside Ben's sedan, leaned across the wide seat and cranked down the window.

"No questions, just follow."

Ben started to open his mouth, took one look at the house, and then simply nodded. Jonathan felt hope seeing Ben show a bit of backbone. The man was going to have to find all a father's strength to get to the end of this ordeal.

Jonathan drove a few blocks, until he found a space big enough for both cars to park. Grabbing his doctor's bag, he got out and motioned Ben to join him at the side of the road.

"Something's happened and Darla's frightened to death. Who is Kiri?"

Ben gaped at him.

"Ben. Kiri, who is she?"

"She's Rose's au pair."

"All right, I'm telling you this now so by the time we get to the house you'll be past the shock. You have to be strong for your family, understand?"

Ben nodded and actually bit down on his cheek, but he'd stopped crying.

"Kiri has been hurt—I believe killed." Ben gasped but said nothing. "Your daughter's missing."

Ben mouthed the word 'no' but Jonathan continued.

"They told Darla not to contact anyone. That's why she said you couldn't have Rose this weekend. We're going back, but if someone is watching, we can't be seen, so we'll approach from the back. However, I think it best to stack the odds in our favor."

"How will . . . ?"

Jonathan knelt and told Ben to do the same. He took out a pouch from his bag and shook out some dirt onto Ben's palm.

Ben furrowed his brow and rubbed at the small pile with the finger of his other hand. "What—?"

"Consecrated earth," Jonathan replied, taking out a small copper flask.

"Consecra—cemetery dirt?" Ben almost tipped the pile off his palm, but Jonathan gripped his hand and held it still.

"Gail trusted me enough to send you to me, right?"

"Yeah."

"That's because I have certain skills. Right now, I believe—hell, I know—you need those skills. Now, sit tight for your daughter's sake."

Jonathan opened the flask and splashed a bit of water onto the dirt. "Holy water," he said, sliding the flask into his suit pocket. He produced a piece of hematite and pushed it into the mud. "Now, no matter what, hold still."

Jonathan extended his hand out over Ben's and began to rub

his ring finger and his middle finger against each other. He spoke seven words in Greek, and a shadow began to wrap around the two fingers. He moved his fingers rapidly and yet the darkness which entwined them remained motionless.

Ben breathed hard and fast and his eyes grew wide but continued to stay crouched. Jonathan figured the man was literally scared stiff, but didn't care as long as it kept Ben still.

Once a sufficient amount of shadow had gathered, Jonathan breathed on the back of his hand and the smoke fell, disappearing into the mud on Ben's palm.

Jonathan plucked the hematite out of the mud and tossed it into the doctor's bag. He scooped some of the mud from Ben's hand and placing his fingers on the ajna chakra, at the center of Ben's brow, drew a symbol over what was referred to as the third eye. Jonathan then did the same for himself.

Bag in hand, Jonathan stood up. "Keep to the shadows and move quietly."

Ben stood, but looked from his hand to Jonathan's head.

"Move, Ben. Your family needs you."

"Right." Ben nodded and started down the street.

Jonathan swore when he realized that the neighborhood had no alleyways to snake through. Seeing no other option, he vaulted over the four-foot, chain link fence surrounding the first property and started to cross the yard.

Hearing his client's feet slip on the plastic coating of the fence, Jonathan slowed. However, a moment later, Ben was beside him, nodding that he was okay. It wouldn't go as smoothly as he had hoped. Jonathan pushed Ben forward, towards the next property divider.

Ten minutes later, and only three houses from Darla's place, they found themselves facing a six-foot wall of wood planks that ran from street to street. Jonathan crouched down, and with some encouragement, Ben placed one foot on his hands and scrambled over.

He grabbed the top of the fence himself and, swung up, and over, only to find Ben frozen where he had landed. Jonathan feared his client had sprained—or worse, broke—something until he saw the German Shepherd staring in their direction

Jonathan began walking as quietly as he could, confident in the concealment spell he'd cast. The dog cocked its head but continued sitting. Jonathan motioned for Ben to get moving.

Jonathan saw the dog swing its head slowly back and forth with an odd look on its face. It could hear them, and probably had caught their scent, but the spell worked, and, in the darkness, they were hidden from the canine's eyes.

Soon the Shepherd gave up and lay with its paws over its muzzle. Once Ben joined him, Jonathan decided not to risk the chance of injuring his client and eased open the gate which lead to the front, and quietly shut it behind them.

Jonathan hadn't wanted to come at the house from the front. The spell he'd done wouldn't hold up against the glare of the streetlights or the landscape lights illuminating the sterile lawns. He edged into the neighbor's surgically shaped bushes, pulling Ben down with him.

Jonathan took two full minutes to scan the area. He saw nothing unusual—no vehicles parked at the curb, no movement at windows, not even a cat slinking by. Jonathan hated to admit that he'd slunk, climbed, and cast a spell for nothing—but it was true.

"Come on," he said, and straightening, walked briskly to Darla's place.

The back door opened into the kitchen; the only light a low wattage florescent over the sink. They found Darla sitting in the gloom at the dining room table. Before her lay a feast of memories, served up in two-by-five slices. The pictures all featured the same dark haired, bright-eyed child. The newest photos put Rose at two, maybe not even.

"She's such a good girl. Why would anyone do this?"

Before Jonathan could come up with an answer, Ben crouched beside Darla and enfolded her in his arms.

"I didn't think you'd come," she murmured into his neck.

Jonathan had questions, but some of them could be answered with a little exploration and following his nose.

He had learned there existed scents that, once you knew them, once you'd been forced to confront them, you became unable to forget. Having come across those odors more often than he cared to admit, it became possible for him to be his own hound dog.

Jonathan found the corpse in the child's room.

Something wasn't adding up. A good quantity of blood had soaked into the carpet around the cadaver but nowhere else. The body resembled a rag doll, left crumpled in a corner. Despite the blood, he couldn't see an obvious wound. And most curious, even in this small room, the smell hadn't gotten any stronger.

Careful to avoid setting a knee into the dried gore, Jonathan crouched to turn the body over. The stench of rot assaulted him, then. Jonathan forced himself to ignore the smell and placed his hands on the body.

Kiri's clothes, as well as her long brown hair, had become a hardened red shroud. He had to push hard to separate her from the carpet.

Looking about, Jonathan spotted a long-handled hairbrush on the dresser and went to retrieve it. Beside the brush lay a prayer card, and, as the son of a pastor, Jonathan knew its type. He opened it and read the quote: 'I baptize you with water unto repentance, but He who is coming after . . . will baptize you with the Holy Spirit and fire. Matthew 3:11'. Under this was a time and date. Rose had yet to be baptized.

Unconsecrated: the flesh of the fallen.

Jonathan returned to the body and used the brush to move the hair plastered to the dead woman's neck. What he found unsettled him.

At the back of her neck, he saw a ragged hole that looked like someone had bitten down into her very spine, chewed up the hunk of flesh, and probed at the spinal fluid with its tongue.

With a sigh, he ran his hands over his face and swore. He knew of a few things that might make a wound like that, but only one matched with the rest of the evidence—a ghul. Only a ghul could have hidden the body—smell and all. With one last curse, he made his way back to the dining room.

He found the two as he'd left them: Ben on his knees with his arms encircling Darla, her head resting on his shoulder. In soft voices, they spoke to each other, and Jonathan hated to disturb them, but he had to for them to have any chance of saving their daughter—if she still lived. Jonathan believed she did.

If the ghul had just wanted a snack, it would have devoured the toddler in the room he'd just left. It had left with the infant, and more importantly, had bothered to mess with the mother. It wasn't unheard of for a ghul to play mind games, but usually they did so with the intended victims and not for a fast snack already in its possession.

An eastern ghul differed completely from a western ghoul. A ghoul was one of the living dead. It ate only the flesh of humans, usually devouring dead meat, but it would consume the living if they presented as easy prey. Ghouls were like mildly intelligent movie zombies.

But this family had run afoul of a ghul, Jonathan was fairly certain, a type of djinn. Djinn were intelligent, cunning, and, according to Arabic legend, made from 'the fire of a scorching wind.'

Luckily, ghuls were the inbred cousins of the djinn family. He had run into one before, and, though it had not been pretty, he had gotten the better of it. If he had faced one of the other types of djinn, Jonathan honestly didn't know who'd have come out on top.

A ghul would eat human flesh but only of the living, and only to gain the ability to 'become' that person. They were shape shifters, and, like all djinn, masters of illusion.

"It's worse than I imagined. Your daughter wasn't kidnapped— not in the way you think. I'm sorry, but if you want to save your daughter, we have to act."

"They'll call. They will," Darla pleaded.

Ben, luckily, had more of his wits about him. Jonathan didn't know if the difference had to do with Darla living with the stress longer, or because Ben had passed through a mental barrier by witnessing Jonathan conjure. Either way, Ben seemed up to the task, and Jonathan thought he might just be capable of bringing Darla along.

"Darla, when did Kiri start acting weird?" Jonathan pressed.

"How? I mean she—Yes."

"When, Darla? How long?"

It took a moment, but with Ben gently encouraging her to think back, Darla took a deep breath and, wiping at the tears on her cheek with the back of her hand, answered. "Beginning of the week, Tuesday maybe. She . . . there was something about her that made me uncomfortable, but I thought . . . I don't know. I mean, we all have days, right?" Jonathan could hear the guilt in the question. "Times when life is dragging at you. Every job can be frustrating sometimes—I mean, I know she adores Rose."

Darla put her hand over her mouth as she realized she'd used the present tense. "I just thought Kiri was in a mood. I know we all have runs when everything someone says seem to bother you"—Jonathan caught the way she looked sadly at Ben for a moment—"when we don't appreciate what we have." She lightly touched her finger tip to a picture of Rose's sitting on Ben's lap. "I just assumed it would pass and everything would return to how it was supposed to be."

A week gave Jonathan hope. It meant the ghul had invested time in Rose. Jonathan had no time to spare, however.

"There's no one watching the house. Your daughter hasn't been taken by kidnappers. To get Rose back, I'll need both of you to trust me. I'll need both of you to prove your love in blood—literally."

Darla expression clearly showed her confusion and fear. Jonathan could have lied to comfort her, but right now, that wasn't his job and he'd never been good at it anyway.

"Ben, I need you to get a sharp knife from the kitchen, a fair-sized container, and the largest tea towel you can find." Ben looked at him, not quite registering what he'd heard. "Now, Ben."

Ben managed to untangle himself from his ex. Jonathan had no way of easing Darla into what had to happen. He could only hope that Ben would support him, for what Jonathan was about to ask of them would give pause even to those who truly believed in magic.

Wishing he were with Ralph drinking beer and not about to make these people do what had to be done, Jonathan said, "Darla, I need to find your daughter. To do that, I need some of what you three share. I need a part of each of you." He held the knife casually, but in her line of sight.

Ben braved the question. "What exactly are you proposing?"

"To put it bluntly, Ben, I need to mingle your blood with Darla's to form a spell which can lead us to Rose. The incantation acts on the link you already possess with your daughter, a link of blood, of the soul."

Trying to sugarcoat it would be like dribbling honey down the throat of someone you were force-feeding bees to, so he didn't bother.

"I need you both to cut symbols of power into yourselves, forging a binding spell and making you a beacon. It's the only way, Ben, and I warn you now, that it isn't going to be pleasant."

Ben hesitated, but looked hard into Jonathan's eyes. "What do we do?"

Jonathan started by tracing the symbol on Darla's palm with a marker. He left it up to Ben to convince her to cut that very symbol into her own flesh. Jonathan would have made the cut, but for that particular spell to have power, Darla had to be a willing participant.

Jonathan wondered why their marriage hadn't managed to survive, for Ben and Darla still shared something strong, as evidenced by the blood running free from her palm. Jonathan set the container under the wound to collect the blood and set about drawing the symbols Ben would have to cut on his arm. One would match Darla's, but another four would go up his forearm.

Jonathan didn't speak as he drew the symbols. Ben knew the score. He had witnessed Jonathan summon shadow and now watched the blood of his ex-wife as it collected in a Tupperware container.

"Your turn, Ben."

Ben pressed the tip of the knife against his skin near his elbow. He swallowed, shut his eyes, and pushed. Jonathan reached out swiftly and gripped his hand.

"This'll scar no matter what, so just go deep enough to bleed, okay? You're no good to anyone if you pass out from blood loss, or damage your muscle."

Ben nodded, and Jonathan let go. Ben continued to run the stainless-steel edge along the black marker on his arm. He hissed through his clenched teeth and the blood ran in thin rivulets, seeking to fertilize the ground. Jonathan slipped the pristine tea towel under Ben's arm, and, drip-by-drip, the idyllic country landscape printed on it was blotted out.

Once Ben had reached the third symbol, Jonathan knew he no longer felt the pain of each slice; his arm had morphed into one stinging burn. Jonathan could tell because Ben's pace picked up. With each cut masked by the ones before, the work went faster. Jonathan honestly wished he could have saved Ben from the ordeal, but it simply wasn't in his power.

Jonathan stopped empathizing and went to search the kitchen for plastic wrap. He found some easy enough, and a lucky guess discovered the Crown Royal in the cupboard above the stove; the same place his mother had kept alcohol when he was young.

Jonathan returned to see Ben cutting the last symbol. He poured whiskey for each of them, tossed his back, and immediately refilled it.

"Drink, Darla. You need it. You have to hold down the fort. We'll call as soon as there is something to call about."

"No." The sound was almost a whimper. "Don't leave me alone."

"Drink," Jonathan said, sliding the glass towards her.

She looked to the glass as if seeing it for the first time. The hand that reached for it shook, but she raised it to her lips without spilling much. Ben waited to be sure Darla drank, then took a good portion of his without any encouragement.

"Throw back the rest, Ben. Trust me; you'll be glad you did."

Glancing from Jonathan to his ex, Ben did as instructed.

The towel had turned completely crimson now, and the container under Darla's hand had collected a noticeable amount of blood. Telling Darla to go bandage her hand, Jonathan took the towel, dunked it into the Tupperware, and slid both under Ben's arm.

Jonathan lifted the sodden cloth and began to chant in Gaelic. It seemed odd not calling upon his own energies, but he summoned the power that resided in the symbols, the blood, and the innate magic that connects a family together.

Darla returned holding her injured hand, wrapped in white gauze, to her chest. A detached part of Jonathan noticed the tiniest of blooms had pushed through the snowy weave.

"What's he doing?" Her eyes were wide and blood-shot; they looked awful against her ashen skin.

"Let him be, Darla. I've seen—I can't even describe what he did, but we need to trust him. I trust him, and I know that you trust me."

She sunk into her chair, and picking up a photo of Rose, absently took another drink of whiskey.

Jonathan instructed Ben to hold his arm out, and then took the cloth and began to wrap it around the man's arm. He began with one corner resting on the first symbol Ben had cut, the mark of Tsoa Wang, god of hearth and family. He then wound down over St. Anthony's name and the hieroglyph of Bast. He covered the cut for Lovantucarus, protector of youth. The end of the blood-soaked linen Jonathan laid on the symbol in Ben's palm, the match to Darla's.

The moment Jonathan covered that final symbol, Ben screamed out in pain. He went taut, fighting the energy that seared through his body. Jonathan expected it and pinned Ben's arm between his own arm and body. When the magic had completed its course, Ben slumped.

Jonathan relaxed his hold and motioned for Darla to fill Ben's glass.

She put her hand on the bottle but paused. "He's not much of a drinker."

"This is no time for aspirin," Jonathan replied and slid the bottle from her grasp.

Ben gratefully gulped back a large swallow.

"Worst is over, Ben. It's not all over, but you've passed through the nastiest part. That burn in your arm—that faint glow marking the symbols through the cloth—that means it wasn't in vain. Rose is alive, and now we have the means to find her. Finish up that whiskey."

Jonathan grabbed the roll of plastic wrap and began to wind it tightly around Ben's arm, working down from the elbow as he had with the towel until satisfied that it couldn't leak, or shift. He didn't want the blood to dry, but he didn't want Ben to bleed out; the plastic would take care of both.

"Darla, we can't waste time retrieving one of our cars—we need yours."

Jonathan didn't want to admit the all-too-real worry of his Lincoln stalling out. Speed and reliability were essential, so despite his fondness for his steel block on wheels, Darla's minivan presented their best option.

"Take me with you—please." There was no ignoring the heartbreak in her voice.

Ben looked to him, but Jonathan shook his head.

He wasn't ignoring her pain; he was saving her from more.

He didn't know where they were going, or what they might find when they get there. They already had too many variables on this trip for him to play babysitter as well. Making her understand that, to see beyond the immediate need to be with her child, Jonathan didn't know if he had that kind of magic.

It seemed Ben had some magic of his own, however.

"One of us needs to be here for Rose," he said, placing his hand on her cheek. "I have to know *you're* safe."

She drew away from his touch and tears began to slide down her cheeks. She looked away from him, to the pictures of her daughter. After a moment, she bit her lip and nodded. When Ben reached out to hug her, she clung to him.

Jonathan tossed back the second whiskey and then went into the kitchen to grab his bag and wait. She said something to Ben, but Jonathan only caught the word 'safe,' and then Ben passed him, grabbing a set of keys from a wall hook.

Jonathan followed him into the garage but laid his hand on Ben's shoulder when he tried to get in the driver's seat.

"You're in no shape. You can't drive in that pain, plus—you're the beacon. I need you to focus on what that arm—hell, your whole body—is telling you. I'll do the easy part of aiming the car. You have to tell me which direction.

"Why did you two split?" Jonathan asked, as he backed out the car into the street.

Ben didn't look at him but sighed, "I don't think either of us know now. At the time we seemed to have become different people but . . ." He turned toward Jonathan, his face set. "What now?"

"Just go with your gut, Ben. Right now, you're like a radio tuning into your daughter. Which way?"

Ben hesitated. He doubted his own gut; an easy enough thing to do with so much riding on a feeling. One word could consume so much confidence.

"Rose, Ben."

Jonathan spoke slowly, with no demand, no worry. He cheated and used the magic he'd already laid on Ben as a conduit for drawing on Ben's unconscious, this touch of hypnosis.

"Where's Rose?"

"Left," Ben answered as calmly as he'd been asked.

He'd simply allowed himself to know, and Jonathan didn't ask again. He spun the wheel hard, stomped on the pedal, and the Toyota gave a little squeal before shooting down the road.

"Keep talking to me. Keep me heading in the right direction. It's all about Rose now."

They'd traveled a few blocks in silence, and Jonathan worried he'd have to prod his passenger again, when Ben winced and barked out the word. At the next intersection, Jonathan hardly slowed as he spun the wheel. Before long, it became apparent they were heading to the rough part of the city. Jonathan wasn't surprised.

Ben continued to indicate changes in direction a few seconds early by hissing in pain. The effort and pain had turned his face ashen and sweat beaded his brow, yet he managed his job and Jonathan managed the wheel.

↟ ↟ ↟

They'd entered the part of the city known as Blacklight; the area where junkies crawled off to die, where prostitutes who kept their faces hidden sold their wares, and dead men eked out a life stealing the dreams washed into the gutters. That deep in, Jonathan didn't bother with the brake; there, you stop to taunt death or dump the body.

The streetlights were broken out, and flame licked long shadows from trash barrels. Dark shapes refused to betray their true nature, and the eyes that watched them were unlidded and cold. It was here Ben writhed in his seat, his voice straining to escape clenched teeth. Jonathan slammed on the brake and undid his seatbelt. He took Ben's chin in his hand and turned it, so he could look him in the eyes.

"Where's Rose?"

Ben lifted the bloodied arm and pointed. "Fourth floor."

"Let's go get your girl, Ben."

Jonathan took out his knife and, placing the tip under the plastic wrap, slid the blade down the length of Ben's arm. The red sheath fell way like a snake's skin and he told Ben to unwrap the towel. Ben uncovered his wounds, which, though still splayed, had ceased to bleed. He tossed the towel to the floor between his feet as Jonathan grabbed his bag from the back seat.

They got out of the van, and Jonathan stopped long enough to draw a crude figure on the hood with silver-imbued petroleum jelly, making it unlikely anyone, or anything, would touch the vehicle. It wouldn't do to save the child but still be trapped in a version of hell that the city had cultured like a fungus in a petri dish.

Ben already looked better, and Jonathan felt a small sliver of worry slide away, but when his client tried to go first, Jonathan had to shove him to the side. Someone had replaced the glass center of the dilapidated door with bulging plywood, hiding everything on the other side. Jonathan pushed his bag into Ben's arms, slid his Beretta from its shoulder holster, and yanked the door open.

A long hall awaited them, which ended with a flickering bulb at the base of some stairs. Stagnant air leaked out, carrying the odors of mold, decay, and rot. The wet-dog smell underlying all that assured Jonathan they had found the right place.

As he stepped into the hall, Jonathan wondered if he shouldn't have made Ben wait in the car, but in truth, he didn't know what lurked up there. When dealing with djinn, even ghuls, nothing was certain. Ben's presence meant Jonathan could stall and give Ben time to get Rose out of the decomposing nest of rat droppings and blood.

They edged down the hall, past doorways that gaped dark, like missing teeth in the mouth of a fanatic. Just as they reached the stairs, there came a rustle and a grunt. A creature with pale flaking flesh and broken blood vessels rushed at them.

Ben simply snapped out his arm, and his fist connected with a crack that echoed briefly in the building, only to be swallowed by the sagging walls. The thing staggered backwards, a muffled howl leaking out from around the layers of cloth that were wrapped around its hands. As suddenly as it had come, it was gone, enfolded by the black embrace of the building.

"Was that it?" Ben gasped.

Jonathan wanted to grin but couldn't seem to find the muscles to move his mouth that way.

"No. That was just some junkie."

Jonathan saw Ben's relief mingle with shame.

"But you threw one hell of a punch." When Ben continued to stare down the hall where the person had fled, Jonathan put his hand out and tugged Ben towards the stairs. "Come on."

The stairs creaked ominously as they ascended, and as the two of them worked their way up, the treads began to sag more under their weight. At each floor, the landings opened up to a hall. It felt like staring into a corpse's throat.

The fourth floor was just as dark and ugly as the other levels, but the fug had grown thicker, that wet dog smell heavier, and mixed in, the unmistakable scent of rotting flesh. Ben gagged, and Jonathan pulled from his pocket the container he'd used to mark the van. Ben looked at him disbelieving.

"Mint boosts effectiveness. Just rub some under your nose."

Jonathan knew he had to be sharp. He had to be cunning and careful for both of them—for all three of them. The ghul had to know they were there, but it wasn't likely to attack unless forced to. A ghul knew its mortality and used its brain more than brawn. It could assume the form of a dog or of the last one it fed on—in this case, Kiri. It had hidden the body of the au pair for a week with a certain amount of magic it possessed, mostly illusion.

Jonathan indicated silence, grateful the moldering carpet would muffle their footsteps. The smell, more than anything else, tipped him off to which room the creature inhabited: meat and dog—both gone bad.

Jonathan paused outside the doorway to switch weapons. His Berretta would be useless against the ghul, or at least its ammo would. A normal bullet would pass through the djinn with little effect. What damage it did suffer would heal swiftly.

He reached under his jacket and tugged the revolver from the small of his back. After checking to make sure all six chambers were loaded, he nodded to Ben and slipped into the room.

The scene matched the stench. In the far corner, he saw a small pile of meat from no recognizable animal, the bones being too broken, the flesh too corrupted. Near that carnage, Rose lay on her back, smeared with blood, crying and wearing nothing but a diaper. Ben brushed past him dropping the bag.

Jonathan's instincts told him to fire into the other corner—the dark, apparently empty one. Not knowing where Rose really was, or if the ghul held her, he had to restrain himself. Yet, if he holstered his gun to banish the djinn's illusion, he feared that he would fail, his magic not strong enough.

Ben had lifted his daughter from the floor, but the desperate wails of a cold, scared, child continued. Jonathan then saw the way through the trap. The spell that bound Ben and Darla to their offspring could be used for Rose. A phrase reversed the spell, allowing the child to 'feel' the parents.

He spoke in Gaelic, trusting enough fresh blood lingered on Ben's wounds. The child's screams stopped. Ben collapsed to his knees in pain, but the flare of magic had momentarily exposed the truth.

Ben heaved the lump of festering muscle he'd been cradling, which thudded heavily to the floor. Jonathan heard a toddler sob, followed by a faint snarl from the dark corner. Glad that ghuls were slaves to their animalistic sides, Jonathan put two shots into the darkness at the sound of the growl.

The illusions wavered. Jonathan glimpsed the ghul rising and saw what had appeared as piled meat become Rose. Her banshee wails had become pathetic, hiccupped sobs, as she watched her father from a few feet away.

From the ghul: a roar of anger and a hex loosed from a thick tongue. Jonathan felt the djinn's curse dance across his flesh; his eardrums tightened, nearing to rupture, his eyes began to bulge from his head, and his tongue swelled in his throat. Like a collar of fire, the circle of wards tattooed around his neckline leapt into life, searing away the power of the curse. The ghul pushed Ben out of the way, snatching Rose from his arms even as he tried to lift her.

The djinn bled from a shot to the shoulder, and carried Rose one-armed. It resembled the dead nanny only mockingly now, its truer essence pushing through the assumed form. Its papery skin contained a dark glow, as if embers were going cold within it, while bruised, orange cat eyes glared at him.

Watery blood wept from the wound, and Jonathan knew the ghul was hurting. The slug in it, made from rowan wood, impacted like a hollow point bullet and imbedded splinters in a wide swath. In a creature like a djinn, whose essences, it was said, are smoke-less fire—more energy than matter—it disrupted its very nature. Jonathan knew the wound would lessen its ability to cast a sus-tainable illusion.

Unfortunately, they had achieved a Mexican standoff. The ghul had the child, and Ben, though close enough to grab Rose, didn't have the strength to pry her from the djinn's grip, and Jonathan couldn't shoot without endangering the child.

The thing that still confused Jonathan: why hadn't it harmed Rose? Even to a ghul, a child of Rose's age, unconsecrated, was the equivalent of fresh truffles to a Belgian chef—but still, this thing had watched her for a week and only took her when her baptism became imminent.

Jonathan kept the gun ready, unwilling to miss an opportunity to kill the creature if presented. However, he tried to keep a handle on the situation while frantically figuring out what he could do about it. Ben curled and uncurled his fist as he fought the instinct to attack the ghul and retrieve his daughter. In that moment, Jonathan understood the ghul's care of the child.

Jonathan had called the man Ben punched an addict. He'd been right, but it had taken seeing the ghul's concern to make Jonathan realized what the junkie was addicted to—illusion.

Pure magic flooding the senses and fogging the brain could be quite the drug. The djinn had fed that man whatever necessary illusion it took to fulfill its needs. The ghul had taken the child because it needed a host body: a starter sheath for new flesh.

About to birth its own child, the offspring of it and the man downstairs, the ghul had chosen Rose to be its first host body—pure and untainted. But Darla's decision to have Rose baptized ruined her as a possible host. Everything would have happened differently if she hadn't, and Rose would have died before anyone had been the wiser. But, with its offspring not yet ready to enter the world, the ghul had no choice but to steal the child and hide it away for its own uses.

Jonathan lowered the gun slightly, ignoring Ben's look of disbelief.

"No one wins this way. You kill the child, I drop you—we all lose. If you manage to get past me with her, I'll track you down and we're right back here. Any way this goes down, you'll need a new vessel. Give the girl to her father and we all walk away. Find another child; all I care about is this one."

The ghul understood the situation as well as Jonathan did.

"Swear on the child's soul you won't shoot me again the moment I pass her over." Its voice, though guttural, echoed that of a young girl's—Kiri's, Jonathan assumed. "Swear on your father's grave you won't cast anything on me."

Jonathan was getting pretty sick of everyone knowing about what had happened between him and his father, especially when they brought it up to use against him. Still, it seemed the only thing to do at the moment.

"I swear it."

Slowly, the ghul passed Rose to Ben as Jonathan slid his gun into his shoulder holster. Ben held Rose to his chest. He stroked her hair and cooed to her, but his eyes spoke death as he glared at the ghul.

"Come on, Ben. Time to go."

Ben nodded and walked towards him, glancing often over his shoulder. When he reached Jonathan, Ben shoved Rose against him. Even as he grabbed hold of Rose, Jonathan felt his gun come free of the holster. He tried for Ben.

He didn't make it.

One, two shots rang out. Jonathan dropped to his knees, pulling the copper flask from his coat pocket. A third shot, then a fourth.

"In the name of the Father, the Son, and the Holy Ghost," he rambled off quickly and sprinkled the child with the holy water. Rose actually giggled.

Jonathan heard the click of the now empty revolver.

Leaving her on the ground, Jonathan stalked past Ben, who stared incredulously at the creature who was no further harmed than before the bullets had been shot wildly past it.

The ghul had hunched over and Jonathan assumed it was attempting to assume its dog form. He didn't know if it could with the rowan in it, and he had no plans on finding out.

He thrust out his hand, spraying the djinn with the contents of the flask. The blessed water hit the ghul and turned to steam, but the vapor hung—a halo of charged matter. The mist cooled, fell, and, hitting the djinn, vaporized again. Within this fog, the ghul remained motionless, trapped between its natures of energy and matter, trapped in its own belief and the word of myth.

Jonathan grabbed the gun from Ben. He wanted to smack the man with it, but settled for yanking on the back of his shirt collar.

"Those bullets were handmade. Not only are they expensive, but they took a great deal of time to make. Time I'd rather have spent drinking to forget incidents like tonight."

Jonathan jammed his gun back where it belonged and scooped up Rose himself. Descending past the second floor, Ben came around enough to demand his daughter. Jonathan happily complied. The minivan was outside as they'd left it, but at the door-way Jonathan stopped.

"Get in. Call Darla. Tell her you have Rose and that she's fine. I'll be a moment."

Jonathan turned around and searched each room of that floor until he found the wasted man, huddled in his rags, weeping over a busted nose.

"Here, let me."

The man whimpered and tried to push himself deeper into the corner. Jonathan moved his fingers and a green glow appeared. The energy flowed like grass in the wind and Jonathan reached out.

"You've had a bad turn," Jonathan said, helping the healthy, confused man to his feet. "But now it's time to go home."

With his free hand, Jonathan pulled out his cell phone and punched in a number.

"Hey, Ralph. Yeah, almost finished for the night, still good if I swing by with a few cold ones?"

Jonathan opened the passenger door and helped the man in. "Great. I could use the company, too. Speaking of company, I might be bringing someone along—tell ya about it when I get there."

* * *

TOMBSTONE
Scott E. Tarbet

<Strongly Encrypted Email via UltraLock>
Sent: Sat 8/3/2013, 9:11 PM

This here house is my tombstone. It stands above my grave. Hain't nobody alive in it—just me. I'm buildin' it with my own hands: I laid ever' stone carried from my own fields, hand-split ever' shingle from forest king snags I felled myself, turned ever' spade-full of earth. My own self. All alone."

Dear Doc:

That's what I heard when I played back the digital recorder right after that very first session.

You, of all people, will understand how excited I am. "Fit to be tied," the old man would say. This changes everything. Our entire field of study just took a quantum leap.

Congratulations, by the way: to read this you've had to get you-know-who in the university's School of Electronic Security to decrypt it, and she had to crack multiple layers of security on my office computer to get the key.

Love her to pieces, trust her with my life. I bet she already scrubbed all this from the servers and brought you this email on a thumb drive. Burn it after you read it. I'll bring all the original research documents with me when I come back.

It's going to sound paranoid, but I've redacted anything from this whole long email that reveals any of our identities, or exactly where I am. That I'm on the Texas-Louisiana border is inescapably obvious from the transcript, but the Sabine River is 510 miles long, the swamps and forests are deep, and I'm miles from any paved road.

I need to stay off the radar until my research results are iron-clad, and you and I agree I'm ready to publish. But I suggest you talk to your buddy at the *Journal of Paranormal Research* and alert him to hold space. You'll soon see why. But, as the old saw goes, just because you're paranoid doesn't mean nobody's out to get you.

The national security implications of my research are plain. The Federal government has had parallel research going back at least 70 years. Just the encryption possibilities inherent in the communications transcribed below will probably drive the NSA berserk. So all this isn't paranoia, it's just healthy, realistic caution.

I've encrypted and uploaded the recordings to the raw data folder for this project on the Department's secure server. You-know-who will help you access them. *Please* listen to them as soon as you can and give me your thoughts by return encrypted email. I'll make the trek again into cell range in a few days to get your thoughts.

Paranoia probably isn't the only mental illness you'll initially wonder about as you read this transcript. But as my post-doctoral advisor, you've known me a long time. You know I don't drink or do drugs, and you've never seen any sign of bipolar or schizoid disorders or any of the possible physical causes of auditory and visual hallucinations.

As a psychological professional, I've carefully thought through all of that, held myself up against every standard I can think of, and I am one-hundred percent confident that all of this is real.

The physical and documentary evidence I've accumulated is overwhelming.

Here is the transcript, exactly as it came out when I first played back the recording. I've tried hard to recreate the way the old man sounds, which I find somehow both very familiar and yet somehow alien—a voice from another time—and a place both strange and yet . . . home.

TRANSCRIPT 2013.08.20-21.01
(wmv file https://129.215.50.40/2013.08.20-21.01.wmv)

This here house is my tombstone. It stands above my grave. Hain't nobody alive in it—just me.

I'm buildin' it with my own hands: I laid ever' stone carried from my own fields, hand-split ever' shingle from forest king snags I felled myself, turned ever' spade-full of earth. My own self. All alone.

I mixed ever' bucketful of cement. I heated and twisted and soldered ever' rod of cast iron. Maybe the hardest was learnin' to make winda glass. But I got plenty of time.

So far, it has took me eighty-seven years. Don't fault me. You're young, but I was kinda old when I started—seventy-two—and dead at seventy-two is still seventy-two.

That's how old I was when my ungrateful spineless wretch of a daughter, my evil witch of a granddaughter, and her snivelin', weak-kneed husband the banker boy, put me in the ground. That was 1926. A lot has changed since then. But not me. A hundred and fifty-nine years since I come to this earth, and I'm still here.

If you was to stand here and it was 1927, now, or '30 or '40 . . . now that woulda been somethin'. And there was them that done just that. Folks come out here from town sometimes—kids mostly—and fellers that had a little shine to party with, just to stand around and watch field stone rise up off the ground and set itself down in the mortar on top of a wall. They got a kick outta that.

The king rafter—now, that woulda been a sight, but there weren't nobody here in '46 when I finally figgered out how to rig the ropes and pulleys to get it up there all by myself. Right proud of that, I was.

These days I guess there ain't a whole lot to see from the outside 'cause all the work is on the inside. But right soon—next ten years or so—it will be time for new shingles again. That's always a sight to see.

Anyways, folks learnt right quick that it don't bother me none for folks to watch. I never bothered with 'em if they never bothered with my house. But if they messed with my house they was gonna get run off.

I done that a couple of times, and folks got scared enough they stopped comin', even though I never hurt nobody—not serious, anyways. Threw a few rocks and sticks is all. They got the point.

Been a long time since anybody come out this way. Now the road is all growed over. Only the wild pigs remember where it was.

But you—you heard all the stories, read all them old reports, maybe you even talked to some of them self-same neighbors who act like this farm—*my* farm—don't even exist, 'cause they been told since they was bitty children that you don't come on this land lessin you're tetched. They know better. I reckon you don't.

[transcriber's note: copies of corroborating reports from the local newspaper and sheriff's office reports spanning decades, describing incidents on the property, have been uploaded to the secure server.]

You ask fer my story, you with your fancy cameras that see in the dark, and microphones you string with wires all around the place, and sound recorders you can hold in the palm of your hand, and your fancy Greenpeace backpack with a dangly name tag cut in the shape of the airplanes I see fly overhead, up there where they're practically nothin' but a white streak of smoke across the sky.

But I see like when I was fifteen years old. Ain't nothin' wrong with my eyes. And I can read, by gum: that luggage tag says you come from New York City. New York gosh-dang City. Like anythin' good ever come out of New York City. Except maybe the Brooklyn Dodgers.

And your electric doo-dads got the name of a fancy Scottish university painted all over 'em. I reckon we fought the War to End All Wars for them folks. But somehow we keep having to go back over there and fight some more. Or so I heard a bunch of years back. Afore you was born, I guess.

So here you come, all the way out here through the skeeters and ticks. You got yer flimsy little tent and a sack to sleep in and the clever little stove that heats up food outta silver pouches. You sit here outside my house three days and nights, without once knockin' on the door like civilized folks, talkin' to me without knowin' am I even listenin', like you're talking' to the wind.

But you tell me over and over that you respect my privacy and my history and that you just ask for my story. Like you got some right. That just 'cause you have the same name as me and a PhD by your name, you think that will make me willin' to talk to you. You got gumption, I'll give you that.

Paranormal researcher, my Aunt Fanny. Fancy name for a busybody, if you ask me.

Know what I bet? I bet the oil companies sent you here. Or the timber companies. 'Go out there to that farm,' I bet they said, 'and see what's what. See if all the reports all these years is true.' But you—you got your own reasons for comin', I reckon. Ain't just the paycheck.

Well, it ain't gonna do them companies no good, cause they ain't gonna get rid of me or explain me away. I'm here. I'm real.

But you, Mr. Paranormal Investigator, you are in luck. You might just get famous. You might just get your face on a magazine or maybe even get to talk on the radio, you bein' the scientist feller that can prove he talked to me, what with your cameras and sound recordings and all.

I ain't sure it's gonna work, but we'll give it a try. Won't hurt me a lick to set and talk a spell. Ain't talked to no one since I died—no one who could actually hear me, anyways.

Wait now—I take that back: I did talk to my daughter and granddaughter two weeks after I died, and knowed darn well they could hear me, but they wasn't in no mood to listen. And they hardly count anyways, them bein' blood kin and all. But with you, it might just work. If you're really a PhD paranormal researcher, maybe, as the Good Book says, you got ears to hear.

So, I expect I'll just sit down on the porch here and talk and we'll see how much yer fancy microphones and cameras pick up.

You see the river right over there: that's the Sabine, the dividin' line between East Texas and Louisiana. This farm, all one-hundred-twenty-two glorious God-blessed acres of it, sits right smack on the west bank of the Sabine, straddle a pretty little creek that runs through a good pond and down to the river.

Lunker fish in that pond, I bet—not that I ever bother 'em. Good game, plenty to keep a family fed—if there was anybody here to feed, which there's not. Old-growth piney woods and forest meadows on one side, farmland on the other. Beavers, coyotes, muskrats, possums, wild pigs—even cougars back in the day.

My people have a history here. Lots of my folks born, lived, and died on this land. Lots of kin planted in the little graveyard right back there behind the house.

My great-granddaddy come up the river way back when there weren't nothin' but Indians and Mexicans and Frenchmen for miles around. He trapped from the top of this hill for three seasons, fell in love with the place, married my great-grandma and hauled her up here from New Orleans, and went to farmin'.

My granddaddy was born and bred right here, went off to fight the Mexicans with Sam Houston and never come back. My daddy done the same in the War of Northern Aggression with Colonel Terry's Cavalry. Got hisself shot out of the saddle at Gettysburg.

[transcriber's note: corroborating copies of the land deed, birth notices, obituaries, census records, and Civil War newspaper reports, including notice of the afore-mentioned death, have been uploaded to the secure server.]

So I farmed this land, boy and man, from the time Daddy left to the War—I was nine years old—'til the very day I died. Along the way, I married a good woman, had a good life. Had a son. But he didn't make it to his first birthday. Only had the one daughter, and only the one granddaughter. But by golly, that was plenty.

Right around Aught One they hit oil down to Beaumont and all hell broke loose. Big oil. Millions of barrels of it, all over this part of the country. Hundreds of carpet baggers runnin' around for years buyin' up the right to drill on peoples land. Come at me directly too many times to count.

Three of them fellers come right up here to the farm. First one I was polite to—country polite just like I was raised. Set him down, offer him a little snort from my fruit jar, which he got down without chokin', so I figger he's okay. But then he starts in on the sales pitch, got more and more high pressure 'til I had to run him off.

Second feller didn't get no shine before he got run off. Third feller didn't get on the porch. Nosir. I tolt him he looked okay for a city feller and he was okay by me, but my ol' shotgun just weren't up for visitors that day. He took my point and cleared out right smart.

After that, I put me up a No Trespassin' sign, put some buck-shot through it myself just to make the warnin' clear, and the carpetbaggers stopped callin'.

One of 'em, though, some high-falutin' oil company geologist, finally got to my granddaughter at a fancy party in town and tolt her she would be rich if she talked me into signin'. She convinced her mother, and, even though I hain't heard boo from neither of 'em in the better part of a couple of years, they started ridin' all the way out here from town ever' Sunday, near eight miles. That was a lot further before motor cars, you know. New York City boy like you—one who thinks a long walk is down to the corner market for the newspaper—an eight-mile buggy ride is a long ways. I ain't saying it weren't a long way for us back in the day, but then we didn't know no better.

Anyways, when them women got the oil fever, they got to lookin' at the half of the farm on the other side of the creek where the old growth forest is, and the greed got that much worse. "All the neighbors are selling the mineral rights, Grandfather!" come the drumbeat, week after week. "Papa, all the neighbors are selling their timber to be clear cut. Don't fret over trees, Papa; they're just plants. They'll grow back," she'd say. Yeah, maybe someday, after we're all dead and gone.

Well—dead, anyhow.

Now, I ain't a stupid man. Back in them days, I watched my pennies—had to—and watched sharp for ways to make more. Another mule woulda helped, and maybe a hired man now that I was slowed down some. But I watched my neighbors sell their oil rights. The drillers would swoop in, cut roads through all the trees, spill drillin' mud and chemicals and waste oil all over the ground, kill ever' good plant in sight and let weeds come back up instead.

The landowner would get a few thousand dollars, maybe build a new house, maybe buy his wife something purdy. But sooner or later, he was right back to where he was before: a dirt farmer scratching out a livin' hand to mouth. But, now they was scratchin' on ugly, scarred, wrecked land. Them scars ain't never healed.

Nosir, that ain't for me. I owe the land more than that.

And them that sold their timber was worse off yet. I don't know if you ever seen clear-cut land, but it don't look like nothin' more than an old mangy dog that mean boys has got a-holt of and shaved. Sorrier than a drowned cat. Now, I'll grant you, the trees has come back to my neighbors' lands—but spindly shadows of their ancestors ninety years ago, harvested and harvested again for pulp ever' decade or two, all the stumps just left to rot so walkin' through the woods ain't walkin' through the woods no more; it's climbin' over one old stump after another.

But my old-growth trees is still there, and now even the sixty acres I was farmin' when I died has eighty-seven year-old trees on 'em—not ancient forest, primordial forest they call it—but grand old trees that are home to birds and deer and foxes and coyotes. No cougars yet, but Good Lord willin', someday we'll see 'em back again.

Anyways, the very next time the girls come out from town, banker boy with 'em, as soon as they was settled on the porch of the old frame house that stood right where I'm buildin' my new stone house now, with lemonade nice and cold with real ice from my ice house, they started in on me. "Papa, we feel that . . ." and "Grandfather, it would be in your best interest if . . ."

Criminy the airs they put on! Papa! Grandfather! Don't know where they come up with calling me that, but it weren't from me or the missus.

And that no-account banker spoutin' on about investment opportunities and return-on-investment blah, blah, blah.

About how I could get electricity and indoor plumbin' and be just dandy modern and comfortable. Made me right sick at my stomach.

I finally stood up and told 'em, "Now, you all had your fine say, and I do appreciate your opinions, but it's time for you to listen to me, 'cause I'm the one with the say-so: ain't nobody gonna drill on my land, and ain't nobody gonna cut my timber. Over my dead body." And I walked out, out into the trees, and didn't come back to the house 'til they was long gone.

I've wondered ever since if that's when they decided they was gonna do it, or if they had already decided, or if they cooked it up after they left that day. However it was they come up with it, it was over my dead body, all right.

Turns out my daughter and granddaughter was livin' way high on the hog in town. They was runnin' up bills my granddaughter's husband couldn't pay, even with his fancy salary from the bank. He had taken to swindlin' widows and orphans and churches and anyone else that would let him.

The whole house of cards was just about to crash in around his ears unless he found a way to lay hands on some cash, quick. And gettin' rid of me was the way they figured to do it.

When they come back the next Sunday, they acted all sugarplum sweet and like nothin' never happened the week before, only they brought along a dinner of my favorite fried chicken and lemonade and sweet buttermilk and rhubarb pie.

I'll never know exactly what bite had what poison in it 'cause it all tasted right good to me, but ten minutes after I set down to eat, my stomach tied up so tight that it doubled me right over. They set there all cool and calm as cucumbers and watched me try to stand up. When I started to spew blood, they even skooched back so they wouldn't get splattered, then skooched back some more when I keeled off my chair onto the kitchen floor.

It took a long time to die and hurt real bad. It got harder and harder to breathe, and I fought harder and harder to keep doing it, until, all of a sudden, breathin' weren't hard no more. Nothin' hurt—not even my lumbago.

I was standin' there right by my own head starin' down at myself all curled up tight in a ball lying on the floor, my poor dead face all blue and wound up in a scream like my jaw was gonna tear off. I felt right sorry for that poor ol' thing lying there, all wore out and twisted and dead.

Granddaughter stood up and started givin' orders about cleanin' up the mess and haulin' me in to my bed, sent her husband to town for the doctor with a story about how my poor old heart finally give out. And me, standin' there listenin' like I had no good sense, rooted to the floor of that house as if I really was planted there.

Right after the banker was out the door, my daughter crossed the room for the mop and pail and doggone if she didn't walk right through me! I meant to get out of her way—I honest injun did—but somehow my mind just weren't right, as if I just naturally expected her to see me and step around me, which o' course she didn't—walked right through me.

I didn't feel nothin' but a push, like a breeze went through me, but she sure did. She let out a squeal and went to babblin' about how somebody like to a poured ice water down her neck, and it being such a hot night and all.

The granddaughter come over and grabbed her mother by the elbow like a toddler and give her a tongue lash like she was one, too, how she was just panicky and she better shut up before she had to give her a slap and give her something to cry about, 'cause she better believe she would.

Now, this might sound funny to hear, 'cause it sure does sound funny to say, but hearin' her talk to her own mother that way kinda tore somethin' loose in me. You'd think getting kilt with poison mighta done it, but you'd be wrong; hearin' that girl sass her mama was the last straw.

I never did hold with slappin' a child. Though, maybe if I hadn't a' spared the rod so much my daughter wouldn't a got spoilt so bad and I mighta stayed alive a few years more. And I probably wouldn't be here now.

I never had lifted a hand to my granddaughter in all of her days, but now somethin' snapped and I hauled back and slapped her face. Hard. It didn't hurt me, but by gum, she sure enough felt it. Her head snapped around and she spun back all wild-eyed and backhanded her mama, who was bawlin' too hard to know what was goin' on.

Probably she thought somehow her mama had managed to smack her one. But no, it was me. So I did it again. And again. And now I was startin' to enjoy myself just a little, because I finally spoke up.

"Ever since you was little I knowed you was evil. You was a awful, hateful, spiteful child. And now you've growed into a greedy, money-grubbing monster, and you have kilt me. Damn you to everlasting hell!"

She heard me sure enough. She spun like a top, lookin' around the room, and looked down at my body, lookin' for where the voice was comin' from. Well, sir, that's not where I was no more, so just to make a point I walked up and give her a good hard shove that sent her sprawlin' over backwards, right on the part of her that shoulda been paddled when she was little. She scrambled up and backed right out the kitchen door, screamin' like a banshee, and run off outta the light.

Didn't take her mother long to follow her, neither, and neither one come back in the house 'til the banker come back with the doctor. Then they poked their heads in and looked around real careful before they would follow Doc and the banker in the door.

Ol' Doc—knowed him all my life. He was a good man, and I could tell he smelt a rat, what with me lyin' there all twisted up and vomit all over the place, and me not in my bed and nobody doin' nothin' about cleanin' me up. But he was just a good old country doc and there weren't nothin' he could do but take their word for it.

I tried pattin' his shoulder to let him know I was there, but no luck—I couldn't feel him at all and he couldn't feel me nor hear me neither, him not bein' kin. I said howdy to him, which him and the banker didn't hear, but the girls sure did, because they jumped, then tried real hard to act like they didn't hear nothin'.

So, he pronounced me dead, which I sure enough was, all right, and had the banker help him hoist me up into his wagon to take me into town to lay me out at the banker's big brick house right on Main Street. My daughter and granddaughter followed right along behind in the little surrey they come out in.

I tried and tried to go along, but danged if I could get up on that wagon for all my tryin'. I really wanted to see what else they was goin' to do to me. So, then, I tried followin' the wagon down the road, but whenever I got close to the property line, my thinkin' got all fuzzy and old-like, and pretty soon I'd find myself walkin' back toward the house without knowin' how it was I got goin' that direction.

I done that three or four times that first night—walked toward the property lines on all sides, and pretty soon figured out I weren't goin' nowheres. I was stayin' on my own land. But that was just fine, since I didn't want to go nowheres else when I was alive, why should I now that I was dead? Just for curiosity? No thanks. Not worth the trouble.

Do I miss not walking off the property? Nope. A hundred twenty-two acres makes for plenty of nice walks in the woods. I got everything I need.

Well sir, next day the banker was back again without the women, to get papers from my ol' roll-top desk, insurance and deeds and such, and with a hired man along to fetch some things of her mother's that my daughter wanted. Stuff didn't mean nothin' to me, so I just let 'em in and out without botherin' with 'em.

But I have to wonder if the women thought that 'cause the banker and the hired man come home and didn't report nothin' that day, and nothin' happened at the funeral neither, that give 'em the false confidence that lead to what happened after. 'Cause it turned out the same the next day, when the funeral procession come marchin' real slow up the hill to bury me with my people on the top of the hill behind the house.

Here come the preacher, looking all mournful and solemn and important, and all the relatives and friends from miles around, a few of which I actually liked. So I didn't think it would be right to act up when they was all up there to mourn over me.

Besides, when I was alive—leastways when my wife was alive— I tried right hard to be a Christian gentleman. She tried hard to make me one. I went along with it, and drove her all the way to church in town each and ever' Sunday, sat through the preacher's hell fire and damnation hullabaloos, and even put a little somethin' in the plate when it come around.

After my better half got took by the influenza epidemic . . . well, me and the Almighty wasn't on speaking terms after that. Me and the preacher didn't have nothin' to say to each other neither. And now that I was dead and hadn't seen no sign of my wife or the fires of hell or the clouds and harps of heaven, it was even harder to be good for the sake of bein' good. Didn't seem to be no percentage in it.

But still, I thought, if this here was just a stop-off, and I was gonna see my wife after the funeral, well then, no sense in pro-vokin' her. She was the sweetest, kindest, most Christian woman that ever drew breath, but you didn't want to cross her and make her lips go all thin and her get real quiet and frosty.

So I behaved. Didn't see her that day, though, and ain't seen her since. Only thing I'm sad about. Ain't totally give up neither though I guess, 'cause I heard all them stories about ghosts and whatnot getting released from bondage finally. Who knows. Certainly not you or me.

Anyways, it was the middle of the day, bright broad daylight, when they showed up again the next Sunday. I don't know if they thought what happened the night they kilt me was a one-time thing and buryin' me meant I had gone away to hell or heaven or wherever, or if somehow they thought that it being light meant I had to go away and hide or somethin', but that ain't how it works. I'm around all the time, never sleepin' and never leavin', so I heard 'em comin' a long ways off and was waitin' on 'em.

I set down at the kitchen table, right where I was settin' when they done me to death, and watched 'em walk in the door. They was a little skittish at first, ready to bolt, but when nothin' happened right off they set in to goin' through the drawers and cabinets and the old chifferobe, seein' if there was anything they wanted to take, chatterin' along like a couple of monkeys like they wasn't murderous hags and thieves.

Right soon, I got what I was waitin' for 'cause they set to talkin' about the oil company survey crews fixin' to come out from town to start in on drillin' my land, and the lumbermen comin' right behind 'em.

Like I said, I still thought of myself as a kind and good man. So, I ain't proud to say that when them two shrews got to gloatin' about how much blood money they stood to get for killin' me, all the nice things they was goin' to buy and see and do, places they was gonna go . . . well, it got to me, and I got to feelin' right mean and non-Christian mostly.

Granddaughter, she allowed as how now that I was gone, what reason did they have for hangin' on to the old place at all? Why not just sell it for everything they could get out of it? Didn't mean nothin' to 'em. It was just dirt.

Finally, I stewed just about long enough. I stood up, and made sure I pushed the chair back from the table so's it scraped good and hard, 'bout twice as far back as I really needed to. You coulda heard a pin drop, them two women froze so stock still, starin' at that chair. 'Course they couldn't see me walk behind 'em to the pots and pans, but I made darn sure they could hear me—nice heavy steps.

I stopped, just to let 'em think about things a bit, then I screamed at the top of my lungs, "Never! Never! Never!" and I went to throwin' pots and pans and plates and cups, even the coffee pot, makin' the air right thick with flyin' cookware.

Boy, did they scream and scramble! Pelted all over with heavy cookware I reckon you would scream and scramble, too. Right out the door they went, right into the surrey, and whipped that poor horse all the way to the property line, and probably beyond.

Well, sir, I hoped that was the end of it, but that weren't no good. But then you already knowed that, or you wouldn't be here now, would you?

A week later, just as the women had said, here come the survey crews. I can tell you I made things right warm for them boys. There weren't no marker that they could pound into the ground that I couldn't pull up and throw into the bushes as soon as their backs was turned. There was no tripod for their little survey telescope that would stand up for more than a minute before it would wind up on the ground, the telescope's lenses smashed. Shoulda heard them boys tie into each other the first few times that happened! Pretty soon it dawned on 'em that it weren't just accidents, and they got real real quiet.

Them Model A Ford pickup trucks they come in was the first automobiles I ever seen, but I'm right handy, so it didn't take me long to figger out how to yank out wires and slash hoses and puncture tires. Smashin' windows was lots of fun, too.

It didn't take much longer than the mornin' for 'em to decide they was wastin' their time and equipment and get their behinds back to town. It was a good piece of work for them boys to get them trucks home after all that. They wound up scroungin' parts from one to make the other run, so they could pull the wrecked one out of here with a chain.

Their boss weren't with 'em that first time, though, and sent back another crew, cussin' out the first bunch for a pack of super-stitious fools, and dockin' their pay. The second crew didn't talk about nothin' else all mornin' but how them other poor yokels thought the place was haunted and lost a day's pay, but they didn't fair no better, and this time the boss was with 'em, so I reckon I made a believer out of him all right 'cause I never seen that bunch back out here.

Same thing with the ones who come to stake out the timber haul road—they thought it was goin' to be easy duty, but they never got nothin' at all accomplished. Pretty soon the word got back to the murderers that things out at the farm was just impossible and the entire contract was in trouble. I guess they figgered more dras-tic action was required, more foolishness. So here they come again.

It had been right quiet and peaceful for several days when I heard the rattle of the surrey comin' up the hill at full gallop. They didn't come in the house at first, not like they done the last time, but they run around the house in both directions. The smell of kerosene came through the open windows and the rattlin' of one empty can after another.

I hollered out to my daughter, "Would you burn down the house you was born in? Are you completely gone to the devil?"

She screamed back at me, "I'm a murderer! I stood by while they kilt you! I'm going straight to hell! What do I have to lose?"

"Shut up, Mother!" her daughter screamed at her, "You idiot! Can't you see you're just making it worse?"

I run out on the porch, and they both heard me comin' and spun around. My granddaughter had a ridiculous huge Roman Catholic crucifix in one hand, a big ol' Colt Navy revolver in the other, and her mother held my wife's big ol' Bible that she had carried to the First Baptist church in town ever' Sunday for so many years.

I couldn't believe my eyes, so I stopped stock still and just started laughin'. Them two murderers was so ridiculous, tryin' to hide behind the gew-gaws of religion, that I couldn't help but laugh. 'Course, under the circumstances I suppose it come off diabolical, like a demon laughin' from hell.

With a scream to wake the dead the granddaughter swung that crucifix at the spot she figgered my head would be, and 'course it went right through. I laughed again, backin' through the door into the front room, and the two of 'em come right after me, mistakin' that I was backing away for me bein' afraid, which I wasn't. I was just plain amazed, and more than a little amused. What did they think they could do to me now? Kill me again?

The daughter raised that Bible high over her head and started rantin' at me to be cast out into the fires of hell. I was laughin' so hard, I swear if I coulda wet myself, I woulda. You know how it gets when you get to laughin' and can't stop—only when you're dead, your bladder don't threaten to let go on you and your stomach don't start hurtin', so you just keep on laughin'.

Then somehow that ol' Colt Navy went off, and the kerosene got sparked, and, suddenly that old dry timber house went up with a woosh like a box of lucifer matches.

I don't mind sayin', Christian gentleman or no, it was right satisfyin' to be right in the middle of that fire with them two gettin' what they so mightily deserved. I think about that a lot.

They screamed and screamed, battlin' each other to get out the door, but they had soaked the whole porch with kerosene, and all the way round the bottom clapboards of the house, so the roarin', smoky flame drove 'em right back to the middle of the room. In the end they both died right where I did. One on top of the other.

It was the afternoon of the next day before the banker showed up lookin' for 'em. I had unhitched the horse from the surrey and fed and watered him—it weren't the poor brute's fault he had to haul them witches out to keep tryin' to kill me over and over.

You can bet the banker was a mite perplexed how come that horse was standin' in a stall in the barn, all content with fresh hay and oats and water, when there was them two smolderin' corpses lying in the smokin' ruins of the house, right there in plain sight for all the world to see.

Here come the preacher again, this time with half the town, to bury what was left of them two women in the family plot. There was lots of sighin' and cryin' and shakin' heads at the poor banker's tragic loss all in such a short time—his wife's grandfather dead of a tragic heart attack, then his wife and mother-in-law dead in a tragic accidental house fire. It was all just too accidental and tragic. Tragic. Right.

[transcriber's note: copies of corroborating newspaper reports and sheriff's office reports have been uploaded to the secure server.]

I imagine you're wonderin' if I saw them two women after they burnt. Answer is no, but you can bet I hope they just keep right on burnin' wherever it is they went. Kin or no, they was murderers. They certainly wasn't bound to the land like me. Could be anywheres.

The next survey crew that come out to the place got the same send-off as the first two. And the one after that and the one after that, ever since. I let 'em hang around a bit whilst I listen to their gossip and get some news about the outside world, before I run 'em off and pull up their survey stakes. But no oil company or timber company has never took nothin' off my place, because they can't never finish their surveys.

Well, sir, whilst the oil company and the timber company had the money all tied up in court, some of them widows and orphans and churches that banker was gyppin' cottoned to what he'd been doin' to 'em for years, and his whole scheme come a tumblin' down after all.

The sheriff come to see him, right there in his fancy office at the bank, figgerin' to lead him out in handcuffs. But banker boy, he asked to visit the toilet, and splattered his brains all over that nice white porcelain with a Derringer he kept tucked in his desk.

So none of them widows or orphans or churches never got a chance to take their money back out of his hide. Not that there was much hide on that scrawny, cowardly no-account. He was so concerned about nothin' but his own reputation that he blew he brains out and never once thought of providin' for the little boy he had at home . . . you know—the one they named after me when they was still tryin' to flatter money out of me. Your granddaddy. The little boy that went off to live with his father's kin Back East somewheres. The one you're named after.

I didn't hear about none of that 'til the next time a survey crew come up and was talkin' amongst themselves about how just plain weird the whole affair was and how the banker's estate, with all the oil and all the timber and land, was all tied up in court, and they was tryin' to get money for widows and orphans by sendin' out survey crews. But of course I couldn't let that happen, not even for widows and orphans, 'specially since there weren't nothin' in it for my kin.

About due to happen again, I reckon, which is why you're here. Still won't do 'em no good. I reckon God will let me stay and protect the land until it's back in the hands of kin, back in the hands of them what honors it. After that, who knows.

[transcriber's note: copies of sheriff's office reports have been uploaded to the secure server, along with copies of the notices to the estate from the oil and timber companies officially cancelling the contracts that I pulled during a visit to the probate court clerk's files.]

Well, that's my story. When you check your cameras and sound recorders, I do hope you can hear me. Maybe even that you heard a word or two whilst I been talking, which just might be, us being blood and all, because you just been sittin' there staring into the trees, silent as the grave, the whole time I been talkin'. Long time.

If you did hear, tell them company fellers leave me alone to build my house. It goes up slow, one little bit at a time, built without hands the livin' world can see. I'm in no hurry. Because it's not really a home—it's a tombstone.

<Strongly Encrypted Email via UltraLock>
Sent: Sat 8/10/2013, 9:11 PM Subject: Recordings

Dear Doc:

I'm dismayed, but hardly surprised, that you haven't been able to hear the voice on the raw recordings. As the old man suggests, maybe when I get back to the university I'll be able to electronically wash them and make them intelligible. For now, all I know is that his voice is plain to me. But there seems to be a genetic component to that understanding: his daughter and granddaughter and I could all hear him, while his grandson-in-law, the doctor, and you cannot. More research is needed.

Speaking of genetics, thanks for running interference for me with my mom. I'm sorry she called you out of the blue when I had been out of cell phone coverage for a couple of weeks and hadn't called her. Bad son.

Even more, thanks for not letting on that I was back on her side of the Atlantic, especially not that I am out at the old home place. As you can guess, they used the stories that have come down in her family about this place and the events here to frighten small children into good behavior. She would probably have a stroke if she knew I had set foot anywhere in the State of Texas.

I've called and IM'd several times to keep her calm. Don't know what the fallout will be when she learns what this has all been about. The old man says, if she's anything like her grandma, she'll be madder than a biddy hen dipped in a horse trough.

I promise I'll be back to the university very soon, and that I will subject myself to the most rigorous psychological testing that you and the rest of our colleagues can devise. At the moment, I wouldn't blame you in the slightest if you suspected me of being wildly delusional. If it weren't for the recordings and other documentation I've uploaded to the server, I might suspect the same thing.

I hope all the evidence puts your mind at ease. I swear I didn't know any of this before the old man told it to me. All I had were old family boogey man stories. I've tracked down all the old documents and newspaper reports—everything you'll see in the uploaded files—since the old man first told me his story.

One other bit of news: I'm going to have to delay my return to the university for a couple of months. After a lot of soul searching over the last two weeks, I have come to the conclusion that whatever the impact on my professional career, I need to see things here through to their conclusion.

The connection to the land that has grown in me in the weeks I have been camped here is hard to put into words. The old man, my grandfather's great-grandfather, who built the stone house, is here. His great-grandfather before him is buried here, and lots of folks from the generations in between. His mother, wife, daughter, and granddaughter are buried here, too. That's a lot of family history. Nine generations in all. How could my soul not be attached to this place?

As you know, I was raised in a Manhattan co-op, barely ever setting foot on the earth, let alone feeling any attachment to it, much like my mother and my grandfather, who was ripped from this place in his infancy. This has been very much a homecoming for me, physically and spiritually.

The upshot of it all is that circumstances compel me to take on myself the careful stewardship the old man has borne for so long, so faithfully, and so well. It's not just the land; it's the family. Nothing could feel more right.

Three days ago, after discussing it with him, I packed up my tent and moved my belongings into the house—not that there was that much to move in.

He had no idea, of course, that the contracts with the oil and timber companies had been cancelled long ago. Turns out it was way before my mother was even born since there was a survey crew out here, but he had lost track of time. "Time flies when you're havin' fun," he says. I think he truly believes that saying is original to him.

The house is quite comfortable in a pre-electric sort of way. As it turns out, in his heart of hearts, the house was always a hopeful thing, always waiting for someone to come and love the old home place and agree to be the next steward. That next steward is me.

He knows and accepts that I won't live here full time right away, but he also knows that I will cherish it and care for it all my life, and will pass it down to my own kids.

I've installed a new solar generator, and a friend from over near Elkhart has helped me install a new pump and tanks for the well. The old man is anxious to get on with the electrical and indoor plumbing—as a matter of fact, as he has built the house, he has even carefully left space for the wiring and pipes, and plenty of access to install them. It won't take us long now that the two of us are working together. He figures as soon as the place is ready for me to move in with my future wife and family, he'll be ready to move on.

We should be done by Halloween.

* * *

GHOST TOWNIES

E. BRANDEN HART

Warm out today," Jimbo said as he and Dean climbed the library steps.

"Was warm out yesterday," said Dean, handing his friend a handkerchief. Jimbo took off his cowboy hat and dabbed the sweat from his forehead. "Prolly be warm tomorrow, too. Now, go on up there and look in dem doors to see what we're dealin' with."

"All right," said Jimbo as he continued climbing the stairs. "But I coulda sworn I heard screamin' a second ago."

Dean shielded his eyes from the sun and scanned the horizon. He remembered a time when the street in front of the library crawled with pedestrians, traffic, and ice cream vendors, but not anymore. "I don't see anything."

"Holy crap—how many people died in this library?"

Dean shrugged and spat on the ground. "Looks like a few dozen. Prolly more roamin' 'tween the shelves."

Jimbo squinted and looked through the tinted glass on the front doors of the Corsicana Public Library. "One, two, three—I think that's Ms. Tremble over by the magazine rack. Remember how she use ta holler at us for gettin' up in her tree? Four, five, seven . . ."

Dean double-checked his supplies: four flashlights in his tool belt and one twelve-inch Maglite in his hand. In his fanny pack

(Jimbo called Dean "Mary" whenever he put it on) were enough backup batteries for the flashlights to last a year. The front pockets of his jeans bulged with matchbooks from every restaurant and hotel in town. His shirt pocket was crammed with a pack of cigarettes and a Zippo lighter with "Go Screw Yerself" etched on the front in flowing, gothic letters.

". . . forty-four, forty-five, forty-seven. Wow. I count forty-eight of 'em in there. Wasn't you sayin' there was only a few dozen?"

"Forty-eight *is* a few dozen." Dean turned his Maglite on and off a couple of times to check the charge. Still pretty bright; probably had at least a few more hours in it. "Well? Should we go in?"

Jimbo sighed. He picked a piece of fuzz from his long-sleeved flannel work shirt and watched as it floated toward his snakeskin cowboy boots. "I don't like this. Most a' dem's prolly Huggers, an' I hate dem guys. Almost all of 'em are roamin' around, but goin' nowhere. One of 'em even keeps lookin' this way. He looks pretty pissed off."

Dean shook his head. "Nah. If he was truly pissed off, he'd've been out here by now."

"I don't know . . ."

Dean grabbed Jimbo by the arm and spun him around so they were looking at each other. "I don't know either, but what I do know is, unless we get to the property records in the old fallout shelter in there, we're gonna be goin' to houses one by one for the next twenty years before we find one where not a single person has died.

"I don't know about you, but I'm not willin' to wait that long to find a place where we can sit around at night, drinkin' beer an' playin' poker without worryin' whether one of these things is gonna pop up outta the floor all of a sudden wantin' a hug 'cause his mommy didn't love him enough or whatever the reason is that they do that."

Dean paused and took a breath. "An' I know yer gettin' sick of not havin' a place to lay down or call yer own. An' I definitely know yer tired of not havin' a workin' toilet in the mornin', what with yer irritable bowel syndrome an' all that."

Jimbo shrugged Dean's hand off his shoulder and turned away. "It ain't my fault I can't process dairy like normal folk."

"I know, but listen, buddy, if we're gonna get any kind of a good night's sleep in the rest of what is probably gonna be a short an' miserable life together, we need to find a place where nobody's died. We've been searchin' for almost three weeks now, an' I'm tired. Now, I know there's a lot of 'em in there, but we have to go inside this building if we want to find a clean house. There ain't no two ways around it."

Jimbo looked at the ground, saw a small rock, and kicked it as hard as he could. It clanged against the metal frame of the library door. Some figures floating inside wandered in the direction of the noise.

"I know," Jimbo said, shaking his head. "I know yer right! Ever since we was boys in the first grade, you've been right about every-thing. That's why you got valediction when we graduated high school."

"Valedictorian."

"Whatever. It was you who came up with the idea about flash-lights, an' it was you who came up with the idea about the library, an' the records they keep in the old fallout shelter. An' I know yer right! There's just somethin' I don't like about it."

Dean looked through the filmy glass and into the library. The things in there realized someone was outside, and several mean-dered toward the door. He turned his Maglite on and looked his friend in the eyes again.

"Jimbo, you're the bravest man I've ever known. Even twenty years ago, when we was just playin' on the monkey bars, you were the first one who tried to do a flip off of 'em, remember that?"

"Yeah . . ."

"An' remember how afterward, when you were in the ICU, after they realized you weren't sufferin' from massive head trauma an' that was just the way you normally talked, remember how you tol' me that the next time, all you had to do was jump a little further an' make sure to tuck yer chin in more, that you knew you could do it?"

"Yeah . . ."

"An' remember how, that next week you tried it like that, an' later that day we were in the ICU again, an' you reached out an' grabbed that nurse's behind?"

Jimbo chuckled. "Yeah . . ."

Dean put his Maglite by his side, shook his head, and put his hand on Jimbo's shoulder. "That was one of the bravest things I've ever seen another man do. Just reach out like that an' grab some woman's hiney?"

"Well, it was a purdy nice one."

"You bet it was! An' ever since that day, I've been waiting to find my own behind to grab." He looked inside—three or four Huggers were floating slowly toward the door. He had to get this over with and get in there before the front hall was flooded with them.

Dean spat on the ground. "I'm lookin' at this library like you looked at that nurse's rear end. I intend to grab it an' squeeze it an' even though I know it's gonna be a little scary, I'm gonna remember how one day, when he was in a hospital bed with a broken vertebrae an' internal bleeding, a seven-year-old boy named Jimbo McGovern saw a posterior he liked an' grabbed it. An' that's what's gonna get me through this day."

Jimbo didn't say anything for a second. Then he smiled and said, "Yeah. Yeah! You're right. Let's do it! An' who cares about those guys roamin' around in there? We'll chase 'em off 'fore they know what hit 'em."

Dean clapped him on the back and checked his Maglite again.

"You bet," he said while Jimbo checked his own gear. "An' you gotta remember: they're just ghosts."

"Yeah, I know," said Jimbo, adjusting his tool belt.

"Just lonely, old ghosts—pathetic really—who had the misfortune of dyin' on the premises of the Corsicana Public Library."

"Yeah, I know."

"An' all they really want is a hug. They're sad creatures. We should pity 'em instead of bein' scared of 'em."

Jimbo nodded, secured his tool belt, and looked at Dean. "All right, bro, I'm ready."

Even though he knew it was fine, Dean checked his Maglite one more time, just to be sure, and muttered, "Let's do it."

As they opened the doors to the library, Jimbo grabbed Dean by the shoulder and said, "What about the ghosts that can actually bite ya? Should we pity them, too?"

"Sure," Dean said, and smiled. "We can pity them, too. They only got one chance at a good meal, an' that's you an' me. An' after three weeks without a shower, we prolly both taste like crap."

❧ ❧ ❧

It was easier than Dean thought to get past the ghosts and into the library offices. Jimbo had a close call with a Biter, but by the time it got near, he had already started flashing his light. The Biter let out a childish moan and drifted away, a fine, gray mist falling to the ground in its wake.

"Must've died sad," Jimbo said as he watched it go, while Dean picked the lock on the fallout shelter door.

"You'd be sad, too, if you died in the library." His unwound paperclip finally hit all the tumblers, and the lock clicked. "After you," he said to Jimbo as the door swung open over a set of old wooden stairs that descended into the fallout shelter's gaping, black maw.

Jimbo looked at Dean, then down again into the darkness. He scratched his head and scrunched up his eyebrows, and Dean laughed to himself. Since they were six years old, Dean had seen Jimbo wear the same expression any time he was trying to make a complicated decision.

Jimbo turned on his flashlight and pointed it down the stairs. "Holy hell!" he screamed, and dropped the flashlight.

Before Dean could say anything, the Hugger was on him. It flew up out of the stairwell, shrieking like a child with a dirty diaper, bone-thin arms outstretched for an embrace. Dean fell backward against the wall and dropped his Maglite. It rolled away and bounced down the stairwell, casting a small pool of light this way and that as it tumbled end-over-end.

Instincts kicked in, and Dean tried to push the Hugger off him, even though he knew his hands would pass right through it. But he could feel its weight, something he had felt a dozen times, but that still didn't make sense to him. And he could see its head, mostly exposed skull with small roots of hair sprouting from the top in random spots, as it slowly descended toward his shoulder in the final attack of a Hugger.

"Jimbo!" he screamed, already feeling the cold creep through his body as those bony arms slid behind his neck. "Jimbo, we've got a situation here!"

All at once, Dean was bathed in light and heard the Hugger start to whimper. "That's right!" he screamed as he felt the arms slowly release him. "That's right! Go get yer hugs from someone else!"

Jimbo started laughing and walked toward where Dean sat on the ground. Two flashlights secured in his belt loops shone steadily on the Hugger, along with two more in his hands.

"That's right, you jerk!" Jimbo yelled. "Might want to get off my friend, just like I got off my momma last night!"

Dean looked at Jimbo and cocked an eyebrow. Jimbo thought for a second, then continued.

"I mean, just like I got off *yer* momma last night!" Jimbo stopped, scratched his head, and said to himself, "Got off *on* yer momma last night? Got off *of* yer momma last night?" Then, turning to Dean, "Hey, Dean—"

"Just keep shinin' the lights at 'im, Jimbo."

"Oh, right."

By the time Jimbo was next to Dean, the Hugger was already starting to flee, slowly making its way out of the office and into the library proper. Jimbo helped Dean up, dusted him off, and looked down the stairwell.

"After you," he said, smiling.

Dean set his jaw, turned on his Maglite, pointed it down the stairs and yelped. Jimbo doubled over with laughter.

"You just screamed like a little girl!" Jimbo said. "What's down there that's gotcha so scared?"

"A girl," uttered a voice from the bottom of the stairs.

That time Jimbo yelped. He turned to Dean and whispered, "Did you hear that?"

"Yeah."

"Think it's a Truly-Pissed-off-Dude?"

"Nah," replied Dean, pointing his Maglite down the stairs to illuminate the darkness again. "It's a chick."

"A Truly-Pissed-off-Chick?"

"This 'chick'," said the voice, "*is* going to be truly pissed off if you gentlemen don't get me out of here."

Dean peeked around the doorframe. The young woman was curled up at the bottom of the stairs, rubbing her ankle.

"I think it's broken," she said. She winced, sighed, and ran a hand through thick, red hair that fell in tight curls around her shoulders. "I've tried dozens of times, but I can't climb back up by myself. Plus, there was a freaking ghost blocking my way, so I've probably gone insane and you're both just figments of my imagination."

Dean turned to Jimbo. "You better go on down there an' get 'er then."

Jimbo nodded and said, "Let me just tell 'er I'm comin'." He stuck his head through the doorway.

"Ma'am, my name is Jimbo, an' this here's my friend, Dean, an' ol' Dean is gonna come down there an' getcha. He's frail from too much time studyin' an' not gettin' laid, but he assures me that you aren't nearly as heavy as other girls he's carried around from time to time, an' on top a' that . . . "

Dean ignored Jimbo and started descending the stairs. "Ask 'er if she's got a friend," he heard Jimbo whisper as he shone his flashlight into the darkness below.

❦ ❦ ❦

"How bad is it?" asked Jimbo between bites from an apple.

After Dean had helped the woman up the stairs—she refused to be carried—he had perched her up on the desk to examine her swollen ankle.

"S'not terrible. Not broken, either," said Dean. "Just a really bad sprain, like that time you messed yers up when you got caught lookin' in Sally Kramer's window an' fell outta the tree."

"Oh, yeah!" Jimbo smiled. "He's right, ma'am; that fall weren't nothin'. I was back climbin' trees in two, three days tops."

"That's encouraging," she said, wincing as Dean touched her ankle.

"Tender there?" he asked.

She nodded, then tugged at the neck of her sweatshirt. "It's hot in here."

"A/C's prolly been off for about two weeks," said Jimbo. He took one last bite of his apple, threw the core to the ground, and sat down in one of the office chairs by the desk.

"You can't put that there!" yelled the woman.

Jimbo stood back up. "Sorry, ma'am, I didn't realize—"

"Not you; you can sit wherever you want. I mean your apple! You can't just throw it on the ground! This is a library, not a dump!"

Jimbo looked at Dean for explanation.

"She doesn't know," said Dean, shaking his head. He rolled down the leg of the woman's jeans and stood up. "Ma'am, exactly how long were you down there?"

"You mean how long was I stuck in a fallout shelter, screaming for help and being held captive by what looked like a freaking ghost who did nothing but moan and cry and go up and down the same four or five steps over and over and over again?"

They both nodded.

"I think at least two days before the electricity went out. I work for the Daily Sun and went down there to look at some old property records for a story I was writing. I had just finished for the day and was walking back up the stairs when this . . . ghost, I guess, popped up out of nowhere and scared the crap out of me. I fell down the stairs; that's when I twisted my ankle. There were a bunch of MREs stashed down there, and, thankfully, a working toilet. I spent most of the time screaming for help, but nobody came until you two showed up. What the heck is going on?"

"Ma'am, I don't know how to tell you this."

"Just tell me," she said, jumping to her feet too quickly. Dean steadied her and held her shoulders until she shrugged him off. She limped toward a small refrigerator in the corner, opened it, and took out a warm bottle of water. "Just tell me what's going on." She took a long drink of water, then said, "And quit calling me ma'am. My name is Jess. And I want to know what hap—"

A terrible screech filled the air, an inhuman tapestry of noise that made the hair on all their necks stand up. Jess covered her ears, Jimbo looked at his watch and began counting the seconds, and Dean took one of the empty office chairs and started banging it on the desk.

Jess looked at Dean, then at Jimbo. "What is he doing?"

Jimbo stared at his watch for a second longer, then knelt beside Jess. "That sound you heard? That's a Truly-Pissed-off-Dude." He turned his head, spat on the floor, and continued. "Now, you've been down in that fallout shelter without talkin' to anybody, so this is gonna sound weird, but ma'am, I mean Jess, we've gone to hell in a handbasket, pardon my language.

"See, the world's been taken over by ghosts—or, at least, this town has been. We haven't heard any news from the outside for a few days, an' radios an' TVs don't work. Most of the time, the ghosts ain't so bad. They stay in the little area around where they died, kinda like yer friend who was goin' up an' down dem stairs. As long as you have a flashlight on you, they'll pretty much keep to themselves. But some'll actually attack you. My momma, God rest her soul, died when she got bit by one."

"And the ones that bite are called Truly-Pissed-off-Dudes?" asked Jess, rolling her eyes.

Jimbo shook his head. Dean had managed to break one of the wooden legs off the office chair and had moved to the next one. "Nah, the Biters ain't too bad, an' you can usually outrun 'em. Plus, they make noise wherever they go, so they can't really sneak up on ya."

"Better hurry it up, Jimbo," said Dean over his shoulder as he broke off another leg of the chair. "That thing only sounded a few minutes away, an' we still need to get her walkin'."

Jimbo continued. "Right. So, like I was sayin', dem Biters ain't as bad as you'd think. But the Truly-Pissed-off-Dudes? Every one of 'em's different. Some just wanna scare the crap outta ya, an' others just wanna tear up any building they come up on. Most of 'em, though, just seem to wanna kill anything that's alive."

Jess's eyes darted from Jimbo, to Dean, then back to Jimbo. "So, Dean is making stakes? Is that how you kill them?"

"I'm makin' you a splint," said Dean, now working on the fourth and last leg, "'cause we need to get out of here as fast as possible."

"Wait a second . . ." Jess started, but she was drowned out by another one of the screams. It sounded closer and even more horrible than the first.

"Prolly a couple a' minutes at the most."

"I know, Jimbo. Now, throw me that duct tape an' come help me get this on her."

Jess pushed herself out of the chair and stood up, balancing on her good foot. "Guys, I can walk; I don't need a splint. See?" She hobbled around for a few steps, then winced and sat back down in the chair.

"Stay there," ordered Dean. He took the tape and the chair legs, knelt in front of her, and started positioning them on her leg. "Jimbo, come hold these in place while I start taping 'er up."

At this, she struggled a little, and winced again. "You need to go easy, Jess," said Dean as he wrapped tape around the makeshift splint. "We're gonna need you to do more than walk here in a minute or so."

Jess looked back and forth between the two of them. "What . . . what are you going to need me to do?"

"We're gonna need ya to run," answered Jimbo as he tore off another strip of tape with his teeth.

In the main room of the library, the Children's Reading Corner exploded in a shower of books and cheap plaster.

All three of them turned to look through the office window into the library. "Aw, man," said Jimbo, "I used to love readin' books there! Or at least pretendin' to read books there!"

There was one more scream, this time from the area where Dean used to read to Jimbo from "Clifford the Big Red Dog." As the dust settled, they could see something there, silhouetted against the sunlight outside, over seven feet tall, and floating a couple of feet off the ground.

"Welcome to Ghost Town, Jess," said Dean, and spat on the floor again. "Only been here thirty minutes an' you've already met yer first Truly-Pissed-off-Dude—or TPOD, for short."

Dean looked at her and smiled. For a second, she smiled back. Then he picked her up in a fireman's carry, watched the shadow in the distance slowly start floating their way, looked at Jimbo and yelled, "Run, before this one decides he wants to have his way with ya like the one we met at Walmart yesterday!"

Jimbo gave a little yelp, and without looking back, darted through the office door and out into the main room of the library. Dean took a deep breath, repositioned Jess on his back, and followed.

† † †

The TPOD started gliding faster as it saw the two figures streak out of the door to the office and start running toward the other end of the building. It screamed again—it screamed at every convenience, since screaming was one of the few things it enjoyed those days—and floated after them, gaining ever closer, until it was gliding alongside them. The TPOD floated up to Jimbo, who stopped so quickly his shoes skidded on the linoleum, then turned and started running the other way.

The TPOD stopped for a moment, watching Dean continue his dash toward the front doors. Which one should it chase? Dean was a great choice—he was already burdened by the person on his back, but the TPOD kept thinking about the one who had run the other way. He seemed pretty dumb, and the dumb ones were always the most fun to play with.

It looked towards Jimbo, who was running toward the hole the TPOD had made in the wall, screamed again (how it loved doing that!) and shot straight up through the ceiling in an explosion of cheap paneled wood and cotton-candy insulation.

♦ ♦ ♦

Dean still couldn't believe that the TPOD had just floated along beside him—had it just wanted to intimidate them for a while, like a cat playing with its meal? He pushed through the front doors of the library and out into the waning sunlight, and was so deep in thought he didn't even hear Jess' screams. Once he did, though, he didn't stop running.

"Stop!" she screamed. "Let me go!"

"Got . . . to find . . . a dumpster . . ." huffed Dean through ragged breaths.

He jogged toward the edge of the library and turned down the alley it shared with the Baptist Church. "There!" he shouted. Jess shifted to see what he was talking about: a black dumpster that was overflowing with trash. It shimmered and moved in the light.

"What the?" He knew she would understand as soon as she heard the buzzing. It was a green dumpster, just like all the other dumpsters in the city. But it looked black because of the flies.

"Oh, no," she said as he jogged closer, "I'm not going in there." But just then, there was another explosion. Dean stopped and looked up in time to see the TPOD flying up into the sky directly above the library.

"Why does he keep busting through stuff?" asked Jess. "I thought ghosts could, you know, walk through walls and float through ceilings."

Dean panted, but held her tight. "They can, when they want. They can also cause a lot of damage when they want. Think of the

'TPODs' as rampagin' elephants. They make yer friend from the fallout shelter look like Casper."

The TPOD began its mad descent, swirling through the air in waves of gray and black, not resembling anything remotely alive. Then it took form again as it exploded back through the roof of the library, where Dean heard Jimbo's unmistakable voice scream, "Crap—not again!"

"Here," said Dean as he carried her to the dumpster. "Get in."

"Nuh-uh, no way."

"Jess, let me put it this way. I was raised with manners. I was raised to treat women with respect, to be kind to 'em, to make sure they was always taken care of. That's why I've got ya in my arms right now, ya see? But that is one angry ghost, an' he's looking to kill or scare or do god-knows-what to any human he can get his hands on, an' right now, that includes you an' me.

"Now, you can do one of two things: you can get in the dumpster, where he won't be able to see you, an' then you can help me in there, an' the two of us can hope that Jimbo joins us momentarily, or I can put you down an' you can take off while I crawl in there myself. Either way, I know that in the dumpster, with the lid closed, I'm in a place where the Dude can't see me, an' that's the best kinda place to be if you want 'em to go away."

Jess looked up at him and swatted some flies away from his face. "You know, you seem like a nice guy, Dean. Sorry I was rude back there. You can understand how being locked in a fallout shelter for three weeks with a ghost, being saved by some rednecks, and being chased down by another ghost who demolishes libraries might make a girl a 'tad ornery,' as you would put it. But I do appreciate you rescuing me."

"Not a problem, Jess," said Dean.

"Good. Now put me in the dumpster."

✦ ✦ ✦

Jimbo had almost made it to the big hole where the TPOD exploded into the library when the roof about fifty feet behind him collapsed in on itself.

He looked up and saw the TPOD gliding down from the ceiling and looking around the library, its bony face set in a permanent grimace. "Crap, not again!" Jimbo yelled, almost slipping on a copy of "Hoots, Toots, and Hairy Brutes" that he used to pretend to read and laugh at to impress Dean.

The TPOD turned toward the sound and flew at Jimbo, who turned at the last minute and sprinted into the library's "Romance" section.

"I hate this section," he mumbled to himself. He thought of all the half-naked pirates, princes, stable boys, and knights that adorned the covers of the books, flexing their muscles and always about to kiss the beautiful girl, who was typically in some kind of distress. "Creeps me out."

He reached the end of the shelves, turned to his left and his right and, seeing no sign of the TPOD, turned down the "Pet Care" aisle and started sprinting. He caught a glimpse of one of the book covers: a small puppy playing with a tennis ball that was almost as big as its head. Jimbo smiled. He liked puppies.

Jimbo looked up just in time to see the TPOD scream and plunge toward him from where it had been gliding silently above the stacks. He pivoted slightly, just enough to catch a glimpse of the TPOD's face. It looked normal for the undead, with a mostly unhinged jaw gaping at him, and strips of flesh hanging off of its body in several layers. The apparition was larger than most, though, and a dull red glow pulsed in its eye sockets.

Jimbo faced forward again, running faster, and swore that he felt the TPOD's cold hands grasping for him, barely touching the back of his neck. However, when he looked over his shoulder again, it was gone.

He slowed down to a jog and looked around. The hole the TPOD had made in the wall was only ten feet away now. "Where'd it go?" he asked.

Just as he was about to reach the hole in the wall, he spotted the TPOD floating directly above him. They locked eyes and the TPOD plummeted straight toward him, screaming the whole time. At the last moment, Jimbo jumped to the side, slipping on a copy of "Goodnight Moon" and crashing to the library floor.

Jimbo just barely saw the TPOD plow into the cement floor of the library in a shower of concrete and rock that spewed from the hole it had made. Without looking back, and without looking down in the hole, he scrambled to his feet and stumbled outside through the opening the TPOD made when it burst into the library. Jimbo regained his footing and sprinted to the right and down an alleyway. He spotted a dumpster and ran toward it, fought his way through the cloud of flies swarming it, held his breath, opened the lid, and jumped inside.

"OW!" screamed Jess.

"SHH!" shushed both Jimbo and Dean, holding their index fingers to their mouths.

"But he landed on my bad ankle!"

"Sorry about that, ma'am," said Jimbo.

"I told you, quit calling me . . ." but the last of what she said was muffled. Dean held his hand tightly over her mouth and leaned his head as close to hers as possible.

"It may not be able to see us, which might save us, but it can hear us, which will probably give us away. So, if you want to get out of this alive, you need to sit tight, without talking, until me or Jimbo says otherwise. Got it?"

"Got it," she whispered. "Just one more thing, though."

"What?" asked Dean.

"Your hands smell okay for a guy who's lived through the Ghostpocalypse."

Jimbo chuckled. "Just because we haven't showered in three weeks doesn't mean we've abandoned all notions of personal hygiene."

And with that, the three of them waited in silence, listening for any indication that the TPOD had left the building.

❦ ❦ ❦

That night, with the rotten stink of the dumpster still clinging to their clothes, Jess walked in between the two men, eyes wide as she took in the abandoned storefronts of Main Street.

"Moon's bright tonight," Jimbo noted as they passed Hawkin's General Store.

"Yup," said Dean, spitting on the ground. He glanced sideways at Jess. "Sorry, ma'am," he said. "Ol' habits 'n all."

Jess snorted, cleared her throat, and spat. It soared into the air before them, splattering on the concrete about fifteen feet away.

"Atta girl!" said Jimbo. "Where'd you learn to do that?"

She wiped her mouth with her sleeve, then reeled in disgust as she remembered, and tasted, where the sleeve had been. "My grandfather owned a farm when I was growing up." She spat again, this time to get the taste of garbage out of her mouth. "When my mom wasn't around, he would take me out into the pasture and we'd have spitting contests."

Dean laughed. "Sounds like we had the same grandpa."

They stopped to look around. Main Street was abandoned except for the three of them. The squat storefronts were lined up tight against each other, like refugees huddled together for warmth. They hadn't seen a ghost for almost five minutes. "Looks like as good a place to stop for the night as any," Dean said. He unslung his backpack and started opening pouches.

"What?" Jess asked, panicked. "Right here? Out in the open?"

Dean shrugged. "Doesn't matter if you're out in the open, locked in a bank vault, or safe in yer own bedroom."

"It's about where they are," said Jimbo, taking his flashlights out of their holsters. "Or, I reckon, where they was when they died."

Jess shook her head. "I don't understand."

Jimbo took off his own backpack. He fished around inside, pulled out a small camping pillow, and tossed it to her. "Take a seat," he said. "We'll set up camp, fix up some grub, an' fill you in on what dem undead jerks have been up to since you've been locked in that fallout shelter."

⦚

"Dinner" was two cans of Vienna sausages apiece, a can of beans between them all, and a bottle of whiskey. They heated the beans over a Sterno, then sat in a triangle around the faint flame, passing the bottle around.

"How can you guys drink so much of this stuff?" asked Jess after a particularly long pull off the bottle. "Tastes like battery acid and sweatsocks."

"Bet it's helpin' that ankle, though," said Dean, taking the bottle. Jess nodded and rubbed her ankle for the first time since she sat down. Jimbo took the bottle, took a swig, and nodded to Jess. "Let's see it," he said, taking one more swig before passing it back to her.

She put the bottle down on the blacktop, pulled up the leg of her jeans, and sighed. It looked bad. The whole ankle was swollen to the size of a small tree trunk, and it was a dark purple at the center with a bluish-yellow tint on the outside.

"Ouch," said Jimbo, turning his face.

Dean winced and shook his head. "That's gonna need time to heal," he said. "We gotta get to a safe place where you can put yer feet up for a few days, and fast."

Jess lowered her jeans back over the ankle. "I think I'll be okay to walk if I can just rest it for tonight." she said. "But what if that thing comes back, the . . . T-PAD?"

Dean shrugged. "T-POD, an' if it comes back, we'll run again, just like last time. But it's not like bein' inside the library did a whole lot of good for us. Might as well be out in the open where runnin' is an option."

Jess picked up the bottle and took a long, painful drink. "Tell me what you know," she said, the whiskey burning in her belly. She handed the bottle back, crossed her legs as best she could, and gazed at the two men impatiently.

Jimbo sighed and stared at the pink and purple flames of the Sterno for a minute or so. Finally, he began.

"Here's what we know so far: 'bout three weeks ago, I was at Roadside, the icehouse right outside of town, just mindin' my own business an' hustlin' college kids at pool. One of my buddies comes in—he's a reservist with the Guard—an' he's all upset about somethin'. He's tryin' to talk to anyone who'll listen, sayin' weird stuff 'bout little green men, an' the army coverin' things up, an' how if we knew what was about to happen we'd all be freakin' out!

"He ends up gettin' so excited that he knocks over a beer. It spills onto this guy named Buck Nasty. He's a feller who basically lives at the bar an' could prolly bench press a Cadillac. An' he's not known for havin' a good temper. So, Buck Nasty picks my buddy up by the collar of his shirt an' says, 'Listen, you piece of—'"

"Jimbo!" Dean interrupted. Jimbo looked up with a start. "Why don'cha skip to the part where yer buddy gets taken away by those guys in suits."

"Oh, yeah. Anyway, about that time these three guys walk through the front door. They're all wearin' black suits, sunglasses, an' those little weird things in their ears so they can talk to each other. An' they see my buddy standin' in the middle of the room, screamin' 'bout mind control factories, an' black rights in space, an' Hitler's frozen sperm, an' all this other weird conspiracy stuff, an' Buck Nasty's still there, screamin' an' callin' him things like—"

"Jimbo!"

"Sorry, sorry. So, these guys in suits come grab my buddy by the arms, lift him up like he's a feather, an' carry him outta the bar.

"We go back to drinkin', 'cause, hey, weird stuff happens at the Roadside all the time, right? Well, about two in the mornin', we hear this screamin' sound from outside—kinda sounds like a runaway freight train, kinda sounds like a kid cryin', an' kinda sounds like the last scream of some dyin' animal. At first, I thought I was just drunk an' dreamin' it, but everyone else was hearin' it, too. We ran outside; turned out to be one of the smartest things I ever done.

"It was a night kinda like tonight, with a bright, full moon. Me an' about fifteen other guys stood out on the gravel parking lot, boots scrapin' the rocks, all tryin' to figure out what it was and askin' the waitresses to bring our beers outside when Merle, the bar owner, shouts, 'Look—it's over there!'

"We all turn an' look where he's pointin', an' there's this thing streakin' across the sky. I couldn't make out what it was. A couple of the jaded old timers shrugged an' walked back in the bar.

"The rest of us just stood there, though, not 'cause we wanted to know what it was, but 'cause it was gettin' closer. When Merle had pointed it out, it was just a tiny fleck, a gray dot in a black sky. Now, it was a circle, an' it was screamin' our way.

"I'm still not sure why I ran, but as soon as I saw that thing gettin' closer, I turned an' sprinted off in the other direction toward the woods. Most of the guys followed me. I kept lookin' over my shoulder, an' the thing kept gettin' closer. We'd made it about fifty yards down the road when the screamin' got so loud I thought my ears would burst. I stopped to catch my breath, an' one of the other guys shouted, 'It's almost here!'

"I turned just in time to see this white streak swoop out of the sky an' straight into the north wall of the icehouse. As soon as that happened, it exploded out the south wall, leavin' a big ol' hole where the wimmins room had been. It was over in a second, but as I was standin' there, scared outta my mind, the only thought goin' through my head was, 'I could'a sworn that thing had a face.'

"All the other guys ran back to the bar, but I didn't move an inch. I dunno why." Jimbo stopped and looked into the distance.

Dean leaned over to Jess. "He was probably too drunk to do much else."

Jess giggled.

Jimbo continued. "It was prolly on account of how drunk I was, the reason I just stood there. But I knew in my gut that goin' back in that bar was bad news. An' as soon as I saw what done happened when the guys went back there . . ."

He shuddered and sat forward, crossing his arms across his stomach.

"It was a Truly-Pissed-off-Dude. One of the truliest. I watched as it destroyed that bar an' every one of dem men who walked back in there." He paused and looked at Jess. "I'll spare you the details, ma'am, but have you ever seen roadkill after it's been sittin' out on the road for a coup'la days? How it looks all crusty an'—"

"What Jimbo's tryin' to say," Dean interrupted, reaching for the bottle. Jimbo took one last swig, handed it to him, and laid back to look up at the stars. "What Jimbo's tryin' to say is that the ones we call the Truly-Pissed-off-Dudes are the worst of the worst. They're the ones we're constantly runnin' from."

"Because they're the only ones that can actually kill you?" asked Jess.

"Nah," said Jimbo. "They can all kill ya. But the TPODs are real jerks about it."

Jess gave up. "Tell me more about them. Everything."

Dean smiled, took a long pull from the bottle, and sat it down between them.

"So far, we've found three kinds of ghosts. They're all different from each other, an' they're all pretty nasty. The first, an' easiest to deal with, are the Huggers. We call 'em different things—Roamers, Walkers, Loafers—mainly 'cause in the beginning we didn't realize they were all the same. They're the ghosts of people who died sad, usually feeling sorry for demselves. I guess that's the way most people die, 'cause they're everywhere."

"Wait," Jess interjected. "How do you know they died sad?"

Dean glanced at Jimbo, snorted, and spat on the pavement. "'Cause we recognized some of 'em. We already knew they died sad."

He continued, "The good thing is, dem Huggers can't go much farther than fifty feet or so outside the radius of the exact spot where they died. So, they're pretty easy to avoid, an' if you get trapped by 'em, you just wave yer flashlight around an' they go away. But if ya get surprised by one, if one of 'em catches you, it'll start huggin' ya, literally huggin' the life outta ya. We figure this is on account of how pathetic they are, but it ain't pretty when it happens, an' we've both seen it happen.

"Then there's the Biters. They're like Huggers, 'cept they were a little more confident when they passed. They can usually go 'bout a hunnerd, two-hunnerd feet away from where they died, an' they can actually physically hurt you. If they get at you bad enough, they can kill you, like they did with Jimbo's mom, God rest 'er soul."

"Amen," said Jimbo, still gazing at the stars.

"We've both been bit a coupla times. Here's one on my arm, an' Jimbo's got one on his leg."

Jimbo laughed from where he lay. "Dean got bit first. I stayed awake all night with a rifle pointed at him, convinced he was gonna turn into one of 'em."

"I had to remind him that if I did turn into a ghost, the rifle wouldn't help, 'cause I'd be pretty pissed off an' do my best to haunt him for the rest of his life.

"An' that brings us to the Truly-Pissed-off-Dudes. We gave 'em that name the first time we were together and saw one 'bout a week ago." Dean turned, spat, and said, "We were walking into town, little bit after noon, an' saw this grayish streak fly across the sky an' explode into one of the tall buildings downtown. Jimbo pointed an' yelled, 'That looks like that dude from the icehouse, Dean! He was truly pissed off.' So, the name stuck.

"You can't do anything about 'em, 'cept run. They seem to enjoy bustin' down buildings more than anything else, but every now an' then they'll turn on ya. The best advice is to run as fast as you can an' find a small, dark, enclosed space to hide."

Jess reached out, and Dean handed her the bottle.

"So, the Truly-Pissed-off-Dudes, the TPODs, they're all the people who were angry when they died?"

"Truly angry," said Jimbo.

Jess uncrossed her legs and stretched them out. "So, where did all the people go? Did they all get killed?"

"Most of 'em are dead now, we reckon. It happened so fast an' nobody knew what was goin' on. People kept tryin' to find shelter, but they'd get panicked an' make mistakes. It's hard to find a place where nobody ever died before."

"Oh, is that why you came to the library? To try and find records of a house where nobody had died?"

Dean nodded. "Only way we figured to narrow it down some.

We've been goin' in an' out of buildings for three days tryin' to find a place. It's amazin' all the different places where people die in this world."

"Well, nobody's died in the Kramer house," said Jess.

Dean put down the bottle. "The one right outside the city limits?"

Jess nodded.

Jimbo sat up on his elbows. "How do you know?"

"Like I told you, I work for the Daily Sun," she said. "I did a story on Maddie Kramer not too long ago—her family's owned that house for five generations. One of the things she was proud of, given how old it was, was that nobody had died in it before."

"Not a single person?" asked Jimbo.

Jess shook her head. "Not a single person; I confirmed it in the town records. She insisted that everyone who lived there died doing something important and meaningful, like fighting in one of the wars, or examining a wheat thresher while it was still running."

The two men looked at each other. "That's about seven miles outside of town, prolly about fifteen from here," Dean said.

"We could make it there in half a day," said Jimbo. Turning to Jess, he said, "It's the best lead we got. We'll give it a try."

"I just don't like it out in the open like this, not even for one night," said Jess, hugging herself.

Dean stood up and stretched. "I don't like it any more than you do. But right now, we got no choice. Tomorrow, we'll make the trek to the Kramer place, and hopefully, we'll be able to stay there, at least for a while. But tonight, try to get some sleep and give that ankle a break. You ain't gonna do us any good if we have to carry you while we're runnin' from somethin', an' we've been doin' a lot of runnin' these past few days."

Jimbo yawned. "He's right. Just take it easy. We'll get movin' tomorrow, but, for now, we've found a place that's quiet an' don't have no ghosts. Even if it is out in the middle of the street, well, that's good 'nough for me."

Jess laid her head down on the pillow and stared up at Dean. "I want to find a place where I can take a shower."

Dean nodded. "A shower'd be nice right 'bout now. Even a lake would do. They should have both at the Kramer place, though I ain't sure whether it's pump water or city wat—"

An abrupt snore woke Jess up. Dean was sitting and staring at the dwindling flame of the Sterno.

"Everything okay?" he asked.

She nodded. "I fell asleep while you were talking, didn't I?"

"You've had a long day. Don't worry about it. Go on back to sleep, 'cause tomorrow's gonna be even longer."

"I'll try." She adjusted her pillow and laid her head back down. "But I don't know if I'll be able to with Jimbo's snoring."

Dean laughed out loud. "Jess, Jimbo doesn't snore."

She looked to where Jimbo was stretched out, sleeping quietly. "Wait, you mean that was . . . no way. I don't snore."

Dean smiled, yawned, and stretched out on the ground. "Must've been my imagination." She heard him chuckling. "Now let's both get some shut-eye. We've got a long road ahead of us tomorrow."

Even though her cheeks were burning, Jess was back asleep as soon as she closed her eyes.

‖ ‖

"Dean!" shouted Jimbo. "I hear screamin'!"

They were about two miles outside of town in a grassy field that stretched off into the eastern horizon without breaking. Small hills dotted the landscape. Jess and Dean were still walking up the hill Jimbo had scaled seconds before. Her ankle was better after a night of rest, but tender enough that she leaned on Dean as they climbed.

"Hold on, let me get up there," Dean called after Jimbo. Jess let go of his waist and wobbled a bit, then stood upright, wincing just a little.

"Go on," she said, "I'm coming, just not as fast as you yet."

Dean arched his eyebrows and grinned. Jess pursed her lips and shooed him away, so he turned to jog up to where Jimbo stood. At the top of the hill, he could see clearly in all directions. The grassy plain stretched into the horizon, freckled here and there with tight copses of junipers and oaks. To the south, the dark green of the woods marked the edge of the city.

Jimbo spat, then looked out across the field. "It's comin' from the south, an' we need to head northeast to get to the old Kramer house." He squinted his eyes and pointed to where the woods stretched out below them. "See that little glint over yonder? That's the roof of their farm house. It's brand new; I helped put it up a coupl'a months ago."

Dean cupped his hands around his eyes and saw the little pinprick of light in the distance. "It ain't too far," he said. "What, a mile or so, ya figure?"

Jimbo shook his head. "Prolly two, maybe three. Could get there in a half hour or so. Jess is doin' pretty good on that foot. Thing is, I dunno know if we even got a half hour."

The wind blew Dean's hair into his eyes. He pushed it away, then listened. He could hear something, but it might not have been anything more than the whistle of the wind.

"Jimbo, maybe there ain't a problem? Maybe it's just the wi—"

As Jess crested the hill, there was a loud *pop* from the south. They all turned towards the sound.

"What the . . . ?" said Jess and Jimbo simultaneously.

Dean watched as what looked like a tiny toothpick flew into the air above the middle of the woods, followed by another, and another, and another, the tiny path of destruction raging in their direction. It cleared a straight line through the forest, and Dean could swear he heard the whistling get louder.

"Jess, Jimbo—tie up," said Dean. He leaned down and started to mess with the laces of his shoes. Jimbo was already on his knees retying his.

"What?" said Jess. "What do we need to 'tie up' for?"

"'Cause we gotta start runnin'," said Jimbo. "That there line ya see coming straight at us through the trees? That's a T—" Something slammed against Jimbo's shoulder and knocked him to the ground. Dean helped him up as they watched Jess slowly jogging away.

"Got a bum leg, might as well get a head start!" she yelled over her shoulder.

Jimbo and Dean looked to the forest. The line of destruction was still approaching. "It'll break the tree line in a minute or so," said Jimbo. "Then it's probably got 'bout twenty minutes 'fore it gets here, rate it's goin'."

"Twenty minutes; we could be two miles away by then, even with Jess's ankle."

"Unless it changes course."

"Why would it? Looks like it's just havin' fun tearin' up the forest. If we get out of here quick, it won't even see us."

Jimbo wasn't listening. Dean followed his wide-eyed gaze to the edge of the woods, where a man had emerged, though it was hard to tell at such a great distance, and was running their direction.

Dean sighed. "Well, looks like the TPOD's already got himself somethin' to chase. We better get outta here before that guy sees us, else that TPOD'll be chasin' us instead of him."

Suddenly, the man slanted and started running to the northeast. Jimbo and Dean looked out toward the farmhouse. Jess was about five hundred yards away and moving at a steady clip, but was on course to intersect with the man and the TPOD in a couple of minutes.

"Crap," said Jimbo and Dean at the same time. They started running.

Jimbo stumbled down the hill, tripped, somersaulted, and then sprung clumsily back to his feet, taking off in a dead sprint after Jess. Dean was a little more careful and caught up with him quickly.

"I lost sight of her!" Jimbo yelled as they ran.

"Me, too!" Dean had watched as Jess, still ahead of them, disappeared over the crest of the next hill.

"Screamin's stopped though!" yelled Jimbo, and Dean listened carefully as he ran. Jimbo was right; the air was mostly silent, and this time he really was sure he could hear the whistling of the wind. He slowed down and turned back toward the south, looking at the edge of the forest. From where he stood, he could no longer see trees shooting up into the sky. Everything had gone silent.

"You should probably keep runnin'!" yelled Jimbo, and at that moment, a noise like thunder broke the silence. Three or four nearly identical "cracks" sounded, and before Dean even saw the tree trunks that had been thrust out from the front line of the forest like splinters from a kicked-in door, he saw the TPOD. It was all gray, screaming agony and self-pity, floating off toward the man who had emerged in front of it, and in the direction Jess had been running.

Dean passed Jimbo but didn't stop to say anything. The air hummed with the screams of the TPOD, and his own. He didn't even realize he was screaming until he started coughing and almost fell forward from doubling over.

He started running again. "Got to get to Jess," he repeated to himself. He still couldn't see her and assumed she was just over the crest of the next hill. With her ankle, he should have caught up to her by now. The wind had picked up, and it carried the oscillating screams of the TPOD. He couldn't quite tell where they were coming from—ahead of him or behind him—but he could tell they were getting closer.

Dean crested a hill, and panic started to rise. He swung his head back and forth and saw nothing but grass and forest to his left and the barn to the northeast. The roof of the barn had been a pinprick when he and Jimbo had looked at it earlier, but it was now a large mirror, reflecting the light straight at him so that he had to squint. The barn was now only ten minutes away, at most.

Dean looked out to the east. The TPOD was there, cutting through a field of tall grass and leaving nothing but shriveled husks in its wake. Dean followed the TPOD's trajectory to the running man they'd observed earlier, probably still about half a mile ahead of the TPOD and heading straight toward the barn.

Jimbo came huffing and puffing up behind him. "Jess . . . where's . . . Jess . . . ?"

Dean shrugged, still catching his breath, and turned to face Jimbo. "Lost sight of her, dunno know which way to go. I hate to say it, but I'm thinkin' we might need to stay here for now. That TPOD's still chasin' whoever that was, an' I think we're probably fine."

"But what about Jess?" said Jimbo. "Think she's somewhere safe?"

Dean put his hands on his knees, shook his head. "She's probably gone off over—"

He felt a sudden, immense pain in his head. It quickly made its way to the back of his eyelids, and he muttered, "What the hell?" before falling into an unconscious heap, sending clouds of dust from the dry grass swirling skyward from where he landed.

● ● ●

". . . Ain't never listened to advice from a woman before, but I thought, well, there's a first time for everythin'," Dean heard when he woke up.

Dean's head pounded with ferocity unlike any hangover he'd ever had. His eyes throbbed, and he was concerned that they were going to pop out of his skull. For a second he could think of nothing but the sound they might make—*pop pop, pop pop*—then he shook his head to get the thought out, which made the pounding even worse.

"So, I started headin' down here." It was the same voice that had woken Dean up. "Good thing I read yer story. Surprised other folks don't remember this was the only place in town where nobody'd died."

He tried to turn over, felt a wave of nausea, and vomited onto . . . what? Sheets? He felt around him, getting his hands in the vomit, but nonchalantly wiped them on his jeans and continued his examination. He was on a bed, there was no doubt about that, and in a room, which meant that he was probably in a house.

". . . an' it shore is nice for you kind folks to share yer beer with me." Dean concentrated, but didn't recognize the voice.

"Ain't our beer. There were ten cases of 'em downstairs. I's just wish it was culd . . . coll . . . less warm." That was Jimbo's drunken slur.

The conversation was interrupted by a loud, obnoxious snore. Jess.

It was so dark in the room that Dean could only see the outlines of random objects. He tried to roll over again, the other way this time, and made it up onto his side without the nausea coming back.

He was in a bedroom; there was a bedside table, and a glass of water had been placed there. He brought it to his lips and drank for several seconds. Slowly, he lifted himself off the bed and tried to stand. For a brief second, he teetered backward, then toward the wall. He put out a hand, steadied himself, and craned his neck toward the source of the conversation.

The door to the bedroom had been left open a crack, and a low light crept in around the edges. It flickered occasionally, and for a second, he watched it intently, thinking, *We're here. We're in the Kramer house.*

"So lemme tell ya 'bout the time I damn near 'lectrocuted the mayor's poodle," he heard Jimbo say, and at that moment, his legs buckled and he fell to the floor.

"Dean!" yelled Jimbo from the other room. Dean heard two pairs of feet scrambling along the floor toward him. "Say somethin'!"

Dean breathed in deep, mustered all his remaining strength, and screamed, "Get me some ibuprofen an' a bottle a' Wild Turkey!"

"Sounds like he's okay to me," said Jess sleepily. A moment later, she started snoring again.

***

Dean sipped on his whiskey and held an icepack to the back of his head, trying to remember what a life without pain felt like.

"Start over," he said to Jimbo.

"Start over where?"

"Right after Jess threw the rock at me."

Jimbo reclined in his chair and rolled his eyes. They all sat around a small coffee table in the living room of the house. Jimbo and Rowdy, a short, muscular man who Dean guessed to be thirty or so, had made makeshift lanterns out of empty beer cans and some votive candles they'd found at the house, and these were the only light in the otherwise darkened room.

"She didn't throw the rock at ya, Dean," said Jimbo, looking over at the snoring Jess with some measure of sympathy. "She meant for it to hit the ground next to ya. She's got bad aim, is all."

Dean shook his head, grimaced, and reminded himself never to do that again. "Regardless of her aim," he took another sip of whiskey, "she threw the rock toward me, hit me, I blacked out, an' then?"

Jimbo pulled a pack of cigarettes from his pocket and lit one. He inhaled, and said, "An' then, several things happened at once.

"Jess started screamin' something fierce, yellin', 'I killed Dean!' an', 'I'm sorry, I'm sorry' an' limped over to where I was. She had hidden behind a tree fer some reason, an' I finally got her to tell me she'd been tryin' to get our attention by throwin' the rock. I got her quieted down, but it took a couple of seconds, an' that's when we heard the crash.

"The TPOD had taken off on its own; got tired of the chase, we reckon. Rowdy had been runnin' toward the barn. He seen the barn when he came out of the forest. You remember seein' that, don'cha, Dean?"

Instead of moving his head, Dean just mouthed, "Yes," and Jimbo continued.

"Last I saw, that TPOD was at least a mile away from the barn. But between the time you had yer accident an' the time I turned around again, it had done tore the barn up. Must've covered a mile in less than a minute. Poor Rowdy, I could see 'im still standin' in the middle of the field, an' we was both just watchin' as that pitiful TPOD kept plungin' in an' out of the barn, wood splinterin' away in every which direction, crackin' louder than thunder every time he hit it.

"After a minute or so, Rowdy looked up at me. He was prolly a half mile away from us, an' I couldn't make out much, but I could've sworn I seen him give me a thumbs up. Then he started walkin' up to us."

Rowdy shifted in his seat and groaned. "Ain't a big deal. Once dem things—the one's you call TPODs—get a buildin' destroyed, they get bored an' leave to go find somethin' else to do. All you have to do is lead 'em to some place that's still intact, wait for 'em to do their damage, an' then yer safe."

Dean thought about telling Rowdy that if that was the case,

they shouldn't have had any trouble with the TPOD in the library, but thinking hurt, so he stopped doing it.

"Plus," Rowdy continued. "You had that fine woman over there with you. Man, I could see how hot she was from a mile away! Had to come check out what you guys had goin' on."

Jimbo looked down at his beer. Dean forgot about pain and stared at Rowdy. "Say that again?"

Rowdy laughed, then gestured to Jimbo for a cigarette. "Hey man, don't get all crazy or nothin'. I get it, she's yer girlfriend. I hear ya."

Dean's headache didn't seem as bad anymore. He looked at Jimbo and raised his eyebrows. Jimbo simply nodded.

"Listen, Rowdy?" said Dean. "I appreciate all the help you've given us, we all do. An' yer more than welcome to stay the night; we owe ya at least that much. And tomorrow mornin', we'll pack up whatever supplies we can find in this house, and we'll see ya on yer way."

"Wait a second," said Rowdy. "You mean you guys're kickin' me out?"

"Look, we don't want no trouble," said Jimbo.

"Oh," said Rowdy, smiling, "trouble's gonna be the last thing we have in this here house." Rowdy shifted in his seat, then quickly produced a handgun and pointed it at Dean. "In *my* house."

It was a Magnum, and if Rowdy shot him with it, they would have to repaint the walls and the ceiling.

"Bang," said Rowdy, and pointed the gun right between Dean's eyes.

Dean didn't flinch, which wasn't hard since he was certain if he did, Rowdy was going to pull the trigger.

"Now, you listen here," said Rowdy. "Yer friend Jimbo seems to get this, but I want to make sure you do, too." Dean looked at Jimbo, who stood up, still looking at his beer, and walked out of the room and into the kitchen. "You guys may think you've been on yer own fer a while, but you haven't been—you've had each other, see? Me? I've really been on my own. Lost my whole family to this.

"Not you guys, though. Yer soft. What's happened out there is so messed up that you forgot what a messed up place the normal world can be. But I didn't forget, an' I came prepared. I knew I'd run into people like you—people who just wanted to find someplace safe, but hadn't given any thought to what they'd do when they got there.

"Well, I ain't one of dem. I've always known exactly what I'd do if I ever met new people. I'd take over, that's what. An' that's what I'm doin' right now." He smiled and spat on the wooden planks through his yellowing teeth.

Dean closed his eyes and started counting to himself, backwards from one hundred. He knew if he listened to a second more of Rowdy's speech, he'd snap and attack, gun or no gun.

Rowdy continued. "Now, only 'cause I like ya, kind of, I'll tell you what I'm gonna do. I'm gonna head upstairs and catch some shut-eye. You jerk-offs can all sleep down here, on the floor. An' then tomorrow mornin', we'll have ourselves a nice little chat about who's in charge around here."

Rowdy started chuckling to himself. Keeping the gun pointed at Dean, he stood up, drunkenly stumbled and crumpled back down into the chair. He leaned his head back to laugh some more, and that's when he saw Jimbo standing over him with the poker from the fireplace.

Before anyone could do anything, Jimbo screamed and swung the poker down, but he missed his mark and hit Rowdy on his shoulder, rather than the head. Rowdy winced, but obviously wasn't feeling much pain, because he stood up, cocked his head to look at Jimbo, and hit him across the face with the butt of the pistol.

Jimbo fell to the ground motionless, and Jess jumped at the noise. "What the?" she mumbled. She opened her eyes, looked at Rowdy pointing a gun at Dean, and screamed.

"Aw, ain't no reason to scream, honey!" Rowdy said, keeping his eyes on Dean the whole time. "At least, not yet."

Dean remained where he was, watching as Rowdy slowly backed away. If only he could think straight, he could figure a way out of this.

"On second thought," said Rowdy, "maybe there's no need to wait until tomorrow. Maybe I'll just finish ya off right now, so me and the little lady here can spend some time gettin' to know each other."

At least he'd come back as a TPOD, Dean thought, 'cause he'd never been more pissed off in his entire life.

Rowdy pulled the trigger. There was a bang.

ı ı ı

Jess leaned into Jimbo, who had one of his arms around her waist. Their shadows fell over the long, uncut grass of the yard outside the house. The sun was hot, but a soft wind made the day bearable.

"I can't believe he's dead," whispered Jess.

Jimbo shook his head, spat on the ground. "It's a damn shame. I just never expected it. Sorry for the language, by the way."

Jess leaned her head on his shoulder. "I know I didn't know him long, but I can't describe this feeling."

Jimbo nodded. "Yeah, s'kind of weird, bein' so relieved that someone you barely knew blew his own head off 'cause he didn't know how to clean a gun."

"Exactly," she said.

The front door of the house opened, and Dean walked out onto the porch and started toward them.

"Think he'll be okay?" Jess asked Jimbo.

"Who, Dean? Yeah, he'll be fine. We've been in worse jams before. Did we ever tell you 'bout that time we was thirteen an' snuck into the dressing room at Darleen's Dress Emporium, an' my irritable bowel syndrome started actin' up an'—"

"Once yesterday, and twice two nights ago," said Jess.

Jimbo laughed. "Then what're ya worried for? That was way worse than this."

Dean walked up to them with his hands on his hips. "Well, he's in there."

Jimbo and Jess looked at him expectantly.

"He's a Hugger," Dean said. "An' a pretty desperate one. He can't go but about two or three feet from where he died, but he keeps reachin' out for you just the same. That guy really, really wants a hug."

Jess walked toward Dean. She buried her face in his chest and wrapped her arms around his neck.

"So glad you're okay," she mumbled into his shirt, then pulled away and looked him in the face, concerned. "You are okay, aren't you?"

Dean winced as she reached up and lightly touched his face under the long, jagged wound sliced open by the gun shrapnel the night before. They had all worked together to clean it and stitch it up with the sewing supplies they found in the house, but he knew a scar was forming, a scar he expected to wear the rest of his life. Every time he saw it in the mirror, or ran his fingers over it, he would remember how concerned Jess looked when she was sewing it shut.

"Aside from the fact that I can still smell gunpowder, I'm okay, ma'am . . . I mean, Jess." He chuckled. "Sorry. Ol' habits an' all."

She smiled and wrapped her hands around his waist. "And I'm sorry I hit you with a rock."

Dean put a hand on her cheek, leaned down, and gave her a quick kiss on the lips. "Don't mention it," he said. "Been in worse jams before. Did we ever tell you about the time we went to Pizza Town, an' Jimbo got the jalepeno an' bean pizza, an'—"

Jess grabbed Dean's face, his stubble tickling her palms. She pulled him down and kissed him, a long kiss that made Dean stumble.

"Was a little worried I might never get to do that," she said after she pulled away.

Dean smiled. "Let's just make sure we get a chance to do it again."

"I hear screamin'!" Jimbo yelled from behind them.

Dean and Jess turned. Jimbo pointed north, where the imposing woods stretched out into the horizon. Here and there, trees flew up out of the forest like twigs being thrown by a toddler. Dean counted at least five different places where TPODs were destroying the forest and coming their way. He shook his head—it only hurt a little to do that now—and looked down at his shoes.

"Well, boys an' girls," he said as he bent down, "guess it's time to tie up . . ."

He was almost knocked over by Jess and Jimbo as they ran past him on either side. By the time he had his laces in double knots, they were already on the other side of the house, running toward the fence that marked the edge of the property.

"Gettin' a little tired of all this running," he said to himself. "Stupid ghosts."

Jess and Jimbo, now the size of ants in the distance, stopped and turned his way.

Dean smiled and ran toward them.

* * *

CROSSROADS
Neve Talbot

Rob understood his brother's love for the road, especially, as then, in the dead of night. Like himself, Nate had never been one for large crowds. On the road, one was utterly alone. The growling 454 V8 of his brother's cherry 1977 El Camino Classic and the steel-belted radials humming on the blacktop lulled to silence all the demands that sucked the life out of him. They slipped away like the endless blur of the dotted white line that streamed beyond the windshield.

Except, there he was, bringing up the rear of that cross-country cortege, behind his sister Sarah's Suburban, driven by her ass-of-a-son, Bertie; returning home with Nate's ashes, hurtling at 75 miles an hour toward the madness: the boss, the job, the mounting bills and overdrawn bank account, the constant chaos of three small children he couldn't afford. The labyrinth of life with no easy way out.

Toward Annabelle—his own sweet Nan—and that look of dread in her eyes: anguish that assaulted him, and reticence that held him at arm's length. Pleading for answers to questions she dare not voice, nor even understand.

● ● ●

Rob jerked awake, jolted from a deep, dreamless sleep by something—the baby? He couldn't remember. Nan had started whining just before ten, which degenerated into a fight, as usual.

To avoid another relentless demand to hash it out, he put off going to bed until he was certain she slept.

He turned in very late, and the fog of his fatigue melded to his brain like his kids' sticky hands to his skin. Scarcely lucid, he ignored his transient bob to the surface of consciousness, and surrendered again to the depths of slumber.

Her voice prevented it, however . . . a low murmur . . . hesitant . . . wary—scraps of sound distorted by the cobwebs of his sleep-deprived brain. He rolled over, pried open his eyes, and forced the numerals of the digital clock into focus. 04:00. Good grief. He had to be up in two hours. Couldn't she cut him some slack?

He turned toward the wall and faked unconsciousness. He was tired of bending over backward to make her happy, and for what? No matter how he tried, he couldn't figure out what the devil she wanted.

He recoiled from her touch as she reached out to him. "Rob." She spoke gently, a catch of tears in her voice. Blast. He couldn't do this tonight. This morning. She could sleep all day if she wanted, but he had to go to work. He moaned incoherently and pulled the spread up around his shoulders, blocking her out. The light on her nightstand shattered the darkness. He swore beneath his breath and dug in. Not tonight. He'd get his own way for once.

"Rob," she insisted, jiggling him. "Baby. Wake up." She prodded him in the back with something hard. Pushed beyond his patience, he hurled a glare over his shoulder at her. She flinched with the force of it but fought to appear unaffected. "Honey, you need to take this." Was that pity in her eyes? Pity?

Rob looked from her face to his mobile phone in her outstretched hand and back to her face. He felt his stomach drop through the floor. Good news never called at 4 a.m. He watched her blink back her welling tears, but she could not hide the fear and heartbreak. That look he knew only too well.

"Bobby Daniels?"

"This is Rob."

"Mr. Daniels—" the tinny voice on the other end of the line hesitated. "I'm sorry about the hour."

Rob flung his legs over the side of the bed, turned on his lamp, pushed the mop of unruly hair back from his face, and hunched over the receiver. He knew Nan couldn't help reaching out. It was who she was. He felt her drawn to him, then hesitate, repelled by the palpable shield of animosity pulsating around him.

Blazes! He needed some space. He couldn't breathe.

"Excuse me. Who is this?"

"The sheriff of La Plata County, Mr. Daniels—Durango. Durango, Colorado."

"How can I help you, Sheriff . . . ?"

"—Gutierrez. Tim Gutierrez. The reason I'm calling you is . . . well . . . your wife tells me you have a brother by the name of Nathan Daniels?"

"That's right."

"The thing is, your name has ICE next to it in the phone we found."

"What kind of help does Nate need, Sheriff? I'll do anything I can."

"That's just it, Mr. Daniels. If what we found is your brother, he's beyond anyone's help now."

⁃ ⁃ ⁃

Ahead, Sarah's Suburban drew up to the flashing red signal at the intersection, the headlamps lighting up the reflective signs at the junction. "In fifty feet, turn right onto Highway 288," the GPS on his phone instructed.

Rob slowed the El Camino and saw his sister glance over her shoulder to ensure he obediently followed. In the rearview, from the glow of the dash lights, he could see Bertie's vigilance—his eyes peeled for Rob's least deviation from protocol. Defy his mother? That would never do.

It had played out the same that entire expedition—Rob tagging along, doing Sarah's bidding, her perfectly trained terrier properly at heel. They both treated him as if he hadn't a brain in his head, and maybe he didn't since he ran her errands and put up with Bertie's laziness and smug superiority.

And for what? To return home for more of the same. To endure Sarah's constant criticisms—so she could put him properly in his place. So Bertie could gloat over his failures. All while Nan silently castigated him for not standing up for himself. Why wouldn't he grow a pair?

She thought he should man up? Rob agreed. For once, he would make his own choices. He wouldn't be their doormat for the sole purpose of keeping the peace. He had that one golden opportunity to break free without answering to anyone, and he meant to take it. If he didn't right then, he knew he never would.

Rob flipped on the blinker and turned left.

"Recalculating," the electronic voice announced with disgust.

Rob picked up the phone to discontinue the navigation, when it blared a Twisted Sister riff. He cursed under his breath but answered it.

"What are you doing?" Sarah demanded without ceremony.

"I got an engine light," Rob lied. "There's a gas station a couple of miles up the road."

"We'll follow you. Bertie, turn around." He watched in the rearview as the Suburban made an abrupt U-turn in the middle of the highway. Just like Sarah. The world always bowed to her convenience.

"No. It probably just needs oil or something. You go on. I'll meet you at the motel in Santa Fe like we planned."

"We shouldn't split up. Nathan's dead because that car—"

"Don't you lose your deposit if you miss the check-in time? It's already ten." Rob smirked at the silence on the line. Remind Sarah how much more her own way cost her, and you won the argument. The Suburban slowed again and pulled over to the side of the road.

"Keep your phone charged and don't get lost," she finally ordered. "We have to be at Galveston when the folks' ship docks."

"I'm a big boy now, Sissy," Rob answered caustically. "Long pants and everything."

A barked command, more grousing from Bertie, and the Suburban squealed through another U-ie, then peeled out down the road. Rob floored the gas. The engine roared, the tires sang on the asphalt, and he watch as the Suburban's taillights quickly vanished into the night.

╵ ╵ ╵

Their cramped townhouse sat a single flight of stairs higher than the street. Rob stood at the bottom, with his duffle in one hand, the doorknob in the other. He gazed at his wife who stood at the top, the baby balanced on her hip. By the time he finished his final phone call that morning, spreading the bad but truly unsurprising news, Nan had anticipated both Sarah's plan and timetable, and had begun managing the unmanageable.

A large cooler sat at his feet, stocked to feed an army: hoagie sandwiches, lettuce and tomatoes packed separately to keep them fresh, carrot and celery sticks he wouldn't eat, apples and oranges peeled and sliced like she fixed for the boys, granola bars, animal crackers, little bags of corn chips and tiny fruit cups she put in Luke's lunch box, anything else her trolling through the pantry could produce on the fly.

He'd rather just stop at McDonald's, but he couldn't deprive her of her busyness. He couldn't have stopped her if he tried.

But, there she was, gazing down at him with that look, and he had nothing. "There's really no need for you to go."

"I know," she answered. She lied. He knew she believed he needed her to hold his hand. To wipe his nose and dry his tears when he cried, and cradle his head on her breast while she murmured, 'He's in a better place,' or 'He's free now. Free from everything.'

Lucky stiff.

"I'd just be in the way."

Rob blinked at her and remained silent.

"There's not room enough for me anyway." Another lie. Sarah's Suburban could seat nine comfortably and still have room for the State of Delaware. 'The last thing your sister wants is me there,' she left unsaid. 'The last thing I want is eighteen hours trapped with all fourteen of Bertie Mulligan's groping hands.'

Nan knew herself the outsider in that family affair and it stung. She grieved for Nate as much as anyone—probably more than most. They would never let her in, though, no matter how often she proved herself worthy of their respect. They all knew Bertie smeared her reputation as payback for her rejection, but they hid behind that holier-than-thou excuse to freeze her out of their little clique.

But, Rob couldn't give her what she wanted just then. He scarcely held things together as it was. He didn't have the strength to take on her grief as well. Let Sarah insult her with her distance and spare him the effort.

Just that once, he could put to good use Sarah's disdain for her sister-in-law, and her demon spawn's lust for his uncle's wife. He would take Sarah's officiousness and Bertie's hypocrisy over a cloying, self-sacrificing little wifey assaulting him with cow eyes for a thousand miles, needing so desperately for him to need her.

The kids needed her. Let her dote on them. Blast. He thought he would suffocate.

"I'll go with you, Dad."

Rob attempted a smile and ruffled Luke's thatch of straw-colored hair. Seven years old and already trying so hard to be a man. How could he look at him with eyes that understood everything? Or, at least thought they did. "I'll ride shotgun."

"No. You need to take care of Mom and your brothers."

"Matt can watch Charlie."

"Luke—"

"Luke," Nan instructed at the same moment. "Take Dad's duffle out to the truck." The boy squared his shoulders as he hefted the burden, nodded firmly to Rob, and then disappeared out the door, leaving the pair staring silently at one another. Sesame Street nattered in the background.

Rob knew he should fix this—thing—between him and Nan, but he couldn't get a firm grasp on it. She needed him to apologize, but how could he when he didn't know what for? "Annabelle—" He couldn't find the words.

But then, actions always spoke loudest between them. He found it so much easier to speak with his touch. Then, she would answer with her response: the slight quiver of her skin as he grazed his fingers over the softest places, the catch in her breath, the arch of her neck, her dark, hooded eyes surrendering to his assault. Impulses washed over him as, from ten feet away, the friction between them melted in the crackling heat of pheromones that drew his feet to the first step.

The horn from the Suburban shattered the early morning stillness. "Go." The word caught in her throat and he knew not from grief. He swallowed hard when he met her sultry gaze. She would have given and taken the life affirmation they both needed so desperately just then, even if he had only ten minutes to spare. But he didn't, and the horn blared.

"I'll call you when we get there."

"It's probably not even him. The sheriff said he had blond hair."

The words offered Rob no comfort, but rather the reverse. He hadn't told her everything Gutierrez said. He could never do that to her. The thought of his brother's dark hair bleached blond by the blistering desert sun had churned in his stomach all morning.

Despite the comfort Nan couldn't offer him, at least her words dispelled his mood. He wouldn't have to endure Bertie's knowing leer. Sarah wouldn't give him that look—the one that said, 'you're nothing but a randy kid who was hot to get into some trashy girl's pants. Anything that would hold still would have done.'

♦ ♦ ♦

Rob downshifted, released the clutch, and laid on the gas at the apex of the turn. The El Camino leapt out of its coast and attacked the mountain. Its high-beams split the night as they flashed over stone and through the trees as the road banked around the side of the canyon. The breezy, brisk night purged the stench of vomit, blood, and sweat—the final remnants of his brother's last hours—from the cabin as it streamed through the open windows. Rob felt renewed, refreshed, clean. He felt free and laughed out loud.

A sharp turn, and the cardboard box holding Nate's ashes slid across the seat. Rob reached out and grabbed it, then settled it more securely in its place with one hand. "Sarah should have sprung for the urn at the mortuary," he told it. "Mom would have liked it. Who knows if they'll ever send that monstrosity Sarah ordered on eBay?"

Another turn. Clutch. Downshift. Gas. Power through the arc. Another purr of the engine as the muscle car responded to Rob's deft handling. It hugged the curves like a cat winding around its owner's ankles. Like Nan, when he came up to her from behind and—

He shook his head to break free of the thought. "Remember that road trip we always meant to take?" he said instead. "Remember how you promised to teach me to drive a big rig—between spring and fall semester, after I finished my first year at UT? Remember? Back before I messed up so bad? . . . But, I trashed all that and you . . . you didn't do so well either, did you, bro?"

Rob downshifted as the grade steepened. The sound of rushing water from a nearby creek, coupled with the night breeze washing through the trees, prevailed over the low growl of the engine. The mountain air, sharp with pine, sweet with aspen, and smooth with sun-warmed stone, rushed over him and eased his agitation.

"I'm sick and tired of 'someday' always meaning never," he complained. "Maybe it's time we just drive and see where the road takes us. You were the smart one, Nate. You knew enough to leave the baggage behind."

⵻ ⵻ ⵻

Gere always called Nate "little brother." He was five years older. But, no one ever called Bobby that. Gere and Nate just called him 'the kid'—the kid that came as a surprise nine years after Nate. To Sarah, he was 'The Embarrassment.'

Bobby and her son Bertie were both ten. Of course, to Sarah, Bertie did everything better. He was smarter, faster, taller, stronger, more coordinated, more . . . everything. Even two months older.

Nate filled his pad above the garage with the cool stuff Mom banned from the house and Dad swore would mean Nate's ruination. Bobby wished he hadn't bragged to his best friend, Todd, that he could get it, but, if he didn't show up, Todd would tell Bertie that Bobby was a coward, then Bertie would go running to Sarah.

And, Sarah never lost an opportunity to tattle on Bobby. She was a full twenty-one years older, but she would tell Dad for certain sure, and then Bobby would really catch it.

So, he pressed himself against the wall inside the apartment door as he hesitated. With one final glance through the glass toward the house, he shoved the stuff up his shirt, took a deep breath, then sprinted down the stairs and away from the fluttering curtains of the kitchen windows.

Bobby headed toward Dad's workshop beyond the garden, at the back of the lot. Nate always lit up behind it—Gere too, that one time a year ago when they made a rancid sweet sort of smoke from the tiny cigarette, when Gere was home from the Army.

When they caught him watching, Nate snapped at Bobby to get lost, but Gere laughed and sent him to raid the pantry for munchies. Nate got angry. He said Bobby was the smart one. Gere quit laughing.

Nate never had much use for Bobby, but he always stuck up for him. Always.

Bobby ducked around the workshop to where Todd promised to wait for him. "Nothing to it," he crowed to his friend. He sat next to Todd and pulled the chilly cans from beneath his shirt.

He shouldn't have been surprised when Bertie stepped through the back gate. He only lived two doors down, and Todd had never been able to keep a secret from him. Bobby tried to love Bertie, but . . . Dad said Bertie was Bobby's cross to bear.

Bertie was—Bertie. Like grabbing a beer, then spraying the rotten-smelling foam all over them. That was Bertie. Swigging a mouthful—that was Bertie. Choking on his own swagger was Bertie, too.

Bertie tapped the Marlboro on its end like they did in the movies. Then, he flicked the lighter and took a long drag. He looked about to hurl, but if they chickened out, Bertie would never let them live it down.

All of the sudden, a jet of water knocked the cigarette from Bertie's lips. He jumped to his feet yelling dirty words Bobby had never heard before. Todd looked about to pee his pants.

Bobby forced himself to look up: first the scuffed leather boots, then the faded Levi's. The choke chain clipped onto a belt loop and tucked into the back pocket that bulged with a wallet. The garden hose in the grease-stained hands and the pressure nozzle shooting water past him.

He looked beyond the frayed denim jacket and oily blue work shirt, into Nate's stern face. Those fierce eyes peered from beneath a thick hank of black hair and pretended to see nothing but Bertie.

"Cut it out," Bertie hollered. "I'll tell—" Bobby wished he could raise one eyebrow like Nate. It shut Bertie up.

Silently, Nate turned off the spigot as Bertie and Todd scampered out the back gate. He smashed the pack of sodden cigarettes in his fist. He dumped both cans of beer out onto the ground, then crushed them and tossed them into Old Lady Mitchell's aluminum collection over the fence. He cuffed Bobby upside the head. "You're the smart one, dimwit."

Bobby thought how Nate's eyes looked like Dad's whenever Bobby disappointed him. Bobby scuffed at the dirt and Nate ruffled his hair. They walked through the garden to the house. Nate paused at the bottom of the garage stairs. "Hey, kid," he shrugged. "Wanna learn some riffs on my guitar?"

❋ ❋ ❋

"So, how far are we going?"

"Ignorance and apathy."

"You don't know and you don't care."

Rob glanced over at Nate. "No, I don't. Do you have a problem with—" He slammed on the brakes and the tires squealed to a stop on the pavement. "Holy sh—!"

Breathless, his heart racing, he stared at the empty passenger's seat—empty, but for the box of Nate's ashes. His hands shook from the sudden rush of adrenalin. Every muscle in his body went limp and he dropped his head onto the steering wheel. "Get a grip, Bobby," he muttered to himself. "Don't go losing it now."

"And don't sit here in the middle of the highway, either," Nate answered. "You'll get run over by a semi, and I'm rather partial to this car."

Slowly, cautiously, Rob turned his head toward the bucket seat and the sound of his brother's voice. And, there he sat, just like he had the right, appearing as solid as the last time he had staggered into town.

When Rob thought about it, Nate appeared considerably more solid, as that last time had been when Sarah spearheaded an intervention and dragged Nate into a rehab center. Or, better to say, Rob and Bertie dragged him to the rehab center, as Nate was too inebriated to stand.

From there, he had gone to California to live with Gere and his family. Gere had managed to sober up and get a life, and was determined that Nate would do the same.

And, they had thought he succeeded. After six months as Nate's twelve-step sponsor, Gere helped him find a job. A good one. The first he had had in a long time. Nate was on the road to recovery. At least, that's what they all thought—even Nate.

"Yo." Nate gave a casual wave as Rob met his eye. Rob closed his own against the sight.

"I either need to eat or sleep, or both," he muttered. "Probably both."

"Probably," Nate agreed. "I don't think you've eaten a full meal in three days, and you left the cooler and all Nan's hard work in the Suburban for Bertie to snarf."

"Damn."

"But, you didn't want it in the first place—or her either, for that matter—so what do you care? Hell. Let Bertie have the whole package. . . . As for sleep . . . whose brilliant idea was it to drive back tonight, anyway?"

"Guess," Rob grunted. "I'm probably dreaming. The stress is finally affecting me."

"That's another good excuse." Rob refused to answer, and silence reigned in the cab. However, when Rob again mustered the courage to look, Nate still occupied the passenger seat. "Or, you could have fallen asleep while driving, jumped the guard rail, and plummeted to your death down the mountainside, but haven't figured out you're dead yet."

"If only."

"That can be kind of tricky, you know—figuring out you're dead. Everything is so . . . real. How are you supposed to tell?"

"Make sure to let me know when you figure it out."

"Or, I could be a hallucinatory manifestation of your subconscious mind wrestling with the moral dilemmas before you, caught, as you are, between the very real and understandable evolutionary instincts of an adult male Homo sapiens to disseminate his seed as widely as possible for maximum propagation, and the opposing reproductive needs of the female of the species to create a stable, safe environment for her offspring, supported, protected, and maintained by her mate."

"That one," Rob agreed. "And, I need some sleep. And food. And coffee."

"How do you know for sure? How can you be certain that I'm not actually what your overwrought imagination insists that I am, vis-à-vis, a real ghost?"

Rob sat up and looked his brother in the eye. "Because the real-life Nate doesn't even know what vis-à-vis means, let alone use it correctly. He never talked like that. He never talked so much in his life, period."

"How do you know? You're nine years younger than me. How do you know what I read—?"

"Besides the warning labels on cigarette wrappings and beer cans—and obviously without any comprehension?"

Nate stared at him a moment, seeming to feel the burn. "Are you going to get my car out of the middle of the road or what?"

Rob shifted into gear and the El Camino lurched into motion. "Like we've seen another car in either direction for the past half-hour," he grumbled.

"Easy on the transmission, Cochise. Those parts aren't so easy to replace."

Rob floored the gas and shifted hard through the gears until he reached an easy cruising speed of ninety miles an hour. Time and again, he eyed the passenger seat, but his dead brother displayed no inclination to vacate it. "What are you doing here?" he finally demanded.

Nate shrugged. "You invited me, remember? Road trip?"

"And you last accepted an invitation of mine . . . ?"

"Admit it, Bobby. You need me, so I'm here. It's what I do."

Rob barked a laugh. "Since when?"

"Since always."

‡ ‡ ‡

Rob stood in the chancery of the Magnolia First Baptist Church, the most imposing building in town, bar none. Not even City Hall overshadowed it. It was the place where the 'right' people were seen.

"Settle down, will you?" Nate groused from where he sprawled in a chair nearby. "I swear, you need a good, stiff belt."

Rob looked to him expectantly, and Nate wagged his head. "Oh, sure. Now you want my booze, when there's a limited supply. You were too good for it last night, but today . . ." Rob took a long draw from the flask his brother produced, then coughed and sputtered as the cheap whiskey scorched its way down his gullet.

"Easy there, Poncho," Nate instructed. "Save some for the rest of us." He took a swig himself, then restored the flask to its place in the inside pocket of his morning coat. "Besides, it won't do to have you smelling like a distillery in front of the good reverend."

"Nor Nan neither," Rob agreed.

Nate laughed, and produced a much appreciated breath mint. "And no slurring your wedding vows." The whole exercise proved useless, however. Rob felt like he would crawl out of his skin with the waiting.

After a long stillness and another mile of pacing, Rob thought, Nate spoke up. "She'll be here, Bobby."

Nate held his brother's eye, refusing to give voice to his greatest fear. "Thanks for coming down," he said instead; "—for standing up with me. For taking off work and everything."

Nate rose and straightened Rob's tie. "Where else would I be? A man stands by his brother when he walks to his execution." Rob twitched an anemic smirk, and Nate caught him in a headlock and scrubbed at his hair. "I wouldn't be anywhere else in the world, kid. You know that."

Rob pushed him away, then fished in his pocket for a comb. Nate watched him in the glass as Rob put himself to rights. "I'm just sorry Trina couldn't be here," Rob observed.

Nate snorted in derision. "Trina? In the same county as our sister? In a church? I think not. Besides, the very word 'wedding' gives her hives. You can bet she and her girlfriends are having a blast without me."

"Gere brought his flavor of the week all the way from California, and her kids to boot."

"His idea of a test flight, but it will never get off the ground. Take my word for it." Nate held Rob's eye in the mirror. "Marriage isn't for everyone, you know. It's not all fairytale castles and knights on white chargers. It's a big step—a hard thing, even for grownups."

Rob turned to him. "You think I'm making a mistake."

Nate shrugged. "I didn't say that."

"But you think it."

Nate sighed. "It's just—you're so young, Bobby. What's the rush? What about all your plans? You've got your scholarship and everything. She'll be here when you get back."

"Will she?"

"Dude, if you don't know the answer to that question, this church is the last place you should be."

"Nan loves me."

"Yeah, but do you love her? Do you love her enough? Sometimes, it seems like getting the better of Bertie and her mother is the whole point with you—like this is all some big tug-of-war and Nan's the rope; like you're just doing this for bragging rights."

"It's not like that."

"Then, why can't you wait? Why can't you finish school first? Don't you want Nan to go to college?"

"There's no law that says she can't go to school just because we're married."

"Tell me the truth. Why did you have to run back here at the last minute—during Easter break—to do this whole white wedding thing? She's not—"

"Annabelle's not that kind of girl," Rob pounced, incensed.

Nate held up his hands in placation. "I didn't think so, but, you have to admit, this whole thing looks shotgun to me—and a whole lot of other people."

Rob waved his hand vaguely at the door. "We didn't want all this. We planned on going to the courthouse. All this other crap *was her mother's idea. She's the one that's all worried about what people will say if we didn't do it 'right.'"*

"Why not just go, then? Go play house at school without destroying your life."

"Because Annabelle's not that type of girl."

"If you're just trying to rescue her, little brother, you're not doing either one of you a favor. Trust me on this."

"It's not like that. I love her . . . I need her."

"To scratch an itch."

Rob pushed past Nate and plopped into a chair. He leaned his elbows on his knees, hid his face in his hands "We were in art," he said at last. "She played some trick on me—you know. Girls. High school. We were laughing. She was close—in my space. At that moment, I saw her. I knew she would be the mother of my children."

Nate chortled deep in his chest. "I bet you did."

"It wasn't like that . . . well, there was plenty of that. But, this was more. My soul knew—like a shaft of light shining down on her, I knew."

"Divine revelation."

"Mock all you like, but I knew. She was barely sixteen, and I knew."

Nate amended his tone. "I understand, kid. Maybe it's the jealousy talking."

"Scares me spitless."

A tap came at the door and Dad stuck his head around it. "Boys. It's time."

Nate helped Rob on with his jacket, then straightened his tie one more time. Together, they walked through the door to the knave.

"Last call, little brother," Nate murmured. "There are a lot easier ways to get lai—"

Rob wheeled on his brother. "Do you know Annabelle at all?"

As he spoke, the organ music began and the audience rose. Rob craned his neck to see around the crowd, but the creak of the door and their admiring gasp taunted him until Annabelle came into view.

His heart leapt to his throat when he caught sight of her, when the whole room melted into a misty fog. Her frothy gown drew in all the light and created a halo of white around her. The warm, heady scent of jasmine and gardenias wafted on the early spring breeze, and mockingbirds sang in the trees.

He held her in his eyes as her father escorted her slowly down the aisle, until she flushed under the intensity of Rob's gaze and ducked her head. Yet, her shyness could not dispel her gentle smile or the glance she stole from beneath her feathery lashes. Even beneath the veil, the sun glinting through the tall windows set her dark hair ablaze. She took his breath away. No one else in the world existed but her.

"Forget what I said, kid," Nate murmured under his breath. "Snatch this one up while you've got the chance."

† † †

Free of the skeletons of the ancient, weatherworn mountains, the El Camino sped down a long, straight stretch of highway. Under the inky dome of the star-washed sky, the land appeared an aphotic void. The gleam of headlights called the road into existence ahead of the humming tires, then again banished it into nothingness in the dark behind them.

Nate's MP3 player nested on the dash, blaring his old Highwaymen album—Johnny, Willie, Waylon, and Chris. He propped his boots up on the dash and appeared to sleep, the bill of his trucker's hat pulled over his eyes. Rob noted the irony but said nothing. At least the apparition had held his tongue for half an hour.

A pair of yellow hazard signals flashed on the shoulder ahead. As the El Camino closed the distance, the shadowy silhouette of a popped hood and trunk became apparent. "Tough place to break down," Rob said to himself. His headlights shone upon a 1965 GTO as he pulled over and slowed to a stop. Nate tipped back the bill of his hat and grunted.

"I thought you were a new man," he needled, as Nate reached for the flashlight in the glove box.

"Just because I've decided to finally take control of my life doesn't mean I've forgotten how to act human."

A pair of long, shapely legs appeared from within the muscle car. "Hot damn!" Nate cursed. "Good call, kid! Now that's one fine piece of—"

Rob slammed the car door on his brother's lewd remarks, but nervously ran his fingers through his hair, as the shapely curves of a young woman wearing a short, tight skirt followed the legs out onto the roadside. Her loose blouse, open at the neck, ruffled in the night breeze and offered generous glimpses of cleavage.

"Can I help you, ma'am?" Rob asked, advancing on the car.

The woman's silky laughter seemed as natural to the desert as her high cheekbones and sun-browned skin. "Only if you don't call me 'ma'am.'" She swung her long black hair over her shoulder, and her dark, almond eyes glittered in the starlight. "I'm Allie."

"Allie? You don't look like—"

"Like?"

Flustered, Rob pushed at his hair, and took a step back. "I mean to say, you don't look like you're from around here. From back east, maybe?"

A sly smile crept over her stunning face. "And you're the expert? What do people from 'around here' look like?"

"Well, they wear jeans and cowboy boots, or maybe cut-offs and Birkenstocks." He shrugged sheepishly. "I'm not from around here either, but after two days, you're the first person I've seen in four-inch stilettoes."

Allie laughed again, and it felt like cool water on Rob's frazzled nerves. "Point taken," she smiled. "My apologies. I thought you were going to say I don't look Hopi. I'm not—Cherokee, actually— but still. I think I ran into one too many hicks today. You can call me Foot-in-Mouth, if you like."

Rob shrugged as he kicked at the spare tire leaned up against the car. "I wouldn't go that far. How about Runs-on-Flat instead?" She laughed again, and he felt his ears burning. "No jack?"

"Alas, no jack. This is me, the airhead, feeling foolish for not checking when I bought it."

"No worries." Rob quickly retrieved the car jack from the El Camino. "Old car, new to you. Seems like an understandable oversight."

"Yeah, but after what I paid for that Ph.D., I should be smarter. I think I'll get my money back."

"Ph.D., huh? In what, Doctor?"

Allie leaned up against the fender. "Archeological anthropology with emphasis on pre-Columbian Native American art forms and their influence on societal evolution and tribal migration."

Rob grinned and looked up from cranking the jack. "What? Do your Birkenstocks have a flat too?"

"I left them back at Stanford, actually, in the trunk of my Prius, next to the car jack."

"You definitely took the right turn back there, kid," Nate chortled. He winked broadly at Rob as he squatted beside the car, from beyond the long pair of legs that filled Rob's sight. "I bet we get some action out of this good deed."

The jack slipped off an over-torqued lug nut and scraped Rob's knuckles. "Crap!" He felt Allie's eyes on him. "Sorry." He looked up into her face and she smiled. She reached out and pushed his thick hair back from his eyes. "You're kinda cute, you know that?"

He huffed and went back to his chore. "Cute isn't exactly what I was hoping for," he confessed. He bit back his curses as he leaned all his weight on the lug wrench. "But, no one ever described me as suave and debonair." The tire nut gave way, and he lost his balance, landing in the gravel. "Right now, I'd settle for anything less than clownish buffoon."

"Don't be so hard on yourself." He looked up again at the sound of her sultry voice. "Cute's not so bad, especially when it compounds kind, funny, and self-deprecating."

"Not manly?"

"I can't believe you just said that," Nate taunted. "Did you actually just say that?" He whistled and mimed an airplane in a tailspin with his fingers.

"Oh, definitely manly," Allie answered. She traced her finger along the line of Rob's jaw. "But, I was saving that for when I convince you to save the whales."

Rob felt his face flush and was glad for the dark, then turned all his attention to replacing the tire. It was easier to ignore Nate and his helpful coaching that way.

The repair made, Rob moved to drop the damaged wheel into the well of the GTO. "Don't hold it like that, Bubba," Nate commanded. "You're going to—"

"Fricking-frick-frack!" Rob cursed as the heavy rim smashed down on his hand. He jumped back to pace off the searing pain, and Allie burst into giggles. He glared at her, the humor escaping him.

She failed miserably at containing her amusement. "I'm sorry," she smirked. "It's just—you're so funny. Do you ever actually swear?"

"Not if I can help it," he ground through his teeth.

"Well, come here, Boy Scout. Let me see it. I tend to stay prepared myself."

Rob forced a smile. "Except for flat tires in the middle of the desert in the dead of night."

"That," she agreed. "Except for car jacks."

Rob couldn't tear his eyes away from Allie as she absorbed herself in cleaning the gash in his hand. Her exotic perfume filled his senses, and he fought to keep his imagination under control.

"So, what are you doing all the way out here at this hour?"

She looked up into his face, surprised—almost as if she had forgotten he was there. "Oh. You know. Sometimes I just need to drive to clear my head."

Rob nodded. "Sweet ride."

Allie smiled. "Thanks. Got it for a song."

"I should hope so, without a jack."

She laughed again. "Muscle cars are sort of my thing."

"I get that."

"So I see. How long have you had yours?"

Rob shrugged. "Not mine, really. Just driving it for my brother."

"Where?"

"Home. He . . . couldn't." She held his eye a moment, waiting for more, but he looked away.

"There," she pronounced. She closed her first-aid kit with authority. "It's not perfect, but it will do until you can get it looked at." She smoothed the tape over the gauze. "It should stop bleeding."

"Thanks."

"No, thank you. I'm sorry to tease you." He thought maybe he should take his hand back, or step away, or something, but just stood there, frozen. She looked up into his face. "I should send you on your way."

"You should . . . you should be good to go on the spare, but it's pretty worn, so get that flat fixed and back on as soon as you can."

"Yes, sir," she smiled. "Hungry?"

"Famished, actually."

"Let me buy you supper. I know a little place not far from here. They're open late. We can take my car."

Rob stepped back from her and wagged his head. "No. I'll follow you. I can't leave him behind."

† † †

Rob stared at the linoleum with its pattern worn bare in distinct pathways, the antiseptic steel tables and sinks, the institution-green walls. The worn, vaguely neglected look of a small-town hospital barely scraping by delivering babies, sewing stitches, and setting broken bones. Cold. Soulless.

He examined everything—anything—to divert his eyes from the black body bag in the morgue drawer pulled out from the wall, and the eight-by-ten glossies of the scene that the sheriff had scattered on the steel table. Rob could only manage a single glimpse of the photos, but that was enough for him, and more than adequate to send Bertie vomiting into the sink. Rob had known from the first it was Nate.

He scarcely heard as the coroner droned on about the results of the autopsy. He didn't give a flip about the finer points Sarah insisted on arguing over, or the way she told him to do his job, or Bertie's insulting condescension to Sheriff Gutierrez and his men, bluster to gloss over his epic fail.

Rather, he fingered the large, chained wallet Nate always used. His thumbs explored the worn leather as his mind wandered through fond memories until, scalded by the jagged feel of deep canine tooth marks, he dropped it back into the box of his brother's belongings. "Did you get all of it?" he asked abruptly.

"That's everything we found on his person, Mr. Daniels," the coroner answered.

Rob wagged his head. "No. I mean, did you get all of . . . him?" He didn't want to think about the answer. "I would like to see where it happened," he added before the man could respond.

"Murdock thought you might," Sheriff Gutierrez answered; "—the rancher who found the car. He has to drive out there today and will wait for you over at the diner 'til ten."

ı ı ı

The sputtering carburetor and red check engine light brought Rob round from his morbid musings. The El Camino coughed and jolted. A semi-tractor bearing down on him from behind blared its horn as it swerved around his abrupt loss of power. Its load of new cars bounced in their grips as the trailer wobbled and yawed its way to restored equilibrium. A parting gesture in the driver's side mirror assured Rob exactly what the trucker thought of his erratic driving.

Rob had followed Allie out onto a state highway, busy even at that time of night. If Nate had taught him anything, it was to get off the road and out of the way if you break down. So, hazards flashing, the El Camino hobbled along the shoulder until he came to a ranch exit. That would do, at least, until he could check under the hood.

Maybe the hopelessness of Allie's taillights disappearing into the stream of rushing red ahead of him propelled him further down the road. Or, maybe that last Mountain Dew got to him. Or maybe he just couldn't deal with one more problem that day. But, when the El Camino choked and rattled its death gurgle, he had left the headlights flashing past on the highway beyond the horizon.

Rob released the car's hood latch, then cursed at the empty glove box.

"Have you got another flashlight back here, Nate?" he demanded as he scrounged through his brother's effects in the truck bed.

Nate declined to answer. "Now, that's the Nate we know and love," Rob told the ether. "You only turn up when it darn well pleases you, not ever when you could actually be useful."

His cell phone vibrated in his pocket, and Rob dived for it hopefully. Maybe Allie finally noticed she had lost him.

However, Nan's face on the caller ID triggered a reflexive response of annoyance. "Calling it a day. . . . I love you. <3" Why was it whenever she said that, it sounded like a plea? Even in a text message, he could hear her tone.

Allie doesn't have your number, dimwit, Rob chided himself.

Aggravated by the reminder, he tapped off the screen and pocketed the demonic device. It was too expensive to hurl out to the scorpions and rattlesnakes where it belonged.

Rob found himself on the hood of the El Camino, reclining on the windshield and staring up into the vastness of space.

"You're sitting on my car."

Rob eyed his dead brother who lounged next to him. "So sue me."

"You'll ruin the paint. You better treat her right."

Rob shrugged. "I have to sell her, you know—to pay for that." He jerked his thumb over his shoulder at the box of ashes in the cab.

"Damn shame."

"You should have thought of that before you up and died."

Nate grunted. "I want you to have the Stratocaster."

"That guitar and this car are the only things of value you own."

"Muscle cars are a hot commodity. Keep the Fender."

"Funerals are expensive. Cremation or not, the folks will want your headstone next to their own. And, they're still paying for your rehab."

"I thought you weren't going back."

"I don't have to go back to sell your stuff."

"But you are going to saddle the folks with Nan and the boys.

'Happy 50th Mom and Dad. Hope you had a fun cruise. Now, here. Take my family. I don't want them anymore.' There's responsible for ya."

Rob sat up to confront his brother. "Where do you get off telling me how to live my life? When was the last time you held down a job, for Pete's sake? When was the last time you paid your own rent? If it wasn't for Gere and Sarah, you would've been living on the streets. If it wasn't for the folks, you would've been dead!"

"News flash—"

"You know what I mean. You don't know what it's like, Nate. I'm suffocating. I need air."

"Well, maybe if you pulled your head out of the sand, you'd breathe better."

The phone rattled down the hood as it suddenly began to vibrate. Rob grabbed it just as it slid off the edge. "What?" he demanded.

"Where are you?" Bertie's snide tone felt like chewing glass.

"None of your fracking business." Rob jumped to his feet and began to pace.

"Ha. I knew it. You aren't coming home, are you? Have fun whoring around, buddy boy—that is, if you can get anyone besides Annabelle to have you, which I doubt. And don't worry about that sweet piece of—"

"Say another word, Bertie, and I swear—"

"You'll what? You're already gone. I always knew you'd get tired of her. After all, she never was the type of girl a man married. Oh, wait. I forgot. You never were a man. But don't worry. She'll do well enough for herself after I give her a proper education."

"Stay away from my wife, Albert Mulligan," Rob ground through his teeth, "or, as God is my witness, I will make you wish you had never been born."

"No worries, dude. I can wait. She won't be your wife much longer, right? I'll make sure to give her the message."

The line went dead and Rob shrieked with frustration. Before he knew it, his five-hundred-dollar corporate smart phone sailed out into the darkness. He stood and stared into the pitch black after he heard it hit the sand.

"That was brilliant," Nate observed dryly. "How are you going to call a wrecker?"

"How am I going to call Annabelle?"

"Why do you even care?"

❦ ❦ ❦

His Nikes firmly planted in the gravel, Rob sat in the bucket seat, his head in his hands, but his brother refused to relent. "You haven't figured it out, have you? You still haven't got a clue. And I thought you were the smart one."

"Says the corpse."

"And you're not the walking dead?"

Rob had no reply. There were times when he yearned for oblivion. Nothing matched the blackness that crippled him after Annabelle broke their engagement, but the occasional bout still festered in his soul.

"How am I supposed to get anywhere or do anything when every hour of every day is filled with bills and babies and bosses? At home or at work, the incessant nagging is just the same.

"What about what I want? What about my dreams? I had plans, Nate. I wasn't supposed to be this . . . this nothing."

"Be very careful, Bobby. Don't be in such a rush to change your present that you cast off your past and destroy your future."

"My past has already destroyed my future. Who the devil gets married at nineteen?"

"I was there, dude. You dragged her down the aisle, remember? Why did you ask her the second time? Why did you push it?"

"She wasn't supposed to say yes."

"Closure," Nate accused, his voice dripping with contempt. "You wanted closure but meant to make Nan the bad guy. It backfired on you." Rob huffed and paced frenetically. Nate wouldn't back off. "And here you are, shackled to a girl you don't love and kids you don't want, trapped by those pesky marriage vows and hating her for it."

"It's so easy for you to judge," Rob retorted; "—always telling me I have what every man truly wants. But you never went out and got it, did you? All you did was blow into town a few times a year, act all taciturn and tragic, and then run away again. You even had to flirt with my wife because your girl kicked you out.

"I've got news for you, Bubba. Playing with the boys for half an hour and setting the table for dinner isn't real life. Hell. You couldn't even handle that much. How many times have I bailed you out of the drunk tank after one of your visits, and never breathed a word to Nan? So don't get all self-righteous on me about running away."

Rob paced and pushed back at his hair, uselessly attempting to get something in his life under control, especially his tongue. But, there was nothing for it. The truth was the truth, and he had to vent it.

"You forfeited all right to tell me what to do when you hid away, Nate. You didn't even have the decency to tell the people who love you that you were sick. You died because you were too afraid or too proud or too stubborn to ask for help. You ran away instead. I dunno. Maybe you were just plain too stupid."

"And how is what you're doing any different? I never thought you were that guy."

"I've made my decision. It's done. I just have to . . ."

"'Have to what?'"

"Find a way to tell Annabelle."

"Don't you think she knows? Do you really think she needs Bertie's help to figure it out? You claim she doesn't have to say a thing, but you hear her loud and clear. What makes you think she doesn't understand you just as well? What do you think those nightmares are all about? The ones she disturbs your precious sleep with?"

Rob wheeled on his brother, opened his mouth to repulse that acerbic tone, then clamped it shut and turned away.

"You've been living with one foot out the door since before Charlie was born. If you're going to leave, do you both a favor and get it over with, but you know that without Annabelle, you'd be me."

"You can go to hell."

"Oh-kay. If you insist."

Rob jumped at the sound of the silky voice behind him, and spun on his heel toward the road. "Allie. What are you doing here?"

"More to the point, what are you doing here? If you want to ditch a girl, Bobby, you'll have to find a more effective way than showing up on her doorstep."

"What? You live around here?"

"I wouldn't say 'live', but it is one of my favorite haunts. There's a little cabin about a hundred yards up the road where I stay when I come for research."

Rob's brow twitched in confusion. "Research?"

"I study cave paintings, remember? Mammoth, bison, hand prints . . ." She tipped her head to the surrounding hills. "Lots of interesting nooks and crannies up in those bluffs."

"Oh. Right." Rob laughed nervously as she advanced on him. "Um. How did you sneak up on me?"

Allie looked back toward her GTO, still rumbling on idle, its headlights shining onto the gravel. "I was going to ask you the same question, but, obviously, you were preoccupied. Who were you yelling at?"

Rob shrugged sheepishly. "Haven't you ever had an argument with someone who isn't there? You know exactly what they'll say, and they say it in your head—"

"—and then, when you really do see them, they can't figure out what you're mad about."

"That."

"No. I've never done that," Allie grinned. Rob began to relax.

"The dude's a stubborn son-of-a-gun. Loves to argue."

"So, who won, then?"

"The jury's still out."

"What are you doing out here in the middle of nowhere?"

"I had to get off the highway. The car—I need to look under the hood, but, it's too dark."

"What? The Boy Scout has no flashlight?"

"Actually, you were holding my flashlight the last time I saw it."

Allie leveled at him a crooked grin. "Drat! You've uncovered my nefarious plot for world domination."

"By stealing all the flashlights?"

"Exactly. One flat tire at a time."

Flashlight in hand, Allie chattered and kept Rob laughing as he ducked under the hood of the El Camino to see if he could get it started. However, after several attempts, the cylinders still refused to fire.

"Are you sure you know what you're doing?" she called from the driver's seat when uselessly turning the ignition, again.

Rob stepped around the car and leaned on the fender, scrubbing the grease from his hands. "Muscle cars are sort of my thing," he shrugged. "Heck. Cars are my thing."

"Yeah?" Allie came to lean against the car beside him. "You repair them?"

"I design them—at least, I did."

"Did? What happened?"

"2008—Wall Street. Detroit." He shrugged again. "Life. I finished three paid internships with them, and they moved us up there when I graduated. I had only been on the payroll a few weeks when it all hit the fan. I had a promising career. They were going to pay for my master's degree. Then, all of the sudden, the company didn't even exist anymore. And nobody was hiring after that. Nobody."

"That was five years ago. So, what do you do now?"

Rob snorted his disgust. "I'm a draftsman for an industrial pump company—offshore drilling, that sort of thing."

"With a degree in automotive engineering?"

"Student loans don't wait. Bills need paying. Like my dad says, you 'get 'er done.'"

"You man up."

"Something like that."

"And no self-pity."

The words stung, and Rob ducked his head. "Well, maybe just a little."

Allie moved closer and leaned on his shoulder, and Rob allowed her to settle against him. His heart raced in his throat. He felt his face flush and his knees turned to jelly. Every inch of him came alive and burned with anticipation. His imagination followed through to the situation's logical conclusion, and his arm crept around her waist.

"Beautiful night," she murmured softly.

"Among other things," he answered. She turned her face to his, her eyes hooded, her full and inviting lips just parted, expecting him to close the distance. When he hesitated, she reached up to pull him to her, but he caught her hands, then stepped away. "Sorry."

"I thought we connected." She didn't sound annoyed or hurt, which only made him want her that much more. With her, everything was . . . rational. They didn't have to decipher anything or try to guess what the other really meant—what they left unsaid. They just communicated.

"We did. We do. You're smart and funny and drop-dead gorgeous. I like being with you. It's just . . ." He paused, searching for the words. She watched him expectantly. "It's just, I can get that anywhere."

She laughed. "Oh, yeah?"

"No, I mean—I think you're fantastic. You're unlike anyone I've ever met, but I've had smart, pretty girls come on to me before. Girls at work flirt with me. I could take them out. They would—one actually told me she'd take whatever—they know I'm married but still want to hook up, but I'm not that guy."

Allie's understanding smile gave him courage, and he pushed on. "I'm not that guy who thinks it's funny for his toddler to flip off somebody. The first time I heard a foul word come out of my baby's mouth, I swore he would never hear another one from me, so I try not to curse. I'm not good at it, but I try.

"We have no social drinkers in my family. We have teetotalers, or drunks, or recovering alcoholics, or . . ."

"Or?"

"Or dead. I've seen how it destroys us. My grandfather died when I was really young, but I remember him putting my dad through hell, as his father did before him. It's in the genes or something, and I don't want that, so I don't drink. I don't care if people think I'm square or preachy or boring. I know who I am, and I'm not that guy."

"And you're not that guy that picks up chicks—"

"I'm not that guy that finds himself conveniently separated when a fabulous woman is attracted to him—who uses her to scratch an itch. I'm not that guy who thinks it's okay because it doesn't mean anything. If it doesn't mean anything, why betray the people who trust you? Doesn't that make the betrayal that much worse?"

"Are you separated?"

Rob fell silent a long moment as he took her hand from where it rested on his chest. "I don't think I am—at least, I don't think I am until she knows it, too."

Allie smiled sadly. "I think you're probably right."

"I'm not that guy that disappears in the night—that just walks away and lets everything he held together fall apart. I don't leave the mess for others to clear away. That's not who my parents raised me to be. That's not who I want my boys to be."

Allie reached up and kissed his cheek. "It's been nice knowing you, Boy Scout."

Rob caught her in his arms and kissed her soundly. "I really, really like you," he murmured in her ear. "I want to know you better, to get to the point where it would mean something—something amazing, but . . ."

Allie smiled up into his face. "But, the timing's not right."

"Not now. Not yet. Maybe not ever. I don't know."

"I wish the world made more like you, Bobby Daniels."

Allie ducked around him and bent under the raised hood of the El Camino. Before Rob could get her the flashlight, the engine revved, cracking the silence of the night, then settled into the low growl of its idle. She emerged, grinning.

"You just have to know what you're doing." She again kissed him, then patted his chest as she stepped away. "When you do, you know where to find me . . . or, send me that brother of yours."

❦ ❦ ❦

The hot desert sun battered his head and singed the back of his neck as Rob stood on the dirt road, surrounded by sagebrush. He stared at the cigarette butts scattered on the ground around the tire tracks of a large vehicle, accentuated by boot prints treading a path in the dirt.

His mind filled with images of the broken-down El Camino parked on that isolated ranch road, miles from the highway or anywhere else, Nate weak and dehydrated, pacing back and forth and burning smoke after smoke as he tried to figure out what to do.

After rehab, Nate got clean. He got dry, free of the hard liquor that ultimately destroyed him. But it took him too long to get that way. Still smoking two packs a day, getting sober wasn't enough to save him. Because of the rot-gut, the damage had been done. No one knew he bled to death in that godforsaken desert, at the mercy of the buzzards, the coyotes, and the sun.

The coroner had it all worked out. Nate had probably been bleeding from his ulcer for weeks, if not months, before it burst into a severe hemorrhage and he vomited his life out onto the driver's seat and the ground outside the car door.

"He was a trucker." Hopelessness and futility echoed through the emptiness of Rob's soul and hollowed his voice. "He was headed to Chicago and a new job."

Murdock nodded. "A lot of big rigs come through here," he observed. "The One-Sixty gets pretty busy at night. A man would have to get off the road a fair piece to escape the noise and get some sleep."

"He just wanted some peace and quiet."

The weathered, old rancher kicked at the blood-clotted dirt, unhappy evidence of one man's last hours. "Your brother—he was a fighter, son. His battery was dead, his phone was dead, he was sick as a dog, but he cleaned up the mess he made in his truck as best he could. He found something to put water in, then went looking for it. He didn't quit. Not by a long shot." Rob looked up and met the man's gaze. "Come with me."

Rob allowed Murdock to take him by the shoulder and steer him back the way they came. Together, they followed Nate's distinctive boot prints a mile down the road, until they veered off into the desert toward an abandoned cabin a hundred yards out into the sage. "He must have seen that old place on the drive in and came looking for a well."

They walked until they reached a barbed-wire fence that stood between them and the shack. Sharp, new cuts in the rusty metal opened up a span between two weatherworn posts tipped helter-skelter in the loose sand.

The area had been trampled by human and animal, but the deep impressions of his brother's fall remained in the sandy soil. Rob reached down to free a snag of denim from the barbed wire, then stared at the frayed, sun-bleached fabric and tried to make sense of the whole nightmare.

"He was all tangled, son. His boots—the wire—we found him lying just as he fell. There just wasn't enough of him left to get up. Every time I think of it, I could kick myself. Had I looked into it the first day I saw the truck, maybe—"

Rob looked up, startled. The man pointed to caves halfway up the butte rising beyond the cabin. "When I saw that El Camino a week ago, I thought it belonged to folks hunting arrowheads. We get a lot of them—day-trippers, mostly, sometimes the college long-hairs." He sighed and again pushed at his hat. "I only come out this way every three or four days or so. I didn't call the sheriff until the other night, when I saw his car hadn't moved."

Rob nodded but stared at the scene so vivid in his head. "He was so alone."

Murdock again grasped Rob by the shoulder. "Come on, son. I'll buy you lunch. Rita at the diner makes a mean pecan pie."

‡ ‡ ‡

The breeze chased billowing clouds across the sky and rustled through the trees surrounding the splash pad. Rainbows shimmered with each gust of mist as the brilliant summer sun glimmered on the dancing jets of water. Children's laughter glittered as brightly as the sunshine.

Rob watched Annabelle play with Charlie in the spray, smiling her reassurances as he sputtered and gasped when droplets hit his face. Matt splashed in circles around her, and Luke chased some squealing little girl in and out of the fountains. Rob knew then and there that when he thought of joy, he would always recall that moment. Certainty came like the rays of light lancing through the clouds, gleaming through her dark hair and setting it afire.

"Without Annabelle, you'd be me." Adrift. Apart. Alone.

So alone, no one knew he had gone.

The sound of her laughter banished Rob's brooding. She had never appeared more beautiful than at that moment, loving his sons. He said a silent prayer of gratitude: for the future, for the past. For the rescue from his own stupidity.

"Dad! Dad!"

Annabelle looked up, startled by Luke's call. As she met Rob's eye, her relaxed, easy manner stiffened into apprehension, muted beneath the compelling solicitousness that he at last recognized as a deep and abiding love.

Knowing himself the cause of the anguish in her eyes stabbed at his heart. It drove away the calm of his own countenance and replaced it with the tension of guilt and regret. Pushing past it, he smiled and walked toward her. Luke ran up and tugged his hand.

"Dad! Dad! Come and play!"

"Luke, Daddy's tired," she answered for him as she came. "He's come a long way."

Rob crouched down, doffed his shoes and socks, and cuffed his jeans. "Yep," he agreed, glancing up at his wife. "I'm hot and tired and have been driving for two days. That splash pad is exactly what I need."

↟ ↟ ↟

The sun had begun its descent to the west when Luke dashed toward the El Camino. "I got shotgun!" he called. Matt strained to escape Nan's hand as they followed behind. "Luke! Stay out of the street!"

Rob paused, but shifted Charlie in his arms to restrain the preschooler. "Nan, I've been doing a lot of thinking—"

Annabelle turned to him, cautioned by his tone. She searched his face for signs of treacherous undercurrents beneath his calm façade. The fear that he had lost her trust struck deep. Words of hope and despair, desire and regret surged to the surface, but, as she watched him, guarded and wary, they felt inadequate.

"Do you still have those papers?"

She failed to understand him. "Papers?"

"Grad school—the admissions applications. I agree. I think the one at A & M's the best for us, if it's not too late."

"But you said the tuition—the time—"

"I think I can tap into the corporate matching program. I have to get a 4.0, but the money's a good motivator to find the time. We'll make it work."

"We have the house money to get you started."

Rob wagged his head. "You've been saving so carefully for that. The boys need the space."

"I like the return on this investment," she murmured. She laid her hand upon his chest and met his gaze. Her looks bespoke such faith in him, his tongue failed him.

Rob grazed his fingers down the tenderness of Annabelle's inner arm as they sought, then, entwined her own. He raised them to his lips. Her eyes shimmered with tears of relief and hope.

He knew he had at last come home.

"Matt!" Rob dumped the toddler into his wife's arms and sprinted after the escaped four-year-old.

"Luke, get in the car," Annabelle instructed as she came up to where Rob had parked beside her old beater. "Dad's got to meet Momo and Papaw. He's still got a long drive."

"I want to go, too!"

Rob emerged from buckling Matt into his booster seat. "Actually, we're all going."

Nan balked. "But I'm supposed to get Gere—"

Rob took the baby and put him in the car. "Bertie can go to the airport. Or Gere can take a cab. The folks are going to need us there—all of us. They're going to need you."

"But Sarah—"

He again stood erect to pull his wife to him, his chore abandoned. "Sarah's great at the business, Baby Girl, but she has never understood my mother. She's not jealous of me, or even for Bertie. She's jealous because you have with Mom what she could never manage."

"But it's such a long drive and the kids haven't had any lunch—"

"*I* need you there."

She blinked at him, nonplused, although Rob knew her concerns valid. He tenderly moved a stray lock of hair from her face. He held her eye, refusing to concede the argument. "We'll find a drive-through. The boys will have a nice, long nap."

"No food in the car," she answered feebly.

"Special dispensation," he countered, and her smile of surrender made it all the way to her eyes.

"Sarah called."

Rob tensed at the words and drew her closer still. "Really?" he asked carefully. "When? About what?"

"Yesterday morning. Early. From Santa Fe. She told me about your car trouble, and that you'd be delayed. She said not to worry."

"She did?"

Luke piped up from the back seat. "She called Bertie an ass—"

"Luke!" Annabelle blushed. "Sorry. She apologized for Bertie."

"Really? For anything in particular?"

"She's always apologizing for Bertie—and calling him . . . that, so I really don't pay attention. Oh. She said you left your charger in the Suburban, in case you were wondering."

Rob winced. "Uhh, about my phone . . . I sort of . . . lost it."

"No you didn't, Dad," Luke denied. He scrambled over the car seats to shove the device out the window. "It was in Uncle Nate's car, under that box of dirt. It's dead, though."

Rob stared at it, his stomach in his throat, unwilling to take it. Annabelle did instead. "Thank you, Luke, now buckle up."

As she spoke, it piped a "Margueritaville" ringtone, and Nate's face lit up the screen. Nan dropped the machine onto the concrete and stepped back, thoroughly rattled. They both stared at it until Rob mustered the courage to pick it up. "It's a text," he managed to say over his sandpaper tongue.

Nan ventured a look. "'You're welcome'? You're welcome for what?"

Rob forced himself to laugh. The phone had again gone lifeless. "For finding my phone?" he shrugged as he quickly pocketed it. "That must have bounced around between satellites forever."

"Huh. Ghosts in the machine."

"Yeah. Must be."

"Hey, Daddy!" Matt chimed in.

"Hey, what?" Rob answered. He returned to his chore, and ducked down to buckle in Charlie.

"Uncle Nate was in the newspaper with Pocahontas."

"That wasn't Pocahontas," Luke denied. Rob ignored the instant outburst of bickering to look up at his wife. Her apprehension set a pit in his stomach.

"Bertie's a donkey's nether regions," she pronounced after a moment. She took the paper from Luke, who helpfully waggled it out the window.

HOMETOWN BOY FOUND DEAD NEAR HAUNTED SHACK!

Rob stared at the headline plastered above Nate's high school senior portrait. It sat right next to a snapshot of Allie. There she was, leaning against a 1965 GTO in the southern Colorado desert, with jeans, backpack, trendy boots, and all. She wore that same knowing smile on her face, and her hair in a long black braid drawn over her shoulder. The story filled the front page of the local gossip rag.

"This week's issue," Nan explained. "Came out this morning."

"I . . . I don't understand," Rob at last managed.

"Apparently, someone else died out there—this Alison Clearwater. Fell down a well or something, four or five years back. Locals claim it's been haunted ever since . . . But nobody reads this stuff."

"An archeological anthropologist—"

"—from Stanford, yeah. I don't know how he dug this up. I'm sorry, Baby. Bertie—"

"—was supposed to be writing the obituary, and he comes up with this?" Rob looked up into his wife's eyes, saw her pain and anxiety, and forced himself calm. "Well. Look at that. Bertie's an honest-to-gosh journalist." She smiled at his sardonic enthusiasm.

"Bertie's Bertie," he said, taking her into his arms. "We should feel sorry for him."

Nan's eyes sparkled and danced. "And why is that?"

"Because, I got the girl—smart, funny, strong, amazing, impossibly gorgeous, and oh, so, sexy."

"Oh, yeah?"

"And mine. And only mine—something a man finds once in a lifetime . . . if he's lucky." She blushed, but he held her face in his hands. He first kissed her forehead, then each eye, until, with excruciating tenderness, scarcely touched her lips with his own.

"Get a room!"

Annabelle ducked into him and hid her face, and Rob held her protectively. He feared raising his gaze to seek out that familiar voice but could not deny the compulsion. There, in the park beneath a tree, Nate and Allie stood. Nate snapped an insolent salute and Allie blew him a kiss, but they seemed to wait expectantly—to wait for him.

"Nan," Rob fairly breathed, "Baby Girl—I need to tell you something."

Annabelle looked up at him, her eyes silently assuring him she already knew, but it wasn't enough any longer. Not for them. He had to say the words and she had to hear him say them.

"I've been lying to you and to myself for a long time." He hesitated as the fear again flared in her eyes. He knew he had to blurt it out before he lost the nerve.

"I told you once I thought we were over when I called from school, but that wasn't the truth. The truth is, I was afraid. I saw what I was without you. I saw what I could become, and it scared me to death. I had to have you with me. Right. Then.

"With you to protect, I could be strong. I could be the man I wanted to be. I came running home to you because, for us, I could save me from myself. I so want to be the man you deserve. I want to be that guy."

"Oh," she breathed. Tears welled in her eyes and one splashed down her cheek. He caught it up on his finger, then kissed her long and deep. They lost themselves in the luxury.

"Get a room!" Matt chirped, disintegrating both into sniggers.

"Way to spoil the moment, squirt," Rob groused, scrubbing at the child's hair. He held the door for his wife, but as he did, his dead phone vibrated in his pocket. He glanced over her head to the park, and saluted his traveling companions.

They smiled their approval, then Allie looked up into Nate's face to push the thatch of hair from his eyes. He looked upon her all adoration, and wrapped his arm about her shoulder. She reached up and laced her fingers between his.

As they turned to walk away, Nate took a parting glance over his shoulder. He winked at Rob as broad as his grin, and then they were gone.

"No, bro," Rob murmured softly. "Not alone. Not anymore."

* * *

THE DEATH OF
DR. MARCUS WELLS
J. Aurel Guay

arkness met Marcus' eyes. Something had awoken him. He fumbled desperately for the matchbox on the nearby night- stand. At the same time that his fingers found the small tin, he heard the delicate clink of metal against the hardwood floor. With a scratch, the sulfur tip burst to life, casting a warm glow on the room.

Marcus slid from his sheets and scoured the floor for the ring he had knocked from the nightstand. A glint of diamond and a gleam of gold shone from under his bed.

As he stooped to retrieve the precious object, something be- yond the ring caught his eye. On the opposite side of the bed, a pair of small, bare feet stood by his bedside.

The tiny flame burned down to his fingers, singeing them be- fore disappearing and leaving the room in the darkness. Marcus' heart pounded in his ears. He now recalled being awoken abruptly. Striking another match, he rose stiffly, afraid of what stalked him in his sleep, afraid to find the familiar face he longed for and knew he would never see again.

The creak of floorboards and the slamming of the window behind him broke the dark silence. He spun quickly, and his tiny light snuffed again.

THE DEATH OF DR. MARCUS WELLS J. AUREL GUAY

Nothing but blackness and the silhouette of the swinging window met his gaze.

Was that all? Or had he seen something else disappear from the sill the moment he turned?

With four strides, Marcus found himself looking out onto the familiar narrow streets and crowded buildings under the dark London sky. Three stories below, a post lit the flat façade of the building with the glow of its gas lamp.

It was just another dream.

Marcus sighed, then chuckled at his childishness as he brushed his sand-colored hair from his brow. How foolish he was to leave the window unlatched. Turning back to the dark room, he lit the candle on the dresser beside him. He rested his elbows on the dresser's edge and placed his cheek against his upturned palm. Weary hazel eyes looked back at him from the dresser-top mirror.

"This is becoming a bit much, chap," he spoke to his reflection. Restless sleep and nightmares plagued him of late, and he had imagined seeing her watching him from dark alleys before, but nothing quite so vivid as the vision that had woken him that night. "Perhaps we should go and have that chat with Dr. Martin tomorrow."

As a resident physician at St. Thomas', Marcus wouldn't need an appointment to speak with the chief psychiatrist. Nightmares often afflict those who grieve, he told himself. There likely existed some simple remedy that would allow him a peaceful night's rest.

Marcus picked up the candleholder and walked back to his bedside. The diamond ring still lay on the floor. Picking it up, he sat down solemnly on his bed. As he caressed the smooth circle of gold, he couldn't help but ponder how such a small bit of metal and rock could provide so much solace, and at the same time, bring such pain.

He knew he would not be able to sleep again that night. Fortunately, his occupation never failed to supply work at any hour. Marcus washed and dressed, and prepared to head out into the still-dark streets. His co-workers knew the long and unusual hours he kept. The busyness and bustle of the hospital kept Marcus' mind occupied and prevented it from wandering into memories which he did not yet want to address.

By the time he finished fastening his trench coat, Marcus found himself on the dimly lit street where the chill of the autumn night air nipped at his nose. Realizing he still held the ring, he slipped it into his right coat pocket.

Only then did he remember the warnings issued by the authorities. Over the past month, nearly a dozen citizens had been murdered or gone missing, and everyone in London had been urged to stay indoors after dark. Some even claimed that the infamous Jack the Ripper had returned to plague the city once more.

Marcus pushed through his apprehension, reminding himself that most of the attacks were on women or invalids. In the beginning, many of the incidents had taken place at St. Thomas' Hospital itself, though they had moved into the streets with the addition of guards to the night staff. Surely a grown man had little to fear, and besides—he had no intention of staying alone in his flat until dawn.

Marcus had walked almost halfway to the hospital before he saw another soul. At the edge of the St. James' Park, a man in a battered felt hat leaned against a lamppost. The dim orange glow gave off just enough light to show the way down the dark London street, but did little to reveal the stranger's features. With tattered mitts, the stranger pulled an unlit cigarette from beneath his wiry mustache as Marcus passed.

"Got a light?" grunted the man.

Marcus shook his head without pausing. Not one for smoking, he truthfully did not have a match with him, and wanted only to get to the hospital and out of the damp night air. The voice followed him, louder and laced with malice.

"I said, do you got a light?"

Marcus halted. The hairs on the back of his neck stood on end.

"I'm afraid not," he replied calmly, without turning.

Shadows moved out from the park ahead of him, followed by a pair of rough-looking men. Marcus stepped back, turning toward the first stranger. A wide grin now spread across the man's dirty face. The cigarette rested between the fingers of one hand, while the other brandished a sizable knife. A fourth stranger slipped from an alleyway to join them.

"Now, gentlemen, I'm merely on my way to St. Thomas' to care for my patients. I have no quarrel with you."

Surely these ruffians will respect a physician, Marcus thought.

Marcus bumped against the broad chest one of the thugs that crept from park, and realized he had been backing away.

"Who said any'fing about quarrelin', Mister Doctor?" jeered the first assailant.

Marcus soon found himself bullied into a wooded corner of the park. Outnumbered and unarmed, Marcus had nothing but his wit to save him.

"So this is it, then? The new Jack the Ripper is nothing more than a handful of thugs armed with pipes and sticks?" Any time Marcus could buy himself might serve to create some opening for his escape. Quite unexpectedly, the thieves broke into laughter—all but the knife-wielding smoker.

"Shut it! You damn meatheads," he bellowed at his cohorts. Moving in, he waved his knife at Marcus, the tip coming uncomfortably close to Marcus' chin. His breath stank of tobacco and alcohol.

"You 'fink you know the Ripper?" His bloodshot eyes looked deep into Marcus'. "You don't know nofin'. I seen 'im. And it ain't the Ripper what been takin' people. Whatever else 'e was, Ol' Jackie was a man. What's out there now ain't out for brass or pence like a feller jes' tryin' to get his due . . . "

He reached into Marcus' coat and removed the billfold. "Alls this'un wants is blood. It ain't no man, what's out there. I tell you that, Mister Doctor."

The brash thief stepped away to count the few bills he had extracted while the other vagrants moved in, and before he knew it, Marcus had been relieved of his timepiece and belt. Rough hands rifled through his coat. The thug beside him reached into his right pocket, and Marcus suddenly remembered the ring.

That ring was his last connection to her. For nearly a month now, it had lived on his nightstand, watching over him as he slept. Marcus' muscles tensed and he blocked the vagrant's hand with his elbow. He started to struggle. Whatever else they took, he could not let them have the ring.

Another thug pinned Marcus' hands behind his back, and a forceful blow to his solar plexus knocked the wind from his lungs. Between punches, the thieves continued their rummaging while their leader looked on.

Gasping for breath, Marcus strained against the arms that bound him. Abruptly, his assailants halted to look behind them. Hoping rescue had come, Marcus twisted against their grip to likewise look, only to turn into the blunt end of a spade handle.

Lights flashed in Marcus' eyes. Confusion and noise surrounded him as his vision blurred. The thieves released him a moment later, and he collapsed, his legs limp and useless. His head struck the ground before he knew he was falling.

‖ ‖ ‖

The musty smell of earth and decayed vegetation greeted him when consciousness returned. Silence met his ears. For a moment, he dared not move. A ringing pain reverberated in his temples, and something wet and sticky coated his shoulder and neck.

THE DEATH OF DR. MARCUS WELLS I J. Aurel Guay

Marcus tried to raise himself from the dirt, but gasped as a new pain shot from his shoulder and coursed through his whole being. He must have been stabbed in the struggle. His head swam, and the sickening feeling in his stomach made him wonder how much blood he had already lost.

Fighting against the pain, he looked up to survey his surroundings. Despite all his years of medical training, he nearly wretched at the sight that met him. Before him lay the knife-wielding assailant—or, most of him. Missing an entire arm and most of the other, his open eyes stared into nothing. A gaping hole had been torn in his chest. The remains of the other three vagrants, likewise torn and mutilated, were littered about him. Marcus wondered if he was in a dream.

Then he saw her.

Her sobbing drew his attention. Hugging her knees, a young woman sat at the base of an oak a few paces from the carnage. Thin rags clung to her, and tangled brown hair concealed her face.

"Emily?" Marcus strained hoarsely.

Deep blue eyes looked up into his. Her thin lips quivered.

"Emily, my God. How?" He crawled toward her, fighting against the pain in his shoulder.

"I am so sorry," she whispered, averting her gaze. Those few, sorrowful words spoke a strength into his heart he had not felt in such a long time.

Marcus dragged himself closer, but the woman rose and stepped away.

"Emily!" He struggled to his feet.

She retreated further, turning from him toward the unlit corners of the park.

"Emily, no!" He stumbled after her. She broke into a run.

He forced himself to follow, ordering his obstinate limbs to run after her. She was out of sight by the time he moved ten paces.

In another ten steps, the trees began to sway and his legs became unsteady. He did not know how far he made it before the darkness reclaimed him.

† †

A blazing sun baked Marcus' back as he lifted shovel after shovel of soot and ash. It seemed like digging and sifting black soot was all he had ever known. His face was nearly as dark as the charred remains of the building around him. He wiped his brow before moving a heavy beam out of his way, and picked up his spade again.

There had to be something there. He had to find something, anything that would tell him what had happened to her. His shovel struck another bone. He had found many already, but none that he could identify as once belonging to his beloved Emily. The femur he cast aside was clearly too large.

He resumed his laborious work, searching for what he feared to find. It did not matter how long he had to search. He would not rest until he had found her remains. Until that time, there would be no peace for his weary body or soul.

On the next shovelful, he saw something glint in the sun as the ash fell from his spade. Marcus dropped his tool, rummaging through the pile until he found the object in the fine silt. The ash-caked object was circular and smooth, save for the protrusion at its top, which reflected through the soot like dirty glass.

Marcus' heart rose into his throat as he wiped it with his shirt-tail. His falling tears cleaned it further, revealing a golden circle and a delicate setting that clung to an elegant diamond.

His knees gave way and he sank back into the rubble, clutching the ring in his fist as he wept. He looked to the sky hoping for some divine solace, only to be blinded by the glaring sun above.

THE DEATH OF DR. MARCUS WELLS · J. AUREL GUAY

¡ ¡ ¡

"Dr. Wells?" Marcus' eyes squinted against the brightness.

"Dr. Wells?" The call came again. A lamp, held close to his face, shone with the intensity of a sun. With a gasp, Marcus came fully awake to a quiet hospital room.

Lying on clean, white linens, he soon noticed the firm pressure of the bandage wrapped around his temples, and saw the white cotton strips that held the dressings to his wounded shoulder. Nurse Pennysmith and Dr. Barrows stood next to him, looking down at him with a mixture of relief and concern.

"What—" he sputtered.

"Relax, Marcus. You are at St. Thomas' now," said Doctor Barrows, placing a hand on his chest to still him. "You were attacked. Was it the Ripper—?"

"You are in good hands, Dr. Wells," interrupted Pennysmith with a glare at the Doctor.

"Emily . . . Emily? What happened?" Marcus blurted. His head swam with confusion.

His companions exchanged worried glances.

"That was a long time ago, Dr. Wells. You are in London, now, remember?" said Pennysmith.

Marcus furrowed his brow. His mind began to clear, and the vision of discovering Emily's ring found its proper place among his darkest memories. The faces of the thugs flashed in front of him—first threatening, then lifeless and torn.

"Yes, of course. Emily is—I dreamed of her."

"The police will be in later to take a report," Dr. Barrows said, while closing his medical bag. "I'll hold them off as long as I can."

"Thank you." He sank back, allowing the pillows on the bed to support his aching head once more.

¡ ¡ ¡

Some two months later, Marcus found himself again walking the street that bordered St. James' Park. Since returning to his duties, he had avoided that route, opting for the long way home instead. He did not want to pass by the place again. He did not want to relive that memory—that dream. But the cold, drizzling rain forced him to choose the shorter path once more, cutting his near forty-minute walk from St. Thomas' in half.

A cat's call broke the dismal silence as St. James' Park came into sight. The strained cry echoed the dark thoughts that Marcus did his best to suppress. Many times of late, he had again considered calling on Dr. Martin but had not yet found the courage to do so.

Lit only by lamplight, the park was shadowed and desolate. Marcus welcomed the silence as he pressed through the drizzle and soon came to the houses and cottages that hedged the park on its far side. Safely past, he ran his fingers through his thick hair, brushing away the anxiety. The patients he would attend on the day to follow soon replaced the fearful images in his mind.

One patient specifically occupied his attention. She was another victim of the killer still loose on the streets. Like him, she had sustained a serious stab wound to her upper body, in addition to many cuts, abrasions, and mild delirium.

However, the unauthorized treatment she received at the hospital caused him a great deal of concern. He would never have known if the patient had not complained of a burning sensation from an injection she had received. Unable to determine what treatment had been ordered, or even who had administered it, Marcus wrestled over the mystery. He could not allow his patients to be jeopardized by shoddy medical practice.

"Dr. Wells?"

Marcus started at the voice, and realized he had leapt clear into the middle of the cobbled street at the surprise. He pondered the feat for only a moment before returning his attention to the stranger that called his name. The owner of the voice was diminutive and older than himself. Despite his startling appearance at Marcus' side, the well-dressed man did not look threatening. The stranger peered at him through narrow spectacles.

"Dr. Wells?" he said again, adjusting the fine bowler hat on his head.

"Yes?" Marcus regained his composure.

"I have been looking for you, good doctor." The man's flat voice betrayed a hint of German heritage. "I am afraid you must come with me."

"Who are you?" Adrenaline coursed through his veins, the events of that terrible night ever present in his mind.

"I am called Otto. It is imperative, for your own safety, that you come with me immediately." Otto's cane tapped on the cobblestone as he stepped toward him.

"I am not going anywhere, but to my home. If it is all that important, you can find me at the hospital in the morning." Marcus turned to leave.

"As you wish, Dr. Wells." The mouth of the mysterious man turned down within the borders of its well-groomed goatee. He tipped his hat.

The scuffle of rapid footsteps told Marcus the stranger was not alone. Movement from the edge of his vision confirmed his fear, but he did not look long enough to see who it could be. Panic filled him as flashbacks of thugs and knives raced through his memory.

His feet pounded the street and his lungs heaved. He would not be herded and cornered like an animal this time. Never before had he raced for his life, and thankfully, he found himself far faster than he remembered. Taking no time to think of where he was going, he passed the park once more and turned down a side street, his pursuers still on his heels.

There were at least three of them by the sound of their footsteps. After the second or third narrow alley, he chanced a look behind. His eyes met those of an assailant in mid lunge. Hit squarely in the shoulders, he fell headfirst to the grimy street.

Feeling a trickle of blood on his brow, Marcus rose to his feet as quickly as he could. Two paces away, his attacker, a young Asian woman, stood ready for another assault. Three others ran swiftly to join her.

From behind, a small arm gripped Marcus firmly around the chest, and a pinch that he knew all too well stung in his neck. Otto's calm voice came from beside his ear as the contents of the syringe emptied into his bloodstream. "For your own safety, good doctor."

Everything went dark.

+ + +

Stiff, aching muscles greeted Marcus when he awoke. Pain throbbed in his temples. This time, it was not a private hospital bed he lay on, but a hard floor. The stale smell of the room matched the weak, grey light coming through its only window. Whether it was dusk or dawn, he could not be sure.

Rolling over, he found a pitcher of water and a leg of turkey on a tin platter. The water was not cold and the meat was not hot, but they were welcome nonetheless. After satisfying his raging hunger and thirst, Marcus inspected his surroundings.

The view from the barred window showed that his room stood some three stories above the street. Between buildings, he could just barely make out the shimmer of the River Thames and what may have been the East India Docks. An overcast sky hung low overhead. He tried the solid oak door leading from the room, but found it, predictably, locked. He shouted until his voice was hoarse, but to no avail.

THE DEATH OF DR. MARCUS WELLS · J. Aurel Guay

Once finally exhausted, he sat back on the floor and considered the faded and peeling wallpaper around him. What could the curious man and his henchmen possibly want with him? The hospital must have noticed his absence by now. A resident physician at St. Thomas' would never miss a shift. The police surely searched for him, likely presuming him abducted by the rampant murderer.

Some hours later, the door latch finally clicked open. An Asian woman entered, and he eyed her suspiciously, recalling how he had been knocked to the ground before everything had gone dark. Marcus immediately thought of overpowering her and making a run for it, until her companion, an incredibly large and muscled man, followed, filling the doorway.

"Comfy, mate?" asked the gorilla of a man. A new plate of meat clattered on the floor, followed by a fresh pitcher of water. The burly stranger did not seem much interested in a response, and gathered the used dishes without so much as a glance at Marcus. He wore a set of common worker's pants and a loose shirt hung from his broad shoulders, but his large, hairy feet were bare.

The woman, garbed in a red robe of oriental styling, strode to the corner where Marcus sat. Ebony hair pulled tightly back framed her square and serious face. Stooping, she grabbed his chin, forcing him to look her in the eye. He did not resist, for fear of her well-muscled counterpart.

"His head is healed already. He is far along."

Her English, though abrupt and heavily accented, was clear. She turned his face to the left, and then the right, inspecting him closely, but not in the manner of a physician. While she worked, Marcus briefly considered making a hostage of her, but he quickly dismissed the idea—besides being unarmed, he could not see himself taking advantage of a smaller woman in such a way. She pulled back his shirt collar and unveiled the black scar on his shoulder. That, too, was thoroughly inspected.

"Sorry we ain't got better 'commadations for ye, mate." The man scratched his full red mutton chops as he waited for his partner to finish. "Give us a holler if this food ain't enough for ye and I'll see what else I can scrounge up. Blokes like us gotta keep up our strength."

Marcus finally found his voice.

"What I want is to be released from here. Whatever you want from me, I can assure you, I have nothing."

The woman stood, seemingly satisfied with her inspection.

"You listen to Gordon. Save your strength." Without another word, she turned, and the pair left the room.

For several days, their routine continued. He received a ration of meat and water three times a day, a peculiar inspection by Chin, as he learned her name to be, and hours of solitude. Marcus plotted dozens of ways to escape, but could find none that did not end in a confrontation with the larger of his guardians. He tried to explain that he was only a resident physician in training and that he had little money. His captors had no interest, however, and kept about their routine. During his confinement, he never saw the mysterious Otto, though he thought he once heard a German accent in the hall.

Cold and alone, thoughts of Emily continually passed through his mind. Her almond face and the smile that once empowered him to move mountains would come to him against his volition. Sometimes, when overwhelmed by memories of her, he would remove her ring from his pocket, where it had been overlooked by his captors. He had kept the ring within reach ever since that terrible night in the park. Its delicate shine brought back memories of her joyful tears and tender embrace the day he proposed.

But, the images inevitably darkened as her rosy cheeks paled and the sickness overtook her, a sickness for which there was no cure. During her days of suffering he had cursed science, cursed medicine, and cursed himself for being unable to heal her. Then, more woeful visions would rise. Memories of her recovery and hope, followed by confusion and grief, would torment him.

One evening, just after the red sunset surrendered behind the dark city skyline, the rattle of the lock and creak of his prison door woke Marcus from his restless pondering. A silhouetted figure thanked someone beyond the entrance as it accepted a chair. Squinting in the light of the oil lamp, he watched the small man carefully position the chair across from him. Otto settled himself into his seat and set the lamp on the floor.

Marcus rose to a seated position while Otto removed his bowler hat and ran a hand across his bald scalp.

"Dr. Wells, why were you on the train from Edinburgh to London three months ago?" Solemn and clearly fatigued, Otto looked more at the floor than at Marcus.

"Please, sir, I have done nothing wrong. Why are you keeping me here?" Marcus begged.

"I told you, it is for your own protection," Otto replied, unmoved by his pleas. "And it also happens that you are the only link I can find to the series of murders that started in your hospital at the time of your return to London."

"It is not me, I swear it. I am a physician. I am not the Ripper."

"Yes, of course," Otto snapped. "You've not progressed nearly far enough for that. Now, answer my question, Dr. Wells. Why were you on that train?"

"Progressed? What are you talking about?" Marcus' pulse increased. But the strange man merely continued in his impatient glare and waited for an answer to his question.

"I . . . I was returning from visiting family," Marcus muttered. He refused to give the details of that mournful journey, least of all to the man responsible for his bondage.

"And you traveled alone?"

"Yes."

"Did you see anything unusual on that train?"

"No." Anger began to boil in Marcus at his inhospitable treatment.

He set his jaw and looked away, as a heavy sigh escaped his interrogator. A scuffing on the floor surprised Marcus when a chair was set down by his side.

"I will leave this with you. I am aware that this situation is less than ideal, but we are working under extreme circumstances."

The strange man paused in his trite apology, and the shadows in the room raced about as he lifted the lamp off the floor. Marcus squinted in the glaring light as Otto's face came so near that Marcus could feel his breath on his cheek.

Otto spoke absently while inspecting him, just as Chin had done many times before. "Pray that we find this beast quickly, that we may move you to more suitable holdings." He paused in his examination. "Curses, we may not have time for—"

A solid uppercut nearly knocked Otto off his feet as three semesters of boxing at university proved their worth. Jumping to his feet, Marcus rushed in to follow up with a blow to the temple. He put all of his strength into the thrust. But instead of the solid impact of knuckle against skull, his fist met the fleshy palm and firm grip of Otto's hand. Still, the smaller man slid back along the floor from the force of the punch. Marcus' own strength surprised him, yet Otto, somehow, held both his footing and his viselike grip on Marcus' fist.

"Very little time indeed . . ." Otto gritted through clenched teeth.

Sharp pains from Marcus' fist drew his attention away from Otto's intense glare. He recoiled at the sight of the talons that drew blood from his fist as they extended from the strange man's fingers.

"Save your strength, good doctor," Otto growled as he released his grip and turned to the door. "You are going to need it."

THE DEATH OF DR. MARCUS WELLS <small>J. AUREL GUAY</small>

A short while later, Marcus heard the creak of the door again. This time, it was Chin and Gordon who entered, bringing with them two more chairs, a table, and rations for the three of them. Chin approached the corner, where he sat nursing his wounds. Seemingly unconcerned by his attack against Otto, she took his hand and inspected his injuries.

"He must like you," she commented, before moving on to inspect his face and neck again.

"Otto is right. It will come soon," she reported flatly over her shoulder when satisfied.

Gordon sighed and sat down at the table where his partner joined him. "I bloody hate this part."

They seemed to think something was happening to him. Recalling the terrible claws of Otto, Marcus shuddered and pushed the nightmarish fantasy from his thoughts. What had he done for his life to be cursed like this? He felt the cool wall against his cheek as he turned to stare blankly at the damp corner and the bits of dust and dirt that had been given up on long ago. His captors waited for something. He racked his mind in search of some answer.

What he would not give to be with Emily now, to see the shine in her sea-blue eyes. He had been so full of hope once, hopeful in their union, hopeful in her recovery. He still remembered every word of her last letter.

My dearest Marcus,

I want you to know that I am fine. In fact, I am more than fine. Despite your scientific doubts, the fresh Scottish air is working wonders on me. I have not coughed in days and my strength is returning faster than the nurse can keep up.

I feel I must tell you, before it becomes a lie of omission, that there has been one small incident. I hope you will not be too alarmed. One evening, before my improvement, I had such a coughing spell that I simply had to get out of doors into the cool night air. I know you would have disapproved, but I was in such a terrible way, I could do nothing else to soothe my lungs.

It must have been a mad animal that came upon me. I was attacked and bitten, but not badly. The doctor checked and treated me thoroughly, and I have suffered no ill effects.

I have waited to tell you because I did not want to interrupt your work. I know how important it is that you do well in your residency. I know you will want to come here immediately and see to me, but please know that I am well. It was weeks ago, and I have since not only healed from the small wounds, but am thankfully recovering from the sickness as well.

I only tell you now because I know you will rush here to check on me. That is just as well, because I want to come home. The Doctor says he will clear me to return in another week. By the time you arrive, I will be free to be home with you, never to be parted again.

Please hurry, my love,

Emily

The rise of murmuring voices interrupted Marcus' despair.

"You played that before!" Chin accused. Turning his head ever so slightly, he found Chin glaring at her companion over a table of playing cards.

"Wha'? Now, sweetie, that ain't no way to be talkin' amongst mates."

"You are a liar and a cheat!"

"If ye don' like the way the cards is played, ye'll jest have to find someone else to play with." Gordon attempted to feign offence as he reached to take a card. A sharp object struck first, forcefully pinning the card to the table.

Marcus sat up. What he had first assumed to be a dagger turned out to be far more surprising. It was a claw-like blade—or perhaps a blade-like claw—nearly twelve inches in length. He followed its crescent shape up to its hinged joint. His eyes widened as he realized that the joint connected it to a slender limb, which in turn, connected to Chin by another joint near her wrist.

"What are you people?" he found himself saying aloud.

Chin's clawed extension retracted slowly, then lay against her forearm and slid into a fold of skin, making it almost imperceptible. An unexpected softness came over her as she bit her lip and avoided his stare.

"We ain't people no more," replied Gordon solemnly over his shoulder. Chin motioned to her partner and their game resumed without further hostilities.

Overwhelmed with shock and fear, Marcus sat as still as stone for what felt like an hour. Were they all monsters? Gordon and Chin did not seem intent on hurting him. Aside from detaining and ignoring him, they treated him well enough, supplying generous portions of food and drink. If they planned to murder him, surely they would have done so by now.

Could he be turning into one of them? Though his mind refused to believe it, he could not ignore the signs in his own body—his surprising manifestations of strength, and his rapid healing—and neither could he ignore ominous remarks by his captors.

Otto had been interested in the London murders. What could he, or that train ride from Edinburgh, have to do with the murderer? Marcus recalled little of that long journey, the last leg of his trip home without Emily.

††††

Arriving in the tiny Scottish village of just north of Sterling, Marcus had gone straight to the small sanatorium where Emily recuperated. His joyous expectation of bringing her home in good health was quickly overturned when he found nothing but black ash where the home had once stood.

Empty looks of fear and suspicion met the panic in his eyes when he burst into the local pub. No one was willing to tell him what had happened. Every face looked away at the mention of the sanatorium, and his pleas got him no answers that night. Over the following days, he pieced together that the villagers themselves had burned the building. They had burned it to the ground to rid themselves of some horror that had happened there.

A week before, while Marcus was still traveling, the home had gone strangely silent. When no one from the house came to the market that week, the villagers called on the recovery home to check on the residents and staff. What they found, they would not say in detail, but it was clear that everyone in the recovery home was dead.

Marcus called on the authorities, but got little help. The law was thin so far out in the country, and had little interest in following a case with no leads. Eventually, Marcus also surrendered. Emily's ring brought him to it. When he found it some days later among the building's remains, he buried all hope of seeing Emily alive again.

He did not remember much of the carriage ride down to Edinburgh the next day, nor much of the train to London, either. The only interaction he had was with a peculiar Scotsman.

Marcus was sitting alone, staring out the window as the solemn moors raced by to the rhythm of the clacking rails. He saw nothing, heard nothing, felt nothing. The broad-shouldered Scotsman walked by him twice, each time eyeing his doctor's bag, before sitting down in the booth with him.

Despite his fairly good size, the man seemed awkward and nervous. The Scot wiped his brow with a pale hand before speaking.

"Yer a doct'er, right?"

Marcus remembered stirring only slightly from his stupor and nodding.

"An' yer headed to London, right?"

Again, he nodded in time with the chattering cabin.

"They have good doct'ers ther'?"

His interest somewhat piqued, Marcus noticed the profuse sweat that accumulated on the man's brow.

"I suppose they do," he obliged.

"An . . . an wha' kind of medicine is it that you do?" The man wiped his face again.

"General medicine. I am a resident, still in training."

"Ah." The stranger looked down at his hands as the padded leather seat bounced beneath him.

"What kind of doctor are you looking for?" Marcus started to welcome the distraction.

"I . . . I dunno, exactly. I'm just a simple fisherman from Dundee. I sometimes wake up . . . " His countenance paled, and his voice came as a whisper when he continued. "It's a dream I wake up from . . . a real terrible thing, it is. An' I can' make it stop."

The Scotsman again looked at his lap.

"It sounds like you just need a holiday," Marcus replied. "Why not go spend some time with your family?"

"They . . . they're dead," Marcus caught a glimpse of the man's reddened lower lid and a glistening in his eye.

"I am so sorry," Marcus replied, empathizing with the man in their common grief. "Here, then—come to St. Thomas' Hospital, near the river, once you settle in. I will see what I can do."

The Scotsman hurried away without responding. Marcus did not see the man the rest of the trip, and the steady motion of the engine soon lulled him back into his unending grief.

◈ ◈ ◈

Marcus bolted upright in his drab prison room as realization struck. The strange man, the talk of the hospital, the deceased family—they all suddenly made sense.

"The Scot!" Chin and Gordon started. "It is the Scotsman! I met him on the train. He—he wanted a doctor, and I told him which hospital I worked at. It must be him."

Gordon and Chin looked at one another.

"What do you know of him?" Chin quizzed.

"He was from Dundee, I believe."

Gordon nodded at Chin. "A Baurcat, jus' like we thought. Near Dundee's where I got mine."

"Is there anything else?" Chin pressed.

Marcus' eyes darted about as he thought. "Yes, his clothes. His clothes were rather small for him."

"Ha! It's gotta be a Baurcat." Gordon slapped his knee. "He's likely as bloody big as me by now."

"I will tell Mr. Otto." Chin rose from the table and quickly left the room.

"Won't take long now, mate," Gordon said mirthfully to Marcus. "Knowin' where he come from, Otto will figure out who he was, and track where he started in the city. He's smart like that, an' Baurcats is easy to predict once you know that's what they is."

"What is a Baurcat?" Marcus asked, glad to be getting real conversation out of someone.

Gordon paused. "Well, Otto usually likes to do the tellin'. We ain't even spos'ed to talk at all, 'til we sees if you can make it or not . . . But it's so close, now, an' if it's true, then we're practically brothers, you an' me." Pausing briefly, he raised his large arm into the lamplight. A sudden change came over the limb.

"A Baurcat's what got me. It's what I is now." His hand doubled in size, taking on a savage new form, producing heavy claws at his fingertips. "An' it's what you'll be soon enough."

Marcus could not help but stare. His own voice sounded choked as he blurted out, "And the woman, Chin, is she also . . . "

THE DEATH OF DR. MARCUS WELLS · J. Aurel Guay

"Naw, she's a werekind, but not a Baurcat. She's what they call a Southern Harpy—hers make her fast an' light, ours makes us big an' strong," Gordon explained before adding with a chuckle, "Jes' don' ask to see her beak or she'll cuff you one. She don' like showin' that bit o' the change."

"But, how? What brings it on you? Is it an infection?" The physician in Marcus surfaced as he pondered the horrific revelation.

"Them's bigger questions than I can tell. All's I know is that ye get bit and it comes. Best t' save that talk for Mr. Otto."

"Can it be stopped? Can it be reversed?" begged Marcus.

"Only if we catch it early, Doc. Otto's got a cure that'll kill the thing inside without killin' the outside. But, it's too late for blokes like us. It takes a couple a months for it to set in, but even though yours ain't come out yet, you'd be a goner wi'out what's inside." The large man's hand returned to its normal size as he spoke. Marcus paused as he thought back to the mysterious injection the attack victim received under his care—certainly the work of Otto and his colleagues.

The door opened, and a new, unfamiliar man joined them, presumably a replacement for Chin. The conversation ended as Gordon pretended he had not been speaking with Marcus. He and the newcomer began discussing the events outside the room and how Otto was going to find the rampaging Scotsman. Marcus gathered that he was amongst a group of monsters led by the man Otto, and that they were hunting for some rogue of their own kind responsible for the recent murders.

His thoughts, however, focused on the revelation of the creatures themselves—and what it meant for him. It was the stuff of fairytale, of legend, of myth. But what he had seen in just the last few hours challenged everything he once thought he knew about fact and fiction.

With the image of Gordon's grotesque change in his mind, Marcus inspected his own hand. The wounds from Otto's claws had nearly healed in mere hours. Could the scar on his shoulder in fact be the bite of this Baurcat? As sleep overtook him and conscious thought gave way to dark and fearful dreams, he struggled to make sense of all the pieces.

† † †

A hand on his shoulder woke Marcus some hours later.

"Here, drink this."

The warm contents of the tin cup forced on him carried a smell of strange herbs that stung in his nose. Otto's familiar spectacles met Marcus' gaze when he looked up from the mug.

Taking the cup, he blinked and wiped his face, pushing away the stupor of sleep.

"We got him," Otto spoke in a hushed tone, "thanks to you."

"The Scotsman, is he all right? Could you help him?"

The man looked at the floor, and chair behind him creaked as he sank down into it.

"It does not work like that," he sighed. The oil lamp on the table, now turned down low, cast only a faint glow that left the walls in shadow.

"I hear you have been talking to Gordon." Otto motioned to the corner where the goliath snored in his chair. Chin had returned as well, and was likewise resting. "If we can catch a spawn early enough, we can kill it safely. But, beyond a certain point, there is nothing that can be done. The werekind takes over, and the victim falls into madness."

"But, what about Gordon? Or you? How have you escaped such a fate?" If Otto spoke truly, Marcus feared for his own condition.

"That is why you must drink," Otto reminded Marcus. "If we cannot catch the spawn before it is invested, the only other choice is to subdue and control it before it controls the host. Then, the two can work as one. There is but one opportunity, and it is up to the host to seize it. It is up to you, for your time has come."

Marcus looked at the contents of the steaming mug.

"The werekind has matured in you, and will be making its first appearance. It will put your mind to sleep while it reshapes your body and goes out in search of its first meal. That is, unless you drink."

"The tincture will block the creature's effects on your nervous system, allowing you to maintain—or rather, compete—for control of your body."

Though not certain he could trust Otto, Marcus could not deny the strange new sensation growing within him. He brought the cup to his lips and allowed the bitter liquid to pass his tongue.

"But, what is it inside of me?" Marcus finally asked. "During my courses, I read of something called a 'virus.' Is it of that kind? Or is it some microbe?"

"No, my good doctor, it is neither of those." Otto pushed his glasses further onto his nose as he poured a second cup. "While we are both men of science, my training was in engineering and physics. I cannot research the creatures as well as someone such as yourself, but I have traveled the globe studying the werekind, as best as I can, in all their varied forms.

"They are certainly a type of organism: multi-cellular, with a nervous system and circulation like ours. They enter the host and spread themselves throughout the body. Working all manner of wonders, they can change a man's metabolism, enhance his im- munity, and even influence his growth. They do not stop there, however, for in order to feed and spawn new generations, they add to the host's body their own organs in secret. When matured, they emerge to redesign the host's structure, transforming him into a veritable killing machine."

A lump grew in Marcus' throat as his nerves threatened to get the better of him. "But how can such a thing be stopped?"

Otto leaned forward in his chair to look Marcus sternly in the face.

"This is where you must be strong. The creature in you is alive—it has a mind, and it can learn. You must teach it to submit. You must be its master, or you will become its slave."

"But how is that possible?"

"We will give you the tools at the right time. Now, rest, good doctor." Otto poured a final cup of tea and sipped it himself.

Marcus sensed the strange feeling subsiding within him, but he had no intention of resting. Apparently finished talking, Otto enjoyed the remains of the bitter tincture while resting one ankle on his knee.

Marcus allowed the cracked, plaster wall to support his heavy head. He stared at the water stains on the ceiling and observed how they showed the outlines of the rafters above. His mind continued to turn over his future. Surrounded by kindly monstrosities, he could only wait to birth whatever manner of creature was inside of him. A sea of fear and curiosity overwhelmed his mind.

Again, his thoughts turned to Emily. How he longed for her, how he wished for the comfort that came from her smile. His hallucinations made sense now. Certainly, the work of the thing inside him wrought the visions of his late fiancée.

A tearing pain shot through his chest, causing him to convulse and cry out. Otto sat upright and the other guards stirred from their slumber.

"It is moving early," Otto said. "Gordon, please fetch the generator."

Marcus heard the creak of the door hinges, but the throbbing inside him consumed his attention. It felt as though his chest would explode. The throbbing turned to a steady pressure as his heart pounded in his ears. He cried out again as a tearing in his sternum began.

With a sickening clunk, his ribs separated and expanded, somehow locking into new positions. The burning remained, but the pressure no longer pulled at his chest. He felt himself taking terribly deep breaths and wondered if it was of his own volition.

"Oh, Emily! Emily, please," he whimpered.

A tender hand rested on his back.

"Was this Emily someone important to you?" Otto asked.

Through the pain, Marcus tried to put words to his grief.

"My fiancée. That is where I was returning from on the train. She died in Scotland while I traveled to meet her. I—I never got to say goodbye," he wept. It was the first time he had said the words out loud. Why the circumstances finally brought his grief to the surface, he did not know. Thankfully, the visceral pain had eased, at least for the moment.

"Be strong, Doctor, for her memory's sake."

With a knock at the door, Gordon entered, carrying a massive metal device. He bore a grave expression. The floorboards shook as Gordon dropped the machine. He immediately sought Otto's ear for private word while Marcus pondered how the device would help him control the creature inside him.

"Another?" Marcus heard Otto's shocked reply. "Are they sure?"

Gordon nodded.

Otto rounded on Marcus. "What of this Emily, Dr. Wells? Are you certain she died?"

"Of course," he replied through the pain. "There was a massacre. They burned the building."

"And you have seen no sign of her since? Not even a glimpse that could have been her?"

"I have had dreams, but nothing more. She died in a village outside Sterling; that's where I was returning from on the train."

"Sterling," blurted Gordon. "There's bloody Jagerunds in them mountains."

Otto gripped Marcus' arm and raised it to examine the cuff of his sleeve. It fit perfectly at his wrist, as it had always done.

"Damn! How could I be such a fool! This is no Baurcat."

A deathly silence filled the room.

"Mr. Otto, the Jagerunds are savage. They have never been tamed." Chin backed away slowly as she spoke. Otto held his fingers to the bridge of his nose as he hunched, staring at the floor next to Marcus.

"We cain't do a Jagerund here, Otto. It'd 'ave been bad enough with a Baurcat. We gotta finish him now," added Gordon.

"Silence!" Otto shouted. He paused a moment more before looking up. "We now have two Jagerunds to consider. We are spread too thin to handle such a feral werekind on the streets of London. We need the doctor. He can do this; I know he can!"

Gordon begrudgingly approached and lifted Marcus into a chair. A new pain scintillated through his body while Gordon produced heavy straps and bound him in place. Otto pressed a hand firmly on his shoulder as he stooped to look directly into Marcus' sweat-covered face.

"Marcus, listen to me. The tincture you drank protects your mind from the beast, but it exposes you to the full pain of the change." Marcus' face flinched and his eyes rolled as a wave of sharp crackling tore down his spine.

"Marcus. Your Emily is not dead." Marcus lifted his pallid face to look at Otto. "She was not murdered—she was the murderer. Not her, but the beast inside. She is a terrible thing now, the worst of our kind, and she has passed her curse on to you."

A rush of memories overwhelmed Marcus' vision. Could the

park—the vision of Emily—have been real? Otto shook Marcus by the shoulders, pulling him from his revelation. His eyes refocused on the urgently pleading Otto.

"You must succeed. You must subdue the Jagerund inside you if you want to save her, free her from her curse."

Working quickly, Chin finished securing Marcus to the chair and attached a strap to his arm by a large buckle. A heavy wire connected the strap to the machine. A loud thud sounded beside them as Gordon dropped a second identical device.

"If we're gunna do this, I thought we might s'well put both of 'em together, like we did that one time."

"Good thinking, Gordon," Otto accepted a curious-looking handle from Chin. Connected to the first machine in the same manner as the strap on his arm, the handle had a mechanical lever along its length. Gordon turned a crank, and the two machines whirred to life.

"This is a device of my own invention," began Otto, placing the handle in Marcus' bound hand. "When you squeeze this lever, you will both feel the pain, but the electricity will hurt the creature within more than it will hurt you. The beast will try to break you. It has already made room for its own lungs to breathe. You must stop it from going further. You cannot allow the transformation to complete until it has learned submission."

Otto continued speaking words of encouragement, but Marcus did not hear them. At that moment, a surge of pain flooded his senses, and something unnatural stirred within him.

Marcus squeezed the handle. Every muscle, from his bicep to his hand, locked as the burning pain surged through his arm. The thing within him cringed, and he released the lever.

The current stopped, allowing Marcus a gasping breath. The strange churning inside him paused only a moment before redoubling with vengeance. The knuckles of his empty hand dislocated as they separated from their joints. The skin of that arm became tight, and a throbbing pain burned in his fingertips as sharp claws pushed their way through.

Another squeeze, and again the jarring jolt of electricity coursed through his arm. He could feel the thing inside him now. He could feel its hunger and rage. The change paused once more. He released the trigger.

The thing within him resumed immediately and with force.

Marcus clenched his fist around the handle a third time, but the surge only fueled the monster's rage. He could feel it in his feet now. A strange pressure in his legs grew until his bones snapped. Marcus cried out and crushed the lever against the handle with all his might, but it was no use. Desperation overcame him as he looked to his companions, and the change overtook him.

Chin backed away, her body altering as she moved, revealing bird-like legs. Her arms took on the appearance of skeletal wings. Her forearms and fingers lengthened, and again, her clawed extensions reached forward from her wrists. Gordon had already changed. His broadened body and his enlarged and clawed hands and feet gave him a savage appearance. Menacing tusks rose from below his jaw.

Only Otto remained as he was. The small man pulled up his own sleeve and thrust his bare arm in front of Marcus' eyes.

"Fight, Marcus!" he shouted as he displayed the grotesque red burn scars that ran from his palm toward his shoulder. "We have all fought this battle! You must not give in!"

A massive, unnatural arm flung Otto across the room. Marcus felt pulling against his sides as a strong hand tore away the straps that bound him. Only then did he realize that the savage limb was his own.

Working in him with full force now, the creature pushed through the ongoing burn of the generators and the smell of burning flesh. Marcus' skin stretched, revealing a darker hide beneath. He watched, a prisoner in his own body, and felt himself hunch over at the creature's will. The sting of a thousand nails tore at his nerves as sharp quills broke through the skin of his back.

The creature straightened, and Marcus' cry mingled its roar as the bones of his face contorted and broke. The Jagerund continued its roar from its deep chest as the transformation completed, and Marcus felt its razor sharp fangs fit together in place of his own teeth.

He could see himself towering over the others in the room. Gordon lunged at him with tooth and claw, but the hide of the Jagerund was too thick; savage teeth clamped down on Gordon. His body went limp and joined Otto in the corner where he lay, still unconscious. Chin darted around the ferocious beast. Striking with her scythe-like claws, she leapt from wall to wall.

The flitting attacker infuriated the beast. Marcus' new body lifted a massive generator and hurled it against the wall, where the fierce woman clung. It caved with the impact, and though Chin escaped, it was not without injury.

Inside the beast, Marcus wept. The Jagerund reveled in its triumph. It lifted the second generator and bashed through the windowed wall to expose the clear night sky. He felt his lungs fill with cold, fresh air. As it stepped into the opening, the beast again roared in victory.

Something caught Marcus' eye. The Jagerund must have seen it too, for they were now staring directly at it. There, on the rooftop across the alleyway, stood a woman. The blue light of the full moon shone on her, revealing her blood-stained rags, and the tears that washed pure white streaks down her dirtied face—her beautiful, almond-shaped face.

Emily.

She lived.

Despite the curse that they now shared, she was alive. What horrors had she woken to when the Jagerund within her surfaced again and again to satisfy its hunger? What despair had she felt when she failed to keep the beast away from humanity, from the ones she loved?

Marcus snarled in hate for the parasites that now infected them both. He could not succumb. He would not succumb. Not while Emily lived, not while she needed him. He would not fail her again. Marcus fought against that other mind within him. He forced himself to tear his gaze from her. Stumbling back from the gaping hole, he fell to the floor. His brutal arms pulled his body forward, dragging him further into the room. Against the efforts of the Jagerund, he looked for Otto. The man was nowhere to be found.

A spark flashed and crackled nearby.

The generator.

It still whirred by the wall where it had fallen. For the sake of his Emily, he would subdue the beast, or die trying. Marcus dragged himself closer to it. Finding the first wire, his razor sharp teeth slice through the protective coating and down into the cold, dense copper beneath.

The creature fought against his will as he reached for the second cable. Gripping the wire in his savage claws, he took the bare metal end and drove it against his chest with all his might.

A brilliant flash and burning pain instantly engulfed all his senses. Blowing Marcus onto his back, the surge coursed through his body like tearing, white fire in his veins. The Jagerund recoiled and cried out in agony.

Everything stilled.

Marcus' ears rang. He could hear the ominous thudding of his own heart.

Thub-dub. Thub-dub. Thub . . . thub . . . dub . . . thub . . .

THE DEATH OF DR. MARCUS WELLS ⸱ J. Aurel Guay

His breathing slowed. Darkness encroached. He could do nothing now. Perhaps death was better than living as a monster.

In his final moments of consciousness, the only peace Marcus found was in the satisfying sense of fear and desperation in the werekind within him. Then the world, with all of its pain and all of its loss, gave way to emptiness, and on the floor of his prison room, Dr. Marcus Wells died.

But the Jagerund did not know surrender.

Thub . . . Thub . . . Thub-dub . . . Thub-dub. Thub-dub. Thub-dub. Thub-dub.

Marcus' heart burst back to life. Gasping, he rolled over. Immediately, the creature within him worked at his limbs, trying to move itself away from the wretched generator. Marcus quickly clamped down on the metal cord again and raised the second wire in his hand.

A newfound terror leapt up in the monster as it gave way to his will.

The Jagerund had saved them both. Marcus felt the heart-reviving adrenaline coursing through his body. The creature would never again risk such a challenge. Death to the host was death to the beast.

Marcus relaxed and lay still on the floor. A painful, but relieving sensation came over him as his natural bones fit back together and found their proper places. Lying face down, he could not summon the strength to move. In the quiet, he gasped, thankful for every strained breath.

A hand rested on his back.

"Well done, Dr. Wells," whispered Otto's voice. "Sleep now, both of you."

For a second time he felt a pinch in his neck. A calm sensation spread throughout his body and he slipped into welcomed unconsciousness.

SHADES and SHADOWS

ꜛ ꜛ ꜛ

Yellow light shone through the translucent ceiling panels of the train station. Marcus watched as at the far end, a pair of parting lovers embraced one another tearfully. A week ago, a reminder of such passion would have sent arrows though his fragile heart. But with the knowledge that Emily lived, nothing would hinder or sway him from saving her from her Jagerund.

He looked to the nearest of the several crates being loaded onto the freight car beside him. It contained one of the salvaged generators, and weighed nearly 300 pounds. Stealing a glance around him to ensure no one was watching, he bent down and took hold of the box. Thanks to the side effects of his condition, he lifted the crate with little strain, and placed it into the freight car among the others.

"Easy there, mate," Gordon chided as he moved a similarly heavy crate. "Too much strain and you'll wake up yer lil' friend. My back's still sore from the last time 'e came out to play."

Marcus smiled at his new companion. From behind him came Otto's terse voice. "And there would be far too many witnesses."

Approaching with his usual quick pace, Otto added, "As long as the general populace believes we are a myth, we will be free to continue our business and bring hope to the hundreds of souls likewise bound by our curse. Until such a time, secrecy is of the utmost importance."

"And what is our plan, Otto?" Marcus asked as he continued to load the smaller crates and parcels. Otto stopped beside him, dressed in his best clothes and bowler, just as Marcus had seen him that first night.

"Gordon and the others will go back to Liverpool to resupply and secure the provisions we will need. You, Chin, and I will follow Miss Emily. She has already left the city, so I'm told, and is heading north. Do you have any suspicions as to where she might be going?"

THE DEATH OF DR. MARCUS WELLS · J. AUREL GUAY

"She has no ties in that direction, save for the sanatorium. The only thing I can reason is that she intends to limit her violence to places it has already impacted, and the least populated of them. My bet is that she will return to the hills near the sanatorium where she was first infected."

"Hmm. It would be unusual for a werekind to return to the territory where it was spawned. But, if she has not yet succumbed to the beast fully, she might be doing as you say. There may be hope in that."

Marcus hesitated. "Should we bring Gordon, or another werekind of strength, with us if we are to subdue her Jagerund?"

"You, of all people, should know that it is no easy thing to restrain such a creature. No, Gordon will oversee things in Liverpool and meet up with us once we determine where she is headed. It will not be force that rescues your Emily. The beast will emerge against us at the slightest hint of a threat, and every time it does so, her mind will slip further from our reach. It will not be your strength that restrains her, but the bond between you."

"And you believe we can cure her?"

"That will be up to your medical talents. I will avail myself to your efforts in any way that I can. But first, we must find her and keep her counterpart from unleashing its rage and revealing our existence to the masses."

"My heart beats for nothing more."

The leather cord that hung around Marcus' neck slipped from beneath his shirt collar as he bent to pick up the last of the boxes. He quickly tucked the makeshift necklace and the ring that dangled from it back under his shirt. He felt the cool metal rest against the burn scars on his chest as he continued. Leaving London, his residency, all of it, behind was a simple decision. Nothing would be the same, not until he had found Emily, not until he had found a way to kill the werekind within them.

Marcus set the last parcel into the boxcar. He could feel the unseen body within his own as he worked. He could feel its hunger, its bitterness. He turned back to the smaller man. "I will find her and I will find a way to free her, to free all of us. I swear it to you, by all that is in me."

Otto smiled. "I believe you shall, my good doctor. I believe you shall."

* * *

ABOUT THE AUTHORS

R. M. Ridley lives with his wife on a small homestead in Canada, raising chickens and sheep. He has been writing stories, both long and short, for three decades, the themes of which range from the gruesome to the fantastical. As an individual who suffers from severe Bi-polar disorder, R. M. Ridley is a strong believer in being open about mental health issues and uses his writing to escape, when his thoughts become too wild. Follow R. M. Ridley online at: http://creativityfromchaos.wordpress.com

Hailing from New England where he lives with his bride, and their two children, **J. Aurel Guay** writes both fantasy and science fiction with emphasis on strong plots and meaningful themes. Having played at writing fiction since grade school, J. Aurel more recently has revived his passion as a coping skill in reaction to graduate school in biomedical science. Soon to complete his graduate studies, he is intent on publishing further short stories and novels. Follow J. Aurel Guay online at: http://www.jaurelguay.wordpress.com

Scott William Taylor grew up in Utah living on the side of a mountain and lives on that same mountain today with his family and a dog that loves cheese. Scott is married with four children. Scott is the author of *Little Boiler* Girl in Xchyler's *Mechanized Masterpieces Steampunk Anthology,* contributor to *Flash* 500 e-book, and creator of *A Page or Two Podcast*. He also wrote the award winning short film, *Wrinkles*. Follow Scott William Taylor online at: http://www.scottwilliamtaylor.com/

E. Branden Hart graduated from Trinity University with a degree in psychology and philosophy. He works and lives with his wife and a neurotic coonhound in San Antonio, Texas. When not writing, he enjoys playing piano, cooking meat, and carrying heavy things around on his back. Branden's writing has been published at *Toasted Cheese Literary Journal* and *Down in the Dirt* magazine, and he is the Executive Editor of Empty Sink Publishing. Follow J. Branden Hart online at: http://audienceofshadows.com/

Eric White has spent his life pretending things into existence. He desires to share stories that not only resonate in the nostalgic memories of the reader, but also reveal the light and dark of what is hidden behind the thin veil of reality. Kelley, his wife of seventeen years, is his muse. His sons, Zachary and Joshua, inspire his imagination. When not writing, Eric is a paraprofessional for children with special needs. Follow Eric White online at: http://ericwhitesmindlikeanoctopus.blogspot.com/

Scott E. Tarbet writes enthusiastically in several genres, sings opera, was married in full Elizabethan regalia, and slow-smokes thousands of pounds of barbeque. In the piney woods of deep East Texas, which are the home of his story 'Tombstone', a native gave him a bumper sticker that reads, "I wasn't born in Texas, but I got here as soon as I could." His novel "A Midsummer Night's Steampunk" will be released by Xchyler Publishing in November, 2013. Follow Scott E. Tarbet online at:
http://www.facebook.com/starbet

As a child, **Neve Talbot** developed the habit of lulling herself to sleep by dreaming up epic tales of fiction. Now an author and journalist, Neve currently lives with her husband in a quasi-reality filled with fantasy, sci-fi, historical fiction, Regency romance, the classics, and history books, suspended between the piney woods and sprawling metropolis of southeast Texas. She plans on exploring the world when she grows up. Follow Neve Talbot online at: http://www.xchylerpublishing.com

Ginger Mann is a flutist, songwriter, composer, and computer systems integrator. If you can't find her doing those things, look for a woman chasing around her small children with a camera. A Texas artist, she enjoys writing for other Texans; especially young voices. The premiere of her song, "River Night", will be performed by a high school choir in North Austin at the same time as the release of her short story, "China Doll." Follow Ginger Mann online at: https://www.facebook.com/ginger.c.mann

Marian Rosarum studies genre fiction as a graduate student by day and crafts dark fairy tales by night. Although she comes from a long line of Cuban exiles and grew up in Rocky Mountains, she currently resides in Virginia with her best friends, a cat named Colonel Brandon, and the many fictional characters who populate her imagination. Follow Marian Rosarum online at: https://www.facebook.com/marian.rosarum

ABOUT XCHYLER PUBLISHING

With inspiring writers, innovative printing strategies, and a progressive editorial staff, Xchyler Publishing plays a key role in defining the emerging domain of independent publishing.

As the first imprint of Hamilton Springs Press, Xchyler Publishing proudly grooms and introduces exciting new authors committed to their craft. Offering complete publishing services, our professional editors, designers, and marketing staff produce books of the highest quality. The success of our authors is our own.

MORE FROM
XCHYLER PUBLISHING:

Look for more exciting titles from Xchyler Publishing in 2013-2014, including:

A Midsummer's Night Steampunk, an action/adventure with a nod to The Bard, by Scott E. Tarbet, November 2013

Primal Storm, Book II of the urban fantasy series The Grenshall Manor Chronicles by R. A. Smith, December 2013; sequel to Oblivion Storm.

Book I of the Kingdom City Series, a dystopian fantasy by Ben Ireland, January 2014

Accidental Apprentice, a young adult fantasy by Anika Arrington, February, 2014

We here at The X pride ourselves in discovery and promotion of talented authors. Our anthology project produces four books a year in our specific areas of focus: fantasy, Steampunk, suspense/thriller, and paranormal. Held quarterly, our short-story competitions result in published anthologies from which the authors receive royalties.

Additional themes include: Back to the Future (Fantasy, winter 2014), Around the World in Eighty Days (Steampunk, spring 2014), Liar Liar (Thriller/Suspense, summer 2014), and Mr. and Mrs. Myth (Paranormal, fall 2014).

To learn more, visit www.xchylerpublishing.com.

Xchyler Publishing Sneak Peek

Primal Storm
by R. A. Smith
Grenshall Manor Chronicles Book II

1.

Everyone who ever lived has known fear at some stage in their lives. For some, the dark. For others, spiders. Or perhaps heights. For every individual exists a tailored nightmare.

The trick is to not let it get the better of you. And Jennifer Winter knew that better than most. She'd been a fighter from her first heartbeat. During childbirth, a rare complication for the modern age took her mother. But Jennifer kept breathing even after everyone had given up on her.

And just a year ago, she clung on again, with the help of a friend, when Death came for her.

She once had strength well beyond that of a mundane being—speed, power, toughness and a ferocious battle posture, traits that brought a bestial warrior to the surface from the depths of her soul.

Now, she may have been perhaps a solid athlete at best. The power she possessed previously had seemingly deserted her. Before she could look after others again, she would have to relearn to look after herself. Through some strange logic, that had led her to the dangerous challenge she had set herself: free-running the rooftops of London.

Whilst bedridden, she demanded to be shown sports and exercise to keep her inspired. Thankfully, her employer by formality, housemate by convenience, and best friend by lengthy history, Kara duly obliged with a series of extreme sports clips, but the one which had caught Jennifer's eye the most had been a short movie on *parkour* versus *freerunning*. She had found it fascinating, *motivating*.

She had set out from her starting point of Grenshall Manor, obscured somehow in Mill Hill, North London, just as it was getting dark. Some basic stretches, which attracted the unwanted attention of a group of spotty teenagers, preceded a gentle jog. Her idea of gentle still allowed her to overtake a few of the regulars in the neighbourhood as they wound down from their commute in the best way they knew.

After a couple of miles, when she reached Islington, she decided to break into something more interesting. It was time for an exercise of balance. She looked to the skies and started to climb the face of a block of flats until she reached the rooftop.

She moved to the edge of the high-rise and rocked forward on to the balls of her feet. One slip and she would have a very long drop down. *One minute*, she said to herself. *One minute without falling*. The first challenge of several.

As it had all her life, the world continued to pick fights for her. When her stepmother entered her life, Jennifer hoped that things would improve. But nothing good came of that. Oh, she remembered. She would never forget.

That was the day the fear started.

When hers became a tale of two stepmothers, however, her life changed irreversibly. The second, the enigma she knew as Alice Winter, had her deal with most of her fears head-on. Like now.

Thirty seconds.

She stood taller, stretched. It felt good.

She'd had a lot of time to think about her past; lots of time as well to consider a new exercise regime. Months, in fact—months of stagnating in a bed in a mansion hardly any living person knew existed until her friends, Kara and Mary, found it. Their discovery of Grenshall Manor yielded much more than a property of significant value, but her part in its discovery ended a day sooner at the hands of a violent, undead entity.

The assault she withstood would have killed just about anyone else several times over.

Her balance was perfect; her strength, better than she gave herself credit for. She stretched out her arms, a movement which produced only the merest hint of teetering on the edge. She looked good for achieving her goal.

Twenty seconds. Not good enough. Push harder.

Still on her toes, she leaned another inch forward, another inch out into empty space. Again, her balance held true. As she endangered herself further, staring out over the cityscape, she chose her route of descent.

Time. Challenge done.

She lowered herself back to the soles of her feet and stumbled backward as she did so. She had spent weeks intensively building back up her calf muscles after their period of atrophy. They did not let her down, but they did ache like hell.

She cursed herself for feeling so weak. She wiped sweat from her brow as she allowed herself a little recovery time, but only a moment. She turned to the left and bolted to that edge of the building. As her feet hit the ledge, she sprung as hard as her legs would permit . . .

Not hard enough. She was going to be a good foot short. She grabbed a satellite dish just in time but misjudged that, too.

Instead of grappling the top, she fought to grip of the bottom of it. The bolts came loose with the tiniest pop and the dish tilted under her weight.

Quickly, she pushed her legs wider and braced herself against the building. She nudged herself upward and shifted her grip repeatedly up the surface of the dish. Her balance returned, her hands reached the top of the dish before it took further strain and she propelled herself to the right. Her feet landed on a balcony railing. She crouched, then leapt for an overhang on the roof. She pulled up and onto her intended target.

Jennifer continued her run, her immediate future no longer mapped. She ached, but that was a good thing. She was still moving. That was the important part. She built up more speed, and propelled herself using all her limbs for the next building—that one slightly lower down than the last. She had the momentum this time, but the ground came at her fast.

Brace!

She hit the concrete first with her right leg, absorbed the impact with an elegant forward roll, then came straight out of it. Back on her feet, she continued at almost full speed to the edge, then flung herself into space. The opposite roof was too far below distance below to roll.

She flailed in the direction of a high pipe on that building. Catching it just before landing blunted the pace of her drop, and with that, she fell safely to the roof. Perhaps not quite as intended, but decently all the same.

Jennifer had already marked her next building. She leapt more confidently, allowed herself no hesitation, and leapt again, that time straight down at an angled wall. She hit with her feet firmly planted on the top. She had to combine speed with balance and ran with arms out either side. The slightest slip would leave her very little chance to react safely.

The first few steps were fine, more momentum than judgement, but the next had her crossing her own feet at a high speed. Just as she had her footwork together, she ran out of wall. Impossibly off-balance and still travelling too quickly to stop, she threw herself into an elegant swan dive to make the most of her motion. She got quickly under control and tucked into a somersault.

She caught another protruding pipe and her feet hit the wall at her own pace. She took another quick look but swung around, then pushed herself clear, and dropped neatly on to a passing truck. One final spring took her to the pavement, just in front of an alleyway. Her feet planted with competent gymnastic form.

She winced as the self-punishment she inflicted decided to catch up with her. Every muscle gave crippling protest. She propped herself against the wall of one of the buildings and rested before pushing on.

Jennifer stepped into a canter, then worked herself into a flat-out sprint for a full minute. She breathed heavily. It used to take her ten to fifteen minutes to get anywhere near as tired. Her stamina had abandoned her on a day in which the fear returned.

That fateful, near-fatal day had been almost a year ago. Of those many months holed up at Grenshall Manor, for half of those, she had been unable to sit up by herself, let alone move on her own steam. Mary, the heir to the mansion and one person she could genuinely say had been through the wars like herself, had looked after her on almost every one of those days, a unique nurse. She kept her company, in touch with the world, and eating.

But Jennifer began to resent being cared for; worse, to develop a strange animosity for her caregiver. She couldn't help but notice that Mary blossomed by the day as she learned increasing control of that dark art of hers.

But more than that, Mary looked genuinely happy in herself. She had, figuratively and literally, laid old ghosts to rest in the time she and Jennifer had known each other—most significantly, as Jennifer assessed matters, the lingering case of her parents' deaths at the clumsy hands of an irrational ghost.

Jennifer had achieved none of this. The mother she never knew a victim of natural causes; nothing more to say on that tale. The woman she most wanted to call her mother after that, who helped her through her darkest days and introduced Jennifer to the basics of her talents, Alice, was taken from her, too. No resolution had come of that, and she no idea even where to start.

Though that pale touch of death had faded from Mary over the recovering months, she had become a completely different person from the one-time half-dead amnesiac she first rescued. The raven black hair had grown full-bodied, a streak of red in there by her own choice.

When not improving her more mystic arts, or working on building repairs, Mary would sacrifice entire days to keep Jennifer company. Sometimes, she would improve her tailoring skills, but she would keep herself busy every day with one thing or another. And for most of that time, Jennifer—hobbled, weak and unsteady. It proved maddening.

The most recent couple of months had been better. At least some of her coordination had returned and she could get around the building. She even helped Mary with her clothing design. But that night in the station, it would not leave her be. Always hitting her when it was it was least welcome. Like when she was catching her breath.

∎ ∎ ∎

"MARY!"

Jennifer roared, enraged into indiscipline, leaping straight at Violet and attacking with her sharp, clawed hands. She pummelled her opponent repeatedly, shredding away at normally vital organs. But that did not slow her opponent. Instead, Jennifer found herself hearing echoed laughter from . . . somewhere . . .

"Rage . . . power . . . madness . . . yes . . . you must join us . . ."

One of her clawed strikes was caught in mid-air and Jennifer's fury degenerated into fear as she stared into shadowy eyes. She moved for the necklace, even now gleaming at her, but a numbing cold washed over her, freezing her in place, leaving her defenceless.

Jennifer grew paralysed when needle-like fingertips dug hard into her arms. Her mind scrambled, her breath shortened, she could think of nothing but the biting chill, the pronounced thumping of her heart beating; slowing rapidly.

As the voices laughed in concert, she lay helpless, unable to cry out, even though her guts felt torn from her—immobilised as darkness encroached upon her sight, a vision of death and shadow no living mortal eyes should have seen; the last thing they would ever see. The girlish giggling continued, taunting her even through that slow, excruciating process . . .

† †

The first day she regained consciousness after that fateful assault, Mary and Kara told her that Violet had been defeated. But that memory lingered, the pain inflicted in that struggle unlike any other she had ever experienced. Every part of the creature's touch felt like raw, unbottled death.

The worst thing about it, though, was that it had taken her out of the fight. She'd left her best friend Kara with no more help than a broken woman as protection—someone she hadn't known for forty-eight hours. Being dead, or just gravely wounded, meant that she could not save them, whatever they faced.

And if she went down, what chance did they have? That would have been two others she couldn't help. And proud as she was of

Mary and Kara for defeating the most powerful enemies they had run into to date, she resented the fact that they reminded her of her failure that day; the most dangerous time either of them had ever faced.

There would be more danger, she *knew* that for a fact. And because of it, she had to prepare. Get herself at least fighting fit again. She amazed Mary with the speed she was able to run, after returning to her feet. "It's a bloody miracle you're still with us at all," she had told her. It especially reminded Jennifer that Mary kicked the life back into her when retrieved from of all places, a morgue. Yet another favour owed.

So it started with runs around the mansion. As she worked on her conditioning, Grenshall Manor's own condition also improved. Every day, Mary and her new staff toiled to restore a former glory— or to add a contemporary touch in a way only the new lady of the manor's artistic eye could. In the more recent evenings, Jennifer helped out where she could, hefting stones and climbing to parts others had difficulty reaching for repairs. It was all good for her natural return to shape.

She'd been running for longer than she thought—now in unfamiliar territory. She looked up, trying to find a landmark, a street name, anything to tell her where she'd gone. It was probably time to head home.

Against the moonlit sky, she saw a flash of shadow amidst the darkness. It had gone as soon as she picked it up, but there had definitely been something. She looked around, and nothing seemed out of the ordinary elsewhere. There couldn't have been anything there. She shrugged and continued running.

She made it ten steps before another shadow flitted by. Too late to be birds. Too densely populated and bright—unlikely to be bats. Too big. Wrong movement. It had just leapt across a building. But cameras pervaded the streets of London. The police would rapidly look into it if they deemed it suspicious.

Her hair stood on end. Then, she closed her eyes as a blinding flash sizzled around her. Vehicles stopped and darkness fell. The visual effect was reminiscent of what she had seen of an electromagnetic pulse. But the rest did not follow.

Physically, she had no evidence of a device of suitable power being unleashed around her. But a quick look around told her nothing new about the situation. The only thing she had seen came from looking up. It was just the one lead. She took it and found a foothold on a nearby building.

Jennifer started climbing, the stone on the side of the building slippery. But, she fought for every grip, and clung with great strength. She wobbled, the balance awkward. Arms and legs coiled, she forced her way up, finally gathering momentum and gaining her stride.

She reached the top and looked across the rooftop. She was alone, as far as she could tell. But this was a better vantage point than where she had been, and, at least she reinforced her technique in the climb.

Surely the emergency power would kick in before too long? Almost as she had the thought, there were a brief flash from hundreds of lights as far as the eye could see. But, as suddenly as they had come on, they flashed off.

What gives?

She saw several flashes of movement. More shadows, climbing the surrounding the roofs nearby. She heard a whizzing sound behind her. Without thinking, she dashed for the nearest extractor fan and leapt over it, forward rolling as she landed. She dragged herself to the edge of the vent and sat up, peering from behind cover.

Jennifer spotted the hook before an individual clad completely in dark, loose clothing and a face mask reached the top. They retrieved their climbing equipment and moved towards her. An electronic whisper sounded as the climber approached. She slid around the opposite side of the fan and watched. He was armed, but as far as she could see, bore no resemblance to any local police team or military squad. She'd walked right into something else.

"Number Four in place," he whispered, not beyond her strong hearing. A year ago, she could have leapt the fan and taken him down before he knew she was there. She still had a chance, but she needed to know more. Staying low, she crawled closer, waiting as he positioned himself on the edge of the roof.

There it was again. That flash of shadow. It went past, well before she had any idea what it was. Still a large shadow. Still flowing.

Then again. An adjacent rooftop. Right by the standing guard. The shadow flickered into sight again, then vanished just as soon as it appeared. She got a better look this time. Person-sized. Wings? No. A cloak was more likely. But the vanishing was more difficult.

She could sense a trail. That smell. She had grown accustomed to it. That was why she hadn't picked up on it faster. It was like . . . distilled *death* to those with senses as acute as hers had been, but it wasn't forgettable either. It was the same stench that Grenshall Manor reeked of, if one knew where to check. Not like Mary. The sense around her had changed.

No. This was more like that awful Gate Chamber Mary had told her about, but she had never seen for herself. Mary claimed to be in full control of it now, but Jennifer could still sense it. Jennifer had no reason to doubt her friend, for anything the rightful owner of Grenshall Manor had said to her since they met had been right.

But it—the shadow—had gone again, whatever . . . *whoever* it was. What she knew: the squad had spread out around the buildings. Yet, she had never checked her exact whereabouts. She intended to do that when she had given up for the day and ready to head home. Hence, it was time to check the nearest landmarks and work it out.

She recognised one of the buildings, not too far ahead. The British Museum. A useful reference point. And one that the intruder had been staring straight at. They were *all* pointing in that direction. She guessed that must have been their concern.

As she stared, the shadow returned, right there. It moved quickly, flitting around down there, near other figures. They had dropped to the ground as she stared. This thing was causing harm. It was time to act.

She leapt on to the fan and then down behind the guard. But she stumbled.

"Wha—?"

She launched an uppercut from the unbalanced stance. She caught him and eased him to the ground, smashing a fist into his facemask. Certain he was unconscious, she dragged him out of sight and slipped him out of his fatigues, putting them on herself. It wasn't a perfect fit, but it would do.

Then she plotted a route and moved back to the other edge of the building. She launched at speed and vaulted on to the fan, then on to another protrusion on the building, before propelling herself with all her strength over the edge to a slightly lower building.

Jennifer knew someone was on that rooftop too, but her landing was sloppy, putting her right in front of him. She punched him hard in the gut and reworked her footing before seizing him by the head and throwing him over her own. She brought a foot down the side of his skull, taking him down and out.

With no time to hide him anywhere, Jennifer left him and ran again. She leapt, looking for flag poles, lowered platforms and hanging ledges—anything to descend quickly but keep from alerting them. Down she went, across and around, but her lack of practice and familiarity with the scenery caused her to slip a couple of times.

For an ordinary person training daily in the art of *parkour*, freerunning, that would have been dangerous enough. For an untrained individual, it was damn near suicidal. To Jennifer, who needed only watch once and was as good as trained, but so very off her game, the risk fell somewhere in between.

Her grip slipped once too often and she fell on her back, winding herself. But she picked herself up and moved before she could bitch too hard about it. There were still too many armed villains in the area. That bump was nothing compared to being discovered.

The nearest guard had heard the fall, try as she might to mask it. She pressed herself against a wall around a corner and waited for him to check. But he looked spooked. They were in communication. At least two of them had failed to report. They were aware they had been compromised. There was no turning back for her now, even if she had foiled their plans.

No such luck. They held their positions but pulled out their weapons. Jennifer leapt in full sprint and, using a fixed camera, swung herself straight onto a lower building. Even as her feet hit the ground, more smoothly this time, she made the connection.

The pulse had put the cameras out of action, as much as the power. The assault was anything but spontaneous, and couldn't have been easily planned. Whatever she had gotten herself into, she could probably have used backup—but that was impossible now. It was either let it happen or finish the job.

She noticed herself blowing again. She was normally better than this. Clinging on to the edge, she lowered herself down and found herself on a hotel, the *Kingsley by Thistle*. A good vantage point. Maybe she could figure out what was actually going on from there.

People milled around below her. They seemed edgy. Many held small objects in their hands, no doubt mobile devices they realised were not functioning at the moment. There was no light coming from them, but her eagle-like eyesight gave her a hint. They had nothing to do with whatever was going on around them. Most were moving away, trying to retreat to find a source of illumination. It was one of the most reliable, most primordial instincts of human behaviour. To find safety.

A tempting alternative, but Jennifer knew such an elaborate operation no doubt meant someone or something was in jeopardy. Against the tide of the crowds, one other person stood stock still, but not dressed as the others she had seen. The individual stood too distant to see in great detail, but her calm poise amidst the upheaval caught her attention. She leaned in for a closer look.

To her left, another of the mysterious squad raised a rifle. Long range. And aiming downwards at the person she was looking at. She powered herself upright, and flew at the gunman, first throwing him off his aim with her lunge. Her momentum took him to his knees, and she wasted no time. She kicked the gun from his loose grip and slipped her arms around his throat, squeezing as he thrashed around to escape. She leaned backwards and snapped her legs around his waist, ensuring maximum leverage and squeezed harder. His resistance quickly stopped as he slipped from consciousness.

"Number Ten: I said take the shot!"

She seized his radio and the grappling hook from his belt. She then ran to the edge of the building, securing the hook and tying the end of the attached rope to her waist. If Number Ten wasn't available to take that shot, someone else would very soon. She took the plunge, rappelling down the building with professional precision. She kept one eye on her target all the way down.

Near the bottom, she could see the intended victim: a young female police constable who had been playing with her radio but had given up and searched the street. She spotted Jennifer's descent, and headed over, pulling her asp from her belt and flicking it to full length. "Stop right there!"

"It's not me you want, Constable."

The officer hesitated, reaching also for another pocket. Jennifer detached herself from the rope and stepped forward.

"Stay where you are!"

"Look, this whole thing's deliberate. Something's up—we haven't time to waste."

"I know."

"Someone just tried to kill you. Someone else will probably try in a moment. You need to move. Right now."

"What do you mean, somebody—?"

"Talk in cover." Jennifer ran to a nearby alleyway and beckoned the policewoman to do likewise. The constable followed with extreme caution.

Jennifer kept a good look around, but was aware of the understandably jittery officer ahead of her. "Inspector Hammond." It was a long shot, but it was the only name she had; the only link that had any chance of saving the woman without resorting to violence. "I need you to stay out of sight, get to the working power and call in. Ask for Inspector Hammond and tell him this is from Dr. Mellencourt's friend."

"Look, I can't just—"

"Whoever this is, they've gone to a lot of trouble to do whatever it is they are planning. I think they're hitting the British Museum."

"Even with the power down, they'll have no chance."

"There's a bunch of them. They're armed and they've got something the museum guards really won't be able to handle. Nor will you."

"And you will?"

"Previous experience. But I need to hurry. Please do this for me."

With that, Jennifer turned and made her way out of the alleyway. "Hey!"

Stop shouting. You'll get us both killed. She turned and threw a finger to her lips before bursting into a sprint.

Jennifer had lost little of her speed and quickly covered the ground to her intended destination. It wasn't going to be easy, but she had to go for it. As expected, the entrances appeared secure, but a closer look inside revealed several guards on the floor. They were motionless, not even breathing. Her physical enhancement may have gone, but her additional senses had not dulled.

More lives may have been in danger in there. She had no time to waste. She tried the front door. Locked. She ran to a trade entrance. Also locked. "Damn." She would have to hit the roofs again.

The presence of several of the robbers on the roof came as no surprise to her. But none were doing anything other than standing on an over-watch pattern.

"Thirteen. Hostile located, directly below. Remember mission protocols. Over."

"You have a better shot? Over."

"Confirmed. Taking now."

All pretences of subtlety now gone, she released her grip from the rooftop as the shooter grazed her shoulder on the way down. She gritted her teeth and supressed a howl as she hit the ground hard. Rolling backward, she cursed as she lay flat, her legs dead from the fall. Anyone else, on a good day, might have broken them both.

She rolled across the ground before the second shot could find its target. She forced herself back to her feet and leapt behind a pillar, just as the third slammed into her cover.

"Seven. Why isn't the target neutralised?"

"Target just leapt off the roof."

"And still moving?"

"Fully active."

"Mission compromised. Prepare to abort."

"Negative." This voice was female, a strong French accent evident. "First team are about to acquire the targets. Deal with the problem. And any witnesses."

If she stayed there, Jennifer was dead. Even if those shots remained inaccurate, the strike team were coming for her. She made a dash for the side, weaving as pot shots smacked around her. But it wasn't as if there was a convenient window. Roof glass was likely her only way in. That was going to hurt. Even if she survived the armed robbers.

She scaled the building again, but this time, searched for the nearest guard. Clinging to a ledge, she edged across until she was closer to a pair of boots. The guard looked in the other direction—but not for long.

With all her strength, she lifted herself further up with one arm and with the second, swept at his heels. He landed on his backside, kicking her in the face, but she clung on grimly. The guard swung his feet at her, but she blocked with her free hand before catching one of his ankles.

She launched the other hand straight at his face. He caught her arm but soon realised his life was in her hands. His delay allowed her to drag herself up. He began a muffled yell, but she rammed her forehead into his nose, then straddled him. She swung several punches until he stopped moving.

The noise had alerted the others. She pulled herself up to a crouch and stayed low as she ran across the roof, looking for any glass areas. Another guard took aim. She threw herself down on the glass and rolled as the shots came in, until she found cover once more.

She waited for the robber to close in and rolled around to the other side of the glass dome. When he came within reach, she launched to her feet and grabbed his rifle, twisting the barrel away before he could raise it, then kicked a hamstring and dropped him to one knee. One well-aimed chop to the back of his head finished the job.

Retaining the rifle, she ran back for the glass roof and took a flying leap to evade a series of shots. With all her might, she slammed the weapon butt into one of the bullet-cracked panes and shattered it. She repeated this several times until there was a suitable gap and then threw herself into the hole, just as a hail of rounds flew over her.

Another long drop, but she was more prepared for it this time and rolled as if it was a tenth of the height. Now, she needed to find the first team. Almost in total darkness, she crouched behind one of the centre exhibits and looked around, hoping for other light sources. Instead, she found another downed guard. She reached for his neck, checking for a pulse. Nothing. She shook her head and looked deep into the darkness. Another body. In a swift but crouched hustle, she checked him, too, on the way past and again saw no signs of life. But he led to another.

She soon picked up a different trail. That cold, abhorrent whiff of death that she picked up on the rooftop. That was the trail to follow. She moved fast, all the while focusing on what was at the end of the scent.

Mistake. The cloaked figure flew out of nowhere and tackled her to the ground, but her momentum freed her as she rolled backward. Jennifer got to her knees, but the shadow moved faster, punching her twice in the face and knocking her backward. As the assailant closed in for the kill, Jennifer swept hard with her leg, and floored the opponent. She crawled forward and leapt—

But the woman vanished into thin air. Jennifer landed on nothing. She tried to re-establish the scent, but a knee connected with her face. The lightning-fast attacker then kicked her hard, leaving her flat. Jennifer heard a sword unsheathing, but even with her sight, could barely see it. Punch-drunk, she offered no resistance as another kick rained in on her jaw and the sword tapped her neck with a cold touch of death she remembered intimately. Panic set in. She knew this was the end.

"Face of war."

It was just a whisper, but it echoed across the museum just as the sword rose. The killer hesitated. Jennifer attempted a sweep on her adversary, but her strike simply passed through the cloaked figure. She doubted a repeat attempt would produce different results. She continued to roll and made a run for it.

The cloaked figure appeared from nowhere in front of her and thrust a powerful kick into her face, quick as a flash. Jennifer fell backward, the ethereal onyx blade against her throat. It chilled to the touch. In her experience, only Mary could move like that. But this person could fight.

A woman with bright red hair emerged, her arm around a tall, lean, tattooed man with a shaven head. Neither were uniformed. The red-haired woman clung to the tattooed figure like glue.

"Are you certain?" the cloaked figure asked. Her voice was accented, possibly Asian.

"He said it. When is he ever wrong?"

"Then why was this so easy?"

The red haired woman frowned. "Do you want to explain to *him* that you killed her? Let him make the decision."

"As you wish."

The cloaked woman swung a rapid kick at Jennifer's head.

"She certainly has resilience." A second and third kick sent everything dark.

2.

Everything ached—an unusual occurrence in itself. On the plus side, it meant Jennifer felt the effects of the fight, simple aches and pains, cuts and bruises, instead of the cold, debilitating torture of months before. At least she felt *alive*.

How long had she been out? A few seconds? A few hours? And also, *where* was she? Lying under covers on an uncomfortable bed which was reminiscent of a ship's cabin, in a room she could barely stretch out twice in. The ceiling didn't look to give her much clearance either.

The next challenge was how to get out of there, wherever there was. She got out from under the sheets—and realised she had been relieved of all clothing, other than her sports underwear.

What?

An uncomfortable situation just became even more so. She looked around for her clothes. The room was sparsely furnished. Other than the bed, not even a rug covered the wooden flooring.

However, on a very low table lay a stunning, blue silk dress. Jennifer lacked Kara's expertise on matters of fashion, but felt quite certain the gown was of exceptional quality, and definitely expensive. *Someone* was dropping an unsubtle hint as to how they wanted her dressed.

As much as the wardrobe demand aggravated, the real question was why they didn't off her when they had the chance, especially if they knew what would happen when she got out of there. Unless whoever held her just didn't care.

Her thoughts drifted on to who the hell the robbers were, and how the cloaked one took her down so easily. That ruffled her greatly. Sure, her condition remained some way off a hundred percent full strength, but she had no idea she was *that* rusty. Her opponent moved faster than anyone she had previously encountered. Organised, disciplined *and* well-equipped; it seemed quite clear the gang members were no common criminals. And some of them also had additional . . . advantages.

She returned to thoughts of how to escape. The walls were impenetrable old stone, whilst the door was wooden but looked solid. Jennifer went over and gave the handle a try, unsurprised to find that it didn't turn far. Leaning hard against it didn't budge it either. It felt unshakeable. If she was anywhere near full strength, it would have been worth testing harder, but at the moment, nothing doing.

She supposed there were some advantages to not running at full strength—opponents would likely underestimate her. Because, besides healing her recent wounds, it was fair to say she was feeling better than she had in a while. Maybe if she just stayed there for a couple of days, they'd have the real Jennifer to contend with. And then they'd be in trouble.

Only problem was, someone clearly wanted her to keep an appointment with them. And she made her own damn appointments.

Justified paranoia rather high, she checked for cameras in the room. A cursory scan, followed by a more detailed squint, revealed nothing. If they were hidden, they'd done a really good job of hiding them.

Cheap perverts ruled out at the least, she went for the dress and dived into it. She began to zip up the back—it was better than nothing after all—but then an idea came to her.

"Hey!" she called, in half-zipped attire, and battered the door. "I'm awake. But I need a little help getting into this thing."

She cupped an ear to the door and heard footsteps close by. A key turned in the lock and she leapt backward and to the left, alert and waiting.

The door opened but not to full width. The guard, dressed as most of the others she'd seen, appeared with nobody behind him, armed and aggressive. "Get ready," he said, a French accent to his voice. "The boss wants to see you."

Good. She was too valuable to shoot. "Looking forward to it," she purred, turning her back to him. "Now give me a hand."

"Stop messing around and get dre—"

Jennifer was already where she wanted to be. She smashed an elbow cleanly upward into his chin, then grabbed his arm. With total control, she twisted it, turning him the opposite direction and drove him head-first into the wall twice. Guiding his unconscious body down on to the bed, she peered outside in all directions. Only one guard in sight—the one she'd knocked out.

Sloppy of them. *Or too easy.*

She wasn't going to make a run for it dressed for an awards ceremony if she could help it. She stripped the guard before ditching the dress in exchange for his body armour and more practical clothing. She examined the submachine gun but dismissed appropriating it as a terrible idea. Instead, she simply relieved him of it, sure to remove the magazine. Using the dress, she tied his arms to the head of the bed and then crept outside, quietly closing the door.

A shout came from her left. Sadly, in French. Checking on a colleague?

She dashed right, staying as light on her feet as she could. She reached the end of the corridor and was again faced with a choice of left or right. Behind her, the guard came into view. She pointed back towards the room at her old prison quarters before darting left. Her cover would be gone in seconds, but at least she would be away from him.

A bit of running took her close to another guard, but she pointed frantically behind her, just long enough for him to hesitate. She threw a fist into his face before he could respond, then swept him to the ground and straddled him, punching him out cold. Jennifer rolled off him and pushed him into the wall, but there was nowhere to hide him, and after she heard the gunman at the room raise the alarm, there was no time either.

Only time to run. She bolted into a corridor: two more guards with rifles levelled. She pounced on the first guard on her way past and took him down with a smack to his booted ankle. Already inside the second guard's reach, she seized his leading wrist, then rolled her back into his body and slammed him to a wall once, then again, before smashing her head right back into his nose. She smacked her forearm into his chin several times until he slumped to the ground.

She took the weapon but removed the magazine and the temptation to fire.

Onwards again. Another choice at the corridor, and a guard near the left side. She raised the weapon before he was aware. "Drop it. Now."

He looked around. Stalling. But her bluff was failing anyway; he knew where to look on her gun. But his hesitation provided the split second she needed. She swung the gun around and smacked the butt into his temple, and followed up with a high kick for good measure.

She moved with stealth through another corridor. The lack of windows or stairs narrowed her options greatly. But better to keep a move on and hope an escape route availed itself.

A staircase at last, leading upwards. That told her she was at the lowest possible floor. And heading up usually led to a point of escape. After a cursory check for hostile activity, she advanced.

The corridor up the flight of stairs was better illuminated. A large door stood at the end of the corridor, solid but perhaps leading out. She ran away from the door and stopped to assess the obstruction in detail. Much as she wanted to escape, a sigil within a brass circle which looked recently defaced caught her eye. Within it stood out a stylistic letter 'W' and an equally ornate Omega emblem behind it.

Perilous as Jennifer's situation was, seeing it changed things.

That symbol struck a familiar chord. She'd seen it before, but associated it with a person rather than a building. She'd never learned what the symbol truly meant. But she associated it with safety, security. Someone she could trust.

The only person she had ever seen with it:

Alice.

Everywhere she went, Alice wore a small brooch shaped as that symbol. Given the general circumstances under which they used to meet, though it was a curiosity, Jennifer had never asked about it. The woman was normally busy saving her life.

But what was it doing in this place? Up on *that* wall? Where the hell *was* she?

Is that why they haven't just offed me yet? Friends of Alice?

They couldn't have been friendly. There were better ways to express that than kicking her in the head. And whatever she did or didn't know about Alice, she wasn't a common thief. She wouldn't have kept them as company either. It just wasn't her. So, whoever these people were, they *weren't* there to help Jennifer in any way. Time to get out of there, then.

She listened for hostile movements, attempting to isolate footsteps, shouting. But her enemy was quiet, if they were around— more than the last lot, at least. She ran to the end of the corridor which offered a left or right choice but no signs of the *right* way.

She crouched and peered around the corner, both directions. All clear. But each had doors roughly equidistant at each end. There wasn't an obvious route to take.

Decision time. It was too exposed there for any real stealth, but there was plenty of room for trouble in either direction. Still, she wasn't going to work out an escape route by standing around.

Turn left.

She charged as fast as she could, making her way to the closed door.

There was a whistle through the air and a crack. Jennifer was on her back, staring at the ceiling by the time the sound registered. She spluttered and choked.

The blow had caught her right in the throat, but there was nobody in sight. She stood alone and frustrated in the empty corridor, with neither a door nor a convenient grate nearby.

Three deep breaths later, she returned to her feet. She couldn't see anyone . . . but sensed there was still someone around.

Concentrate.

Nobody was that damn good. Unless they were . . .

The slice through the wind caught her again, this blow straight under her chin. It knocked her backward and off her feet. She straightened herself up, then smacked the ground and cried out in frustration, knowing exactly who she was up against. Although she didn't, which just aggravated her more.

"Show yourself!" Her opponent did not oblige.

A different approach, then. She listened, even sniffed. She picked up that scent of death, of decay that she had become familiar with over the past year. Try as she might to deny it or escape the fact, she smelled the same stench that lingered around Grenshall Manor, around Mary.

And that was why it took time to pick up on; in the months in which she had barely moved from the bed, she had grown used to the presence of Mary and her Unresting world now. But that knowledge gave her a hint of what she was dealing with.

It probably wasn't a ghost. And not a mindless brain-eater or pumped-up brute like that Natalie or Thomas Barber, puppets of the deadly Violet. Living, then, just like Mary. Only whoever it was could fight—and pretty well.

Jennifer ran the other way and then stopped and sniffed. It was as good as she had. She caught the scent again, but almost too late as something cracked towards her. She raised an elbow and blocked the strike before lashing a jab forward. She caught something, but her opponent left her range again.

"You're a right pain, you know?" Jennifer snarled. She attempted to hold the scent, but the enemy was moving too quickly. She couldn't hold there; reinforcements could come at any moment. She headed back to the door, edging cautiously, not running this time. She continued to rely on her nose, but the smell of death was all around her. The ghost walker could have been anywhere.

She reached for the door. As she got a hand on the grip, her unseen opponent seized her arm and wrenched it around. Jennifer leaned and twisted her body to keep her arm free. She got a punch in the face for her trouble but at least got clear of an arm lock.

She launched another jab in front of her, but connected with nothing. A kick connected with her stomach, then two punches to the face and an elbow floored her again. She swept her leg, knowing where the opponent must have been—in front of her—but again, it was in vain.

"You really should yield, or someone will end up getting hurt." The voice echoed in the air around her, a female voice with a hint of an accent, Indian perhaps.

"It's not going to be me," Jennifer countered. But she wasn't sure of the truth of that statement. She hadn't affected her opponent but had been floored three times, which not many had managed up to that point. And she couldn't even *see* who was hitting her.

She stretched her hands and felt a familiar tickling sensation within them. But they did not elongate into weapons as she desired. The ability to create those razor-like talons that had helped her in the past had deserted her.

She didn't want to lose. But she had bitten off far more than she could chew with her fearless foray into danger. It looked like she had entered the fray too soon, her own strength nothing like she had known it to be in the past.

She'd have foiled an ordinary robbery attempt, no problem. She could handle competent and well-armed guards quite comfortably. But that cloaked menace was another matter. She had no answer to that speed, that movement; the fact that she couldn't just engage in a straight fight.

"I'm *not* going back into that hole." She tried to get up again and leapt for the door, but another heel to the face put her right back down. It was only then that she realised what she had said. *I'm not going back into that hole.* That was what she had said in her early teens. That stepmother of hers. She hadn't felt that weak since those days.

To yield, to stay down, was not an option. It was escape—or die trying. And she knew full well if they wanted her dead by now, she would have been. *Whoever* they were.

"Fine," echoed the voice. "You'll just heal up again anyway." A rush of wind howled around Jennifer's ear and then the air rushed out of her lungs from a hard, unseen, kick to the gut. A flurry of punches and kicks connected, with her no closer to knowing where each blow came from. Her resistance ended as she hit the deck.

3.

An overpowering fruity fragrance assaulted Jennifer's sense of smell and brought her round. She attempted to spring upward but found herself restrained by thick rope binding her to a chair. Anger flooded over her. To be knocked out once in the space of twenty-four hours was careless. Twice was just unheard of.

She stopped thrashing and took in her surroundings. She sat in a dining hall, very old in appearance, medieval almost, but somewhat run-down, deteriorating in places. Yet, the lengthy table before her appeared intact and rock solid. The spread on it most certainly resembled a banquet of times gone by; the only space left on it no doubt to accommodate plates.

As her vision cleared more, the only other individual present at the table caught her attention. Opposite from where she sat at one end, some distance away, a man with dark hair, neat and cut just above the shoulder. Piercing green eyes peered at her, striking even from that distance.

He wore a suit, clearly tailored to his build, athletic but not bulky. He stared at her, assessed, perhaps judged her, as her thoughts again turned to an escape plan. Had her razor fingers not deserted her at a critical juncture, she would already have been free. But then what?

He didn't look overly troubled by her presence, and probably rightly so, considering her latest performances. Her ghostly opponent was nowhere to be seen; a familiar problem. However, neither did any scent of death or decay linger in the air.

Though bound, Jennifer wasn't gagged. "So . . ." she drawled. "How come I'm still alive, then?"

The host laughed heartily, never taking his eyes off her. "Honestly. You have quite a low opinion of us after so short a meeting." He also spoke with an accent she couldn't quite place. Perhaps Italian. "Who do you think I am?"

"Gang boss, maybe?"

"Straight to the stereotypes, I see. Do you see any gangsters around here?"

Jennifer scanned the room. She could probably lose the ropes, but, assuming the ghost walker wasn't there, she wouldn't be far. The armed guards evenly spaced against the walls of the massive hall posed a more immediate threat.

A door stood at the back of the room behind the host, who she knew nothing about, but she saw no windows at all. She heard another door close behind her as well. Perhaps a changing of the guard? But, taken altogether, it meant too many X-factors, a maze of a place and all manner of other difficulties to contend with. It was hopeless.

To make matters worse, she couldn't pretend to be useful to them for much longer, intentionally or otherwise. "So you're not your typical organised crime outfit. But your boys were still trying to raid the British Museum. That makes you robbers—criminals. Stays in the category of organised crime, yes?"

The man twitched and shook his head. He looked disappointed in her. "The weak or dull mind would assume us common criminals. To dismiss my collective as merely lawless rabble, which we are not, would be a grave error.

"What happened to the dress I provided for you? It took a great deal of trouble and considerable expense to find something appropriate, and so well-tailored."

She shifted awkwardly in her seat. The idea of how total strangers could achieve a custom fit made her skin crawl. But she sat straight and glared defiance at her host. "You're right. It looked extremely fetching on the lackey you sent. I liked his attire better."

His pause told her that she'd succeeding in being suitably irksome. But his poker face at least rivalled her own. "I liked mine on you better." She felt dirtier with each of his words. "It cannot be coincidence that we chanced upon such a competent vigilante. Or is it possible that you are simply too dense to realise who it is you chose to oppose?"

She *did* resent that. He *wanted* her to. "Which do *you* think it is?"

He denied her an immediate answer, preferring instead to keep staring at her. After a moment's analysis, he responded. "You know what I think? I think you're someone who went looking for trouble. A part of me hopes you do not find yourself short. However, I would like to know how you lasted as long as you did against my court."

"Court?" An unusual name for any gang, for certain. "In honesty with you, I don't know."

And if I'd been anywhere near my best, they wouldn't have lasted nearly as long against me.

She forced a grin. "You want to untie me? I'm not in any danger of escaping."

The host looked amused but soon afterwards nodded. One of the guards shouldered his weapon and advanced toward her, then released her from her binding.

She considered the escape opportunity: a clean chance to swiftly take out the guard and restrain him. But that would have meant taking a hostage—which wasn't an option—and would result in no advantage that she didn't already have. Also, in that room, whichever direction she faced, she had her back to someone. *And the ghost walker.*

And all this before she took into account the unknown quantity of the suited man at the other end of the table.

Meanwhile, the guard did not take his eyes off her for the duration of his chore. He had a soldier's eye, assessing her assessment. He returned to his post.

Her hands now free once more, she looked down at them and channelled the combative mentality she had such a firm grip on. That irritating tickle ran through her finger bones again, but not so much as a rapidly-growing fingernail sprouted. Thwarted before she started, her attention returned to the other end of the table.

"Thank you," she said, an air of sincerity about her. She examined her captor up and down, trying to work out what, if anything, had got him to the position in which he sat.

It pleased her to know that the ability to see chromatic auras hadn't deserted her entirely. She could extend her sight, sharpen her focus to such an extent as to see the essential energies of just about anything. When she said she had a bad vibe, she meant it like few others. And the skill contributed to her lack of illness in her teens.

From a brief snapshot, she confirmed that nobody was attempting to poison her, and that her captor displayed no obvious special powers or talent she could fathom.

"Well, you appear to have seen sense," the man replied, tucking a napkin into his collar. He snapped his fingers and one of the rearmost guards banged twice on the back door. Within seconds, unarmed staff in waiting attire rushed through and attended the pair at the table.

The table spread was quickly lifted, dish by dish, and they began to serve. Jennifer waved away a plate of prosciutto just as her staffer was about to serve. The waiter nodded and exchanged his plate for a fruit cocktail. His superior glared at Jennifer with some apparent disdain.

"*The Face of War* . . ." He let the words run across his tongue as he examined her further. "The Face of War." Repeating it did not add conviction to his tone. "A fruit cocktail person. Such a thought hardly strikes fear into the mortal heart, does it?"

"I've never called myself anything like that." She lightly rubbed her chin. "That's something to do with why I'm here though, isn't it? That name."

He grinned, folding a quantity of the meat around his fork before forcing every bit into his mouth. "You really have no idea, do you?" Without waiting until he had finished chewing, he continued. "Our organisation has quite recently acquired the services of a relative prophet, Vortext. When he speaks, we must listen, for he has always had something very useful to say on the rare occasions words leave his mouth."

Jennifer's eyes narrowed. She cut a piece of melon into a small chunk and scooped it into her mouth, sure to maintain eye contact. She made a point to finish chewing before answering. "Oh?"

He kept eating even as his servant continued to fill his plate. "He has been an exceptionally reliable find. Both of them were actually, him and that girlfriend of his. But you seem to have inconvenienced her somewhat."

I've no idea what he's talking about.

"Inconvenience is the story of my life. But tell me—what did I do?"

The host twitched, about to say something, but he restrained himself. "Nothing insurmountable."

She snapped with predatory speed. "Then why mention it? Is this something to do with me being the 'Chosen One'?"

He glared at her, ashen. "Do not mock that which you fail to understand."

She leaned forward on the table. "If I'm that important to you, I can mock freely. You already told me you're keeping me alive for a reason, so you can hardly force me to take your threats seriously."

The host relaxed, perhaps a show for her benefit. "You are only alive as long as it takes to exhaust my investigation, so enjoy your bravado while it lasts. If only you could see the painting I had back at my home. It carries the title, *The Face of War,* and I have it dated in origin from the sixteenth century."

"So?"

"So it looks exactly like you. That is no doubt why Vortext mentioned it. He is an impressive creature, I must say. At the moment, that painting is my most valuable treasure. And I believe it holds great secrets. If only we could unlock them."

Her eyes narrowed. "Not a gang boss but an art thief, then? One with serious resources, at that."

"Art?" he smirked. He took a moment to shovel some of his food down. "I—*we* seek the world's truest treasures. Creations well beyond plebeian understanding."

"Like a painting with someone who bears a passing resemblance to me? Tell me, what did you get for your troubles in the end?"

He shook his head. "Nothing, thanks to your interference. We had spent weeks working out the logistics of that operation, and had a strict deadline. Your running loose disrupted our schedule beyond repair. Things mobilised rather quickly."

"And yet you had enough time to carry me."

"I told you: when Vortext speaks, my court listens."

"You keep saying that," Jennifer snorted. "What are you, some kind of prince or something?"

He grinned. "Yes. You have already met some of my court."

Jennifer leaned forward, and gnawed on the fruit in front of her. "*Whose* court?"

He stood and waved one of his guards towards the door, then gave a sweeping bow. "I, madam, am Gianfranco Manta. And in the places I walk, I am very much a prince. Please, let me introduce the Manta Court to you." His face dropped into a scowl. "So that you don't get any more ideas of running away."

Suits me. I'll get a better idea of what I'm up against.

"I would be honoured." She gave a mocking bow in return. He ignored the baiting. From the rear door, the ghost walker entered, fully corporeal. She remained wrapped in the grey cloak, which veiled the wearer exceptionally well. She walked close to Jennifer and gave a smug look, then took her place at the table some distance to the left of their guest.

Even though fully physical, the woman's movement was wraith-like, and she kept sheathed within her flowing robes a sword. Jennifer spotted its bejewelled hilt. It reminded her of that knife she had seen Mary with from time to time within Grenshall Manor.

Though not wishing to turn her back, her attention returned to the door as a tall, dark-skinned man walked in, slim but wiry. His head was shaven, imprinted with tattoos of a design she couldn't pick out. In contrast to the overconfidence she had seen in the woman, he looked distant, to the point of being elsewhere.

A striking young woman held his hand. She wore a bright red dress, with hair, boots and lips to match. She held her forehead with her spare hand, and no sooner had Jennifer noticed the action then her own head bristled with a fierce itch.

Jennifer distinctly felt they had previously crossed paths, and she couldn't attribute it to the memory of Manta's recent words. But that couldn't have been right. And yet, something about her struck familiar, like perhaps they had been together for some purpose or other. She attuned her chromatic vision to sense whether any other tell-tale signs lingered.

Feelings of powerlessness, pain, and death all lashed against her in one sharp slam. Her knees buckled and she seized the table for support. She blinked herself back to mundane eyes and it all vanished, as if it were nothing more than savage daydreaming.

Despite her surroundings, the red-haired woman exuded a sense of calm, trust, warmth, and a cute innocence free of any possible threat. But it seemed false, a trick of the mind. Jennifer's instincts screamed danger.

She attributed some of the malevolent presence to a knife-shaped shade she saw pulsing somewhere near the woman's thigh, a well-concealed weapon. However, the power Jennifer detected couldn't hide from her augmented sight. It reminded her in presence of the weapon Mary carried, only more like an evil twin. That made some sense.

The blade her friend, Mary, carried once held the soul-devouring sapphire which contributed to Jennifer's near-death. More infamously set into a necklace, it became the source of power that caused dozens of deaths and a reign of chaos which engulfed London, and brought a raft of undead, ghostly, and otherwise terrifying encounters. On Mary's knife, a hole gaped where the jewel was once embedded.

If that knife was anything like that, and in troublesome hands, then being trapped in this madhouse would be the least of Jennifer's worries.

"So that's what you meant by treasures you're after," she mumbled, looking around. The tattooed man and the redhead both took seats on the right hand side of the table. She reasoned that the ornate weapon of the cloaked woman was probably of some concern as well.

"Let's see." She was louder this time. "We have Vortext, the prophet. The cloaked warrior, over there. And you." She pointed at the woman in red, who clung to Vortext as if he was set to blow away. "What did you do to me?"

Her target looked over at Manta for a moment; not a pleasant look either. But Manta shrugged, gesturing back to her. "Yes, Cerise," he said, tapping his foot. "What did you do, exactly?"

Cerise stopped rubbing her head and cast Jennifer a murderous glance. "She's got something to hide," she said. "And she's very determined to do so. But her life has been far from boring."

"What do you mean by that?" Jennifer asked. Her head itched again.

"I witnessed you take a fall that should have, at the very least, stopped you ever walking again. And you caused us a great inconvenience before and after. Not possible from an ordinary person."

Jennifer reached for the nearest salad bowl but her designated servant intercepted and promptly loaded her plate. It was too much like those months holed up at Grenshall Manor. She could work her own spoon now more than capably. "No, thank you." She gently pushed the servant away. Manta nodded at the door. The servants departed at once. "You got me. I'm a freak of nature."

"Not a freak, no," Manta chimed in. "A special talent, certainly. Possibly even worthy of my Court. *The Face of War*? I should like to find out."

"She easily bested several of your guards," the cloaked woman stated. She sat back from the table, out of reach of the food. "Not me, though."

Jennifer felt the wounding taunt. "Off day," she hissed through gritted teeth.

"Which is why you are sitting here now." Manta poured two glasses of an old, wine, expensive by all appearances, from a nearby carafe, but Jennifer declined, preferring a glass of water.

"I—*we* would very much like to see what you can do on a good day." The three others nodded as one. "Still, it was useful to see the competence of my staff tested."

He took a sip of his drink before raising his glass at his court, one by one, and then at the spare seat on his right. His court each raised nearby glasses in reply. "There is a place here for the right people. I hope you will be able to join us."

"Not interested in being a career thief, thanks. I had plenty of chances for that."

"For whom are you so principled?" Cerise asked. "Who do you truly fight for? What made you move against us?"

"Common decency." Jennifer rushed a glass of water down. "What's your deal? It can't be money."

"Why can't it be money?" Cerise said, looking intrigued. "What we are looking for is highly valuable. It would be a lot easier otherwise."

"Well, that's true. But it means more to you than just that. What's your game?"

"I simply believe in a better world,"

"Yeah right." Even as Jennifer spoke, Cerise's words seemed to take on an ironclad sincerity. Not enough to sway her own opinion, but she was beginning to see how Cerise had found her way into the court. It was all very subtle, but there was something about her contradictory to the effervescent young woman who seemed to be sitting there.

"So, a question for you: what's that symbol about—the one all around the place?"

The three looked at each other for a moment. Then, in unison, they gathered their glasses and refilled them before lifting them in the form of a toast. Manta gave Jennifer a moment to follow suit. She did not move. He shrugged. "To Winter's end!" he cried.

"Winter's end!" the others repeated.

"Yeah, I still don't know what you're talking about."

"Of course you don't." Manta drank heartily, then lowered his drink to the table. "Allow us to educate you. You see, there have been some dangerous threats to humanity running around for many years, threats which your politicians and law enforcement establishments have no understanding of. Like yourself, all at the Court have something which makes them exceptional by society standards. That doesn't make any of us 'freaks'. That makes us extraordinary. Which means we have certain . . . responsibilities to the world around us. You have seen for yourself what the Grey Lady here can do."

"That's an unusual name," Jennifer answered, her mouth thankfully moving faster than her mind on this occasion. She'd thought to mention this wasn't the first time she'd seen such powers manifest, but being as her current state of affairs was as a captive, with no guarantee of walking out of this establishment alive, the last thing she wanted to do was to drag her friends into it.

That said, she would have given anything to see Mary pit her mastery of the ghost realm against the Grey Lady's slippery talents. "If it's not too personal a question, what do you all do?" She was staring specifically at Cerise when she asked.

"I'm their best medic," Cerise answered.

"Uh-huh," Jennifer replied, remembering the hidden knife. She looked at Vortext. "I know what you do. But you haven't told them much about me, have you?"

Cerise leaned towards Jennifer, a most un-healer-like look on her face. "You are something of a mystery."

"Glad to hear it." The detainee mirrored Cerise's actions before turning her attention back to Manta. She already knew all she cared to about this 'Grey Lady', too. "So. You were telling me about this sixteenth century painting."

"There is little more to tell. Though I can easily picture you in the plate armour you—she wears in the painting. You have a warrior's eyes, just as I saw on the image."

"Where she is seen, there is always war."

Vortext blurted the words as if he had just woken up, then just as soon as he had, returned to a catatonic state—a disconcerting experience. "Cerise, shut him up before I do."

She shot Manta another glare but stood up and Vortext stood with her. The two left through the door behind Manta.

"Did he blab something he shouldn't have again?" Jennifer asked, suddenly grinning. "What's all this about starting wars?"

Manta, clearly infuriated, took another hefty swig of his wine. "Well, I am in no doubt about his talent even if you might be," he said through gritted teeth. "What he quoted was an inscription on the back of the painting. Again, I have never allowed anyone to see it, but there it is, word for word."

"Surely it's just another art piece worth a few quid you can shift on the black market?"

"It belonged to my grandfather!" he said, bashing his fists against the table. "I would never conceive of selling it, no matter how much it is worth." He slumped back into his chair and spoke in a far quieter voice. "It's all we had left of him. Of anything."

She was about to press him further, but she caught his sense of loss when he spoke. It was genuine; not possible to fake as one who had felt it as she had. Manta's 'grandfather' sounded as 'mother' did to her, or even 'Alice'.

Alice. That symbol. Had she been part of this?

"That business about the 'dawn of spring'," she said instead. "What are you talking about?"

He looked up at her. "Former residents of this place," he simply said. "We are only going to be here temporarily ourselves. Just long enough to accomplish our second . . . task."

"You're planning another robbery?" She didn't give him enough time to answer that. Too many other questions were burning at her. "Former residents? What happened to them?"

"They were very dangerous individuals. They tried to kill me, my court."

"So we had to act." The Grey Lady turned to face Jennifer, having sat motionless for some time. She looked more through

Jennifer than at her, cold, utterly distant eyes in her otherwise pretty face.

Her mind refused to acknowledge the likelihood, but deep down, Jennifer knew exactly what they were getting at. The former residents had been eliminated. These were not people for messing around.

But neither was she. As against her as the odds were here, she had found herself not just amongst thieves, but murderers, too. That last day she had seen Alice Winter, she was eighteen years old. She had been officially adopted at fifteen, and hadn't looked back from then. When Alice had entered her life properly not long before that, her life had changed. No more bullying. No more injuries from home. None that lasted anyway.

Her adopted mother—the proper one, not the stepmother—wore that symbol; the one belonging to the former residents. And she did not have a callous bone in her body. At least, not that she had ever shown Jennifer.

And she wore *that* symbol. The one that persisted on the walls of this place, wherever that was, and reminded her of the one thing she just couldn't move on from. And her captors saw them as an enemy. She couldn't let them know that. She just couldn't.

"So, you lot, whoever you are, took out anyone who had anything to do with that sigil, because you thought they were a danger to you?"

"That order was a danger to everyone," Manta snapped. She found that rather difficult to believe but held her tongue. "Now, we can get on with our business without people trying to kill us."

Don't bet on it.

But as soon as she had the thought, she remembered she was no killer. Remembered the worst night of her life. "Now that we've worked all that out," she said, swallowing the lump in her throat, "what do you want with me?"

"If you're important enough to be part of a painting my grandfather treasured, then plenty."

"Blonde women who can throw a punch and look good in armour aren't that uncommon, you know."

"Matching your appearance so precisely, they are. He told me as much himself, an old war story."

"Your grandfather fought in a war then?"

"Never fought, no. His was a higher purpose. During the war, he kept a number of treasures safe from the careless bullets and bombs which were loose and everywhere. He had the good sense to move out of Milan, an increasingly dangerous place, and relocate to Berne. Quite a move, I know, but heading to the neutral Switzerland was good for business."

Manta sat up and puffed out his chest as he proudly told the tale. "Glauco Manta was an antiques dealer, which will come as no surprise to you in my field of work. He had many clients. The Nazis paid best and most frequently as they tasked him with finding such things, but Italian interest remained strong of course, even some French.

"He would take care to look only for those on a list given by Nazi experts on such matters, and actually became so good at it that they provided him the rank of *Oberst* and had him work permanently for them.

"But he found this painting, the only thing which survived a bombing in Berlin in 1944. He took it home, kept it from the other things by way of bribery and substitution. He treasured it and researched what he had known of the building beforehand. Just a house with a rich collector, but this was the only painting that remained intact."

"That's lovely, but that means the painting can't have been of me, doesn't it?"

"'She was seen in Constantinople in the eleventh century, Milan in the sixteenth, and others,' my grandfather told my father, who in turn told me. Father said that I should look for her, especially in battle, if I ever was. He was correct. I have been at war. But I still need to know what happens now."

"Clearly, I start a war with you all and fulfil some kind of strange self-fulfilling prophecy your mad self seems to have got into his head."

"See how far you get," the Grey Lady said, just loud enough to be heard, with just enough authority for all to listen. "You have clearly learned nothing from our last encounters."

"I learn all the time," Jennifer said, watching as her adversary rested a hand on her sword hilt. She knew that, even with a table obscuring her view. "And I learn fast."

"As do I," Manta said. "And I should thank you for reminding me why I allowed guests around my dinner table during this critical time." He snapped his fingers once at the Grey Lady who promptly stood, before vanishing in plain sight. "You see, I can afford no such failures tonight as I had last night. It took a lot of work to get out of there with little trace. But how do we improve if we do not learn from our mistakes, hmmm?"

Jennifer whirled round as she heard the door behind her click locked. Within seconds, the other did the same.

"It is a pity that some have failed to grasp this simple principle. And as such, they have proven themselves unworthy to both myself and those others whom they serve."

Manta reached under the table and produced a reinforced briefcase. He dropped it with no regard for the crockery below, and then reached into his inside suit pocket. He pulled out a set of small keys and turned them on locks first on one side, then the other, of the case.

Jennifer stood, alert for incoming trouble, but Manta waved her back to her seat. He moved without urgency, evidently in no hurry. "In this case is enough to pay each of you that which I agreed," he said, loudly and clearly addressing his guards. He gained the attention of each of them, holding and rotating the case so they could all see inside.

Then, he snapped it shut and dropped it on to the table, which scattered food all over the floor. "But I called each of you here because you *failed*."

The guards stepped back, alert to Manta's sudden change of tone, and looked at each other, perhaps in the hope that his words were being directed somewhere specific.

"You had the simple task of stopping her from escaping. But she put each one of you down easily. And yet she insists she is not the Face of War, nor one of us. How can I trust you to guard me? How do I trust you to protect me when one unarmed woman embarrasses each of you?"

A mixture of reactions followed. Some guards hung their heads, others shook theirs, and a couple backed away in anticipation of treachery. Those few edged towards their weapons. Jennifer suspected they were probably the ones with the right idea. She lowered herself near the table, but, certain the focus of the others present lay elsewhere, she decided to keep it that way.

Manta returned to his seat, one hand on the case. "Seeing as I have set aside this money to pay you all, it shall remain that way—to whoever can walk out of here with it."

Immediately, one of the men readied his rifle in Manta's direction. But no sooner than he had found his aim, he began to gurgle. Jennifer saw no outer wound on him, but he coughed blood and collapsed to the ground, motionless.

The smell of death. It filled Jennifer's lungs again just as the guard next to him toppled forward, also coughing blood. He hung at a strange angle, as if leaning by the chest on something, but she saw nothing there. After a couple of seconds, he fell forward, just as the last.

One soldier ran for the door behind Manta. This time, she saw the ethereal figure thrust a shadowy blade straight through his back and out again. It left no hole in his armour, no marks at all, but he fell just as sure as if skewered.

The cloaked figure vanished again, and just as Jennifer worked out where she had gone, two more guards fell down dead. The remaining three armed themselves and dropped into a crouch, trying to pick a target. Two of their heads bounced away from their bodies as they dropped forward.

The Grey Lady appeared to Jennifer's left, central by the table with the blackened blade in her hands, bloodless. Her smile made Jennifer quite literally nauseous. It wasn't just the deaths; something else had occurred beyond her sight. She could see its residue—a pale red glow around the killer that would have been lost to more natural eyes, but there was no mistake. Those killings had done something to her, given her strength. By taking theirs.

The cloaked assassin turned her attention to the last hireling, the only one not in body armour. Jennifer recognised him, now this punishment was going on, as the one outside her cell door. He shook his head before releasing a double tap in the Grey Lady's direction. She stood, untroubled by this attack which either missed, or more likely passed right through her ghostly form. She sheathed her sword and gestured to Manta.

Manta tapped the case. "Nobody else left," he said to the survivor. "Go on. Take it. Walk out of here. You've earned it, and as I say, I put the money aside for you all."

"B-but . . .she'll kill me," the guard babbled.

"No. Actually, I had other plans to see you dead. But I would have hoped, given your background checks, that you would have been more than capable of such a simple matter."

"You told us not to shoot her!" he protested.

"I also told you she was not to escape," Manta hissed. "But I'm giving you several options here. A chance to prove yourself. See? She's even put away her weapon. What possible danger could a man as tough as you be facing?"

"Enough!" she called out. "If you're doing this for my benefit, I've seen enough. Let him go."

The Grey Lady turned to her. "Weak," she said in a spectral whisper. "So soft of heart. You could never be the Face of War."

Manta threw his hands into a shrug. "Maybe not. But we have an hour before the next job. And so you know," he turned to Jennifer, "this was for my benefit, not yours. I can't surround myself with security which cannot do its job." He returned his attention to the sweating guard. "I am offering you an opportunity to prove yourself. I suggest you take it."

The guard squirmed, but looked around. Jennifer recognised the signs of one attempting to escape. Not long ago, it had been her. But they wanted her aliveat least for a time. Manta had just signed the guard's death warrant.

Manta calmly turned to Jennifer and held a hand toward the panicking guard. "The honour, Face of War, shall be yours." The guard raised his weapon and backed to the door, but no longer knew who to target. His gun point wavered between Manta and Jennifer, a fact that only seemed to augment the host's calm. "You should hurry up and kill him, brave warrior. He has a gun to you. It's you or him."

"What?" She couldn't work out what Manta had up his sleeve to protect him from gunfire, but his hand remained up. The guard's gun arm veered left and right, still trying to make his chosen shot count. "I'm not going to—"

"Look out!" Manta cried, and lowered his hand. The guard appeared to receive a sudden nudge off-balance and he stumbled, then fired an unsteady volley in Jennifer's direction. His shots missed both targets wildly.

Jennifer stood and vaulted on to the table, running straight for the guard. As she leapt off, an invisible force swiped her off-balance and she fell forward. She corrected herself against the wall and fell into a backward roll. As she returned to her feet, the invisible attacker grabbed her by the jacket collar and kicked at her hamstring, dropping her to her knees. As she tried to correct herself, she felt herself dragged back by the hands and took another series of punches to her chin. Before she could recover, the ghostly figure lashed her to the nearest table leg and then disappeared out of sight once more.

The guard seized his opportunity and tried the door handle, but it did not budge. Manta waited with a patient grin as he tried to force his way out with no success. Seconds into his struggle, he found himself suspended in mid-air, grabbed by his collar and thrown with some force back into the centre of the room. The ghost woman rematerialized close to him even as Jennifer thrashed to get free, but the binding, quick as it had been, held firm against her efforts. She did not stop trying.

"Disappointing," Manta proclaimed as he hung his head. "But very well."

The Grey Lady returned her attention to the mercenary. She lowered her hood and revealed a cold, resentful visage. She looked down on him in every sense. "Come on. All you have to do is defeat me, and you can go free."

He looked at the money still on the table and saw that he would still have to get past her to acquire it. He thought better of it and raised his rifle. He fired two rounds, but his target had once more become translucent and closed in on him.

With minimal effort, she drew her sword and sliced his weapon straps clear, then disarmed him and kicked the gun away. Her body solidified and she rehoused her blade. "Guns. Unsporting."

Jennifer slammed her hands against the table, drawing blood as she attempted to escape the rope. But she made little progress.

She watched the desperate man draw a survival knife and charge the cloaked killer. She easily sidestepped his clumsy lunge, then grabbed his hair and rammed her knee into his face three times.

He dropped his knife, and it bounced right by Jennifer's feet. She reached for Fate's gift to her and seized it with her soles, then drew her knees upward. In her struggle, she noticed the Grey Lady turning back to face her, her opponent restrained in a brutal-looking arm lock.

"Now," she said to Jennifer, "*this* is for your benefit." She applied an instant and significant increase of pressure and snapped his arm, then dropped him limp to the ground and let him scream. Jennifer edged the knife a little closer to her, but still far from her bound hands.

Manta banged on the table. "We need to hurry this up," he told his henchperson. She nodded with a sneer and zeroed on the mercenary. He dragged himself to his feet and made a dash for the door. The ghost walker grabbed his ankle and tripped him. She leapt forward and brought her feet neatly down on the base of his spine, to another painful-sounding snap.

She seized control of the howling man's head and stood, hauling him like a doll as he whimpered and thrashed with his remaining working limbs. She forced his head in front of the money case and shook it for him. She then wrenched it hard to the left and shoved him on to the money.

Though her victim already lay definitely dead, she drew her sword and pushed it straight through his spine. It did not pierce skin but appeared to pass straight through, as ethereal as Jennifer had seen its wielder.

As the killer stood proud, Jennifer flicked the knife upward just above her head and into her hand. She started to cut but she could not miss the pale-red mist which encircled the killer, emanating from the onyx blade.

Once free, she went first for Manta. He did not even flinch. Just as she approached, she felt a deathly cold blade against her throat, ghostly by sight but razor-sharp to the touch. She stopped dead in her tracks.

Manta spoke without the merest change in his tone. "You have a great deal of fight in you," he said; "but too much mercy for those undeserving of it."

"Nobody deserves to be murdered like that," she responded. "That wasn't a fight; that was an execution."

"They were unworthy to call themselves my protectors." He waved the blade away, and it vanished. Jennifer knew that its wielder had done the same but probably wasn't far away. She had no control of her situation, and that irked her beyond belief.

"But very well. You have entertained me enough that I will offer you the same opportunity. Tomorrow, when we have what I came here for."

Jennifer felt relief that she had not been turned loose to be hunted down and slaughtered like an animal, as she had just witnessed. She had to hope another day would see her grow stronger. That morning, she had been feeling better than she had in many days.

But, a sense of hopelessness nagged at her, guilt that she had put the guards in that position in the first place and that she had failed to get them out of it. Unless she was feeling significantly stronger, an extra day's stay of execution would end up being just that.

"Indulge me," she asked, grabbing at anything she could. "Where is 'here', anyway?"

"You are in an old headquarters of our gravest enemy," Manta said, looking far too assured for Jennifer's own good. "We are in Gien."

That sounds French. How the hell did we end up in France?

We can't be too far in. I must've been out for a couple of hours. I've learnt something, anyway.

"Why here?"

"It's a good base of operations to reach the Louvre." His lips upturned. "And this time, we shall be doing so without your interference. Put her back in her confinement, will you?"

"Turn around and head to the back door," said an echoing voice. She knew to whom it belonged. It had none of that force of terror that Mary was able to invoke about it, but even so, the disembodied nature of it still caused a little nervousness. Jennifer could not fight an opponent she couldn't track, or harm. No recourse other than obedience presented itself.

As she got to the door, Manta clapped twice. A lock clicked. The door opened and the red-clad Cerise sauntered in. She stared at the defeated Jennifer with an uncomfortable allure as she walked past. Though undoubtedly attractive, the situation did not lend to such a reaction and Jennifer knew it well. Other forces had to have been at work.

Jennifer settled herself, but Cerise already appeared satisfied with her reaction. The woman half-bowed to Manta, but with some noticeable grievance; not to having given deference, but something about the manner of delivery. It almost looked as if she'd made a mistake and was torturing herself over it.

"They're yours," Manta informed. "I still don't know what it is you do with them, but clear up the mess."

"Don't I always?" Cerise's lips upturned almost flirtatiously.

"And hurry up. We need everyone ready in forty-five minutes. I want the crown."

Crown?

"Keep moving." The echoing voice nudged her into action again. With one last look back, she observed Cerise dragging the two headless guards out of the other door with considerable strength, whistling a tune as she did so. She dumped the bodies through the door and then reached for the knife Jennifer had seen about her earlier. The door closed.

Jennifer wondered what they meant by all they had just said, whilst keeping an eye on her route back to the room in which she was being detained. She needed a means of escape before she, or anyone else, died for nothing. The heads on the floor taunted her, reminded her of failures there and in the past.

I'm so sorry.

***Watch for the full release of Primal Storm,
Book 2 of the Grenshall Manor Chronicles
by R. A. Smith, in December, 2013.***